# One in Vermilion May Live

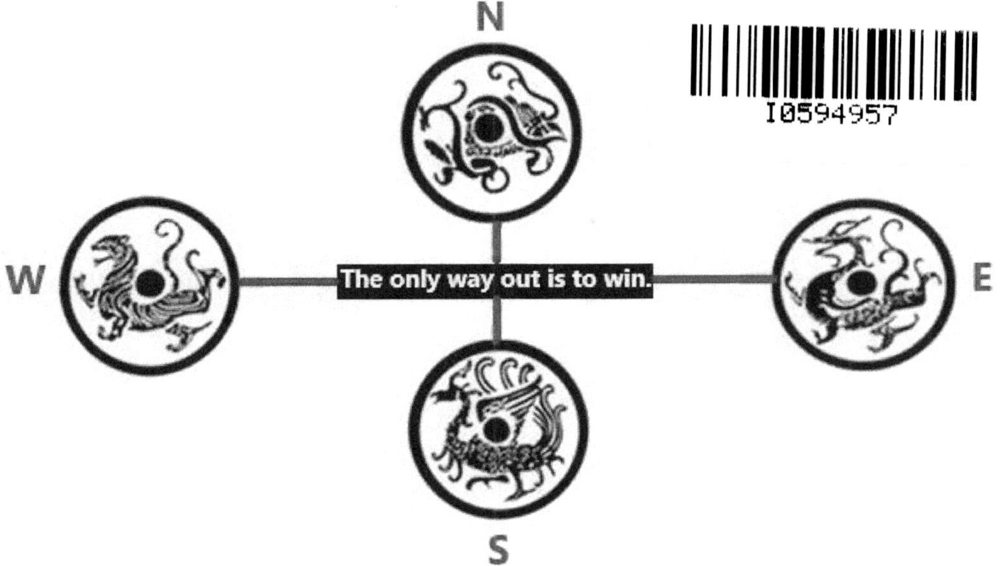


Jennifer Jaxxon-Louis

Book 1

Blowing Up The O'Grady Kids

Book cover by Evgeniia Gurcheva

Several interior illustrations by Ishani Samarathunga

Other graphics created by Jennifer Jaxxon-Louis

ISBN: 979-8-9922987-
1-0 (PDF eBook)

ISBN: 979-8-9922987-2-7 (EPUB eBook)

ISBN: 979-8-9922987-3-4 (Paperback)

ISBN: 979-8-9922987-
4-1 (Hardcover)

ISBN: 979-8-9922987-5-8 (Future Audiobook)

Printed in the United States of America.

First printing edition, 2025

Website: https://authorjenniferjaxxonlouis.com

**A Twista' Sista' Kinda' Book**

In this series of books, you will find the twisted stories of two sisters intertwined or twisted.

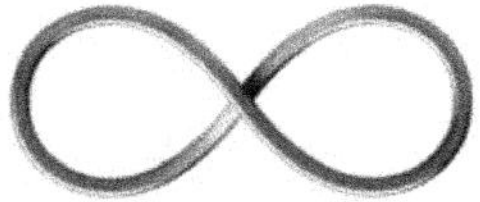

To Greg, Peter, Bobby, Marcia, Jan, Cindy,

Mike, Carol, Alice, and Cousin Oliver.

The real O'Grady's.

Thanks for everything.

And of course, for Mom

and

the two mysterious women

who saved my life.

## Upcoming Releases

Two in Vermilion May Die (Blowing Up The O'Grady Kids, #2)

What Happened in the Janitor's Closet – A Novel of Short Stories

Three in Vermilion May Lie (Blowing Up The O'Grady Kids, #3)

The Killer Ratio: How U.S. Law Murdered My Mom

Tomorrow and Today, a World Away

Somebody Else (Burning Harbor, #1)

Clues to a Killer

Compound Fracture

Zero Life Points

The Last Movie She Ever Saw

Back to the Butterflies

Angel Number 41

Minders' Keepers

Rubber Band Ball – A Memoir

Scenes from a Slot Machine – A Memoir's Sequel

I Woke Up in My Book

To receive a monthly newsletter and participate

in contests and giveaways, sign up for

Jennifer Jaxxon-Louis' Reader's List at

https://authorjenniferjaxxonlouis.com

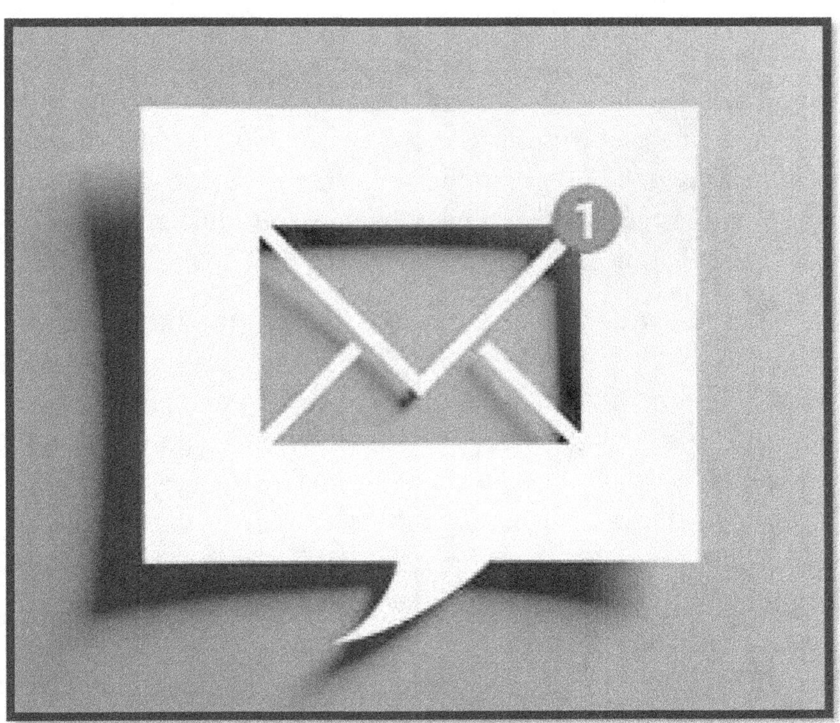

## Author's Note and Acknowledgements

Many things inspired this story. One was the thought that someone could use nanobots to hold others hostage from the inside. To me, that would be a truly terrifying situation because someone could force others to do whatever they wanted, threatening them with painful or even fatal consequences. Another was Lois Duncan's novel *Ransom* about a bus full of teens who are kidnapped, which made me think of of the very memorable bus tour I took from Metro Detroit up to Michigan Tech in 1991 when I was a junior in high school. The three ideas came together like smoothie ingredients in a blender.

At that time, in early 2023, I'd just finished reading *The Hunger Games* trilogy, binge-watched *The Squid Game* series while taking copious notes, and was happily immersed in the show *Sons of Anarchy*, and they all contributed to this story. I knew I needed a criminal group for my plot, and an outlaw motorcycle club was perfect. I was familiar with them because of *Sons* and from the many years I spent in several biker bars in Fort Lauderdale and at biker events all over Florida.

In addition, I used *The Brady Bunch*, one of my favorite shows ever, because I wanted to have six rounds for the game in the story, and I found that having the six wholesome Brady kids as villains was a hysterical juxtaposition. I also used other characters from the show in strategic ways. Of course, I could not directly use the show's or characters' names, so I came up with The O'Grady Kids and made similar names. I figured, if one was a fan of the show, they would get all the fun references, but if they weren't or it was before their time, it would be inconsequential. It was also my way to pay tribute to this amazing show that was very influential to me growing up. My sister Nicki and I have a lifelong, ongoing argument about the wonky layout of the Brady house, which we know is a disjointed TV set but still try to make sense of anyway.

Through fun Internet research, I discovered the Four Auspicious Beasts of the Chinese Constellation: the Azure Dragon in the East, the Black Tortoise in the North, the White Tiger in the West, and the Vermilion Bird in the South. They were perfect for my game in the story because they had directions associated with them which could define regions, and their images could be shown on the coins that needed to be collected in each round. The Vermilion Bird also inspired the title of the game and the book.

I was already stoked about this story concept, but what really set it on fire was author Dan Brown's great advice in his Masterclass on writing thrillers. He said to think of the best locations you can possibly imagine as he did in *The Davinci Code* and then stretch your story along them like a canvas on tent poles. Therefore, I used real-world places that are as chaotic as possible to ramp up the tension while helping readers to better relate and provide a more authentic feel. I grew up in Metro Detroit and will always be a Detroiter no matter where I live, but I also went to school in the Upper Peninsula of Michigan at Michigan Tech in Houghton, visited Cleveland often because my sister lived there, went to Mackinac Island (and got sick eating too much fudge), and resided near Fort Lauderdale for seventeen years. I found ways to incorporate all these areas into my story, and boy, were they fun to research in greater depth.

I attended Michigan Tech in 1992, majoring in structural civil engineering like Darla's character. This amazing school changed my perspective on many things, and I fell in love with the region near Houghton in the Upper Peninsula of Michigan, quite different from where I grew up in Metro Detroit. It's the prettiest place I've ever been, rivaling Juneau, Alaska, where I visited once, and it is unique in so many ways. I have set other novels there in a fictitious town called Burning Harbor north of Houghton, taking advantage of the Canadian cultural influences and extreme weather conditions which make things quite interesting. I am currently working on an adult thriller series called Burning Harbor with the first book entitled *Somebody Else*, a story I've had in my head for twenty years.

I also studied at Lawrence Tech in Southfield, Michigan after I left Michigan Tech, deciding I preferred to major in architecture rather than engineering, and then I finished at Wayne State University in Detroit with a bachelor's degree in developmental psychology. Long story. Later, I attended the University of Michigan for my first master's degree in math education. I honor all these wonderful institutions of higher learning in my story and thank them for all I learned.

As a former math professor and now an academic advisor, I hope this series inspires teens to major in STEM areas because there is a real need to improve technological and other innovation for the betterment of society. However, this story also serves as a warning, casting a humorous yet terrifying light on how well-intentioned technology can become catastrophic in the wrong hands.

There are several people who helped me achieve my goal of publishing this tale I wrote.

First and foremost, I would love to thank my mother, Beverley Susan Siegel, who always believed in me and was there for me. She was a teacher who changed careers and became one of the first women in the IT department at Chrysler's headquarters near Detroit. She wrote some of their original software. Ironically, she and I switched places because I went from programming into teaching. She was also a single mother who raised three daughters all by herself, exemplifying a strong and honorable woman with a heart of gold who would literally give you the shirt off her back. I owe everything I am to her. I wish she could be here today to see me publish my first novel, but I hope that wherever she is, she's doing a happy dance along with me. I have written a memoir that features my mother, entitled *Rubber Band Ball,* which I will be publishing in the future, as well as its sequel *Scenes from a Slot Machine*. Stay tuned.

I'd also like to recognize Corewell Health William Beaumont Hospital in Royal Oak, Michigan, where my mother was a frequent patient my entire life. They always took excellent care of her, and so I pay great tribute to the hospital and staff in my story to thank them for saving her life countless times.

In addition, I'd like to thank the two mysterious women at Topeekeegee Yugnee Park in Hollywood, Florida on November 6, 2015 who I never saw but saved my life when I was having a massive heart attack after running six miles. I don't know how to find them — I've been trying for years — but if you can tell people, maybe word will get to them somehow to know how thankful I am to them and how I wish the best for them. The full story is on my website at https://authorjenniferjaxxonlouis.com under the BLOG tab.

I wanted to have wonderful artwork in my book, not just to look great and give the reader more information, but also to differentiate between the two interweaving stories so it would be obvious whose viewpoint it was. After many tries, I finally found a wonderful illustrator in Sri Lanka named Ishani Samarathunga. She is extremely professional, creative, and talented, with excellent reviews on Fiverr from other authors who she has worked with for many years. Her drawings are amazing, and I plan to hire her for future projects. I highly recommend her to other authors. She was an absolute pleasure to work with. I also worked with the very talented Evgeniia

Gurcheva to develop my front and back covers, and I got assistance from Rodney Hatfield about how to market my book.

I wanted to find some younger sensitivity readers to review some of my more controversial content, and I encountered this wonderful soul who calls themselves "Hallowed" on Fiverr. They told me that they loved reading so much, they offered their critiquing services at very low fees – practically free – to help writers be better. This person gave me great feedback and suggestions, and some of the best compliments I have ever received. I am thankful for someone like this who truly helps others because they care about literature, ideas, and good writing so much, and I will seek their help again in the future. Similarly, I hired someone named Theo M. on the same website to do a complete analysis of my book, and they gave me some excellent feedback and pointed out things I would have never noticed, so I am quite grateful for their wonderful contributions and thoroughly enjoyed their hilarious reactions throughout.

I also met a fellow writer named Becky Wells Phillips on one of my author Facebook groups, a beautiful African American woman who writes about her experiences with racism in the US, and she offered to read my Neo-Nazi passages and give her honest opinion. I felt it was important to have people of different cultural and racial backgrounds review my work, and I am quite appreciative for her time and excellent feedback. In addition, another author named Sandra Edwards Foster-Graham generously reviewed my story.

Immense thanks also to Mr. Paul Martz. This wonderful author is the new members liaison for the Speculative Fiction Writers Association critique group, affiliated with Rocky Mountain Fiction Writers. When I joined, he took special interest in my book because although we both reside in Colorado, he grew up near me in Metro Detroit and attended Michigan Tech about a decade before I did. He offered to beta-read my book. He caught inconsistencies in spelling and logic, made wonderful suggestions, and helped me craft a better story. Paul donated his time and effort without expecting anything in return even though I kept offering just because he wanted to help me, and I am quite grateful to him for his generosity and fabulous insights.

In addition, I want to honor Deborah Rose Campagne — my Aunt Debi — who was highly influential in my life. She was my mother's younger sister whom she raised, practically a fourth sister to us. Later in life, she became a Red Wings superfan. I used what I knew from her to write my hockey scenes.

Keondra, a character in the story, has a mother based on my aunt, who both wore diamond Red Wings necklaces, named their pets after all the players, and kept careful stats during every game. I love and miss Aunt Debi so much, and I thank her for all she gave me my whole life.

Another person for whom I owe tremendous gratitude is the great author and agent Joyce Sweeney. I discovered them around 2012 when I took their online writing class. I had no idea at the time that they lived right near me, so I got to meet them and attend several of their writing workshops. Joyce, an accomplished young adult author, poet, playwright, children's picture book expert, and now literary agent, changed everything I thought I knew about writing. They included me in their critique group where I learned so much from them and the amazing authors who participated and are now all published. One of the best things I gained from Joyce was their Plot Clock technique, which they have published and can be found online. I use it religiously when developing a story because it is extremely helpful and easy to follow, better than any other method I've tried. I highly recommend it for any author who wants to develop a solid and engaging plot, as well as Randy Ingermanson's The Snowflake Method, which I use in conjunction with The Plot Clock to create a solid story concept and outline.

I'd also like to thank the authors Tracy Woodman (Lee Woods) and Matt Posner who interviewed me for their podcasts around the time my book launched to help me promote it.

Also, a tremendous thanks to Tammy Pope, a wonderful therapist I found, who has been extremely giving of her time and help. I am immensely grateful to all these people and could not have gotten through without them. Writing this book also saved my life in many ways, getting me through some very dark days.

Lastly, I'd like to thank you, Dear Reader, for tuning in and checking out my story, the first in a series entitled *Blowing Up The O'Grady Kids*. I hope you enjoy reading it as much as I enjoyed writing it. You may crack up but also cry. I highly advise you to have tissues nearby.

# MICHIGAN

## THE GREAT LAKES STATE

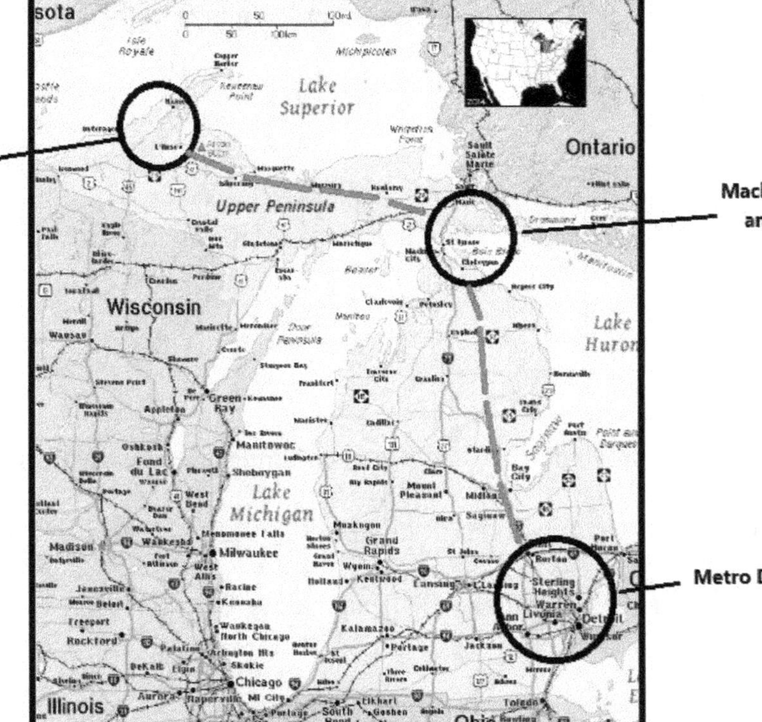


MICHIGAN TECH
Huskies
UNIVERSITY

Mackinac Island and Bridge

Metro Detroit

# Today's Vocabulary Lesson

Bubbe — Yiddish word for grandmother – rhymes with "cubby" – used by many Jewish people.

Zayde — Yiddish word for grandfather – rhymes with "lady" – used by many Jewish people.

Mackinac — an island between the upper and lower peninsulas of Michigan and also the name of the long suspension bridge that connects the two peninsulas – pronounced "Mackinaw"

Euchre — a popular card game at Michigan Tech – pronounced "yooker"

Houghton — the city where Michigan Tech is located – rhymes with "boatin'"

UP or U.P. — stands for the Upper Peninsula of Michigan – pronounced "yoo pee"

# Story Parts

# PART 1

## DAVINA'S ESCAPE

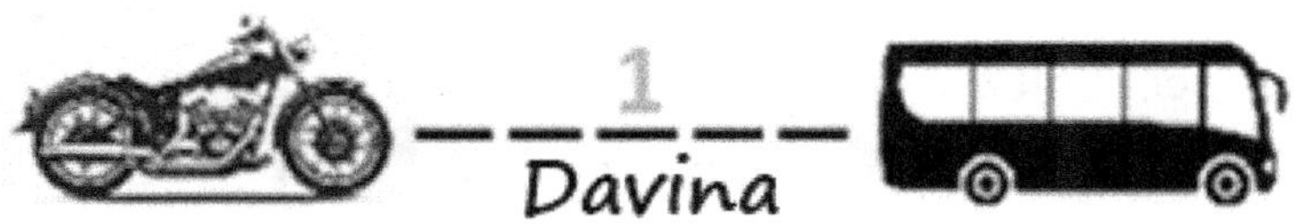


## Thursday, December 6, 2029

On an ordinary Thursday in December 2029, I'm riding the school bus home thinking everything is fine. Just as I'm on the brink of solving the extra credit Calculus problem that has driven me crazy all week, my hologram phone watch screams, "Holla' for Your Hollaphone!™" and I practically jump out of my seat. Everyone around me glances up from their own Hollaphones while my heart gallops in my chest. A text from my bestie Antonia says we have a situation, and she's very distressed.

I press my watch's flat black circular face with a ridge of pink and blue rhinestones that everyone says is super cute. An inverted triangle of light splays from a tiny hole in the center. Seconds later, a hologram phone materializes all shimmery and glowing on my wrist.

"Holla' for Your Hollaphone!™" my watch calls again.

MetaApplesoft's new hologram phone watches are only supposed to sing while the holographic rectangle solidifies into a regular smartphone, but mine has a mind of its own. My friend Niyah thinks it's a glitch from getting it wet, but Antonia insists it's possessed.

I swipe the sound down, but Holly, the virtual assistant, serenades me yet again as I take the phone off its base to call my friend. When Antonia answers, Holly interrupts our greeting, singing the jingle three more times.

"Geez," Antonia says. "Get that thing fixed already. That Holly chick is seriously wigging me out. Anyway, Radesh texted that two of the triplets, Eks and Wai, tested positive for Covid-28, while Zee's appendix burst last night. They're doing okay, their mom says they're on the mend, but none will be at the Nerd Bowl Semifinals this weekend."

"You freaking serious? With Radesh out for his aunt's funeral, that's like half our team!" A knot forms in my stomach as I realize that our captain and now our three strongest members are suddenly gone before the biggest tournament of the semester.

Antonia sighs. “Yeah, and none of the rest of us math and science geeks know jack about art, politics, sports, or history, which are like half the categories.”

“Oh, man,” I moan, anxiety ballooning in my chest. “Right. It’s just you, me, Leon, and Isaac left. We are so screwed. With all the strong teams this year, we might as well kiss our six-year streak as Michigan Nerd Bowl champs goodbye.”

As soon as the words are out, I realize where I am and whip around to see who may have heard. No one is paying attention, all focused on their Hollaphones as the school bus enters the ramp for I-696 East. I sigh with relief. Nobody gives a crap about the fate of our Nerd Bowl team, most not knowing or caring that we have one.

But I do. Blowing my bangs off my forehead, I try to think of anyone who knows about that crap to possibly recruit. I can’t let this thing my parents can finally brag about me to others, that I’m part of this winning team, suddenly not be true. Or else they’ll revert to what they used to say before I joined: *Here’s our daughter Davina, born two minutes after Mallory, and her hair is more orange than red, whereas Mallory’s is more red than orange.* They’ll rely on physical differences, of which there are few, because Mallory always outshines me — without trying, I might add — in everything I do.

“So, me, Leon, and Isaac voted,” Antonia says. “Congrats! You’re now our interim team captain.”

“*What*?” My palms break a sweat. “You decided this already?”

“Yep. It was unanimous.”

I wipe my hands on my jeans. “But this is only my first year!” I sputter. “Most of you have way more experience. How did I get such an honor?”

“Everyone thought you’d best know how to fix the situation.”

“*Me*?” I shake my head with disbelief.

“Yeah you.”

“Not sure what I did to earn such a vote of confidence, but I deeply regret whatever it was.”

Antonia giggles. “Come on! You’ll be great. Ooh, Trystan’s coming my way. Gotta’ fix my face. Kisses.” She hangs up to go flirt with the guy she’s been into forever who doesn’t know she exists while I collapse my super-singing Hollaphone into my wrist.

I book an appointment with the MetaApplesoft store in Twelve Oaks Mall to fix my Hollaphone, then shut it off for some time alone. With my Calculus problem forgotten, I stare out the window braiding my hair while considering possible solutions to our tournament dilemma. Puzzling over why I was chosen to lead the rest, it suddenly occurs to me that perhaps I’m being hazed by the Nerd Bowl team, and this is my first test.

A chill washes over me, and I start to obsess about this possibility. I’ve heard rumors of things they’ve done in the past. Not sure why I thought I was exempt just because I’m Antonia’s friend. My parents’ judgmental faces flash before my eyes, always preferring Mallory the graceful dancer who twirls circles around me on the dance floor and in school, and I spring into action. I start a list on my Hollaphone of anyone who might help save my reputation as a member of this unknown champion team. I’m about to call the first person when I get another text.

This one is from Mallory. *Need car tomorrow too. Teaching Aqua Zumba before school, subbing five classes after, even Flamenco. Many teachers out with Covid-28. Get another ride.*

I scoff, already super annoyed that Mallory took our shared Jetta before I even woke up today for an impromptu practice with her hip-hop crew, the Majik 8 Balz. I had to rush to catch the bus I didn’t expect to take. That’s why my hair’s so greasy; I didn’t even get a shower. And my nose is quite aware I forgot the deodorant step. Mallory didn’t exactly ask me either, just told me by Hollaphone while I was asleep. Then she texted me after the seventh period bell saying she had a doctor’s appointment, and I needed to catch the bus home.

I had to run to the other end of the school and practically throw myself in front of it to get the driver’s attention as he was pulling away. I wasn’t about to walk three miles in the snow.

I type my answer, my lips curled in a snarl, telling Mallory how unfair her hogging our car is when our parents gave it to both of us for our sixteenth birthday last year. She thinks she's so entitled just because she won that big, prestigious teaching job at her dance studio and works four days a week now. And there's all her practices and rehearsals and performances with her hip-hop crew, but the car isn't just hers. She has no respect for the fact that I'm trying to start an animal rights club at school and —

A distant rumble becomes a herd of elephants, stealing my attention away as a swarm of motorcycles surrounds our bus.

Guys on Harley's wearing black leather vests over flannel shirts descend on us like crows on a half-eaten sandwich. The words "Rebel Demons" on their backs curve over clenched fists with skulls superimposed. Each hollowed face leers at us, becoming a sudden audience as the bikers form two lines on either side of our bus.

"What the hell do they want?" someone yells over the revving of their engines. The stench of diesel fuel wafts through the opened bus windows. I gag and bury my nose into the lapel of my blue and white striped cardigan. Murmuring swells around me as I think of the son of the Rebel Demons leader, this total jerk in my grade named Snake Riley.

I gulp. Is he coming after me?

Seeing red, I search for him in the crowd, looking for his half-shaved head with an elaborate snake tattoo covering his neck and scalp. As I think of him and all the things he did, my fists clench like the one on his family's motorcycle gang logo. Nah, he's supposed to be in juvie far as I know. He didn't even have a hearing yet for his parole. I'm quite aware since I was supposed to go.

But maybe he escaped and is here for retribution, to punish me for what my parents did to him. Did the Rebel Demons already get to Mallory, or is she next?

I crane my neck trying to see, but I really can't tell since all the bikers look alike. They wear the same blue jeans over thick black boots with chains hanging from their necks and patch-covered black leather vests. Many have scraggly beards and rough skin, and the thick silver rings on their fingers and the chrome on their bikes glint in the afternoon light. Getting up from my seat, I strain to see their faces, wondering what I'd do if Snake was among them. Would I have the guts to confront him?

The bus jerks to the left, and I fall onto a guy nearby. Tires screech, people scream, and we crash into a ditch on the side of the freeway, slamming into a huge backhoe left there.

"Hey, watch it!" the guy I've sprawled all over whines.

"Sorry," I mumble, pushing off him. Out the window, there's a hissing sound, and smoke rises at the front of the bus. Or maybe it's coming from the backhoe, I don't know, but I worry one or both engines will soon explode.

Beyond, a row of Rebel Demons dismounting their bikes stretches as far as the eye can see. They're parked around clumps of snow left from the storm earlier this week. Are they all here to help Snake get me?

A shiver embraces me with this possibility as an acrid smell of something burning wafts into the cab, mixing with the fuel from earlier. My watering eyes scan the ceiling lines, locating an emergency exit sign. I grab my bag ready to bolt toward it at the back of the bus when a loud *pop-pop-pop* shatters glass at the front, spinning me around toward the sound.

A few Rebel Demons storm aboard, their gleaming guns blazing. The bus driver, this old guy with a white buzz cut named Gus, shrinks away as they shove a Hollaphone in his face. Gus shakes his head side to side, eyes wide, raised hands shaking. The Rebel Demons glower down at him a heart-pounding minute…………………then move on to the front row.

A huge guy with long grimy hair at the head of their pack shows his phone to a girl from my Shakespearean literature class. She pulls up her sunglasses, squints, then shrugs. Twisting around, her slat eyes scan the crowd. Her head stops my way, and she stares right at me.

I duck down, wedging myself into the foot space between my seat and the next. My heart jackhammers in my ears as I wonder if anyone noticed I suddenly disappeared. Peeking around the seat guarding me, I find several pairs of black boots headed my way.

As the metal chains on them clank against the leather like we're in some western showdown, my heart winds up to spring out of my chest.

They stop and turn, not quite near me yet.

I exhale a few seconds, trying to figure out how to get away undetected.

A hand clamps down on my shoulder.

I jerk around with my breath in my throat to find a boy I recognize from my row of lockers sitting above me on the seat. I'd been so into my Calculus problem that I didn't realize he was next to me. This quiet, dark-haired guy with a baby face and rosy cheeks that don't match his tall frame peers down at me with concerned eyes. I put a finger to my lips, and he nods, then looks forward like I'm not there squished against his knees.

The black boots move closer, maybe three seats away, and my heart and stomach smack a high five.

"You seen her?" one of the bikers demands.

Sure they're talking about me now, I angle around but then freeze. The trial with Snake Riley was eons ago. Why would they want me now?

Eyeing the guns in their hands, I decide I don't want to find out.

Curling into a ball, I try to wriggle under my seat so I can get to the back of the bus, but the vertical supports and long legs of my seatmate block me. Locker Neighbor lifts his knees as much as he can, and I squeeze into the small opening beneath him.

Inching forward on my elbows, I snake around the center pole until most of me is under. Wondering how I'll navigate around each person's legs in my path, I hear, "Hey you under there. Goin' somewhere?"

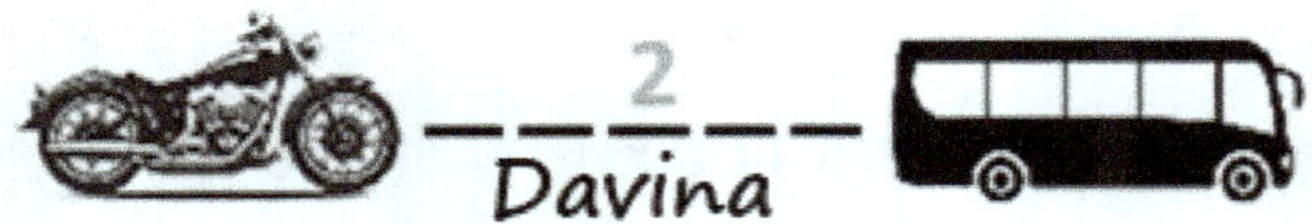


A deer in headlights, I try to decide if I should ignore the voice and press on or back out and face the music.

*Bullets go through flimsy seats*, my mind screams, and I scoot backwards. Unfolding myself, I perch on the edge of the bench and look up to find a Rebel Demon with a grayish beard and cracked brown teeth snarling down at me. The barrel of his gun is inches from my chin.

"You deaf? I'm talking to you," he growls. The stench of cigarettes and beer almost knocks me out.

Blinking watery eyes and holding my nose, my mind cranks out any excuse it can conjure as my eyes fixate on that barrel and only that barrel while everything else fades away. "I, uh, I think I l-lost my contact lens," I stutter. Rubbing my right eye, I study the floor like I'm still searching.

He grunts and nods, then shoves a Hollaphone at me. On it is a picture of a girl from school with chipmunk cheeks, short frizzy hair with the front dyed blue, and several facial piercings that highlight her acne and gold front tooth. Her name is Krystall Nykkolls, and Mallory says she's a second-time senior and the biggest drug dealer in school. Mallory knows too, because her best friend's boyfriend is Krystall's cousin.

I deflate with relief as I realize they're not looking for me. Then, I feel super guilty, because who knows what they'll do to Krystall if they find her? Horrifying images clobber me. It's nothing I want to see.

"Where is she?" the Rebel Demon demands.

Glancing around at all the startled and stone-still faces staring at us, I don't spot her or any of her friends in the crowd. They always sit near the front and are obnoxious and loud, throwing things, launching insults, and playing music that I typically hate, so annoying I can't even concentrate. Shaking my head, I tell him I don't know.

"Where's she hang out?"

“We’re hardly friends with the same people,” I croak around the sandpaper in my throat. “I have no clue.”

The biker raises his gun to my forehead, and my heart stops. “You sure about that?”

I blink yes and otherwise freeze as he studies me. Time stands still while he considers if I’m telling the truth, and I consider the barrel of his gun millimeters from ending my life. As I await his decision, part of my mind wonders how it might feel to be shot while the rest slaps it back into place, not allowing it to go there yet.

He sneers, his steely eyes roaming every inch of me, the scariest lie detector ever seen. After a century, he drops his gun and moves onto the next kid, for now done with me.

I collapse into my seat, gasping for air. Locker Neighbor asks if I’m okay.

Shaking my head, I put it between my knees trying to catch my racing breath as he awkwardly pats me on the back.

“What do the Rebel Demons want with Krystall?” Locker Neighbor whispers.

I don’t dare answer because they’re too nearby. I’m sure it has to do with drugs though. It’s well known that the Rebel Demons run all the guns and drugs in Metro Detroit and all over Michigan, and Krystall is supposedly the biggest dealer in school.

The Rebel Demons — probably her supplier — continue their interrogation with people behind me. After everyone denies knowing Krystall’s whereabouts or who she hangs with, the bikers stomp past me grumbling and exit the bus.

Then I notice flames licking at the front windshield.

# 3
## Davina

I scream, and others do too, and then it's a mad dash for the rear emergency door. Someone unlatches it and kicks it open, and we all push at each other, struggling to the front of the line to hop out. The whole "ladies go first" sentiment flies out the window as most of the guys rush before the girls. Locker Neighbor is in the lead, the concern he showed for me a distant memory.

I'm one of the last in line to leave, and then I remember my new tablet in my backpack at my seat. I turn to get it, but the fire has breached the bus shell and is coming toward me at alarming speed.

That's when I see a trail of something wet leading to the front of the bus. Did the Rebel Demons pour gasoline on their way out *and set the bus on fire?*

I spin around and charge toward the remaining few trying to get out the door, shoving them through the opening. I finally hop out, and a girl I pushed tells me to watch it with a nasty look.

I hear a whoosh behind me and turn to find the bus that we just escaped completely engulfed in flames. Stepping away, my greasy hair ready to singe, I turn to her with a sneer. "Sorry I rushed you there."

She shoots me an even nastier look. I leave her with her unfortunate personality and put as much distance between myself and the inferno of a bus as possible. Gulping fresh air, I stomp the ground, thankful for it under my feet, as the Rebel Demons race away on their Harley's.

I stand beside my bus mates on the shoulder of the freeway as cars whizz by. Fingers are lightning on Hollaphones as everyone tells friends what happened. One girl near me whips out a microphone from her bookbag and her friend films her with his Hollaphone as she does a report for our school's MeeToob news vlog, *What's Up South Farmington?* The driver Gus tells someone nearby to call the police as he dials our school, and minutes later, a Channel 7 News chopper appears in the sky.

Word sure travels fast.

While waiting and freezing in the frigid December afternoon — my warm coat I left on the bus now ashes along with my new tablet — I videochat with my mom to tell her what happened. Quite shaken up, I pace in my little area to warm my limbs. My teeth chatter as I recount everything with a good amount of shivering and my singing Hollaphone butting in.

Mom wants to come get me, but I know she teaches tonight and it's hard to find a last-minute sub. I tell her not to worry, they'll soon rescue us. She only agrees not to come after the new bus, some police, and a fire engine arrive.

As firefighters unwind hoses to spray the flaming bus, a few police officers board the new one to ride with us. They interview everybody about what happened. The whole time, my mind replays the awful things Snake Riley did to my family. I wish he and his Rebel Demons would just leave us alone already.

A while later, I stumble home from my bus stop, my head pounding. I take turns between freaking out over having a gun in my face and almost incinerating on the bus, obsessing over my hatred for Snake Riley, worrying about Krystall Nykkolls even though I barely know her, and wondering what the heck to do about the Nerd Bowl Semi-finals this weekend.

As I turn down my street with my head spinning a tornado of competing thoughts, it finally dawns on me to let my Nerd Bowl team know why I'm so late for our Thursday afternoon meeting. When I switch on my Hollaphone and dial Antonia, my phone watch sings to me repeatedly. Hanging up, I send her a quick text and shut the damned thing off again.

# 4
## Davina

A half-hour later, I'm settled into my parents' office next to the kitchen since the desktop in my bedroom keeps shutting down and my new tablet's a piece of toast. I'm surrounded by shelves full of neurobiology and biomedical engineering texts, magazines and journals about nanotechnology and artificial intelligence, and all The O'Grady Kids paraphernalia my parents collect. They're obsessed with that sitcom from their childhood that now plays all the time in reruns.

I go through my Nerd Bowl handbook reviewing rules and procedures as I scarf protein bars and kale crisps. The figurines of all six O'Grady kids plus their mom, dad, and hot maid stare at me from the shelf as I chew. Super creepy with all eighteen eyes on me, plus four more with my parents' new Cousin Tolliver and Tigger dog figurines. My nervousness over the bus incident converted to hunger with the availability of decent snacks. Suddenly I'm ravenous, although all that staring by the O'Grady's is bringing my anxiety back.

Spotting the cupcakes Mom brought yesterday from her favorite Jewish vegan bakery on the kitchen island, I start to get up, suddenly needing frosting, but then everyone logs into the meeting. Fiddling with the webcam atop my monitor, my image sharpens in its little square. I appear in my South Farmington High School Nerd Bowl 2029 t-shirt I got when I joined this year.

Grumbling that the cupcakes are too far away, I slip on my headset and adjust the mic. "Hey, can you all hear me?"

"Stupid asshat," someone says. My head whips to the window to find Mallory's best friend Liza out near our pool yelling into her Hollaphone as it hovers near her face in Float Mode. She peers at herself in a kitchen window to fix a comb holding back half her magenta-striped, pink bob while she and her boyfriend Dave trade other fun insults. They seem to enjoy fighting more than getting along.

I wonder if they know that the Rebel Demons want Dave's cousin Krystall Nykkolls. Perhaps that's what they're arguing about.

Antonia, my Brazilian friend who constantly chews gum to prevent overeating, nods from my screen while her jaw works and her cheek divots plunge. "Yep. Hear ya' clear as a bell. Now, am I hallucinating, or did you just call one of us a stupid asshat?"

"Gosh no. Sorry. No, that was Mallory's very loud friend." Liza stomps past the pool toward the family room where Mallory's Majik 8 Balz hip-hop crew is practicing,. She yells into her Hollaphone as she flings open the French door.

I wriggle my fingers at Isaac and Leon on my monitor, and they wave back. I tell my team about what happened on the bus, skipping the whole worrying about Snake Riley part, and we discuss it a while. Everyone reports what they already saw on *What's Up South Farmington?* and heard from friends.

I'm sick of thinking about it even though the disturbing thoughts keep poking through my mental gate. "Okay, enough of that," I declare, cutting off Isaac with whatever he was saying. "So, guys, what the heck are we going to do about Saturday's tournament? We'll totally tank unless we can somehow pull off a miracle. I mean, I barely know the difference between a soccer ball and a football, so count me out for the sports category, and I can't distinguish between Picasso, Rembrandt, or Dali either. They're all just paint."

Leon raises his hand, clearing his throat. "Since there are four areas we don't know and four of us, we should each choose two to study in case someone else gets sick or dies or something. We have tonight, all day tomorrow, and the car ride early Saturday morning. It's four hours from Farmington Hills up to Traverse City, so we should trade off driving every hour to maximize our study time."

Isaac brushes his brown hair from his eyes. "I think we should learn as much as we can in one new area, not dilute our focus between two. And we should still try to get subs if we can bribe them enough. How much do we have in petty cash?"

"Not much," I say. "Like fifty bucks. Antonia, what do you —"

The theme song from The O'Grady Kids, the show my parents love, suddenly blares from the family room across the kitchen. "*Do-do do do-doooo!* Here's a fun tale of a super cool gal who was bringing up three kiddos of her own…"

Mallory pushes furniture out of the way with her crew members near a big screen TV showing the six O'Grady siblings. The faces of Craig, Skeeter, Robbie, Marci, Janice, and Sandy appear on the sides of a grid with their parents Mark and Karyn on the top and bottom center squares. Their hot maid Allisyn walks around the perimeter in her sexy French maid's uniform, lovingly touching each kid on the nose with her feather duster as they grin back at her. After, she floats on a cloud to the middle square and does a group hug with the whole family, her arms becoming cartoonish and encircling everyone in a big heart. It's beyond cheesy.

Then, her head pops through and she winks at you, and you're left wondering why, so you stay tuned, but you never find out. My parents said it's the most popular question on the O'Grady Kids fan site they run. What the heck is Allisyn winking about? There are pages and pages of hilarious responses.

I'm about to yell at Mallory and her crew to turn down the sound when Liza points a remote at the TV and does it for me. She storms outside on her Hollaphone yelling at Dave again.

I return my attention to my Nerd Bowl team on my screen, and we get into a debate about the best way to prepare for the tournament. Just as I'm dialing this girl who may be able to help, I hear: "One, two, three-ee-and-a-fo', Rocket and Poppit be knockin' on yo' do'!" The bass from the family room speakers kicks up until I can feel it in my jaws. Although Leon's lips move on the screen, I can't tell what he's saying.

"Sorry. Call you right back." I rush out of my parents' office, across the kitchen, and into the family room where Mallory, Liza, and four other girls are pop-locking. They move around all jerky-like as if they're plugged in with frayed electrical cords. I lower the speaker volume.

All six stop in mid-pop, or lock, not sure, and glare at me.

"Hey, what gives?" Mallory huffs with hands on her hips. She's wearing one of her many Majik 8 Balz t-shirts, of course with Twista' Sista' in hot pink over the eightball. That's her crew nickname ever since she perfected her head-spin, the highlight of their act.

"Sorry. I'm on a Zaam call in there and we can't hear."

Mallory twirls her rust-colored ponytail into a bun. "You know we practice here every Tuesday and Thursday night while Mom and Dad teach. Why aren't you up in your room?"

"Computer's all jacked up. My new tablet just burned up. And no one else's computer will let me log in except Dad's. My stupid Hollaphone won't stop singing to me, so I can't even use that."

"But tryouts for America's Fave Dance Troupe are in two freaking days and Santos just threw all this new choreo at us," Mallory complains. She doesn't even ask why my tablet burned. I wonder if she's heard. "We gotta' practice and this is my last chance. I can't rehearse tomorrow because I'm subbing lyrical, ballet, tap, jazz, then freaking *Flamenco* if you can believe it. Been seriously learning from InstaTok all day between classes. I'll be totally wiped after."

"Well, more power to you, but I need to be able to hear my teammates and vice versa. So, can you keep it down a skosh and lower that bass so that I don't have any more heart palpitations?"

"But we need to *feel* the music to get a feel for the music. That's why you should do your thing *upstairs*." Mallory points toward the ceiling like I don't know where it is while turning up the bass and lifting one eyebrow, yet another thing I can't do.

I flash her a tight smile, not wanting to raise my voice in front of everyone but having no choice. I shout: "*As I said*, my computer is acting up. We have an emergency ourselves with —"

Mallory puts up a hand to shush me while turning down the sound, then flicks her fingers to shoo me away. "I don't need to know. Go back to your big, important meeting and leave us alone." Her stony eyes dare me to say anything else while some of her crew members smirk.

Irritated she puts down everything I do, I spin on my heel, my skin prickling from her always getting under it. Taking a couple deep breaths, I try to calm myself enough on the way back to Dad's office to continue my meeting. Between her and the bus, I pray I don't burst into tears.

I grab a cupcake on my way, hoping it'll help.

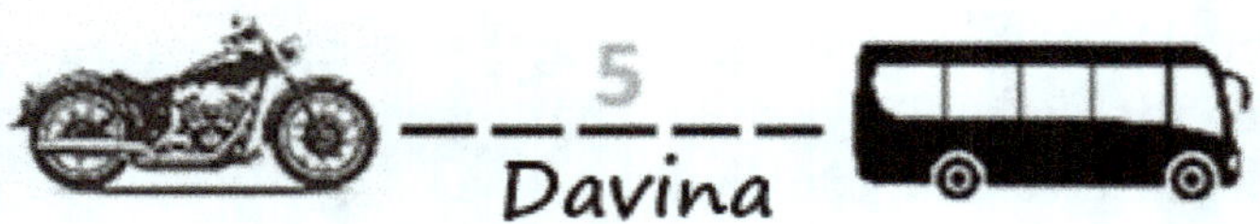

# 5
## Davina

“Hey, Davina, want me to come over later to fix your computer?” Isaac asks from my screen. “Maybe we can go for a smoothie after, you know, and then we can study together tomorrow after school if you want, like quiz each other over at my place or something. My parents are out of town.” Isaac winks at me like Leon and Antonia aren’t right there.

Ugh, so awkward. Ever since those two rum punches and a little kiss at Antonia’s Thanksgiving party a couple weekends ago, Isaac acts like we’re going out. Although he’s nice enough, I’m just not feeling it the way I imagined for my first boyfriend, like at all, maybe even into the negatives. It might just be that when he laughs, he kind of looks — and sounds — like a walrus wrestling a fish in its mouth. Once noticed, it cannot be unnoticed. Also, kissing him was like smooching wet clay.

Although I’ve been politely obvious about my disinterest, Isaac hasn’t gotten the hint. Now, he’s cornering me in front of others and pressing me to make plans. Antonia even commented when he did it earlier this week, saying it was giving Nerd Bowl a weird vibe. We’re meeting soon to strategize.

My mind is a pitching machine spewing excuses, and I slug one at Isaac. “My parents’ lawyer is coming over when they get home from teaching. Snake Riley may be released from juvie soon, so they need to prepare a victim statement to prevent that, and I said I’d record them. Probably not a good night, but thanks anyway.” He doesn’t need to know that all really happened yesterday. I kick myself, wondering why I brought Snake up again when I wanted to stop thinking about him. He’s on my mind way more than he should be, which is never. Pisses me off even further; everything about that guy irritates me.

Isaac’s face falls. “Yeah? Wow, time flew by. How long’s it been since the trial?”

“Like eight months now.”

“Who’s Snake Riley?” Leon asks. He just moved to Michigan this summer, so he’s clueless about most things.

"He's a junior like me and the son of the leader of the Rebel Demons," I tell him. "The same biker gang that messed with us today on the bus looking for Krystall Nykkolls. Snake went to juvie for attacking my parents this past Valentine's Day."

"Seriously? Why'd he do that?"

I shrug. "Who knows? He never talked the whole trial." I sigh, my blood still boiling about him being so tight-lipped after all he did, further torturing us by making us wonder why. He never admitted anything or apologized. "That day," I tell Leon, "after my parents exited a Detroit Symphony Orchestra performance and were searching for their car, Snake came out of nowhere and pushed my dad into traffic where he was nearly flattened by a semi. Dad's old hip and leg injury was made much worse as he escaped, and he needed surgery. Then, Snake shoved my mom over so hard that she fell against a concrete bench, breaking her front tooth and cutting up her face. Then, he literally ran over her, stomping on her head and giving her a bad concussion that she still gets dizzy from all this time later."

Leon's eyebrows shoot up. "Oh wow. No way."

"Way. After a root canal and implant, which cost a fortune and were quite painful, Mom had two plastic surgeries on her face but needs more. They won't be able to fully erase her scars until the new nanobot technologies get advanced enough to repair skin tissue. The doctor said she may have to wait like five to ten years. Meanwhile, now she looks like a patchwork quilt."

Antonia clucks her tongue. "I still can't believe someone could do that, especially to your mom who's so pretty and nice. She's like maimed from him."

I nod. "I know. Still can't believe it either. Snake didn't just almost kill my Dad and take my mom's looks, but he stole Mom's evening bag, the one that my Bubbe beaded and stitched for Mom with her arthritic hands shortly before she died. Bubbe even sewed a secret message into the lining only Mom would understand. God, I hate that Snake bastard. Wonder what he ever did with it after he spent her cash."

"Probably sold it for drugs," Isaac says with a snort. "Or another stupid snake tattoo."

"I just can't believe Snake would mug my parents over a little cash when his Rebel Demons are loaded with all the money that they have coming in." I shrug. "Doesn't make any sense."

"It's such BS that he's going to come back to school, and you'll have to like *see him* in the halls." Antonia shakes her head, her nostrils flaring. "Nice payback after you like saved his life and all."

"I know, right?" I sigh about the prospect of ever encountering him again. "I wonder what he has against me and my family. Like, did something happen I don't know about?"

"You saved his life?" Leon asks.

"Kinda', yeah," I say. "During outside lunch in fourth grade, I'd started eating my vegan bologna sandwich when this huge Doberman wandered onto our playground and went after Snake — back then he was Jonah — who was playing tetherball with his friends. The dog pounced on Jonah so you could barely see him. His screams were ear-shattering as the dog started mauling him."

"Oh God," Leon said. "So, what did you do?"

"I just ran over and threw my bologna sandwich at the Doberman, and then Mallory and all the other kids followed suit. The dog forgot all about Jonah, chomping his way through a minefield of PB&J's and ham and cheese's, which allowed Jonah to run to safety. He never once thanked me, and I figured he either thought someone else saved him or he was the rudest person ever. After what he did to my parents, I know that Jonah 'Snake' Riley is a bad seed from a no-good family, plain and simple."

"God, sounds like it," Leon says. "What a jerk."

I wasn't aware they made people as bad as him until I encountered him in all his snake-filled glory, sitting in court with a frown on his face as he studied his table. I got to stare for the entire two-day trial at the tattoo of a snake wrapped around his neck going up the side of his half-shaved head, like right onto his face and everything, with a forked tongue that dips into his pierced eyebrow. Jonah got it sometime in middle school, and from then on, everyone started calling him "Snake." I shudder, so disgusted. I can't imagine why *anyone* would mark themselves up like that, for a cool nickname or otherwise. It's so stupid and gross.

"You got that right about Snake being from a no-good family," Antonia says. "My cousin Carlos bartends at this biker bar over on Gratiot.

He says Snake's family's motorcycle club, the Rebel Demons, are responsible for a lot of the crime in Metro Detroit and all over the state. They've got chapters in Flint, Battle Creek, Ypsilanti, Jackson, Lansing, Cadillac, and tons of other places too. They're called 'one-percenters,' the baddest of the bad, and you never want to mess with them, or they'll mess you up, like maybe permanently."

I picture Krystall Nykkoll's face contorted with fear — obviously someone who did mess with them — and my heart skips a beat.

I shove the image away and nod. "Oh yeah, my parents' lawyer told me that too. She's well acquainted with the Rebel Demons, always in court with them over one thing or another. She thinks since Snake turned seventeen while inside, he'll probably drop out of school and go do Rebel Demons stuff — whatever that entails — and I'll never have to see his ugly snake-tattooed face again. God, I hope she's right." I exhale, thinking about how I was sure he'd escaped juvie and was there on the bus for me.

Shaking my head, I again try to purge my worried thoughts for Krystall Nykkolls and return to my Nerd Bowl meeting. "So, guys, let's do quiz questions from the four categories we don't know, and then assign each one to whoever scores the highest in that subject. Hopefully, we don't suck as bad as we think."

"Sounds good," Leon says. "I got some Nerd Bowl questions here. Topic is politics. Okay, what is the Democratic stance on using nanobots to optimize genetics in unborn babies?"

Isaac shrugs. "Against?"

Leon makes a buzzer sound. "Democrats totally support this. You living under a rock?"

We attempt five more questions, answering none correctly. As Leon asks another, the music from the family room cranks way up again. "Drop it like you *a liar*. Drop it like you *on fire*. Drop it like you *be higher* – what? – higher – what? Higher than high, lower than low. On the flo', yo', less go!"

I groan. "Seriously?" Running back to the family room, my fingers clench, ready to strangle my sister.

Mallory dances over to the speaker so that she's blocking it by the time I arrive.

"Hey!" I reach around to turn down the sound, keeping my hands from my sister's neck only because I have witnesses.

She shifts her body to stop me.

I go the other way, but she's quicker, and then it becomes a game as Mallory moves all around, her body a shield.

When she throws her arms above her head and thrusts her hips this way and that, I do the only thing I can think of without getting violent…I tickle her.

Mallory tries to ignore me, but I continue until she can't stand it and keels over laughing while swatting me away. "Stop!"

Giggling, I slap-fight with her and push past to the volume control, turning it down again. "Hey, sorry, I know you need to like *feel* the music and all, but I've got to —"

A scream outside drowns me out.

My eyes fly to the French door which leads to the yard. "What the —"

Mallory bolts toward it and whips it open as the shrieking continues.

I hurry after her to the edge of our pool where Liza stands pointing. I follow her finger to the shimmery water below, past the leaves and twigs and a stray innertube drifting lazily from an afternoon breeze, to find a body face down in the deep end. Its head is circled by a halo of blood.

My heart vaults into my throat. Who the hell is that?

Me, Mallory, and Liza all gawk at each other, then return our gazes to the floating body as the rest of the Majik 8 Balz join us.

Its head pops up, and the person in our pool gasps for air as a gash on their forehead leaks red into their eyes.

Shock steals my breath as they flail their arms, their mouth opening and closing like a fish but nothing coming out. They sink under, then struggle to the surface before it occurs to me that the person in our pool is the missing drug dealer Krystall Nykkolls — and she can't swim.

How did she even get here?

Some Rebel Demons at the side fence shake the shoulder-high gate. Finding it locked, one climbs the rungs and hoists himself over.

As Liza dives into the pool to save her boyfriend's cousin, Krystall lunges for the side and pulls herself onto the ledge, practically springing out of the water. She takes off for an opposite fence and scales it like she's Spiderman, clamoring over as a few Rebel Demons charge after her. They have more trouble than Krystall but eventually disappear over the same fence using our BBQ as a springboard.

Liza hops out of the pool and grabs her Hollaphone, tapping the screen. As we hear a *pop-pop-pop* in the distance, Liza says, "I gotta' tell Dave. Sure hope his cousin's fast — if she's still alive."

# PART 2

## MALLORY AND THE TECH TOUR

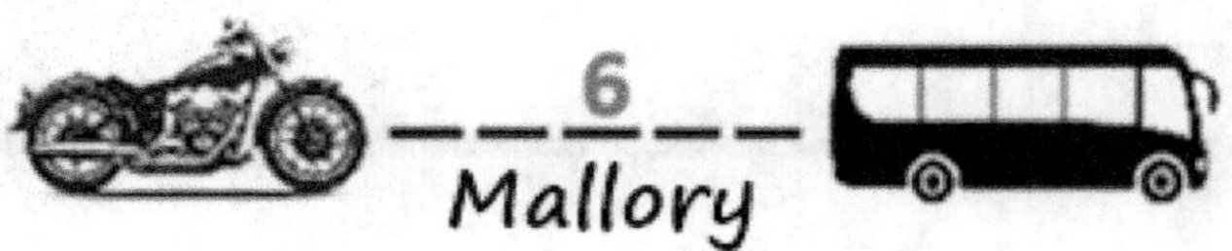


**Monday, January 7, 2030**

It's been around a month since anyone saw or heard from Krystall Nykkolls. Her face is plastered on flyers around town and websites all over the OuterNet. No one knows if the Rebel Demons got her or not, but it has given the people who host *What's Up South Farmington?,* our school's MeeToob news vlog, great material this whole time. They've interviewed police officers, people at Buddy's Pizza where Krystall worked, and a bunch of students who knew her, but no one is saying where she went. I've helped my best friend Liza and her boyfriend Dave, Krystall's cousin, asking around and putting up flyers. So far, we've only heard speculation and gossip.

Dave's aunt, Krystall's mother, reports the police have no leads and say the Rebel Demons insist they haven't seen her each time they've been questioned. The bikers supposedly stopped the bus and ran through our yard after Krystall because they needed to discuss a business matter. They claim she redesigned their website, but part wasn't working right. She seemed to think they were upset with her and ran off, disappearing in the shadows behind our house. They supposedly haven't seen her since.

When I asked why the Rebel Demons weren't arrested for what they did to Davina's bus, crashing it and maybe even setting it on fire, Dave's mom laughed so hard, she spit Vernor's ginger ale out of her nose. She told us through her tears that the Rebel Demons own most of the judges and cops in town, so it's a non-issue. That's why they were so ballsy to even do it. I asked how Snake got put away in juvie most of this year if they're so influential, and Dave said he must have had a new judge they didn't get to yet.

I haven't helped Liza and Dave as much lately though because two weeks ago, right before winter break, my Zayde, my mother's father, had a major stroke. I spent a lot of time at the hospital with Mom, who isn't taking it very well. Her brilliant father, who she admired her whole life and tried to emulate, suddenly doesn't know anything and is blind. He went from the most intelligent person Mom knew, a theoretical physicist and professor at the University of Michigan in Ann Arbor, to the intelligence of a one-year-old in a matter of seconds that the stroke lasted. She just can't wrap her brain around it yet. And with my Bubbe now gone, he has no one to help him when he gets out of the stroke rehab. Mom says he might move in.

The day I return to school for the spring semester in January, I get a text from Mom during fifth period. She asks me to come home in the hour before I teach my lyrical class at Miss Sylvia's Dance Centre. She and my father need to talk to me.

"Is it Zayde?" I ask through text, bracing myself for bad news. I suffer through half of physics wondering how it will feel to find out he passed. Bubbe was hard enough last year.

Mom finally answers as the bell rings. *No, he's about the same. His occupational therapist says he's making a little progress even. Yesterday, he was able to hold a spoon and feed himself some applesauce.*

I sigh with immense relief and sadness until she texts: *We'll tell you later, but don't worry.*

So of course I do. My parents never miss work, and now they'll both be there in the middle of the day to talk to me instead of teaching? No, something's up for sure.

When I arrive home, seeing their cars in the driveway sets my heart a-flutter and I rush inside. "What's going on? Is Davina okay?" Although she and I aren't exactly close and never were, which people always comment is rare for identical twins, it still concerns me.

Mom's eyes are jazzed about something. "She's fine. Here!" She shows me her Hollaphone, a huge grin on her face. It's the first I've seen since her father's stroke.

Peering down, I see an email from the SAT people. Results for a test my parents made me take. Big deal. "This is why you're home early and made me come before class? I already saw they sent it."

"No, but how did you do? I can't log in to see."

"No idea. I didn't check." I tap my watch to splay my Hollaphone, then sign in. Glancing at my score, I shrug. Even though it does nothing for me, it'll make them happy.

My parents look like dogs whose frisbees are about to be tossed. "Well?"

I hold my phone out to them, and they're sharks on a bloody leg. Hugging me, Dad twirls me about like he's a merry-go-round while Mom shrieks in my ear. "Perfect score on the ACT *and now* the SAT! It's a miracle! Well done, well done! Can't wait to tell *everyone*!"

They're as excited as I would be if I'd landed a role dancing on Broadway.

"We're so proud of you!" My parents bury me in a suffocating embrace.

I duck out and back away. "Okay, okay, great. Is there anything else? I need to get to the studio."

My parents peer at me expectantly. "Really? No excitement at all?"

My shoulders bob. "Big whoop. Doesn't get me any closer to becoming a professional dancer, does it?"

"No," Mom says, "but it could bring you tons of other things, like full rides to college, inspiring mentorships, and other great opportunities!"

I twirl my finger. "Not on Broadway. K, so what do you want to talk about? I need a snack before class, so can we make it snappy?"

My parents' faces fall, but I can't fake enthusiasm even with all the work I've been doing to improve my acting technique.

"Well?" I turn toward the pantry and search for something that won't upset my stomach while teaching.

Mom shoves her Hollaphone in my face.

I back up and squint at the screen. "Michigan Technological University Preview Tour 2030. Leaves on Saturday. Yeah, so?"

"Davina shared it with your mother on Twitbook, and Mom signed you up!" Dad beams like he's telling me great news.

I push the phone back at Mom. "What? Why would you do that?" Has she been smoking crack? Although my parents are so enamored with Michigan Tech that they've talked about it my whole life like it's the best place on Earth because it's where they met, fell in love, and became biomedical engineers, they know my whole reason for living is to dance, *not* be an engineer.

"I even got you into the last slot for the Mechanical Engineering Spotlight Tour!" Mom practically burps exclamation points. "You'll get to talk one-on-one with students and professors and get an extended showing of—"

I could kill Davina. I can't believe she sent this to Mom knowing how crazy Mom is about her alma mater. She probably did it to get me back for everything she's always resenting me for, constantly trying to stir the pot between me and my parents. "Really? This is why you made me come home? Why you're both not teaching?" I shake my head, so incredulous. It's like my parents were invaded by body snatchers or something.

"Yes!" Mom says. "They were advertising on Twitbook, and I paid the $500 fee and the extra for the Spotlight Tour, and now you'll get to go with real students to all the major core classes and —"

"You know very well that the day after graduation, I'm moving to Manhattan. I don't want to major in any tech area, or even go to college right away, if ever. I'll do anything to make it on Broadway, to fulfill a lifetime of working my tail off to achieve this goal. Have you ever heard me or watched me dance? Do you know me at all?" I shake my head, wondering if intense worry about Zayde has somehow compromised their brains.

"We've discussed this," Mom answers. "We've researched the odds. You know it's such a longshot. You need to stop living with your head in the clouds and do something more practical. You're getting old enough now to start making some important decisions."

"Head in the clouds? Seriously? Come on. Someone's got to make it on Broadway. Why can't it be me? I'm not going to give up because it's challenging. That's why I'm here on this Earth, to be that dancer who everyone wants to see, to make everyone happy, to be me. I need to go *now* when I'm at my prime and have the best chance against so much competition. I've explained this a million times, but clearly, you don't listen." I scoff. "You're the ones with heads in clouds."

I've been training ever since my parents took me to magical productions of *42nd Street* and *A Chorus Line* on Broadway when I was five. So, in a way, it's their fault. I knew as I watched the dancers with their beautiful legs, pointed toes, and spangled costumes twirling and swaying and lifting and shimmying while twinkling their jazz hands and singing great songs that I *wanted* to be up on that stage, that I *had* to be on that stage, that it was my *calling*, my *purpose*, my *destiny*. Stars were forever in my eyes after that trip, and *that's* where I want to be — not stuck in some damn lab behind a computer screen.

"Mallory, we know you enjoy dancing," Dad says, "but considering all your academic accomplishments, we'd really like you to get serious about your future and reconsider."

"*Get serious!?!? Reconsider!*?!? Not become a dancer and choose a technical career? Uh-uh, no way. Are you really even saying this?" My eyes practically bug out of my head. "You've paid for lessons for me all this time and come to many of my performances. You know I've worked my butt off my whole life preparing for this. How can you think I'm *anything* but serious, and more importantly, why wouldn't you want me to do what I love?"

Mom leapfrogs over Dad. "Because you've had perfect scores on every single test you've ever taken, doing better than even your sister who is so advanced. And you know you put in no effort while she works her tail off. Imagine if you tried? Your superior intellect would be *wasted* if you spent your life simply *entertaining* people. Don't you see? You could be doing something truly *valuable*, contributing to the advancement of society!"

My jaw drops. "So, I'm being punished for it? Because not dancing would be a punishment."

"Punished?" Mom asks. "You've been given a gift, a gift you must use!"

"Yes, I've been given a gift. Maybe. Whatever." I sigh and roll my eyes. "But even so, like, isn't giving people great joy while inspiring them to be creative and exercise for better health and be romantic and all the other amazing things dance can do something that helps society too?"

"It's not the same. Doesn't matter as much," Mom says like she's the be-all and end-all of what should matter.

My parents are beyond clueless. I think of how dancing makes me feel in my very soul, the way it fuels me and inspires me and makes me stretch to my very limits — maybe like facts and figures do to them — and I cannot imagine doing anything else. "You've never been moved by dance like me, so you don't get it," I tell them. "You think you know everything because you have doctorates and I'm a stupid idiot."

"That's not true," Dad says. "But in this case, we know better about you and what you can do."

I huff at his nerve. "Well, just because I'm good at math and science doesn't mean I like them."

"You should think about more than what you *like,* but what you'd be best at with your strengths," Mom says. "You could contribute so much with your extraordinary intellect, even working with emerging nanobots and other artificial intelligence technologies!" Her eyes light up as she mentions her newest area of research, which she wants to discuss with everyone, like even the kid manning the Taco Bell drive thru.

Mom's nanotech talks are like taking ten bottles of sleeping pills. I form my fingers into a gun and blow my brains out. "Uh, no thanks."

"But they're now using nanobots to target bad tissues and cells in cancer patients, eliminating the need for chemo and radiation. We're on the verge of finally, *finally* being able to *cure cancer* for real, all because of nanotechnology. People dying from cancer will soon be a thing of the past! Can you imagine?"

"That's great but —"

"*And,*" Dad says, "some psychiatry faculty at Wayne State University's Medical School are using bots to continuously monitor and adjust serotonin, dopamine, and other levels in the brain. Soon, mental illnesses like bipolar disorder, schizophrenia, and borderline personality disorder will become obsolete, allowing those afflicted to lead normal lives. Nanobots are here and they're revolutionary. Doesn't that sound exciting?"

"Sure, but —"

"Don't you want to get on the ground floor of all this?" Dad asks. "You could become a pioneer like Madame Marie Curie who discovered radium, polonium, and radioactivity. She won the Nobel Prizes in physics and chemistry for making huge strides toward treating cancer. *Or* you could be like Lady Ada Lovelace, daughter of esteemed poet Lord Byron and a brilliant mathematician. She wrote the first computer programming language in the mid-1800s before computers were even invented."

My eyes widen. "Really? How is that even possible?"

Mom taps my SAT score on my phone. "It is for those with minds like yours, who can see how to make the future better. *You* – not even Davina – but *you* have a mind like theirs, we're sure of it, maybe even like Archimedes of Syracuse himself. His mathematical and engineering discoveries and inventions from around 250 BCE are still used today with little improvement, and he didn't even have a calculator! We didn't name our dog Archie after him for nothing."

As if on cue, our black and brown rat terrier Chihuahua comes by and humps my leg.

"We know you love to dance," Dad says. "And you still can on the side, but this is more important, don't you see? You could become another Lady Ada or Madame Curie!"

I groan, gently shaking Archie from me. It's a lot to live up to.

Mom clenches my arm. "And we don't want you in a few years after you've tried and failed on Broadway, or even if you've succeeded. We need people like *you* with off-the-chart math and science aptitude *now*. The U.S. lost its foothold as the world leader in technological advances. We need kids majoring in STEM areas like never before. Your participation, dear Mallory, is necessary for the success of our whole country!"

I don't answer because I'm thinking through a difficult tap sequence I've been trying to master: *heel shuffle-heel toe, heel shuffle-heel toe, heel shuffle-heel shuffle-heel shuffle*-JUMP-*toe*.

My eyes come into focus. Beyond my parents, Davina is down the hall struggling to open the garage door that always sticks as hurt paints her face. Didn't realize she was home yet. She must have heard everything. A wave of guilt almost knocks me out. The door pops open, and Davina slips away before I can say anything. Out the living room window, I spot her running down the driveway to Antonia's car wiping her cheeks.

Serves her right for sending Mom the notice about this Tech Tour that she signed me up for.

I'm sure Davina resents what she just heard because she knows it's true as much as we do, but I can't not be me for her sake. I mean, should I throw test questions and pretend I can't dance just to make her feel better? I can't help that I got certain abilities she missed and she feels she must compete with me in everything, joining the maximum number of school clubs they'll even allow. She's even trying to start an animal rights group only she cares about. It's never even a competition, and it's not my fault that I always win.

Mom nudges me. "Maybe even one day, you'll figure out how to use nanobots to help Zayde recover from his stroke!"

I glare at my mother, crossing my arms. "Don't you dare. That's so low. Don't use him to get me to go."

Dad squeezes my shoulder. "Just check out the school before you decide. Go on the Michigan Tech tour your mother booked. I know you're not a fan of the cold, but it's so great up there, I promise you'll be pleasantly surprised. Will you at least do that? Do it for your mother?"

Oh great. He threw in a "do it for your mother." I glance at Mom, noticing how old she has become in the weeks since Zayde's stroke. She hasn't kept up with her roots, and the gray line there in addition to new wrinkles across her scarred face has aged her at least ten years. Her exaggerated pout strums the strings of my heart — but not enough to play me.

"Look, it's going to be cold in New York, and I'll have to deal with it there which sucks, but hell, I'd wear a string bikini and live under a lean-to in a blizzard for Broadway. But to attend Michigan Tech and study engineering in those extreme weather conditions?" I shake my head. "No thanks. If I wanted to major in something nerdy, I'd go to Lawrence Tech with you guys, or preferably the University of Florida where it's warm. But I'm going to Broadway, so it's a moot point." Before they can say anything else, I grab my bag, a package of almonds, and my water bottle, and head toward the foyer.

"Mallory, please go on the tour and give it a real chance," Mom calls. "You'll love it there! We promise!"

I shake my head, a wry smile on my face. "You guys are too much. Nope. Sorry. I won't go. And next time you have five hundred bucks to just throw around, I could use some new toe shoes, leotards, and tights."

Dad catches up to me at the door, his lips stretched into a thin line. "Mallory, if you won't do as we ask, you leave us no choice but to discontinue all the financial assistance we provide for your dance costumes and competitions. We won't help you if you can't at least consider what we're saying."

Tears fill my eyes. “Like even our Spring Break Showdown in Cancun that we’ve been planning *all year*?”

“And the European Exhibition next summer,” Mom says. “Please go on the tour. That’s all we ask.”

The strings that my parents have been supporting me by are suddenly frayed and ready to snap. “The final payment for Cancun is due next week! I can’t flake out! Everyone’s counting on me.”

Dad puts his arm around me. “Then do the Tech Tour, give it a real chance, and we’ll talk when you get back.”

Shaking him off, I slam out the front door and escape to my lyrical class.

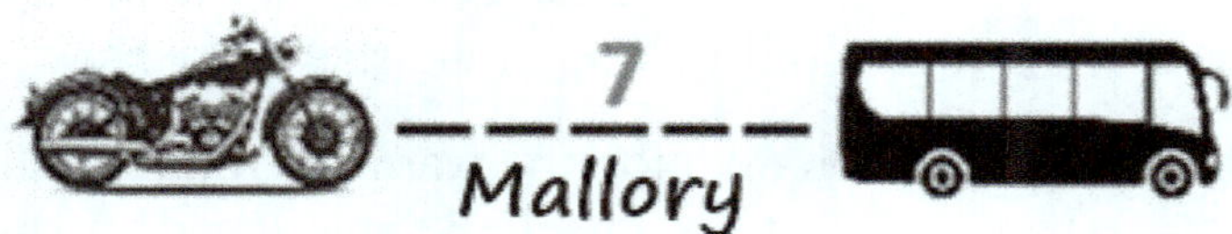


**Wednesday, January 9, 2030**

I grasp the ballet barre that I helped Dad install in our basement, my self-appointed dance space. Standing in first position, heels together, toes pointed outward, I listen as my warmup music plays from my Hollaphone hovering in Float Mode. Stepping right, I land in second position and do a grand plié, my knees bending outward so that my fingertips sweep the floor. I straighten my legs and stretch my right hand over my head toward the mirror as the early sun angles through the upper windows and blinds me.

Focusing on my breathing, I push my body into deeper and deeper stretches, hoping to shed the negative feelings that have kept me in a chokehold all week. As I lean forward into an arabesque, balancing on the little square tip of my toe shoe, I fume about the Tech Tour that my parents are trying to rope me into. Damn Davina, sending Mom the link to it knowing she'd make me go. And right at the beginning of the term too when I have so much to do. Plus, I'm choreographing two new routines with Santos for our debut on America's Fave Dance Troupe in a few weeks. I kick forward, catching my foot high above my head, then leave it in place and arch my back, grabbing onto the bar and touching my ponytail to my calf.

Miss Sylvia still hasn't responded to my email that Mom forced me to send, letting her know I won't be teaching next week because of the Tech Tour. I've probably blown it with her by taking so much time off with little notice. Now, she won't tell her Broadway buddies about me as she promised when granting me the spot as her junior dance teacher. Maybe she'll even blackball me. I've heard she does stuff like that if you get on her bad side.

My head swarms about me and I lose my balance, collapsing into a pile of tears and toe shoes as I realize how leaving next week might affect me. But then, not going on the Tech Tour will mean losing my funding for Cancun and Europe, and I don't want to dip into my savings for them, or I will literally have to live in a lean-to on Broadway until I land a job. But as Twista' Sista', I can't not go; I'm kind of the star of the show.

Exasperated, I abandon my morning warm-up routine and rush up to the bathroom I share with Davina. I peel my leotard and unwrap my toe shoes, then shed my tights. Showering, I try to squelch the resentment in my belly about how my parents are suddenly trying to dictate my life. No matter what I say, they have a counterargument. And part of me sees their point, I really do, but I cannot imagine giving up dance for any reason, no matter how good it may be for others. And that makes me feel guilty, like Mom wanted, saying I'd be wasting my real strengths which could improve peoples' lives. A small part of me thinks she's right, but the rest of me screams that I was born to be a dancer, and it's more important to follow your heart than your conscience.

I get out and dry off, then gather my clothes for the day, returning to the bathroom with an eye on the time. I slip into my dark purple sparkly tights, then pull on my black spandex mini-skirt, silver tank top, and off-the-shoulder purple sweatshirt that says *Dance Like Nobody's Watching*. As I start on my make-up, Davina walks in. Fastening the gold pin that Bubbe gave her through the collar of her ruffled white blouse, she glares at me in the mirror.

We haven't spoken since she overheard our parents praising me yesterday. She returned from studying at Antonia's late, and I didn't even know what to say, so I hid in my basement dance studio practicing grande jeté's. She's been down since her Nerd Bowl team lost some big tournament right before Winter Break and are now in third place, and nobody showed up to two animal rights club meetings she held except her two BFF's. Then, Zayde's stroke, so I know what she heard is tough on top of those, but what am I supposed to say? Sorry Mom and Dad know I'm smarter than you? I can't help how they act, or who I am.

I apply paste to my toothbrush and start brushing instead of talking. Glancing over to see her smearing some shiny gloss on her lips, I notice she looks heavier than ever in her fluffy pink sweater she pulled over her blouse. Her face is fuller than mine, legs and arms pudgier, and her belly protrudes slightly. I'm sure it's one more thing she resents me for. She's not fat at all, just not as tight and toned as I am. Yet I dance seven days a week while she goes to the gym occasionally. Maybe I inherited my superior intellect and ability to dance when she cannot, but I earned my slimmer figure. She can't blame me for that, but I'm sure she's found a way.

Her look of hatred intensifies, the crinkle of her nose growing deeper as she runs a brush through her flaming hair.

“What?” I finally say, burning from the heat of her silent accusations. She’s probably even faulting me for having redder hair.

“What what?”

I spit into the sink. “Why are you so mad at me?”

“Who says I’m mad at you?” Davina pulls a polka-dotted scrunchie around her ponytail.

“Mom, who told me that *you* sent her a link for that Michigan Tech tour all next week that she’s making me go on. That was such a shitty thing to do! It’s not my fault that —”

Davina rolls her eyes. “Really? You think I gave her the link so that she’d send *you*?”

She tosses her hairbrush into its bin and storms out of the bathroom as I stare at her, my mouth agape. How did I not realize it before? Of course she sent it to Mom for herself. It’s another way to get our parents to recognize her. She’ll be the one who is enthusiastic about attending the school they love, being the cooperative one when I’m not. And then she and my parents will have something in common that I don’t, their knowledge about all things Michigan Tech. She’s always running a race against me, who is only walking yet still beating her.

Then, I realize I can use the fact that Davina was the one who wanted to go on the Tech Tour to try to get out of it and start formulating a plan.

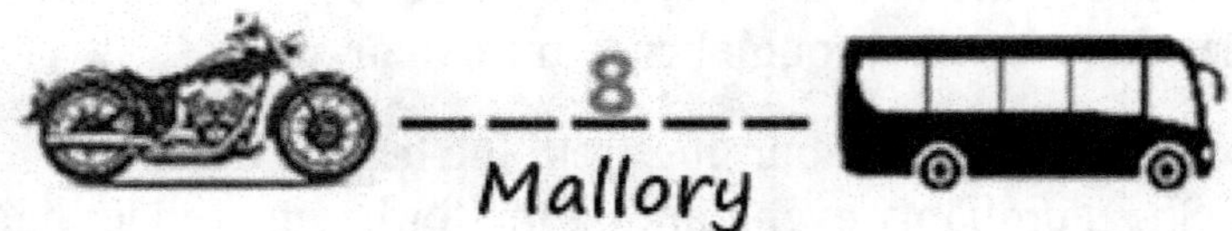


**Thursday, January 10, 2030**

The past two nights, I've barely slept awaiting a response from Miss Sylvia, and then when she finally replied, she told me all the teachers who will be covering for me next week are upset that I ruined their off-time plans. I'm so worried I blew it with her and the other teachers now and beyond pissed my parents put me in such a position. I don't even want to teach tomorrow, afraid I'll run into some of them.

"You know, Davina forwarded you the Michigan Tech Tour link so you would send her?" I blurted to mom when we were packing lunches in the morning. Whatever plan I thought of the night before flew out the window as my desperation overtook logic in my sleepy brain. "She should go, not me."

Mom looked mildly surprised but then shrugged. "She'll probably go there whether she does the tour or not, or to Lawrence Tech, because she already knows she wants to study math and will get a great education at either. Or if she flips and wants to study animals that she's so passionate about, she'll probably go to Michigan State. But it's you who we want to impress. You know very well you're our greatest hope for success."

My eyes whipped around thinking Davina must be there, but I didn't see her. I could faintly hear a song from her favorite band No Ice Cream for Ian coming from upstairs. Whenever I get a compliment, I'm always scared she's there to hear, and her hurt face has become my biggest fear.

I asked Mom why Michigan Tech is making us go on this tour a whole week, right at the beginning of the semester. She said it takes fourteen hours by bus to get there, and they want you to get a good view of their campus and all there is to do, so it needs to be an entire week to get the full experience. When I balked at the long bus ride, Mom suggested I meet new friends and learn to play Euchre, a popular card game up there, like she thinks I'll be attending after next year and will care. Ever since her father's stroke, she's been acting so freaking weird.

Tonight, after finishing my evening practice with the Majik 8 Balz, my parents corner me in the kitchen. Mom slides a box of vegan seven-layer cake in front of me on the counter and grins, knowing this dessert from a Jewish bakery is my favorite thing in the world besides dancing.

"What's the special occasion?" I ask, opening the box and pulling the top layer off a piece. I've only ever eaten this type of yellow cake with whipped chocolate icing between its seven tiers one layer at a time. I allow myself to indulge on my birthday because it's so fattening. This variety spiced with rum is the best.

"I felt bad you're upset about the Tech Tour next week," Mom says, serving us slices. My parents sandwich me on bar stools at the kitchen island.

"Yep. Pretty upset about being blackmailed."

"Please don't view it that way," Dad pleads, handing me a fork. "We want you to be more open-minded, to really think about what we're saying and see what it's like at this amazing school before you reject it."

Mom grabs a framed photo nearby showing her and Dad embracing against a backdrop of a white lighthouse and a blue expanse of water. My parents love it so much at Michigan Tech in the Upper Peninsula of Michigan, or "U.P." as everyone calls it, that every few years, they travel there. After, they go further to the Copper Harbor Lighthouse an hour's drive above Houghton to renew their vows under the Northern Lights. The image shows them holding hands in the very spot where Dad first told Mom he loved her and where they later married, the waves of Lake Superior applauding in the background.

When Dad originally let Mom know how he felt and they kissed, the song "Grandpa Got Run Over by a Beer Truck" by Da Yoopers — a band famous for singing funny lyrics about life in the U.P. — came on Dad's playlist Mom made for him. It became their song, and they played it at their wedding reception to great laughter and throughout my whole life.

Mom puts the picture in front of me. "Remember how beautiful it was when we went to Copper Harbor last time? You could live with all that gorgeous scenery every day while you study up there."

"I've never gone. Always had dance commitments."

"Oh, that's right," Mom says. "That was Davina who came last time and bought you those copper earrings you love."

I feel my ears and realize I'm wearing them. "Yeah, Davina said it was unbelievable up there," I admit. "She described incredible views, especially driving through an ice tunnel formed by the snow weighing down the trees over the road."

The teal and purple rhinestones surrounding my Hollaphone watch flash. I glance to find a text from April, the girl who my boyfriend Blake dumped for me last summer when we all worked together at Olga's Kitchen. I haven't talked to her since I quit shortly after discovering they'd been together before he and I were. It got super awkward with her dirty looks and nasty comments.

She writes: *Hi. It's April from Olga's. Went to my brother's frat party at U of M last Saturday. Saw Blake making out all over the place with some tall, skinny Asian chick with short hair and long earrings. Didn't know you guys broke up.*

My heart cannonballs into my Skechers. Neither did I.

Last Saturday, I'd been ready to spend an entire weekend with Blake in his dorm room at the University of Michigan and sleep with him for the first time. He'd been asking for a while, and I was finally ready to gift him my virginity. Just as I was halfway out the door, he called to say he got Covid-28, and I shouldn't come. I've barely heard from him since, only a few texts to say he felt horrible and was sleeping a lot. I gulp back a wave of tears. Did he really feel horrible because he was sleeping with that other chick a lot?

"Something wrong?" Mom asks as the seven-layer cake in my stomach threatens to come back up.

I'm not about to tell her what I just read. She's always so dismissive of our relationship, especially now that Blake's away at school even though it's only forty-five-minutes away. She warns not to put all my eggs in Blake's basket, even though she wasn't much older when she put all her eggs in Dad's.

I flip over my phone. "No. Nothing." I glance back at my parents' wedding picture in Copper Harbor. "Davina also said it was unbelievably cold up at Tech, much more so than here in Detroit, which I already can barely tolerate. She said it starts snowing in early October and typically goes all the way until May. That's not for me. You know I'm a summer girl."

“Oh, you get used to it!” Dad says. “All that snow and ice make things so fun!”

I snort. “Snow and fun do not belong in the same sentence.”

Dad slaps the island counter, jarring me from my seat. “That’s because you’ve never been to Michigan Tech! It’s all about snow and fun up there!”

His giddiness makes me think that the rum from the cake is getting to him.

“God, we used to barrel tunnels into the snow plowed into giant mounds all over campus and hang out in them,” Dad says with a nostalgic grin. “It was especially fun with a case of beer and a deck of cards so we could play Euchre while watching Star Trek on our portable TVs. We’d huddle together under flannel blankets on waterproof sleeping bags, usually with a pizza or subs, at least until Public Safety chased us away.”

I shudder, my nose wrinkling. “I can’t imagine doing all that in the cold.”

“You get enough people together, you don’t feel it,” Mom insists. “And it’s a great excuse to snuggle up to someone new.” She winks at me.

“I’ll take your word for it.”

I picture Blake and some beautiful Asian girl cuddling under a blanket in an ice cave and a wave of nausea threatens to take me out to sea. Exhaling through it, I text Kari, Blake’s stepsister who is my good friend, forwarding her April’s message and asking her opinion.

“Then, in February,” Mom continues, grasping my hands to stop me from texting, “Michigan Tech hosts its world-famous Winter Carnival, which they’ve been doing over a hundred years to celebrate all the glorious snow. The main attraction is the elaborate ice sculptures that the Greeks and other student clubs build all over campus.”

Kari responds: *No way would Blake cheat on you. April’s full of shit.* She includes a poop emoji. *Besides, if it really happened, why did she wait so long to tell you?*

My heart climbs out of my sneakers and soars back into place. “Great,” I say, pulling away. “Now, I really must —”

Mom shows me her Hollaphone again. “Everyone we knew often traveled over to Hancock, Houghton’s sister city, via the Houghton-Hancock Bridge, the world’s heaviest and widest double-decked vertical-lift bridge. It’s a civil engineering marvel and official landmark.”

I glance at a picture of the bridge on her phone. “That’s nice.” I forward April’s message to the leader of the Majik 8 Balz, my good friend Santos, wanting a guy’s perspective. I type: *Thoughts?*

Dad turns in his seat and unknowingly elbows me. My Hollaphone clatters to the counter.

I snatch it up before Mom can read anything.

Santos responds right away: *April may be telling the truth. Blake cheated on her with you, so why wouldn’t he do that to you too?*

My heart yo-yo’s in my chest while considering what Santos and Kari said as Mom shows me another picture on her phone. A bunch of hockey players pose for a team photo holding some huge trophy. “We also went to a ton of awesome Huskies hockey games at Tech. Always such a blast!”

I put my hand over my heart, hoping to still its bouncing as a million thoughts about Blake collide in my head.

“Or,” Dad says, “we’d battle it out with other students in the broomball pits all over campus.”

“Broomball? What the heck is that?”

“It’s like ice hockey,” Mom says. “But you chase a ball instead of a puck around the ice rink with brooms rather than hockey sticks, wearing sneakers instead of skates.”

“Oh, the bruises we suffered crashing into each other!” Dad says like it was a good thing. He and Mom high-five over my head.

I slide off my stool, moving away before either parent can force me to listen anymore or bribe me with more cake. “I hear you, really I do, and it does sound like a super-duper great school, but it’s not for me. Sorry.”

“Talk to us after you go on the tour next week,” Mom pleads. “I know you’ll change your mind.”

I stalk up to my room, incredulous at how unfair my parents are being, threatening not to pay for things they promised and sinking so low as to try to butter me up with seven-layer cake. They've barely mentioned Zayde all week, suddenly putting all their attention on their quest to change me. And now Blake may have faked Covid-28 to diss me for our first time so he could be with another girl?

While night ticks by and gives way to dawn, I'm dizzy going back and forth, wondering what to do about my boyfriend and how to get out of the Tech Tour. All my supposedly high intellect fails me. Staring at the new day's sun through the blinds striping my comforter, I'm still clueless about both.

# 9 Mallory

**Friday, January 11, 2030**

In my multicultural class, we're doing all these touchy-feely getting-to-know-you activities because it's a new course. For our in-class timed essay today, we were to write about something incredible that happened to us or someone we know. And perhaps since Michigan Tech and my parents are on my mind so much this week, the first thing I think of and subsequently write about is the unbelievable way that my parents met there. They insist no couple could ever, ever top it. I sure hope I never do.

And of course, since I've had no sleep and am in the worst mood imaginable, my teacher picks me to read mine to the class.

Groaning, I trudge up to the front of the room wishing people weren't always making me do shit I don't want to do. Peering down at my paper, I clear my throat. "My mom and dad were freshmen at Michigan Tech in 2001 and lived in the same dorm, having everything in common but not knowing each other yet. They were part of a large group of kids who'd trekked up the hill of snow plowed up so high that it reached the top of Wadsworth Hall."

"Yeah," a boy near the window says. "My cousin goes to Tech. He says the snow up there is insane."

"It was sometime after dinner, with the glaring lights from the dorm the only illumination in a dark and starless sky. While other kids skied and snowboarded on the giant snow mound whooping and hollering, blowing off studying as heavy metal music blared from someone's window, Dad straddled Mom on a long sledding train of about twelve students who took off from the roof."

"Oh man. Sounds like a blast!" someone comments.

"Near the end of their descent, their speed lightning as their sleds gained momentum on the slick surface, the sledders encountered a raised manhole cover in their wake. The train became a hammer striking a broadhead nail, and half the sledders went left while the others went right. My father, right in the crux of the split, was pulled in one direction while his leg, still wrapped around my mother, was yanked in the other and practically torn from his body."

"Oh my God," several people murmur.

"Everyone panicked as Dad wailed like a bear-trapped coyote. They scrambled around as he writhed in the snow, everyone trying to help him. His leg was all twisted and bent at an angle so disturbing that a girl took one look and puked into the snow right next to his head. As the smell mingled with the realization of what happened, he did the same. While the students waited for the ambulance to come and others poured out of the dorm to see what was happening, they tended to my father who cried for his mommy and wished he never decided to go sledding."

"I'm never sledding again," a girl in the front row says, and several around her agree.

"Only Mom thought about how cold Dad would become if his adrenaline slowed enough for him to feel it. The temperatures were dipping below zero by then. Mom ran to her dorm room nearby and returned with the down comforter from her bed, wrapping it all around Dad, whose name she still didn't know."

"As they awaited the paramedics, Mom cradled Dad's head in her lap, stroking it while telling him her favorite math jokes, hoping to distract him. Her corniest: 'What is I times M times A times A? I am a square.' Dad snorted and even grinned despite everything. Mom quizzed him on math formulas and elements from the Periodic Table in chemistry and Newton's Laws of Motion in physics. She taught him how to sing the Quadratic Formula to the University of Michigan's 'Hail to the Victors' fight song and even got him humming along through clenched teeth. Mom did anything that she could think of to occupy him until help arrived."

"When Dad had several surgeries to repair his shattered leg and hip, Mom — by now introducing herself as Barb while she learned his name was Seth — sat by his side and kept his parents updated after they had to return to St. Paul. She got his assignments from his professors and made him lentil and split-pea soup in the crock pot she snuck into her dorm room. She took good care of his gerbil Henry III that he snuck into his since he couldn't get around very well."

"Mom helped him catch up with what he'd missed since they discovered that they had three courses together but had just never noticed each other before. My parents have been inseparable ever since, and to this day, my father walks with a cane and a severe limp. He says it doesn't really bother him though because it reminds him of how he met Mom."

I sit down to huge applause with everyone saying my parents are the coolest ever. I grumble thanks, knowing better as they're about my least favorite people in the world right now, and try to figure out Plan X to get out of the Tech Tour since all the others have failed. My time is running out.

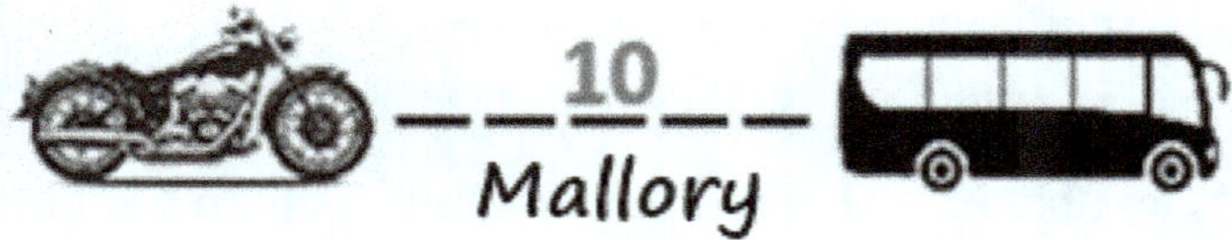


**Saturday, January 12, 2030**

The red light looms up above, bleary and blinding in the haze of the early morning dusk. As I flip on my left turn signal at the head of the line to enter the Twelve Oaks Mall in Novi where the Michigan Tech tour bus will be waiting in front of the Macy's, I wish I could think of something — anything — to escape. My time to get out of it is up, all attempts to stay home while still getting my parents' financial help for Cancun and Europe falling on deaf ears. I need a Hail Mary, but no one even has a ball.

Yawning, I grip the steering wheel tight, my knuckles white, resenting being woken up at the ass-crack of dawn to go on this thing when I could be sleeping. Honestly, I'd rather have a root canal or pap smear than this; I'm on the verge of screaming.

And then on top of it, they made me drive, both saying they had to catch up on student emails. Glancing at Mom beside me appearing so smug as she types on her Hollaphone and my dad in the rearview mirror squinting at his like nothing's wrong, I feel like smacking sense into each of them, making them see things from my point of view. I guess they'd say the same about me, but I've honestly tried. I can't see giving up my dancing dreams for any reason, no matter how noble theirs might be. They're certainly not going to live my life for me.

"Oh, by the way," Mom whispers, talking on the side of her hand like she's telling me a secret even though Dad's right there. "Another added inducement about going to Tech I failed to mention is that over eighty percent of the students are male. It was a nine-to-one ratio when I went, but now, eight to two — that's eight guys for every two girls — which are still good odds. That means not much competition for the hottest guys and could make for a very, *very* fun time." Mom winks while I cringe, not wanting any more information.

"Uh, I have a boyfriend," I remind her, although I'm not sure I do anymore. I didn't hear from Blake at all yesterday. I stopped myself a million times from texting him, unsure of what really happened with that tall skinny girl with the short hair and long earrings — if there even was one.

April's text haunts me, winding a continuous loop through my mind. Blake making out with some girl at the frat party. Blake, who was supposed to be sick when he knew I was going to finally be with him, who chose that other girl over me. Maybe.

As I go to the crazy place in my mind obsessing about every facet of our relationship and what could or could not be true, horns honk. Mom yells at me to drive. I glance up, and the light is green.

"Mallory! Do you hear me? Go!"

I begin hyperventilating, thinking of Blake making out all over that frat party with some chick he just met, when he knew why I was coming up there that weekend. How could he do that to me? And so publicly?

*Or maybe he didn't just meet her,* this other part of my mind taunts, and then I go down that rabbit-hole, wondering how long he'd been lying and how I'd missed the signs.

The honking continues.

"Mallory! The light is green! Turn! Turn now!"

My brain catches up with reality, and I lurch forward.

Right then, a low red sports car behind me zips around my right side, making the left turn before me and scaring me to death.

I slam on my brakes, causing my seatbelt to strangle me as I come millimeters from hitting it. "What the hell!"

A new SUV behind me almost crashes into me now, but I floor the accelerator and my Jetta lurches forward, causing Mom to scream.

The red sports car darts ahead of me into the four-lane loop surrounding Twelve Oaks Mall. I charge after it as my parents yell for me to slow down. The red car weaves in and out of traffic, and I follow, nearly causing several accidents.

The sports car exits the loop and approaches a fancy gray bus sitting in front of Macy's. It parks in a spot, and a dark-haired guy in jeans and a brown leather jacket unfurls from the driver's seat.

He's going on the Tech Tour too? Awesome. I pull up next to him and jump out, ready for battle. "What the *hell* is your problem?"

He opens his trunk and reaches inside. "No problem, now that I made my bus in time." His calm voice makes me want to throttle him.

With dark hair falling over piercing blue eyes and a cleft in his unshaven chin, the guy is way better looking than I want him to be. If I wasn't so pissed and attached to Blake, I'd be trying to get him to notice me. Seems unfair, given how much I hate him right now. "Like, two seconds would have made a difference. You couldn't have waited for me to make my turn?"

"I honked several times. Others did too. You weren't budging, and I had a bus to catch." He slams his trunk and hoists a duffel to his shoulder. "You snooze, you lose. What can I say?" He walks toward the bus while I gape like an idiot.

I barrel after him, but Mom pulls me back by the hood of my coat. "Mallory! What's gotten into you? He could be your future chem lab partner. Don't burn bridges before you even start!"

My eyes shoot her with daggers. "Really? You're *defending* him?"

"No, I'm not, but — "

"And for the millionth time, I'm not even going to Tech, so it won't be a —"

"Are you going on the Tech Tour?" a bouncy voice asks behind me. I spin to find a short girl wearing a Michigan Tech knit hat, a thick blonde braid fringing over her shoulder. She has a black, white, and gold coat over a Huskies hockey jersey, and a matching Covid-28 mask bearing an MTU logo covers her lower face. She dons big, obnoxious sunglasses that seem inappropriate for a dreary January morning when the sun has barely peeked over the horizon.

"Uh, well..." I search my brain for a possible excuse.

"Yes, she's going," Mom says. "She's Mallory Rosenbaum, and she's also signed up for the Mechanical Engineering Spotlight Tour."

"Oh yes, right here," the girl says in a squeaky baby voice as she taps her Hollaphone. "All checked in! Please give your larger bag to my assistant and get on the bus!" As Dad carries my duffel over to some tall guy in Tech gear, Blondie reaches up to put an arm around me and lead me toward the bus door. “We’re going to have such a blast this week, just wait and see! You’ll come back a whole new person, ready to fill out your admissions app!”

Before I know it, I’m standing inside the bus next to the driver, another person wearing Tech gear, wondering how the hell I’m going to get out of here. As the doors shut behind me and my parents and others wave from outside, the driver announces in a lisping voice that we’re going to stop again in about an hour when we reach the world-famous Bronner’sss Christmassss Wonderland in Frankenmuth to pick up more passengerssss.

I sigh a million sighs and glance toward the back, feeling sorry for myself.

The driver continues, her voice booming over a PA system. “Just sit tight, and off we go, up to Michigan Technological University in Houghton, the world’s most beautiful campussss. We have K-Day in September where you can explore over two hundred student-run clubssss. Then, there’s the amazing Winter Carnival in February, where among many exciting activitiessss celebrating the region’sss great snow, student groupssss build amazing ice sculpturessssss all over campussss.”

As I eye an empty seat near a few big guys by a rear bathroom, it occurs to me that I can ditch the tour when we hit Frankenmuth. Then, I can Uber over to Ann Arbor to spy on Blake at U of M, maybe even confront him. My parents won’t know, and I’ll hide out at one of my friend’s houses the whole week if Blake is a cheater, or I’ll crash in his dorm room if he’s not. Maybe I’ll be able to teach some or all my dance classes if I can borrow someone’s car, and then Miss Sylvia and the other teachers won’t hate me. The fare to Ann Arbor will be pricey, but it’s a way better use of my time. Not sure why I didn’t think of it before.

I laugh, glad I finally have an idea after knocking my head against the wall all week. My parents can bite it if they think I’m going to Michigan Tech for even a day. Even if I must crawl there, I’m going to Broadway.

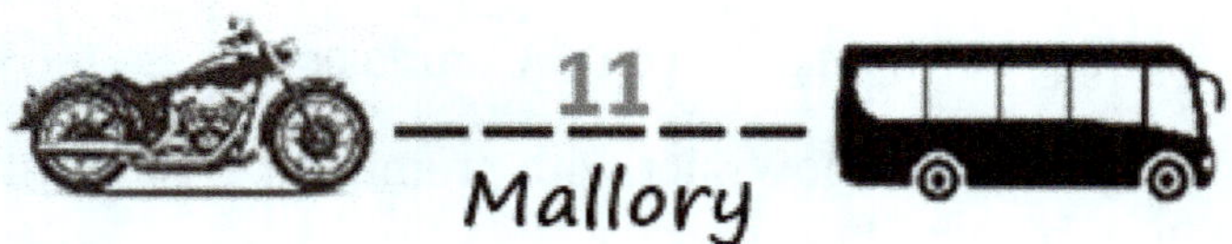


# 11

## Mallory

While heading to the rear of the bus, I approach the jerk with the red car — Asshole Red Car Guy — about halfway down on my right. He pats a nametag on his brown leather that says "Ollie." I scowl as I pass, but then my eyes land on two faces behind him that irk me even more.

It's that bitch Camila I beat out for my job at Miss Sylvia's Dance Centre. She's an attractive Hispanic girl with pin-straight caramel hair and huge almond-shaped eyes I'd kill for. She's with sidekick Keondra, a Black girl with cute braids woven into hearts on both sides of her head but with buck teeth covered in green braces making her look like she just ate a leafy salad.

Camila and I were the final two contenders for the junior dance teacher spot at Miss Sylvia's, and I won over her. Maybe she didn't point her toe, her rhythm was off, her split wasn't wide enough, or I did one thing just a little better because the girl can dance. But I beat her fair and square, and we both know it.

Weeks later, as my Majik 8 Balz was about to perform in the end-of-summer WRIF Dance-Off hosted by Detroit's rock station, Camila threw down her cup of ice water in my way as I rushed to the stage. I slipped and fell on my butt *hard,* pulling out my back and twisting my ankle. I had to go on like that — barely even able to *walk* — after she'd smirked and told me to watch where I was going. Keondra and their other stupid friends snickered like the bitches they are.

After I stumbled around so discombobulated trying to dance through the pain, eventually toppling from the stage and fracturing my arm, we totally lost even though we were the favorites going in. Camila's crew, The Purrrlz Gurrrlz — girls who dress like cats wearing pearls — won. And not just the title and bragging rights, but the freaking $10,000 cash prize, the money we were counting on to fund future competitions. My team was furious with me, thinking I was drunk or something until I told them what happened, and now they have it in for The Purrrlz Gurrrlz, a real West Side Story brewing. And I'm stuck with these two on the Tech Tour? Oh, hell no. Another reason not to go.

My two dance enemies smirk at me.

"*You're* going to Michigan Tech?" Camila asks.

Keondra snorts and elbows her with prominent green teeth as she guffaws like a horse named Ed.

"*You're* going to college?" I return with a sneer. Moving on, I hear "skanky-assed bitch" behind me along with giggling and high-fiving. Whatever.

As I reach the back, I start forming my plan for what I'm going to do once I get to Blake's dorm. He's on the third floor. Will I need rope and binoculars?

While I sit, a girl a few rows ahead lumbers back, barely fitting between the seats, and squeezes onto the bench to my left across the aisle. She wears a gold Huskies hockey jersey and gold ski hat covering her brown curls. The top pom of black yarn resembles a porcupine laying her as its golden egg. "Hey there," she calls with a wave. "I'm Darla."

I glance over and shoot her a half-smile. "Hey. I'm Mallory."

"Aren't you soooo excited to being doing the Tech Tour? I've been like counting down the days ever since my guidance counselor told me about it before Thanksgiving!"

"Uh, no, not a bit. Sorry."

"Oh." Her face falls. I'm a pin in her buoyant balloon.

Her smile lights her up again. "Well, I'm totally majoring in structural civil engineering. It was between that and architecture school. My dad's friend who's a civil engineer said it is the better career choice because it's easier to find good stable jobs, so I'm following his advice."

"Oh. That's nice."

"I'll be designing bridges, dams, and other structures besides houses. I'd really like to specialize in high rises so I can understand why the World Trade Center's central placement of the elevator shafts was the reason the towers imploded so easily during the 911 attack. Interesting stuff, ya' know? So, what about you? What will be your major?"

I force a smile. "I'm majoring in dance."

Darla's face twists with disgust like I said I just ate roadkill. "*Dance?* At *Tech*? Didn't know that was a possible major there."

"Oh, I have no intention of going there. My parents are making me do this tour, but I'm getting off at the next stop so —"

"Oh," she says, her eyes downcast. "I see."

"Didn't mean to…sorry."

She waves a hand with a tight smile and returns to her original seat, pushing in her earbuds.

Whatever. I'll never see her again. And I finally have time to think. As we make our way up to Frankenmuth, a city known for their German-style fried chicken and open-all-year Christmas superstore, the two Tech reps walk the aisles chatting with various people. Blondie who greeted me and a taller one with dark hair poking out of his Huskies hat seem super friendly, but their Covid-28 masks and sunglasses make it so I can barely tell the difference except by their heights and the taller one's scraggly beard escaping his mask. Oh, and Blondie's braid. I pray they don't come down this way. I can't even fake politeness. I just want off this thing.

The college reps engage Darla for a while as my mind churns with plans of escape. Thankfully, they wander away as we pass under an arch with a red and white sign that says "Willkommen" — "welcome" in German — and one below that says "Frankenmuth" in a fancier blue script on a white background.

I stand and grab my backpack, wondering if they'll send me my duffle from under the bus since my name and address are on the tag. Even if not, the sacrifice of a few pairs of jeans and sweaters is worth it to not be stuck at Michigan Tech all week listening to boring lectures about how great my engineering career will be.

The bus stops and two people get on. A short Asian boy with slicked-back black hair and circular glasses and then a tall gorgeous blond guy wearing a Detroit Pistons jersey under his varsity letter jacket. They sit ahead of me on the right, the light-haired guy in front.

I forge ahead, but Blondie stops me. "Going somewhere?"

"I have to get off."

"Get off? Why's that? There are bathrooms at the back, and we'll be stopping for breakfast in two hours. We have water and protein bars now if you —"

"It's not that. It's my personal business. But I need to go." I swallow. "It's an emergency."

"I'm sorry, but your parents signed paperwork saying you cannot leave —"

"I don't care. Let me pass. I know my rights as a United States citizen and —" I try to push past her.

The taller rep stands behind Blondie. "Please, miss, whatever it is, let's sit and discuss it like —"

"Are you *seriously* not letting me off?" I try to squeeze by again, but they block me like bumper paddles on a pinball machine guarding the death zone.

"No one may get off the tour," the taller rep says.

I argue and push, so determined to get to Blake, but then Blondie reaches into her coat and pulls out a huge black gun, pointing it at my forehead. "Kindly sit your ass down and shut your trap. As we said, *no one* gets off this bus!"

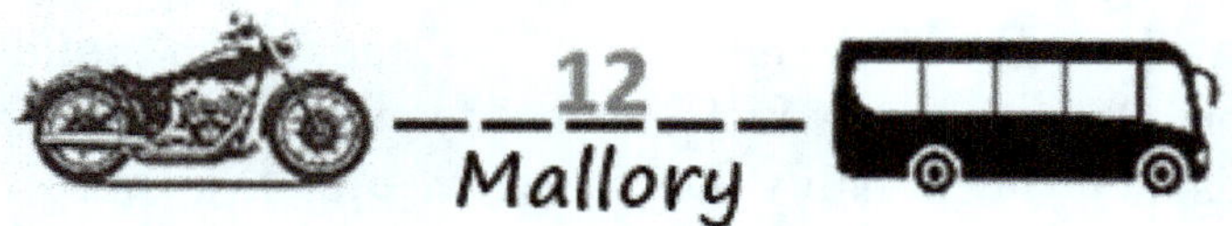


# 12 Mallory

Everyone gasps as the petite representative from Michigan Tech with the blonde braid, the one now with a gun in my face, forces me down until I'm sitting next to Ollie from the red sports car.

He grabs my hand and squeezes.

I glance at him as he mouths, "Be cool."

Three people from the back similarly disguised as the college reps stand with guns, outing themselves as part of this — this whatever this is. Shock chokes me as my eyes go wild, looking from one to the other to the other. That makes six including the driver who are shrouded in Tech gear and holding guns, and now I understand their big sunglasses so inappropriate for a dreary winter morning.

A new reality sets over me like a wrinkled veil as people around me whimper and curse. A whirring sound overtakes them, and everything darkens as shades lower over each window. At the front of the bus, a white screen unrolls from the ceiling.

What the hell? My heart is ready to detonate as I eye the Tech reps waving their guns around.

"Fill this out right away," Blondie says, shoving something at me. I grasp an index card with some text on it and a black and gold Michigan Tech pen. The little rectangular paper asks for basic info like my name, school, year, and hobbies. I'm shaking so hard that I can barely write as a million questions pummel me at once.

The screen ahead brightens, and a group of people appear. Two big guys wearing leather vests with patches all over, their bare arms full of tattoos, stare back at us. Next to them, there is a bald man in a gray suit, a blonde woman with a fur collar smoking a long cigarette, another person in the shadows with gleaming eyes and a triangular pointy hat. Behind them, there's a blur of people whose faces I cannot see.

Blondie waves at the people on the screen. "Hello there, our dearest VIPs. Welcome, welcome! You have been chosen to participate in a new interactive game called Vermilion as our esteemed guests. By playing, you will be able to try out our new 'Invader Patch' produced by our firm, Azure Dragon, Inc., which attaches to existing nanobots and vastly expands their functionality. Don't believe me? Just wait and see!"

"At Azure Dragon, Inc.," another captor says, "our team of dedicated scientists figured out how to harness the bots to do things you would never believe, for all sorts of purposes no one has ever conceived. By playing this game we've created, you will get a chance to see our ultra-enhanced Rover-Bots live in action. In return, we only ask for your generous donations to our company for shares in it, at one percent per hundred grand minimum buy-in per round. This is quite fair considering that the Invader Patch which generates and manages the Rover-Bots will allow us soon, very soon indeed, to rule everyone and everything." Ominous music out of nowhere makes the hairs on my arms stand on end.

The VIPs on the screen bend together whispering.

Blondie clears her throat, but they don't seem to notice. She claps her gloved hands to call for attention, but the VIPs ignore her. Finally, she shoots a hole through the bus ceiling, and we all duck while the VIPs finally stop talking and look up.

Blondie continues in her sing-songy baby voice. "We can disperse the Rover-Bots into municipal water sources, introduce them into grains, wheat, and barley, even feed them to livestock. We can program them in real-time to do all sorts of destructive things, tracking them by unique sequencing. You will be delighted at all they can do, and we're even working on an Invader Patch 1.2! With several amazing add-ons and plug-ins to expand their functionality even further, you will soon see exactly where the Rover-Bots can go. And now, on with the show!"

A thug from the back of the bus comes forward, a black case in his hands, and Blondie takes it from him. "But before we start this game called Vermilion which we've created to demonstrate how amazing our Invader Patch and Rover-Bots can be, let's meet our players, shall we?"

"You are Player #1," Blondie says. She points her gun at a girl at the front of the bus who stands on shaky legs. The girl is so thin, you could blow her in half with a good solid breath. She has short, white-blonde hair held back on one side by crisscrossed pins. Blondie yanks her forward in front of everyone. "Please read your information card."

"My, um, uh, my name is Paige," she says, a tear running past her trembling rosebud lips. "Paige Tellison. I, uh, I'm a senior at Warren Fitzgerald High School and uh, I guess, um, well, I like horses and creative writing and drawing Anime and stuff." She sniffles and wipes her cheek with a jittery hand.

"Great, Paige. Well, since you are Player #1, you will get your injection first." The thug nearest Blondie opens the case and withdraws a syringe with a long needle that makes me feel like passing out. He hands it to Blondie as Paige shrinks back with terrified eyes.

"No freaking way," someone says behind me.

Blondie hands her gun to her accomplice, grabs the syringe, and wraps her arm around Paige's slender throat. Stabbing her neck, Blondie depresses the plunger until all the clear liquid is gone. Paige cries out along with me and several others before Blondie shoves her back toward her seat. Paige clenches her neck with both hands, sobbing as she sits down.

What. The. Fuck.

I exhale, and Ollie squeezes my hand. I forgot he was even holding it. I sneak a peek, and he's shaking his head, warning me not to try anything. The inside of his wrist has the five Olympic rings tattooed there, and I suddenly notice how built he is. His broad chest under his leather jacket tells me he works out a lot.

Next, Blondie forces a butch girl to stand. Her head almost hits the bus roof, she's so tall. She's sporting a Junior ROTC sweatshirt and camouflage pants, with combat boots and a fresh buzz cut to the sides of her spiky yellowish hair. She seems so tough, although her face is quite pretty with nice hazel eyes, tulip lips, and a cute button nose, a startling contrast. She's all badass until Blondie hops up on a seat and puts her gun a millimeter from the girl's temple. The ROTC girl tells us in a small voice that she's Sammi Grayson, a senior at Birmingham Groves High School, and an E-8 Army Cadet Master Sergeant. I have no idea what that means, but she says it like she's important. A taller thug injects her anyway, and then they make my seatmate, Asshole Red Car Guy, a.k.a. Ollie, stand. He comes into the aisle to face the VIPs on the screen.

"I'm Ollie Melson. I'm a senior at West Bloomfield's Andover High and a former gymnast turned cheerleader after a major fall from the high bar gave me a brain injury." Blondie injects him and tells him he's Player #3. Ollie climbs back over me, holding his neck while wincing.

I am Player #4. Standing on jelly legs, I tell everyone I am a junior at South Farmington High School who loves to dance, and then they shoot God knows what into my jugular. I listen to the others, Camila and Keondra behind me who go to Southfield Lathrup High School, Darla the heavy girl from Novi High, and Jiro, the short Asian kid who says he does homeschool and wants to study chemical engineering. Then Troy, the cute Pistons fan across the aisle from me, says he's on varsity basketball at Frankenmuth High. The whole time, I think of the Rover-Bots Blondie just described and wonder if they're now swimming around my insides.

After each of my bus mates introduces themselves and receives an injection, Blondie confirms that they've filled us with millions of *real-time programmable* nanobots that can do a whole host of interesting — and painful — things.

"Millions! Painful? Are you freaking serious?" Darla cries. I twist around and her eyes are tearing, but so are Keondra's and Camila's. Mine start leaking too as we realize what has occurred.

One of the thugs comes at Darla with the butt of his gun. She scoots toward the window and quits complaining.

Suddenly, Ollie next to me clutches his knee and cries out like someone just pounded a spike through his eye. He's all over me writhing around like he's going to die. Then, Blondie makes a big show of punching buttons on her Hollaphone, and suddenly, Ollie stops screaming in my lap and rubs his knee. "It's gone! It's gone! I don't believe it but —"

Blondie presses another button, and Darla starts convulsing, foam coming out of her mouth as her eyes roll all around. She slumps over in her seat so that I can only see her shoulders and head of curls poking out into the aisle. She jerks about like she's having an internal earthquake. Blondie presses more buttons on her Hollaphone, and the poor girl straightens up, wiping her lips, her brow furrowed as she recovers from her seizure. Holding her head, Darla cries until her face is bright red.

Shit. They're programming the bots to do stuff to us like they said. *In real-time*. I've tuned my parents out when they talk about nanobots, but now I wrack my brain to remember if they ever mentioned such a thing was possible. As far as I'm aware, current nanobots are pre-programmed to do specific tasks, not act upon someone's desire, all remotely from a phone like that.

I shudder as potential scenarios swerve through my mind. I'm full of bots that can do *anything* to my insides if I don't comply, that these people — whoever they are — can make happen to me for any reason, or no reason at all. We're now their slaves, subject to their whim. This is *nanoslavery*, being held hostage from within.

I can barely breathe as Troy across the aisle, the cute basketball player who said he hoped to study forestry at Michigan Tech, clutches his chest and keels over. Sweat pours from his forehead as he barfs up icky yellow stuff, some of which lands on my Timberlands.

"As you can see," Blondie says with a grand gesture of her hand like she's presenting a car, "Troy here is suffering cardiac arrest and —"

My instincts kick in and I reach toward him, hoping to administer CPR. Blondie and her cronies stop me with a cluster of guns in my face.

I lift my hands and back away. "But we need to save him! He could *die*!"

"Ahem," Blondie says, "I think it's too late for that."

I glance over, and the basketball player is perfectly still now, his eyes fixed on the bus ceiling.

"What the fuck! Why didn't you stop his heart attack?" I demand.

"Yeah," Sammi the ROTC girl says. "Why'd you save Ollie and Darla, but not Troy?"

Blondie shrugs. "Well, for the game Vermilion you are going to play, which you will find out more about very soon, there is only room for eight. This boy was number nine. It wasn't his fault that he boarded the bus last. Good thing more didn't get on at Frankenmuth, wouldn't you say?" She clucks her tongue and shakes her head. "For some reason, not that many people signed up for this tour. Good thing we got enough, but sadly one too many."

If they'd only let me off, he wouldn't have been, but I don't say anything. Guns are still on me.

Blondie taps her screen, and a sucking sound begins. Right before my eyes, Troy's body implodes, his bones breaking and disintegrating until he's a pile of skin, hair, eyes, teeth, a basketball jersey, and blue jeans, which creeps me out to no end. I'm practically in Ollie's lap trying to get away. After a few more seconds, the rest of Troy fades until the whole cute basketball player from Frankenmuth disappears into a pile of dust. Tiny Blondie sweeps huge Troy off the bus seat with her gloved hand.

"Poof!" she says with an evil laugh, exploding her fingers outward. "Too bad. He was a hottie for sure." She puts an index finger to her mask and sizzles it on her butt.

"What the hell?" Camila and Keondra demand behind me, echoing my incredulity.

The VIPs on the screen whistle and clap like they're watching a great comedy.

"So, VIPs and contestants," a thug says in a deep voice, "Troy's Soldier-Bots collected hydrofluoric acid from his Med-Bots and delivered it to all his organs and bones until they disintegrated, as you saw. The skin, shirt fabric, and everything else sank into the acid left by the bone debris and disappeared. You will be amazed how we've been able to manipulate the Rover-Bots like the Soldier-Bots, which can collect fluids from anywhere in the body — semen, mucus, saliva, urine, whatever — and transfer it to the Med-Bots. These bots can transform the substances into any other of any quantity, giving it back to the Soldier-Bots to distribute. This is deep tech we're talking about like the world has never seen. You'll get to experience it all first-hand like you won't believe."

Blondie motions to me and my bus mates. "You will all be playing a fun game we've designed called 'Vermilion' where there may be at most *one* winner." Dramatic music blares from a thug's Hollaphone. "The person who claims the most victories after six rounds — if anyone makes it that far — will get the antidote to destroy all their Rover-Bots, which is in this amulet." Blondie pulls a silver chain from her cleavage and lets it dangle, showing a green heart-shaped vial of liquid harnessed by a silver spiderweb.

"Or this one," a thug says, producing the same one on his neck.

"Or any of the 2,713 others we sold last month in our Etsy store," Blondie says. "They're very popular."

All our captors reveal the same necklace.

Our kidnappers have an Etsy store?

I peer at each in their clever Michigan Tech disguises and wonder who the hell they are. Who invented this advanced Invader Patch and is using us to prove their technology works to get financing? I wonder if it's someone my biomedical engineering parents know, and maybe they took me to retaliate for something my parents did to them. Perhaps Mom scooped them, or Dad discredited their research. Anything's possible, I'm sadly discovering.

"The losers of The Game will suffer cardiac arrest like Troy did," Blondie explains, "the Soldier-Bots shooting potassium chloride through their veins. But let's focus on good things. The game you will be playing will be so exciting, especially for the VIPs who will be betting on you." She waves at them on the screen, and they cheer.

Huh? Is this all a joke? Am I being Punk'd or something? I peer around, but no one is laughing except the idiot VIPs.

"Now, to summon help in The Game, you will have two game announcers, Mark-Bot and Karyn-Bot," Blondie says. She turns to the screen. "Dear VIPs, you can purchase these customizable Ear-Bots as part of the Premium or Ultimate packages, or separately as an add-on upgrade. We will go over pricing options in the VIP Orientation after a yummy lunch prepared by our Michelin star chefs while being serenaded by No Ice Cream for Ian. They'll be doing a live show just for you."

These mysterious people who took us, who have an Etsy store (?), can get the most popular band in the world to perform a private show? I think of Davina and how they're her favorite, their posters plastered all over her bedroom walls and their music always blaring from her Hollaphone, and then I remember the look on her face when my parents were praising me for my SAT score and trying to convince me to go on this wonderful Tech Tour, and I almost lose it. The mix of emotions pulls me in many directions, and I squeeze Ollie's hand so hard, he finally says, "Ow," and pulls his away.

Then I wonder about the game announcers' names. The parents on The O'Grady Kids, the show my parents are obsessed with, are named Mark and Karyn. A shiver wisps up my spine. Maybe this kidnapping really does have to do with my parents somehow. They happen to be biomedical engineers studying nanotechnology, and I'm shot up with nanobots. And now this possible O'Grady Kids link too? And then, this other connection with No Ice Cream for Ian, which happens to be Davina's very favorite band?

"Okay, Players," one of the thugs says, "Mark-Bot has game instructions so that you'll know what to do during the first round, which happens at 0700 on the morning we get to where we're going. Simply say, 'Mark-Bot, show Game Rules,' then watch the instructional video behind your eyelids. You'll have one hour to ask any questions you wish afterward. Then, you'll rest this evening during Nap Time. When we reach our destination, you'll wake up for Orientation and Prep Time before your first challenge. Mark-Bot will announce the time remaining for various tasks and the bathroom schedule. Everyone clear?"

As the Michigan Tech tour bus rumbles toward a destination unknown, we all mumble through our shock that the directions make sense. I wonder how long it will be until we "get to where we're going," obsessing about where that might be. Eventually, I summon Mark-Bot to watch the Vermilion Game Rules instructional video, terrified about the scary-as-hell situation we're in. How can I possibly escape, how can any of us, when they've got us by the balls from within?

If only my parents hadn't forced me to go on this tour in the first place. Damn Davina for telling them about it. *She* should be here, not me! I seriously can't believe this shit, but it's happening all around me, and I've got to learn how to win it. Because I need to win. I *must* stay alive to get to Broadway no matter what. No stupid nanobots will stop me, I swear. Stupid, stupid nanobots. They won't get the best of me no matter *who* pushes them on me, not if I can help it.

*Dear Reader, To easily access an abridged version of the Vermilion Game Rules while reading, turn to the last page of this book, then three pages before (careful not to read the ending!) and fold down the corners. Alternatively, you could use that cute bookmark that you just had to buy, forgot about, and never used. It's in your sock drawer. ~ Love, Jennifer*

# Vermilion Game Rules

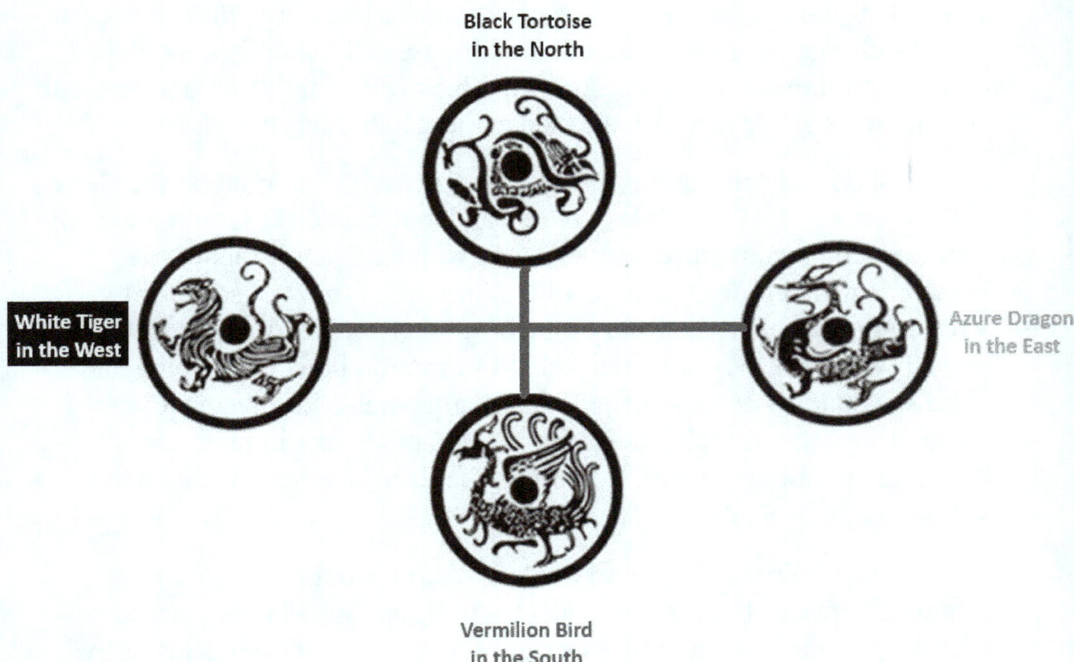

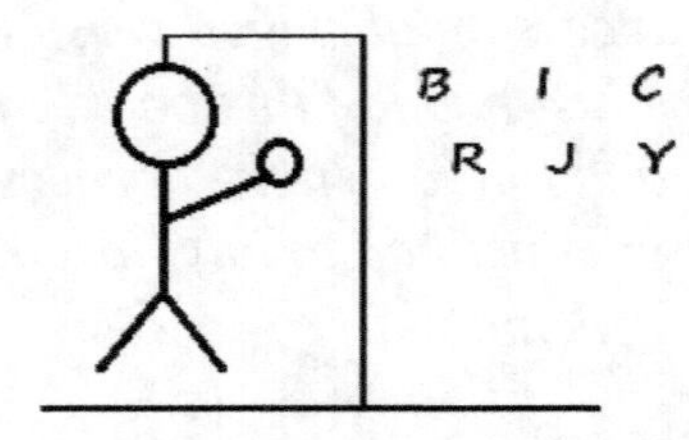


## THE HANGMAN PHASE

Shaking, I close my eyes, my hands clasped in my lap as I sit next to Ollie on the bus. All is black. Suddenly, a disco ball appears above throwing light all over my eyelid screen. A slim, petite woman with short blonde hair long at the collar steps out of the darkness into the circle of a stage light. She wears a pointy-collared blouse full of sunflowers tucked into a mid-thigh brown suede skirt with thick ribbed tights on her legs and pilgrim heels at her feet. A white screen next to her brightens.

She's the spitting image of Karyn O'Grady, the mom on the show my parents love so much, they created and maintain an O'Grady Kids fan site. Goosebumps overtake my arms as I wonder again if this whole kidnapping somehow has to do with them. Then I think of some of the VIPs on the screen at the front of the bus, biker-looking guys in leather vests. I wonder if they were the Rebel Demons and this kidnapping and game or whatever is all somehow tied to my parents involvement with Snake Riley, son of their leader. My parents put Snake in juvie for attacking and robbing them. If that was the Rebel Demons there on the VIP screen, was Snake with them?

The chills multiply until my teeth start chattering, my mind spinning as fast as the disco ball as I try to figure out what one has to do with the other. Is my parents' association with The O'Grady Kids or their beef with Snake Riley or the fact that they study nanotechnology why I was taken?

"Hello, Contestant Mallory," the blonde woman on my eyelid screen says. "I am Karyn-Bot, one of your game announcers."

She's so realistic, but I'm pretty sure she's not the actress from TV who is much older now than this woman. I don't respond, wondering who the hell she really is or who is controlling her, who has taken me and these other kids captive. Her pleasant face turns like day into night, and she glares at me, her nostrils flaring. "I said, hello, Contestant Mallory."

I mumble hello back, in awe of how real her mask or whatever she's wearing looks. Or is she a computer-generated image the Rover-Bots are making me see? It's hard to tell, but she looks so real, whoever she is.

Beside her on the white screen, a gallows platform appears with a rope and noose dangling. Someone with a burlap sack over their head and wrists chained behind them is dragged onto it kicking and screaming. The noose is tightened around their neck, and then the white-masked people who sealed the captee's fate all leave. As the noosed figure flails about, the floor beneath them drops.

Below, text says: "T H E  H A N G M A N  P H A S E," with each letter handwritten on a little blank like in a game of Hangman.

As the person falls, struggles, and eventually dangles with legs still spasming, Karyn-Bot says, "In The Hangman Phase of each round of the Vermilion game, you must collect letter clues to find the four Auspicious Beasts of the Chinese Constellation." Karyn-Bot spreads her arms like she's a gameshow model, bouncing her knees and twinkling her fingers. On the screen appear four gold coins with different animals embossed, the two horizonal and two vertical ones crisscrossed. "They are the Azure Dragon in the East, the Black Tortoise in the North, the White Tiger in the West, and the Vermilion Bird in the South. Get them in the allotted time, which may be different for each of six rounds."

A sky-blue rectangle overtakes the screen. There is a letter "K" printed on it, and underneath, a "3/10." "To find each coin, you will collect clues like this with a letter and a fraction on the back. This means the letter K will be the third letter in a ten-letter word or phrase. The more letters you get, the closer you will be to knowing where to find that coin. Getting to it is a whole 'nother thing. You can check your progress by asking me to 'see puzzle.'"

So, basically, we're playing a deadly game of Hangman? I shake my head, incredulous, wondering who thought of such a thing.

"If you pass the Hangman Phase by getting the coins together on time," Karyn-Bot says, "you and your opponents must walk backward from the fire kaleidoscope — the firescope — that will be formed from the coins until a proper circumference is achieved. When I announce the Vermilion Hour has begun, whoever gets the firescope to the Game Master at the secret finish line within sixty minutes has won the round."

The image is replaced with a skull and crossbones. Red text stamps over it, screaming "Warning!"

"Watch out for your enemies!" Karyn-Bot hisses in my ear. "They want to win as much as you and it is *not* against Game Rules to rob, injure, or kill your opponents."

My heart does zero to sixty in a second flat. I look around at my bus mates and break into a sweat, trying to imagine us at each other like that, enough to injure or kill.

Shuddering, I exhale, trying to squelch the threatening tears, as Karyn-Bot says in a softer, more motherly voice. "Any injuries sustained in a round will be repaired during Nap Time. The Soldier-Bots will carry appropriate drugs from the Med-Bots and repair any broken bones or torn ligaments." A skull and crossbones flag falls from the ceiling over the screen. "If you die, however, there is no Rover-Bot who can remedy that, and you are officially eliminated from The Game."

"Wa, wa, waaa!" cries some game show sound effect.

The skull flag falls, and the screen's image morphs again. Now I'm staring at the spot next to me on the bus where Troy the cute basketball player disintegrated into a tablespoon of dust. I get to relive the pleasure of such a moment as I'm shown the poor guy imploding and vanishing like he wasn't just sitting right there. A banner with the words "The End" waves goodbye. "To reiterate," Karyn-Bot says, "getting killed in Vermilion means you really die."

My eyes pop open and my mind scrolls through a million horrifying scenarios as I glance at my bus mates, my fellow captees. I sure hope not to see any of them in that shape, or be subject to it myself, but judging from how things are going… I sigh, opening my eyes and spotting Blondie ahead in the aisle. It's like she senses it and turns her head my way, her hidden eyes staring at me as I wonder who she is.

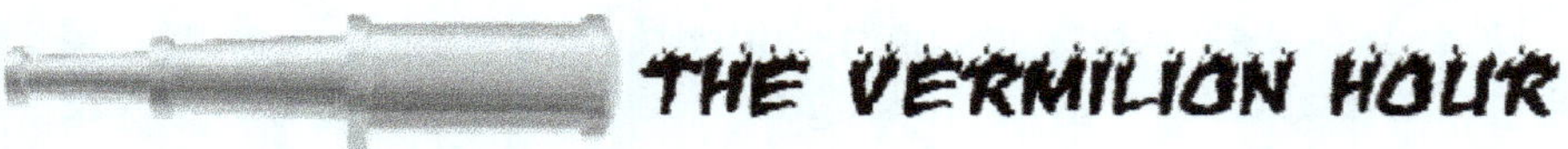

# THE VERMILION HOUR

I clamp my lids closed again to find Karyn-Bot in front of her white screen, the disco lights leopard-spotting all the dark places around. A gold scope appears on the screen with text on it saying, "The Vermilion Hour."

Karyn-Bot puts up a finger. "During the Vermilion Hour part of the round, if no one hands the firescope to the Game Master within sixty minutes, one random player will be eliminated after I spin the Player Wheel."

Next to her, a large wheel appears out of nowhere, one of our names on each colorful wedge. Karyn-Bot spins it and my heart races along, revving up when the dangling arrow above points to the "Mallory" wedge. Wondering if this is a prediction of things to come, my anxiety becomes the hangman's noose.

"The Azure Dragon is the easiest coin to collect, the Vermilion Bird is the hardest, which is why you must get it last. Failure to do so will cause you to face random elimination of one player." Karyn-Bot spins the wheel, and again it lands on my name, sending a wave of panic through me. "Not completing The Hangman Phase and forming the firescope in the allotted time will earn the same result. Random elimination of one player."

The white screen fades, and then my own image appears like I'm looking into a full-length mirror. Around me, a white-dotted egg shape forms and starts rotating as my "mirror me" walks along on the white screen. Karyn-Bot's voice returns. "Game Masters are always watching and listening to you with your Mirror Egg and your Ear-Bots. Be sure to follow all game rules, because we will know if you think we're fools."

My forehead's a swamp while my throat's a desert as I wonder what the heck a Mirror Egg is.

I struggle to breathe as the screen reveals a box of Luckster Gems cereal with Luckster the Leprechaun sliding down a rainbow into a pot of gold. I've never tried it because the gem-shaped marshmallows and oat-n-lard-based coins aren't exactly vegan. Above the box, blood-dripping letters say: Curse of the Leprechaun.

"During the Hangman Phase and Vermilion Hour," Karyn-Bot says, "Luckster the Leprechaun will try to tag each of you with a four-leaf clover." Karyn-Bot's clothing changes before my eyes into different solid-colored pieces that don't match, making her look like a rainbow. A figure emerges from the shadows dressed in green pants and black suspenders, orange curls poking out of his belt-buckled hat and an orange beard covering his chin. His eyes gleam evil as his lips spread into a creepy grin.

"Leprechaun chasing rainbows," he whispers, then swings his arm around Karyn-Bot.

"Ow!" she says, sliding away, a scowl on her face as she lifts her arm to reach something on her back. She dances around, trying to get at it. "Hey! Get it off me!" She finally pulls it forth, and I see a large four-leaf clover made of laminated cardstock, a spike on the back red with blood.

Karyn-Bot's face is scrunched with pain. "If Luckster succeeds in clovering all of you before a victor for the round is named, he will select one gold coin from his pot of gold. Whoever's name is on the front will lose whichever limb is on the back for the next round. So, watch out for Luckster and stay whole!" Luckster high-fives Karyn-Bot and walks over to a black pot with gold coins gleaming as I rub my tearing eyes and wonder if the bots are making me hallucinate. Leprechauns stealing limbs? Really? What the hell next?

My breathing grows more and more ragged as Luckster disappears and then a man emerges into the spotlight wearing an obnoxious Hawaiian shirt, unbuttoned at the top to reveal brown curly chest hair that matches what's on his head. "Hi there, Mark-Bot here." He gives a two-finger salute.

The skull and crossbones reappear on Karyn-Bot's screen. The red text screaming "Warning!" flashes again. "Here are the Vermilion Game Warnings," Mark-Bot says. A Hollaphone appears on the screen in a circle, and then it's crossed out. "You may not use any communication device, attempt to seek help, or tell anyone you're participating in this game. Always wear your provided disguises and do not reveal your identities to anyone. Violation of this warning will result in a family member being subjected to the Punishment Wheel while every contestant must watch."

Another wheel appears, but this time instead of players' names, I see phrases on the wedges like "Puncture Eye," "Burn Body Part," "Submerge in Acid," and "Throw Through Window." Sweat trickles down my spine, and I open my eyes. Thugs and VIPs chat in the distance, but the talking bots in my ear prevent me from being able to listen.

Blondie seems to sense me again looking at her and turns to me. I close my eyes and find a boy of maybe nine or ten with brown curly hair wearing an oversized cop costume. He cuffs the hands of a blonde pigtailed girl behind her who looks just like Sandy O'Grady. "If you are arrested or detained," Karyn-Bot says, "you will have fifteen seconds to escape, or you'll be eliminated from The Game."

The girl stomps the guy's foot and takes off, her hands still behind her, fear scattering the freckles on her face. But, seconds later, she stops, drops, and rolls to her side, then implodes and disintegrates like Troy. Mark-Bot says in my ear, "If you attempt to flee, automatic elimination is a certainty."

"What the hell is this?" Ollie asks next to me.

My eyes open to find his face full of concern as I wonder if the Sandy O'Grady imposter just died.

I start to answer that I have no idea, and I'm still not convinced this is even happening, but a thug takes notice and turns toward us. I close my eyes again to see Karyn-Bot in front of the screen which looks now like a chalkboard, a long pointer in her hand.

The words "Rover-Bot Types" draws itself on the chalkboard.

An invisible hand scrawls "Eye-Bots" in cursive below. Karyn-Bot hits the word with her pointer and says, "These bots allow the Game Masters to see what you see and show images behind your eyelids. They can display things that aren't there and alter your vision for better or worse."

The word "Ear-Bots" slides in from the left. "These bots can allow Game Masters to hear what you hear, play different sounds at various volumes, and prevent hearing."

Text reading "Walkie-Bots" materializes from nothing. "These special Ear-Bots connect to other game players so you can hear one another, providing an internal messaging system. You can summon anyone by saying, 'Walkie-Bot, call Skeeter,' or whatever their name is."

"The Soldier-Bots," says Mark-Bot, "destroy and repair bones, ligaments, and tendons. They collect various bodily substances like urine, bile, mucus, and saliva, and give them to the Med-Bots. These bots transform these fluids into poisons, medicines, hormones, and the all-important dust cloud of highly reflective aluminum or 'lightning sheeting' that makes the Mirror Egg work. Then, the Soldier-Bots distribute new substances to targeted locations."

I'm shown on the screen with that white-dotted ball around me again. "The Skin-Bots form your Mirror Egg," Mark-Bot explains. "They shoot microscopic lasers out of your skin's pores of all different lengths to form an ellipsoid surround. They also emit a fine dust of lightning sheeting. Millions of reflected images captured in the mirrored bits catch on the laser web. The Eye-Bots peeking out your skin's pores assemble them like a huge jigsaw puzzle at lightning speed, and then they read the continuous feed."

A bunch of pixels fill the screen, then rearrange to form a video of some people dressed in all different solid colors with masks and goggles on. They're human rainbows running across some crowded mall food court, the Burger King and Chik-Fil-A signs prominent behind them. "Since the Vermilion challenges occur in public places, the Mirror Egg allows Game Masters to watch while you roam free by accessing the Eye-Bots' continuous feed."

The screen darkens and fades, and suddenly Mark-Bot is walking on a stage toward me in a black turtleneck and green jeans, his hand on his hip, as an overhead light illuminates him. He poses at the end, his lips pouty, eyebrows raised, as a boy looking a lot like Skeeter O'Grady stands at a podium off to the side speaking into a microphone. "This Game Announcer named Mark-Bot provides maps, gives warnings, and does countdowns."

Mark-Bot swivels, juts a hip, and strikes a different pose.

"He can be cranky and likes to lecture. He and Karyn-Bot sometimes bicker, and he always signs off with corny interlude music. It's his thing." Mark-Bot snaps his fingers and spins around, then walks toward a curtain and disappears behind it as a flute twitters over a low bassoon with a bongo beat in the background.

Karyn-Bot now emerges in a rose-pink dress lined with daisies. The wannabe Skeeter at the podium continues. "This other Game Announcer Karyn-Bot provides helpful tips, good news, and instructions on completing tasks. She argues with Mark-Bot at times, but it's because she cares about everyone's welfare. She also signs off with campy transition music, claiming Mark-Bot stole her exit strategy, but sometimes, she's a pathological liar. It's her one little flaw." Karyn-Bot stops at the end of the runway, poses, swivels, poses again, then walks back toward the curtain. Just as she's about there, she trips and sprawls onto her stomach, her short skirt flying up to reveal a red G-string.

What?

Suddenly, Karyn-Bot is standing and leaning on crutches, her right foot casted, next to the white screen, which says: VERMILION GLITCHES.

A video feed of those awful VIPs appears below the words, their faces giddy. "VIPs can bend things to their favor in The Game by applying various glitches — or handicaps — to any player they wish," Karyn-Bot says. "You can suffer up to two glitches per round, each lasting a minute and spaced at least sixty seconds apart."

She points her crutch at the screen, where the words "Spaghetti Arms - $13,000" appears. "With this glitch, you won't be able to pick up or hold anything." A girl on the screen in blonde pinwheel buns resembling Marci O'Grady tries to grasp and lift an umbrella nearby, but she keeps dropping it as her hands and arms fail her. "VIPs must spend an additional $13,000 to assign this glitch to you for that round."

Another girl with barrettes in her blonde hair looking like Janice O'Grady walks across the screen, but when she's about halfway, she slips and falls to the ground like someone pulled the floor out from under her. "With the hobbling glitch, which costs the VIPs $14,000, you won't be able to walk or run, only crawl."

A bunch of bugs overcome the screen, their squishy sucking noises amplifying in my ears as shudders ripple across my shoulders.

"With a tactile hallucination glitch," Mark-Bot explains, "you'll feel that you have roaches or spiders or other bugs or vermin all over you."

I throw up in my mouth a little as I watch the critters crawl all over some guy looking like Craig O'Grady who's flailing all around trying to brush them off.

A loud horn in my ears almost sends me through the bus roof, but it stops as quickly as it started. "With an auditory hallucination glitch," Karyn-Bot says, "a $14,000 expenditure, you will hear loud polka music, an Italian opera sung in high falsetto, a blasting foghorn, or another pervasive auditory disturbance."

Suddenly, a guy in dark clothing with a bird mask of some sort comes at me wielding an axe. He's so real and scary, I shrink away, almost falling out of my seat. "Visual hallucination glitches make you see things that aren't there," Karyn-Bot says. "That'll set VIPs back another sixteen grand."

The screen blackens, plunging me into total darkness. "If you're given a blindness glitch, you won't be able to see anything."

Some green text marches across my screen: *Deafness glitch, also $14,000, will prevent you from hearing anything.*

"With the muteness glitch," Karyn-Bot says, but I can't hear her words. However, they're written on the screen: *With the muteness glitch, you won't be able to talk to anyone, and your hands won't help you communicate. A Spaghetti Arms add-on is required for an additional charge.*

Karyn-Bot dumps a plate of spaghetti over Mark-Bot's head. He looks at me with red sauce dripping down him like blood as evil gleams in his eye. I shiver while wondering what the fuck, and more importantly, why? And even more important than that, is Vermilion how I am going to die?

# PART 3

## DAVINA MEETS PAIGE TELLISON'S FAMILY

**Tuesday, January 15, 2030**

It's been almost three days since Mallory and the tour bus were supposed to arrive at Michigan Tech, and almost four since they left Twelve Oaks Mall. No one can reach anyone on it. Not a single kid, including my sister Mallory, is answering their Hollaphones, and now their voicemails are full of concerned messages. The scariest thing of all is that Michigan Tech says it never arranged such a tour.

The national media is camped out in Houghton now. They interviewed the school's President who said Michigan Tech *used* to do that bus tour years ago to bring kids from southern Michigan to see their school. They'd stopped awhile back and never resumed due to budget cuts.

So, *someone* obviously planned the bogus tour, but no one has any idea who or why, at least that they'll admit. Whoever took my sister and eight other students isn't affiliated with Michigan Tech in any official school capacity, although they may somehow be linked to the university. The authorities are working with them and the people at MetaApplesoft trying to trace who posted the bogus tour on Twitbook. So far, they haven't found anything helpful.

Now, on Tuesday evening around six, Mom, Dad, and I are meeting the other families of the missing in the rec room of a Novi police station near the mall where Mallory and the others boarded the fake Tech Tour bus. The detectives want us to compare information to see who could have a motive for taking the prospective Tech students. All the families are now arriving, exchanging hugs and prayers.

I know my parents must feel super guilty since they forced Mallory on this tour, but no one's saying anything about it, the huge elephant with pink polka dots in the room. I never told them the tour was supposed to be for me, and I'm not sure if they heard it from Mallory. She's on it instead of me, subject to all the potential suffering. This is kind of like ultimate payback for all that she's done to me. No satisfaction comes from such a realization though; I never meant for her to go, and even if I did, I wouldn't have wished *this*. And now whatever happens to her is on me. Why didn't I get my parents' attention before they forced her and say something?

"Oh, Professors Tellison!" Mom calls, waving her hand.

A woman with a Brillo-gray bob wearing a long cardigan over a flowery skirt starts toward us with a sad smile. A balding man with wire-frame glasses and a peppery mustache follows. As they stop to greet others along the way, Mom fills me in. "They're the parents of another missing girl, Paige Tellison. They teach architecture at Lawrence Tech, and we've met them at several faculty meetings."

Paige's picture is among nine enlarged snapshots posted on a board at the front of the room with names written below. I scan the others, but none are familiar from Nerd Bowl.

Paige is very thin with pale skin and white-blonde hair closely cut, cute on her slight frame like she's a pixie girl. Her bright blue eyes match her sparkly blue earrings, and her makeup is nicely applied, her crimson lips particularly striking against her light features. She smiles with a trophy in her hand, her cheeks rosy from pride or too much blusher.

"What's she holding?" I ask.

"She won a creative writing contest for high school students held by Lawrence Tech and got her piece featured in PRISM, their student literature review. Her parents also both won Endowed Teaching Chair awards, her father beating me out for his." Mom pouts, then shrugs. "Then, her older brother Miles won a highly competitive academic scholarship for their doctoral program in geotechnical engineering. Lawrence Tech did a big spread on them in the school paper and they're going to be honored at graduation, the Tellison family and all their amazing accomplishments."

"Oh, wow, that's nice," I say, wondering if Paige was the target of my sister's kidnapping. Perhaps this whole thing has to do with her. Maybe someone she beat out for that writing contest took her and the others. Or it could have to do with her brother for his award or even her parents for theirs. Who knows? Who kidnaps a bus of high school kids and for what reason?

No one yet has any good answers, but the fact that two of the missing kids' parents work at the same college is making the police give extra special attention to Lawrence Tech. It's the only connection they can find so far between the victims except they're all from southeast Michigan and wanted to check out Michigan Tech. Except Mallory, of course, who my very guilty-yet-pretending-they're-not parents forced to go.

Oh, and two other kidnapped girls — Camila Rodriguez and Keondra Williams — are dancers in a rival hip-hop crew, The Purrrlz Gurrrlz, who Mallory beat out for her job at Miss Sylvia's. Some of the Majik 8 Balz said that Camila sabotaged Mallory during a dance competition last summer, which I remember her telling me about after she broke her arm. Many are speculating it could even have to do with that.

I keep wondering if the situation were reversed, would Mallory even come to this meeting or be remotely concerned? Is she now praying for my help and even counting on me to come through for her or doubting I can because she has no faith in me? And do my feelings toward her and how she treats me matter? I rub my aching head, struggling to answer the storm of questions threatening to blow me away.

The only thing I know for sure is it should be me there, not her. The guilt threatens to pound me into the ground, and I wonder again if my parents even know. I'm not about to tell them, not right now, adding another layer of guilt like an extra spoon of hot fudge.

"Seth and Barb, good evening," the Tellisons say, finally reaching our table at the back of the room.

"I wish we were meeting at the Spring Faculty Mixer or even a dreary HR benefits meeting and not under these circumstances," Mr. Tellison says, extending his hand toward Dad.

Dad shakes it. "Chuck, I must concur. This is unbelievable. I mean, how were any of us to know it wasn't a legitimate tour put on by the school? My wife even called to verify details with whoever answered the number in the ad. She *talked* to someone at Michigan Tech, or so she thought, making sure Mallory would have what she needed and signing her up for an extended tour of the mechanical engineering department."

"All the information seemed so official, with logos and nice graphics and whatnot," Mom says. "Whoever put this together sure knew what they were doing, although anyone can lift any online image nowadays with a snipping tool. But why? Is it our connection as Lawrence Tech professors? Did we fail some student who now has a grudge?"

"We thought that too," Paige's mother says. "Or even that it has to do with a rivalry between the two schools, although I don't think Michigan Tech and Lawrence Tech are at odds like Michigan and Michigan State are. I don't really know of any association at all, except they're both engineering schools in Michigan. One's public, the other private, and they're over five-hundred miles apart."

Mr. Tellison shakes his head. "Who knows? Everyone has secrets. Our coming together here today is fine and dandy, but *anyone* could be hiding *anything* that might be a motive. I mean, why *these* kids? Is there something special about one or more of them that made them a target?"

I clear my throat, and everyone turns to me. "I think maybe none of them was the target, nothing about them specifically. The tour was a relatively easy way to gather a significant amount of people all at once, for whatever sick reason. If you think about it, it's kind of genius. If you need to get a group of people together for some purpose, place a simple Twitbook ad, collect $500 from everyone, and bypass jail on the way to Boardwalk. But what is their payoff, anyway? What's their Boardwalk? What are these people who took my sister and the others after?" My voice is shrill and I'm near tears, the incessant worry threatening to knock me flat.

Mom squeezes my arm while Dad rubs my shoulder. "Oh, sorry, Chuck and Rhoda, this is our daughter Davina. She's Mallory's twin sister."

"Nice to meet you, Davina. So sorry about everything." Paige's mother hugs me.

"You too," I mumble, feeling scared for them also and wishing we had a different reason for meeting.

Wondering if Mallory is even alive anymore and if I'll ever see her again haunts each moment. Everyone knows from TV that the first twenty-four hours are the most important in a missing persons case, and we're way beyond that. According to the stats on the board above everyone's pictures, the police are saying it has been around eighty-four hours since they left Metro Detroit. They were due to arrive in Houghton around sixty-six hours ago — if the tour had been real.

We sit at the table lost in our own thoughts, me remembering the handful of times in my life that Mallory was nice to me, until a tall, blond guy with a striped shirt and tie comes up and kisses Mrs. Tellison on the cheek. "Hey Mom, they only had Diet Coke, not Coke Zero. Hope that's okay." He sets a can down in front of her with a big plate of cookies, which he pushes to the center of the table. Picking up one with sprinkles, he bites into it.

"Oh, this is Miles, Paige's older brother," Mrs. Tellison says. "He recently graduated with his bachelor's degree in geotechnical engineering. This is the Doctors Rosenbaum, and their lovely daughter Davina. They're Mallory's family."

We say hello and make small talk until the police start their interrogation. They ask a bunch of random questions, building a huge web of information on the board. The whole time, I think it's like searching for a needle in a haystack. There could be a gazillion reasons why Mallory and the others were taken, and I can't stop imagining what horror they could be suffering. I can barely sit in my seat. This seems such a waste of time, staying here comparing facts that may or may not be true or relevant when my sister and the others are out there somewhere, if they're even still alive. I need to *do* something, *anything*, not just this. But what?

# PART 4

## ROUND 1: CRAIG'S CHALLENGE

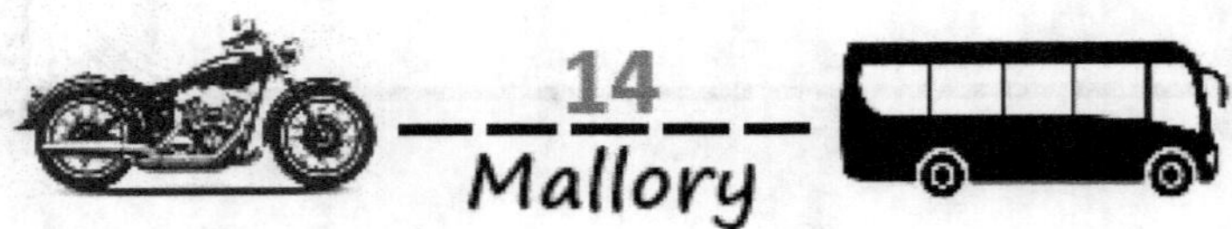


**Wednesday January 16, 2030**

## GAME ORIENTATION

Someone grunts. My eyes squint open in the darkness. There's a long, stocky figure doing pushups past the foot of my bed. I sit up, wondering where I am, as the push-up-er counts aloud.

"Twelve, ugh, thirteen, uh, fourteen, ugh…"

I rub my eyes, trying to make sense of my strange surroundings, and then it all comes back to me. The Michigan Tech bus tour. The "college reps" with their guns. The cute jock Troy whom they made suffer a fatal heart attack and then disintegrated into nothing. With nanobots. The nanobots that are coursing through my veins, swimming all around inside me until they — whoever the hell *they* are — tell the Rover-Bots what to do. The Rover-Bots that can injure someone's knee like Ollie or make someone have a seizure like Darla or suffer a heart attack like Troy. They didn't save him because they only wanted eight people for whatever reason, and he got on the bus last. If only they'd let me off. Why didn't they? Is there some reason they wanted to keep me over him?

It's gotta' be because of my parents. Too many connections for it to be a coincidence.

I lose my breath as tears blind me. Running a finger along my arm, I think of the bots there controlling me from within, lurking millimeters beneath my skin. I can't get them out of me by peeing or vomiting or bloodletting or any other means. They're in there unless I win some game called Vermilion and earn the antidote to blow them to smithereens.

Throwing my covers over my face, I have a good cry, wishing I could force them out through my eyes. I try to steel myself for what will come next, unsure what to possibly expect.

When my eyes stop their annoying leaking and adjust a little more, I pull off my covers to find Sammi, the tough-as-nails Junior ROTC girl with the pretty face, doing pushups on the floor. She switches to sit-ups, bracing her feet under a nearby door. I peer around and see we're not on the bus now, but somewhere else. Somewhere else that's sounds and feels like it's moving.

That girl who was in front of Sammi on the bus, the super-skinny one with the white-blonde hair, lies across from me in the lower bunk of a two-tier bed like mine. People are above us, but I can't tell who from here.

Her eyes pop open. I don't remember her name but smile, at least as much as I can.

She props up on her elbow and cups her bruised neck. "Is this really happening, or did I just have a super fucked-up nightmare?"

"I wish to hell it was just that, but no, you're not dreaming," I whisper.

Someone moves on the bunk above her now. He peeps his head down with a dark head full of nice waves one might want to run their fingers through. "Hey, girls. I'm Ollie." He flashes a perfect white smile like he's a Colgate model. It's Asshole Red Car Guy trying not to be an asshole.

I attempt to return it but can't. Instead, I wave. "Hey. I'm Mallory. Mallory Rosenbaum. I go to South Farmington High."

The girl below him says she's Paige Tellison and she goes to Fitzgerald High.

I scrunch my nose. "Where?"

"It's in Warren, down on Ryan Road and Nine Mile."

Most people I know don't go east of Woodward Avenue if they can help it. "Oh, okay."

Ollie throws his scratchy gray blanket to the side and lunges so that his other hand catches onto the bunk rail above me. He balances on both arms with his legs straight down, knees slightly bent and biceps bulging, then pulls his legs forward into a pike position, exhaling. Swinging his legs down and through, he lets go and lands in a perfect handstand. Flipping around to his feet, he smacks his heels together and raises his arms above his head.

Sammi stops her sit-up to gawk at him. "What in the Sam-hell was that? How'd you do that?"

He bears the tattoo on his wrist, which I remember from the bus is the five rings of the Olympics, an upside-down trapezoid of multi-colored interlinked circles. "I was a gymnast headed to the Olympics. Had a massive fall off the high bar during Regionals freshman year. Pretty much landed on my head and killed my career."

Frowning, he reaches his arms outward so I can see his hairy pits through his T-shirt which is stretched to the nines with his ample muscle. Ollie bends forward and puts his forehead to his knees, hugging himself for a nice back stretch. "I switched to cheerleading, which my friends gave me shit for until they saw I got all the hottest girls in school. Now, they leave me alone. I got a traumatic brain injury though, or TBI. I wanted to let you all know because it looks like we're going to have to work together for part of The Game."

Ollie straightens and slides into a forward split, grabbing his toe. "Sometimes I space out or get real dizzy. Please be patient with me. I'll try my best if you're my partner for anything, but if I flake out, it's not on purpose."

"Yeah, too bad," Sammi says, returning to her sit-ups. "None of y'all are winning anyhow."

Ollie grins at her. "Yeah? You're quite confident there, huh?"

"Hell yeah," Sammi says. "I'm a Cadet Master Sergeant, Junior ROTC, thank you very much. I'm leaving for boot camp two days after I graduate in June. Right after, I'm going to Tech in the Spring where I'll be doing ROTC while getting my electrical engineering degree."

Ollie twirls his finger. "Whoopee."

“I’m in charge of everybody and everything. And I lift weights an hour a day and run for another, plus I swim a hundred laps every morning. When the snow melts, I bike everywhere, doing two hundred miles a week easy. I got the top fitness record for my squadron for the fifth time in a row. I’m pumped to win, *primed* to win, I got it in the bag. Ya’ll are fit, some of you anyway, but I gots the muscle too. And the guts.” She switches to her front and shows off one-armed push-ups done on fingers and tiptoes, then flips us the bird with her free hand. “Suck it, bitches, I’m winning this thing!”

“Oh, okay,” Ollie laughs, flexing his unbelievable muscles shaped by a lifetime on the bars, pommel horse, and rings. He gets to his feet and pivots toward me. “Hey you.” He smiles in a way that turns me into a puddle suddenly, which I don’t expect at all.

“Hi.” My heart’s all annoying, reacting to the fact that he’s a total hottie, but then my brain throws an image of kissing Blake, and I kick myself. But then I think of Blake all over that tall skinny girl with the short hair and long earrings, and I give Ollie a second look. Purely from a dancer’s perspective — I swear — I admire his well-toned physique, but he’s still a jerk, also known as Asshole Red Car Guy.

“Hey, sorry I was a dick to you before all this,” he says like he’s read my mind. He holds the bars above my bed, hovering so I can view his sea-blue eyes. “I was so cranky. Didn’t have my coffee and I’m like not a morning person at all. I could have been more patient. Can ya’ ever forgive me?” He grins and I’m an ice cube on hot pavement.

I force nonchalance to my face and perch my chin on my bent knee. “Thanks for saying so. That’s cool of you. Yeah, we’re good.” I return his fist bump. “So, what are we going to do? I mean, from what I saw in the Game Rules video, you can’t even call anyone or get help, no Hollaphone, nothing.”

“I know,” Paige says, coming over. “And they’re like listening and watching us all the time with those Ear-Bots and that Mirror Egg thingy and —”

“Good morning, Vermilion Contestants!” someone says in my ear. “This is your Game Announcer, Mark-Bot. I show maps upon request, give warnings, and count down your time.” The older male voice sounds just like the O’Grady Kids dad I’ve heard so much in my life, and I wonder again if our kidnapping has anything to do with my parents’ obsession with that show, maybe with some crazed fan they attracted from their O'Grady Kids fan site. I close my eyes, and behind my lids, Mark-Bot is there in his favorite plaid living room chair wearing another obnoxious Hawaiian shirt, this one with flamingos. He gives me a two-finger salute.

A strange kind of interlude music plays, sounding like maracas shaking over twangy desert guitar music. I open my eyes as Camila, Keondra, and Darla appear from around a corner.

Camila says, "WTF?" and shrugs.

We all shrug back.

A female voice sounds in my ears. "Good morning, Vermilion Contestants! I am your other Game Announcer, Karyn-Bot. I give clues, help, and directions. I also announce good things because you know how I always take care of my family." She continues under her breath. "Even though Allysin technically does everything for no money and must wear a uniform despite cleaning for our family for years and —"

"Now, Karyn-Bot, get a grip," Mark-Bot says. "We've discussed Allysin's wardrobe before. It's what the housekeeper of a reputable architect like me *should* wear. What would the neighbors think if we let her run around in blue jeans and a work blouse?" A laugh track plays like there's a live audience.

"Now, Mark-Bot, we will discuss it later in the living room while I knit and you read your news blog, always giving important moral lessons as we wait for Marci and Craig to return from their dates. Anyway, Contestants, we will start the bathroom schedule now according to your number. If you forgot from the bus, look behind your eyelids to see."

I close my eyes, and the number four appears. Good, it's earlier. My mouth is a sewer, and I really need to pee.

"Contestants, we'll continue orientation for twenty more minutes," Mark-Bot says. "You should review your Game Rules. Then, we'll begin Prep Time, another hour, where you should discuss your strategy to collect the coins in The Hangman Phase within the three hours you will get for that part."

"There are six challenges," Karyn-Bot says, "and you will not know their locations until you leave Home Base, except for today. Since this is the first, I gave you a little clue. See? I always take care of my family." A laugh track plays again, this time with applauding and whistling. I close my eyes to see the VIPs on Karyn-Bot's screen happy as clams, watching us on some big TV while munching on popcorn and drinking from colorful glasses with twirly straws.

"Any questions?" Mark-Bot asks.

Darla raises a shaky hand.

"Yes, Darla," Karyn-Bot says.

How did she see so quickly? I search around for cameras but then remember we're being watched through our Mirror Eggs.

"I don't want to play." Darla starts bawling. "Can I just go home?"

I burst into tears too, hiding my face with my hands, my steeliness melting under the blowtorch of reality. Ollie embraces me, patting my head onto his shoulder. "It'll be okay, Mallory, I promise," he whispers. "We'll get through this." He smells like nice soap. I lose myself for a second in his muscles surrounding me and his unbelievable scent.

Pushing away, I try to breathe as Mark-Bot tells Darla, "The only way you go home is by winning Vermilion, and you must play to win." A crescendo of music erupts in my ear. "And don't forget," Mark-Bot says in a movie-announcer voice, "in the end, only one in Vermilion may live."

My heart bucks and flails as I look around and realize that only one of us will be standing at the end — if any of us makes it that far. I notice loud and clear that he said *may* live, not *will* live, and I swallow hard as I realize we all might die. The song *Dust in the Wind* that my parents love takes on a whole new meaning, and a shiver courses through me as I wonder if what I'm picturing, all the bits of me scattering, is a premonition of things to come.

"Okay, Paige," Mark-Bot continues, "you're up first. Please use the bathroom and be sure to change. Your disguises are in bags on your beds. Remember Game Warning #1: no one can know your identity. Violation will result in Karyn-Bot spinning the Punishment Wheel with the consequence applied to one member of your family. You will have exactly seven and a half minutes, Paige, for your bathroom time, which starts now! Mark-Bot, signing off."

"Goodbye Contestants, and good luck!" Karyn-Bot says, and then there's more corny interlude music, this one with a trombone, cymbal, and some slithery sounds.

Camila's face twists up. "Like, what the fuck?"

"I know," Keondra says. "What does the show The O'Grady Kids have to do with anything? They were all on that eyelid video of the Vermilion Game Rules too. Isn't this weird enough?"

"This is beyond crazy," I say, keeping my parents' connection to the show a secret for now. I'm not sure yet whom I trust and what it means, if anything. "Is this really happening or am I on some freaky acid trip? Are we all like sharing hallucinations in virtual reality pods?"

"Paige, bathroom time, now," Mark-Bot warns in our ears.

Paige takes a white plastic bag hanging on the slatted footrail of her bunkbed, then disappears around the corner.

"And now we got some crazy leprechaun trying to steal our limbs too?" Keondra asks. "Man, this sucks. Sure ain't what I signed up for. I just wanted to do the Tech Tour."

Everyone agrees it's beyond the worst thing they could ever imagine, us being forced to play this crazy game to the death with Luckster as a bonus.

"What's over there?" I ask, nodding the way Camila and the others came.

Sammi points to where Paige went. "That's a bathroom, and then on the other side, same as yours. Two bunk beds with a water cooler between them. Only difference is this bay has the door, and yours doesn't."

"So, Door Bay and Doorless Bay," I suggest, pointing to each.

Sammi shrugs. "Whatever. All I know is that whoever has us modified this space because I never saw a motorhome laid out like this."

We peer around, our eyes adjusted to the dim light. The door and windows are boarded up with hard black material fastened with a million screws. Another wall blocks off the driver area so we cannot even see who has us.

"Like, who moved us here from the Michigan Tech bus? Who freaking *touched me* while I was asleep?" Keondra does some weird dance brushing cooties off her skin.

I think about it too and choke on my spit. I've never felt so violated — except when they shot me full of nanobots. Someone I don't know *handled me* in my sleep. I begin obsessing about *where* they might have touched, and I feel like doing Keondra's cootie dance too. Ew.

I look to my wrist and realize that whoever it was removed my Hollaphone, and that adds even another layer of outrage. I guess though since using technology is a violation of Game Rules, it's good it won't be a temptation, but still, who has my personal property? Who freaking owns me?

"Hey, Kid, you okay?" Sammi asks. She tilts her head up at someone above me.

I crane my neck around to find the small Asian boy with round glasses and slicked-back hair who was behind Troy on the bus. Jiro, I recall. He's stares straight ahead, his lips quivering as he rocks back and forth like he's in a trance. He doesn't answer Sammi, just keeps gazing at something I can't see.

"*Konnichi wa*," Ollie says. "*Watashi no namae wa Orri desu. Yoroshiku*." His hands fly to his mouth, and his brows arch.

Everyone turns to gawk at Ollie, even Jiro, but then the kid goes back to his catatonic rocking or whatever he's doing.

"You speak Chinese?" Camilla asks.

"No," Ollie says. "Not as far as I know. I'm in second-year Spanish at school. Don't know a word of Chinese."

"No Chinese! Japanese!" Jiro says suddenly, then returns to his silent freak-out.

Ollie's eyes widen even further. "How am I suddenly speaking a language I didn't even know I was speaking?" He exhales. "It just came out of me. How bizarre." He clamps his lids shut. "I think I said, 'Good day. My name is Ollie. Nice to meet you.'" He furrows his brows. "It's on my eyelid screen."

"So freaking weird," Keondra says.

"*Hai. Jiro wa Nihongo to Eigo o hanashimasu*," Ollie says. He clamps his hand over his mouth again and then closes his eyes. "I said, 'Yes. Jiro speaks Japanese and English.'" Ollie shakes his head, a laugh rippling his shoulders. "And apparently now, I do too."

“Dearest VIPs and Contestants,” Karyn-Bot says. “There is one more Rover-Bot we failed to mention because we wanted it to be a surprise. The Talkie-Bot can read minds and translate what someone was going to say into another language, and then the Ear-Bots work with the Eye-Bots to convert what they said and display the words on the person’s eyelid screen.”

“Man, they’re more advanced than I thought,” Paige says. “Working together like that. And reading minds?” She shivers.

“Yeah. It’s like a built-in translator,” Camila says, shaking her head. “This is so wack.”

“But it’s only happening to you,” Keondra says, nudging her chin toward Ollie. “Wonder why?”

Ollie frowns. “No clue. Just wait. Maybe it’ll happen to you too.”

No one knows what to do about Jiro who remains unresponsive even to Ollie’s sudden ability to speak Japanese. He’s unable to calm down. I’m not much better, my heart tap-dancing all around my ribcage. Then, we discuss The Game until my frayed nerves feel like they’ll sizzle out of my body and run away. I thank God when my number is called for the bathroom, wondering why everyone has come out so far dressed like rainbows. Karyn-Bot had been too in the Vermilion Game Rules video. None of us know.

While I pee, I realize I have no idea how much time has elapsed since I last did. Was it a day? A week? Wouldn’t I die if I was so filled with urine? Not even sure how that works. Maybe the Soldier-Bots brought all my pee to the Med-Bots to synthesize into anything they want, like water and nourishment. For all I know, this could be days, or even weeks, later.

I don’t even remember going to sleep. I think hard, and eventually an image of Ollie leaning heavily on me comes to mind, and then I recall behind me that Camila slumped onto Keondra whose head fell against the cold-paned window before my world went dark. Somehow, they knocked us all out. Maybe our Med-Bots transformed our pee into a sedative and then the Soldier-Bots distributed it to send us all to La-la Land.

God, this is insane. Is that all actually possible? And they have Bots that can read minds too, and force us to speak and understand other languages? That’s way beyond anything I could ever imagine happening.

I picture a bunch of O'Grady Kids somewhere in the distance sitting behind a huge control board, flipping random switches and making us do weird stuff just to see. Is this just some huge social experiment, and we're the unwilling test subjects? Cold sweat overtakes me as I wash up. Closing my eyes, I see a clock showing that I only have three minutes left. Drying off, I dig into the bag that I collected from my bedpost and pull out a blue sweatshirt, red turtleneck, thick green fleece pullover, black sweatpants, white long-johns, yellow socks, purple gloves, and orange sneakers. I also discover a turquoise knit cap with a pom-pom on top, dark sunglasses that are more like goggles with a strap, and a fuchsia Covid-28 mask, everything a different color. That's what the others all came out of the bathroom wearing, although their items were different hues than mine. What, the kidnappers drugged us all and then stopped off at Walmart for a bunch of Fruit of the Loom separates?

There are also various toiletries. I tie my annoying hair back with an elastic and change, especially glad for new undies. The last thing I retrieve is a khaki belly bag that hooks around my waist. Inside, there are tickets for a Mackinac Island ferry getting on at someplace called St. Ignace.

We're going to Mackinac Island? Everyone says that this city adjacent to the Mackinac Island Bridge that connects the lower and upper peninsulas of Michigan is incredible. I've never been there. I certainly didn't plan to go like this.

There's also a twenty-dollar bill and several meal-replacement bars. I can't tell if they're vegan and decide I don't care. Suddenly famished, I gobble two down as I'm getting ready, getting crumbs in my bra.

Mark-Bot calls time, and I rush out to join Paige, Sammi, and Ollie dressed like me, all of us freaking rainbows. We each have the glasses, hats, and Covid-28 masks that were such good disguises for our captors, and I wonder for the millionth time who has us, who's designed this weird fight-for-your-life type game, and if it has to do with my nanotech parents somehow being mixed up with The O'Grady Kids and/or the Rebel Demons. I feel like I'm in an updated Hunger Games, but I don't have any special skills like Katniss and a way less-cool outfit.

Sammi is so tough, now doing alternating-arm push-ups on tip toes, and Ollie is super-buff, easily able to lift three times his weight, and I know they're way stronger than any of us. Paige looks so weak, Jiro is shorter than me and I'm only five-three, and then Darla is almost as wide as Camila and Keondra put together. How can they compete in this very physical type of game? The deck is stacked in some people's favor. Not sure if that's intentional, but I fall with the other two dancer girls right in the middle, a place I've never been.

Paige says her clothes are all extra small or kid-sized, and she thinks the bots measured us from the inside. I'm not sure if that's better or worse than some stranger handling me. Neither option is appealing, but at least one has happened because my clothes fit me like a glove.

Paige shrugs. "Who knows what these bots are capable of, but they're totally doing more than what nanobots we know of do, different than I ever heard, like the Eye-Bots showing us stuff behind our eyelids, or the Walkie-Bots which are like an internal messaging system, and especially that Mirror Egg thingy. Oh, and now this maybe internal measuring and Ollie's suddenly speaking Japanese? It's crazy. Admittedly, the Mirror Egg is a clever way to keep track of us so that they don't have to physically interact with us with guns like regular kidnappers. This is high-tech kidnapping for sure."

Ollie agrees that this is unchartered nanobot territory. We all stare at each other while Sammi moves onto scissor-kick jump lunges and Jiro shakes all spaced out above me, ignoring Ollie and his perfect Japanese. No one knows what to do about Jiro or the super-strong motivated ROTC girl or anything else except get ready for Round One.

Next, we discuss strategy. We decide Paige and I will get the easiest coin, the Azure Dragon in the East, while Camila, Keondra, and Darla are to find the Black Tortoise in the North. Ollie, Sammi, and Jiro will work on the hardest of the three, the White Tiger in the West. Then, we'll meet up and tackle the Vermilion Bird in the South together, since Game Rules say we must get the others first or face random elimination of one player.

Everyone found ferry tickets to Mackinac Island in their belly bags. No one has ever been there, but we've heard it's a tourist attraction five hours north of Detroit known for its fudge and saltwater taffy. "They don't allow cars there," Paige says. "Only bikes, horse-drawn carriages, and scooters."

"I think HoverSegs now too," Camila says, referring to the new mode of transportation that has become very trendy for the rich the last two years since no one else can afford them. They convert a Segway scooter with a standing platform over two wheels, a control stick, and a thigh-high cocoon wall into an "airborne" craft. They jump around ten feet long and three feet high nowadays, more "hoppers" than "hoverers" so far.

"My aunt went to Mackinac Island once," Paige says. "She and my uncle took a carriage ride all around the seven-mile loop and said it was breathtakingly beautiful overlooking Lake Michigan and Lake Huron on all sides. It's like Amsterdam with bikes everywhere. My aunt brought me back some maple fudge, which was amazing, although I ate so much, I got sick. It's rich as anything."

Right when I'm about to ask how we'll manage The Hangman Phase and Vermilion Hour while avoiding Luckster the Leprechaun, so no one loses any body part — gulp — Keondra falls out of the bathroom with a huge billow of smoke following her.

"Jeez, I'm out, okay! Sorry I went over time!" Keondra holds a cigarette in her hand, and as tendrils of smoke wander our way, Paige starts coughing like crazy.

I jump up and wave the smoke away from Paige. "Put that shit out!"

Keondra disappears into the bathroom, and the toilet flushes. She returns, her brows angry. "Man, those fucking bots be all shocking me inside! I was just trying to finish my cig. I'm stressed, man, like real stressed. I smoke when I'm stressed."

"It's okay, girl," Camila says, hugging her shoulder. "It's tight. You're alright."

Paige is red and hacking up a lung. I go over and rub her back. She retrieves an asthma inhaler from her pocket and takes a long drag.

"It's obviously not tight," I say. "She's asthmatic."

"Hey, I didn't mean to smoke in here," Keondra says, her palms forward. "Damn bots be all shocking me and shit because I went over. They be serious as a heart attack about they bathroom time, no joke."

"Well, now she's sick," I say, hoping Paige's ragged breathing smooths out.

Paige starts bawling and shakes her inhaler. "I barely have any left," she whimpers. "What'll I do? I need this all the time, even when I'm not forced to run all around and play some crazy game, and I only have this one."

"Well, I didn't mean it," Keondra says. She stomps toward Door Bay with her arms folded across her chest. Camila flips us off with a zigzag of her fingers and a snap before following her. Darla trails after them, choosing their side, I guess.

Ollie shrugs. Suddenly, Jiro jumps down from his bunk like it's raining people and joins Camila and the others, disappearing into Door Bay while we sit in Doorless Bay, gawking after them.

Switzerland Sammi continues doing burpees in her spot near the bathroom, oblivious to anything but her quest to win Vermilion.

"Did we offend?" I ask, sniffing my armpit. "Nope, not me. Must be you." I nod toward Ollie. "Maybe you told him off in Japanese and the eyelid screen showed you something different."

He chuckles. "Maybe. Weird, man, weird. That Jiro kid's like not right up here." Ollie taps his temple. "He's wigging out, different than me and my TBI. Kid's gonna' snap." He mimics breaking a stick in half.

Paige is still panting. "I am too," she manages, bursting into a fresh set of tears. "Guys, I'm sorry. I'm just so freaked, I can't seem to calm down inside, and it's making my breathing worse. Like way worse. I need to chill but I can't."

"I got you," I tell her. I coach her through some breathing exercises I know from dance while Ollie massages her shoulders with his huge hands. Paige struggles through, trying to relax.

"Hey, let's all be on the lookout," I say, patting her back which is so bony, she feels like my Bubbe. "During this challenge or the next, we'll find someone with an asthma inhaler and steal it for you. They can get another one and you can't. Does it matter if it's not the kind you were prescribed?"

"Anything will be better than nothing. Thanks, Mallory. You're awesome." She smiles weakly and pats Ollie's forearm. "You too."

"Thanks," I say. "Let's stick together, and we'll get through. Agreed?"

She nods. "Totally. I mean, I'll help as much as I can. Like, even in the Vermilion Hour, we can assist each other or —"

"Not sure how that'll work when only one of us can win," I say. "But let's at least protect each other from the others if we can."

Ollie nods. "Definitely. I got your backs. You get mine." He smiles at me, or maybe at Paige, and I try not to notice. Why the hell is he so damn sexy? "Is that cool?"

He's got me anything but cool. As I'm trying to reconcile this unexpected new attraction to Asshole Red Car Guy, a.k.a. Ollie, the gymnast-turned-cheerleader with the brain injury who gets all the hottest girls in school, Mark-Bot hums to life in my ear. He announces we have fifteen minutes until the first round, which he calls "Craig's Challenge," the same name as the oldest O'Grady kid. As Mark-Bot signs off, I again wonder about the connections between my parents and our kidnapping and how it could possibly help.

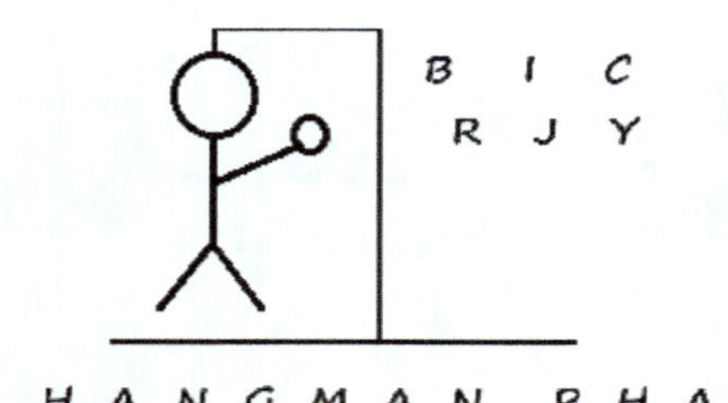


# THE HANGMAN PHASE

The boat says "Shepler's Mackinac Island Ferry," and after I walk down the few steps to the lower level, I sit between Paige and Ollie on a rear bench staring at the frolicking water basking in the morning light. Keondra, Camila, and the others chat in front of us next to people staring at their Hollaphones.

I yearn to grab one, to send a quick message to my family, but I know that someone's watching me through my Mirror Egg. Instead, I fret about how we'll be able to get all four coins in time while avoiding Luckster the Leprechaun who will be there to "clover" us — then maybe cleaver one of us if he succeeds. I embrace myself as a chill ripples through me, trying to imagine such an actuality.

As soon as they released us from Home Base in St. Ignace, a city I've never heard of at the lower tip of the Upper Peninsula, Mark-Bot reminded us that we'd have three hours for this round. As Home Base sped away, I noticed it was a dark gray motorcoach with tinted windows, appearing like a band tour bus. Nice and generic, not very noticeable at all.

"How will we possibly solve four puzzles and gather the coins in time while avoiding Luckster?" I ask, biting my lip. "This seems impossible, like a total setup."

"You guys gotta' haul ass," Sammi says, "find as many letter clues as you can, and get your coins. Then help us with the White Tiger since that'll be toughest of the three."

I nod, but I still feel sick when the ferry docks and we all scatter to our regions.

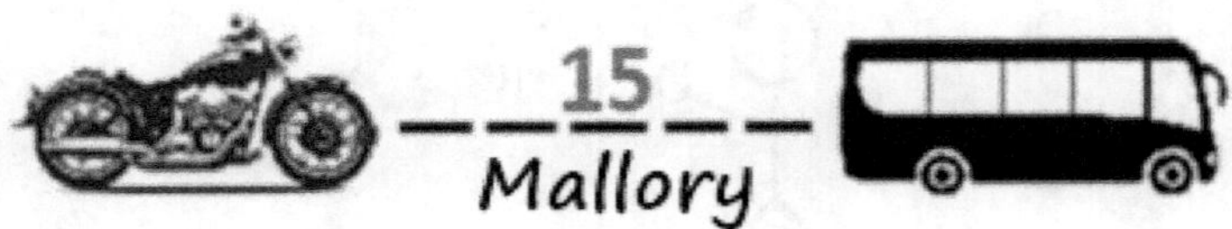

# 15
## Mallory

Paige and I are supposed to get the Azure Dragon in the East, so we follow the map in our eyelids to the eastern region of the island. Since it's impossible to run with eyes closed, we keep stopping to figure out if we're going the right way.

We observe a couple weird things as we go. First, there's a navy HoverSeg with white pinstriping that says "Mackinac Island Police Department" around some official-looking seal. The officer on it leaps along in his navy uniform with his silver badge glinting in the morning light.

"How odd," Paige says. "We don't have any PoliceSegs where I live."

"No, us either. Just regular HoverSegs. I totally want a JagSeg, even though they go for over $130K. All my neighbors have them. I love their new slogan: 'Get one now, no matter how. The JagSeg rules the air.' That alone makes me want one, if I could ever afford it."

"Yeah," Paige agrees. "They are pretty sweet."

Then, even stranger, another HoverSeg has cut-outs of sleighs affixed to its sides. Out the front, two rows of plastic reindeer balance on a jutting pole leading the way. The one in front has a lit red bulb for a nose. As the driver hops on his SleighSeg in front of us snapping his whip to prompt his "reindeer" to fly, I notice his sign: "Winter Wonderland SantaSeg Rides, $20 per half hour." He lands a jump and beams at us with a toothy smile.

I shake my head. "Sorry, not interested."

"Maybe we should," Paige says. "It'll get us there faster."

I remember that we each have twenty bucks in our bags. "Okay, but we need money for food too. This'll take half our funds."

“We gotta’ get the coin,” she says. “And fast, so we can help the others.”

“You’re right.” I raise my hand as the SantaSeg guy bounces away. “Hey!”

He makes a three-hop turn and comes back.

We get on his extended platform and balance somehow, clutching each other for dear life as his SantaSeg leaps toward the east.

He drops us off on some snowy street where there are shops of assorted colors on both sides, mostly pastel blues, yellows, pinks, and greens. They’re all connected, some two stories high while others are three and four. All have high round windows, Juliette balconies, and detailed moldings.

“Okay, let’s split up to find clues,” Paige says. “You take the left side, and I’ll do the right, and we’ll meet at the end. Keep in touch through our Walkie-Bots.”

“Good plan,” I say, patting her shoulder. “See you soon.”

She rushes off, and I turn around to find Luckster the Leprechaun leaning against a newspaper stand, arms crossed, grinning at me. “Leprechaun chasing rainbows,” he whispers in his chilling voice, and I sprint away. He is much faster and tags me with a pat on my back, sending a spike through my shoulder.

“Ow!” I scream, pulling the clover off me. He rushes away, laughing like a joker, to go find some of my bus mates. I fight tears, rubbing my skin where the spike went in. When I can catch my breath, I summon the others through our Walkie-Bots and let them know I’m the first to be clovered.

“Way to go,” Camila scolds with a few choice words, but she’s no worse than I am to myself.

Karyn-Bot prompts us to look behind our eyelids, and when I do, I see a tall sign on the screen which Karyn-Bot the gameshow model is posing near, and it has all our names on it. At the top, it says “Clover Board.” My name, fourth one down, has been crossed off.

“Seven rainbows to go!” Luckster’s voice says, followed by his sinister laugh. “Leprechaun chasing rainbows!”

I shrug it off and enter my first store, my hand clasping my throbbing shoulder, incredulous that I just got stabbed by some guy in a leprechaun costume. Who the hell is he and how is he part of The Game?

I find I'm in a souvenir shop and thumb through some T-shirts on a rack. I see a sky-blue card — I guess that's "azure" for the Azure Dragon coin — dangling from the tag on a shirt that says, "Mackinac Island – You're Always Welcome." The card has an L, and below it, 10/15 and 11/15, which lets me know the tenth and eleventh letters are both L's in the fifteen-letter word or phrase that will reveal the Azure Dragon coin's location. I close my eyes and ask Karyn-Bot for the puzzle, and she shows me the L's inserted into the correct slots:

__ __ __ __ __ __ __ __ __ L L __ __ __ __

I continue along to a fudge shop, then a Hollaphone dealer, a HoverSeg rental kiosk, a drugstore, and others, and I collect clues in all kinds of weird places. Some are duplicates of ones I already found, which infuriates me to no end.

"Mallory, how ya' doing?" Paige asks through our Walkie-Bots.

"Good. Got some letters. You?"

"Fine. Almost done with my row. Check the puzzle now."

Behind my eyelids, I see: __ N __ __ D __ __ K __ L L __ A __ E.

"Any idea?" I ask.

Paige leans against a pole across the way heaving while holding her chest. "I've been studying the map in my eyelids," she breathes. "There's someplace called Skull Cave with the double L. Not sure if that's it though."

I view my map. "Could be, but maybe the word in the middle is 'KILL.' Not sure what that means yet though. There's nothing with 'kill' on the map. It almost looks like 'KILL PAIGE,' except one less letter."

She barks out a laugh. "Yeah, glad it's not that. We need more letters."

"Okay. I'm at some place Harry's that has fancy dresses, purses, and shoes — Ooh, I see a clue. Toodle loo."

I'd been browsing a table of handbags while talking when I noticed an azure card poking out of one. This one looks very much like the beaded clutch that Bubbe made for Mom, the one Snake Riley stole. As I try to get the card out to see what it says, a large man in a pin-striped suit and waxed curlicue mustache approaches.

"That's real nice, isn't it?"

I smile. "Yes, it's pretty."

"Well, the tag says $45, but I can let you have it for a steal at $37, no tax. What do you say?"

I shrug. "I'll think about it."

He stands there with his Cheshire cat smile. I wander away from the table, pretending to check out dresses in the back, keeping an eye on him until he finally disappears behind a curtain.

I return to the table trying to get the clue, but it's wrapped in some plastic holder that is attached inside the bag. I can't extract it since the clingy wrapper is melded to the cardstock.

The salesman materializes from the back beaming. "Ah, you've returned! Shall I ring it up for a bargain for $40 plus tax?"

I know I only have ten bucks, but also that time is counting down. Mark-Bot said we only have ninety minutes left now and I'm not sure if any other teams got a coin. "Yeah, um, sure," I mumble, the words "random elimination of one player" fresh in my mind.

"Wonderful!" The salesman takes the purse and goes behind the counter to ring it up. "That'll be $42.40. Cash or credit?"

I'm not sure what to do, but my instincts say take the purse and run. And so, I do, snatching it from his hands and racing out of the store.

I sprint toward Paige, but when I'm a half a street away, a PoliceSeg swoops in and blocks me.

"Ma'am," the officer says, "we got a call that you took something that wasn't yours."

The purse is right in my hands, so I can't deny it. "Already?"

The salesman is now in front of Harry's shaking his fist in the air.

"I, um, I uh – "

The officer lunges to grab my arm, catching my sleeve.

Suddenly, I hear Mark-Bot in my ears: "Attention Vermilion Contestants! Player #4, Mallory Rosenbaum, has been detained. She has fifteen seconds to escape or will be permanently eliminated from The Game."

I yank away from him and flee, running as fast as I can. The PoliceSeg hops to block me. The officer grabs me again while Mark-Bot continues counting. "Nine, eight, seven…"

My heart chokes me as I try to figure out what to do. He forces my arm to his side rail. His other hand pulls a pair of cuffs from his hip as his PoliceSeg hovers in Auto-Mode.

I try to pull my hand back, but he's too strong.

"Five, four…"

Tears blind me as I attempt to get away. The count reaches two and he's about to snap my wrist into the cuff when a huge snowball smacks him upside the head.

Paige waves in the distance.

With the cop momentarily disoriented, I book out of there and grab her. We duck around a corner where the PoliceSeg can't follow because there's too much snow. We run a few streets over and see he's not after us. Stopping in an alley, we both gasp for air like a pair of fish fresh out of their bowl.

"Nice shot," I breathe.

"All those snowball fights with neighbor kids sure paid off," Paige says through her tortured wheezing.

"Leprechaun chasing rainbows."

Before we can react, Luckster appears from around the corner and clovers Paige, knocking her backwards.

She slips and crashes into the wall, sliding down until she's sitting.

I help her up, pulling the clover spike from her chest, as Luckster rushes away cackling. "Leprechaun chasing rainbows!"

Paige's breathing is more ragged, and she struggles with her inhaler again, shaking it and huffing deeply as she presses her hand to her puncture wound. "Man, it's low," she huffs. "Not sure how many hits I have left."

We spot the PoliceSeg in the distance coming from another direction and I pull her inside a candy shop.

As my mouth waters for the unbelievable blocks of fudge of every color and flavor, Paige coughs and struggles to regain her breath, her inhaler in her hand again. She puffs deeply, shakes it, and gasps that there's nothing left. "I wish I could take off my mask, but it'll be worse if I do." She sputters again. "Both could kill me."

"We'll find you something," I assure her, "even if we must break into a doctor's office or pharmacy. We'll tell everyone when we see them."

"Okay, good. Thanks," she says, inhaling deeply and closing her eyes. A few seconds later, she opens them, exhaling. "So, what's the letter that almost got you killed? Better be a good one."

I pry the azure card out of the plastic inside the purse and flip it over. It's a V in the fourteenth position, and then I'm sure from the map where the coin is, and Paige agrees. After she recovers, we go to find the Azure Dragon in the East, heading north a few streets according to our maps. Clutching each other, we slip-slide along, wondering how easy or hard it'll be. Even though we're missing letters, we're sure now our clue says: INSIDE SKULL CAVE.

As I'm about to summon a Walkie-Bot to check in with everyone and report our progress, I hear Camila in my ears. "Hey, guys. I got some bad news."

"What?" Ollie asks.

"God, not sure how to say this, but well, Darla got eliminated."

"*What*?" Paige puts a hand to her chest. "*Seriously*? What the hell happened?"

"We were trying to get our coin at Friendship's Altar, which is some big rock sticking out of the ground on the northwest tip of the island. It's some big deal who knows why. Then Keondra sets down her plastic bag from the fudge she just *had* to buy, and it blew away. A ranger on an ArmySeg, this one in khaki camouflage, thinks she littered and pulls us over, saying he's going to cite us. He got busy writing a ticket on his

Hollaphone, so me and Keondra got the hell out of there. Darla couldn't move as fast, and he got her, cuffing her to his ArmySeg as Mark-Bot counted down her time."

"Oy, like me," I say. "I had a cop try that with me too, but luckily Paige hit him with a snowball, and we escaped."

"Good for you. Well, not only did Darla drop when her fifteen seconds was up, but then she disintegrated into nothing like that kid Troy, a hissing sound and awful smell coming from her. I puked into my mask as the cop rubbed his eyes with his fists like he just couldn't believe what he saw. Meanwhile, some people recorded it all on their Hollaphones, so now everyone's going to know. Not sure what that means for us since we're supposed to be incognito. Maybe the FBI will figure out it's us, maybe not. It's going to be a national news story for sure though. The chick just up and disappeared on live video."

"God, that sucks," Sammi says. "But sorry as we are about Darla, we got a real situation here. We need your help, especially you three dancer girls. You all get your coins?"

"No," I report. "We found our location though. Ours is inside Skull Cave, which we're nearby. Sounds creepy as hell."

Keondra says they're about to get theirs in or around Friendship's Altar, but they're waiting until that cop leaves and people disperse.

"Well, come as fast as you can. We need you guys as a distraction to help us get the White Tiger coin," Ollie says.

"Where are you?" I ask.

"Some place called Crack-in-the-Island."

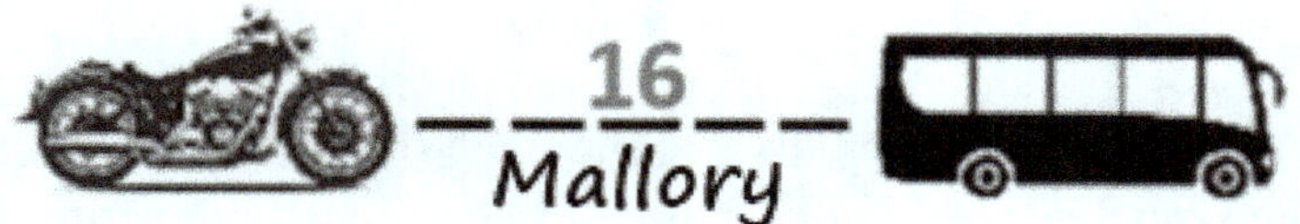


As Paige and I head toward Skull Cave, Sammi reports that Luckster clovered her when she came out of a bathroom, stabbing her through her shin with a spike. Ollie said Jiro got clovered while drinking from a water fountain in the park. I summon the Clover Board to see Camila, Keondra, and Ollie have not been clovered yet.

When we reach the cave of skulls, Paige stops to tie her shoes, so I read a nearby plaque:

> *The small, shallow cave was used as a burial site by Native Americans in the 18th century. In 1763, a fur trader named Alexander Henry survived the capture of Fort Michilimackinac by the Native Americans during Pontiac's War by hiding out there. He later wrote about it, saying the cabin floor was full of skulls. He thought they were from animals, but in the morning light, he discovered they were human, which bothered him greatly thereafter.*

A cluster of them sticking out of the cave's mouth gape at me, and I shudder. "This is so icky."

"Ew, I know," Paige agrees. "I don't want to go in there."

The cave's opening is low and wide, so we'll have to stoop or even crawl to get inside. "I don't like enclosed spaces."

"Me neither," Paige says. "Plus, how are we going to even see to find the coin? I don't want to have to feel inside a bunch of skulls like we're in an *Indiana Jones* movie or something."

An eavesdropping Karyn-Bot says we can ask the Eye-Bots for night vision.

We do, and as we duck into the cave, I question how we'll possibly find the coin in the skull carpet on which we stand. Realizing that every crunch is my foot crushing someone's head makes me increasingly nauseous.

"There it is!" Paige runs toward the back of the cave. Getting on her knees, she wrestles a gold coin maybe three inches wide from someone's teeth. As soon as she gets it out, she drops it, and the coin disappears.

"What the hell!" She tries to pick up a skull near her, but it falls from her hands. "I can't hold anything! What's happening? Why can't I —"

I'm about to tell her that one of the VIPs must have given her a Spaghetti Arms glitch when I hear something. Then, a few somethings. Suddenly, a huge flock of bats screech bloody murder and come at me.

Bolting away, I ditch Paige and dive into the snow in the sunlight, frantic to escape. I peek as an army of airborne rats all black and webby and creepy-as-fuck with red eyes and open mouths burst out of the opening. They swirl around and disappear behind clouds. But then they reappear and dive toward me again. I scurry behind some boulders. Glancing back, I see they're gone. It happens again and again, and I'm not sure if they're real or a VIP-applied visual hallucination glitch, but I'm not taking any chances. I keep hiding behind whatever I can find to shield myself.

They appear again making a beeline straight for me, and one gets into my hair, tugging at my braid poking out from my hat. I thrash around in the bushes I'm in, my heart hammering in my chest, realizing they are real and not a glitch. I try to get to my feet on the icy snow to escape when I feel another bat on my shoulder.

I scream as the claw tightens, scrambling to find my footing.

"Mallory!"

I grab a bunch of branches from the bush and pull myself up, but the bat on my shoulder and the one in my hair won't let me go. "Help!" I try to shout, but fear holds my voice hostage.

"Mallory! It's me!"

I glance back to find Paige there. She's tugging at my braid. "This branch got you." She pulls twigs out of my hair and disentangles my shirt from the stick it's wrapped around.

Realizing it wasn't real bats after all but stupid Eye-Bot tricks, I exhale and collapse into the snow. "Thank God," I cry. "Thought I was a goner." Shockwaves course through me, and I convulse, imagining those bats again. Glancing up to a clear sky, I blink a few times, just to make sure. My glitch minute must be over.

Paige holds up a gold coin. "Got it!" With her other hand, she shakes her inhaler, then lets the coin drop in the snow as she finagles the tube under her mask. Depressing the plunger, she sucks, then sighs. "It's totally done. I'm so screwed."

Grabbing the coin and putting it in my belly bag, I tell her we'll prioritize finding her an inhaler. I alert the others through our Walkie-Bots.

Everyone says they'll steal one when they can. I'm not sure whom I believe. Maybe only Ollie, perhaps Sammi, although she's super competitive, so maybe not.

"Okay, we'll be on the lookout, but get here now," Ollie says. "We need you. We're at Crack-in-the-Island, right near Cave-in-the-Woods in the western region. See you soon."

Paige and I spend the rest of our money on another SantaSeg, eating meal-replacement bars along the way. Upon our arrival, we immediately see why we were summoned.

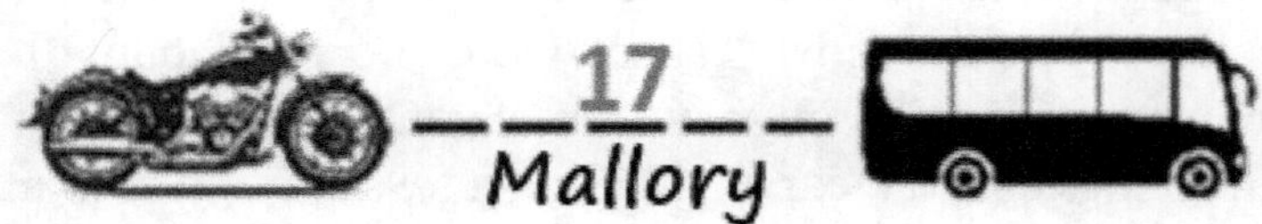

# 17 Mallory

At Crack-in-the-Island, there's a group of at least forty middle-school-aged children and several adults gathered around a tour guide. I peer over a sea of colorful pompons on the kids' hats to find Ollie, Jiro and Sammi waving. They're behind the guide pointing down toward something I can't see.

The tour guide speaks into a mic on a headset, her well-rehearsed voice filling the quiet surroundings. "The Crack-in-the-Island is a natural split in the limestone base on Mackinac Island that was once so deep, people thought it was a bottomless pit. Legend has it that the crack was created when the *Gitchi Manitou*, which means 'Great Spirit' in several Algonquin languages, stamped his foot upon the white man's arrival to the island and created the split. Later, a giant tried to escape to the Under Land. The *Gitchi Manitou* used his magic to trap the giant there, where he's doomed to hang forever."

"What are you telling us?" I ask a Walkie-Bot pointed toward Ollie. Just then, Camila and Keondra arrive, stopping with their hands on their knees and breathing hard. They must've run all the way from the northern region where they hopefully got the Black Tortoise coin but lost Darla. Guess they were too cheap for a SantaSeg or blew all their dough on fudge.

"Good, you're all here," Ollie says in our ears. "We've been trying to get this coin which is way the hell down in this crack, and it's super delicate because it could fall further, so we need to be careful. But they keep running tours through here, and everyone is looking exactly where we're trying to go. While we get the coin with the rope that we stole from a RangerSeg, we need you three dancer girls to distract everyone with an impromptu performance. Do whatever. Make it good. Get them focused elsewhere."

I nod at Camila and Keondra, and they shrug. Camila says it's a great idea, and so we meet, us three dance enemies, and go over what we'll do.

“Just be good and keep them busy,” Camila instructs like she’s in charge.

“You know I’m always good,” I say.

Camila mutters, “Whatever,” and waves me off.

“We have no music,” Keondra says. “I can’t hum that loud.”

“I’ll take care of that,” says Paige. She goes over to some kids and pulls them aside, whispering to them. They play music from their Hollaphones, which sync and amplify the sound. I worry Paige violated Game Rules and indirectly used technology, expecting they’ll cite her, and Karyn-Bot will spin the Punishment Wheel to hurt someone in her family, but no one says anything. Perhaps that’ll come later or they’re okay with what she did.

Meanwhile, Camila and Keondra start a cool stepping routine I totally plan to steal and incorporate into a dance when this is over.

“Move! Move it! Move it to the beat. Move ya’ body to the beat. Move ya’ body to the beat b-beat b-beat beat beat. Move ya’ body to the beat. Ow!”

I start dancing between the two girls but a row behind. All the kids turn, ignoring the befuddled tour guide, grinning as we break into a great groove. I try to complement what Camila and Keondra do, going up when they go down, right when they go left, in sync, on the offbeat, whatever, and people film us on their Hollaphones while others clap along. I feel alive right when I might die, doing hip-hop in the snow at the Crack-in-the-Island, shot full of nanobots and unsure what will happen to me and the others. I try to enjoy dancing for the first time in however long, unsure if this will be my last.

“Uh, guys, this is a tour,” the guide says, but no one is paying attention to her anymore. Even the kids’ teachers whistle and dance in place, shouting “Woohoo!” and “You go girl!” between their hands. Everyone’s Hollaphones are recording, and I know we’ll be online very soon if we aren’t already.

As I twist and pump and glide and crump, punching out an attitude turn into a chasse into a toe-touching split jump, I worry that between people recording Darla disintegrating and now us doing this, they may punish us for outing ourselves and violating Game Rules. Camila and Keondra launch into round-off back handsprings with double-kicking ariels. They get their own applause, especially when they save each other from sliding on the ice into the Crack by grabbing onto a tree root.

Since we're already likely online, will my family recognize my dancing enough to know it's me? I'm covered from head to toe in my ridiculous rainbow outfit, something I would never normally wear. And if so, what can they even do? What can anyone do? Even the FBI can't save us. The only way out is to beat everyone else in this game called Vermilion to get the antidote and disintegrate our Rover-Bots.

You must win to get the antidote, and there *may* be only one winner, if anyone makes it that far.

When Ollie the Gymnast lowers himself into the Crack-in-the-Island with Sammi and Jiro holding the rope and he gets the White Tiger coin, no one even notices. Instead, they're all cheering as I do my famous head spin. Twista' Sista' is back at it again, doing anything I can to be the one who will win.

# THE VERMILION BIRD

We attack the southern region to find the Vermilion Bird coin, all working together now except Darla, who has sadly been eliminated. We gather letter clues quickly, Mark-Bot telling us that we have only thirty-eight minutes left until we compete in The Vermilion Hour — if we manage to collect the last coin. He reminds us that if we fail, we'll face random elimination of one player.

After we study the puzzle board, we figure out that it says GRAND HOTEL THREE TEN.

"It's the Grand Hotel!" Keondra says. "My mom's favorite movie, 'Somewhere in Time,' takes place there! It's about a guy played by Superman — that Christopher Reeve dude who got paralyzed after falling off his horse and did all that great stuff for stem-cell research — and he goes back in time after seeing this woman's picture and —"

"Yeah, great," I say. "Tell us later. Time is running out."

We scramble over to the hotel and up to Room 310.

When we get to the door, we hear a woman's voice behind it. "Ooh, Charles, you bad, bad boy."

There's some rustling and banging, and then a man's voice. "Oh Myra." He groans. "Look what you do to me. But no, not now. We need to meet the McKenzie's for lunch. They're expecting us. Let's do this later and — ooh, you're the one who's bad."

We all break up laughing into our hands — even Jiro who has barely spoken — and we scatter.

"Shit, we gotta get the coin in there with those two?" I ask Ollie worriedly.

He doesn't answer. He's around the corner peering at something.

“What?” I go over to find him staring out a window. Paige joins us, and then eventually everyone else wanders over.

Pointing, he says, “There, that’s their balcony. It’s the fifth one in, from what I can tell.” He checks down the hall and then peers out the window again.

“So?” Camila squeezes past me and into Ollie’s arms as she bends to see. He doesn’t move away, kind of embraces her, which makes my ears hot.

“Our time is running out,” Ollie says. “I’ll go outside and sneak in through their balcony to get the coin.”

“That’s dangerous!” Camila says, twisting around and putting her hand on his bicep. “You think you’re strong enough?” She squeezes his arm as I fight the urge to rip hers from her body.

He laughs. “I bench three-fifty easy. And I’m a gymnast. We climb stuff. I’ll be fine.”

“I’m going too,” I blurt. Everyone turns to me as I ask myself why I did such a thing.

“I should go. I’m more capable,” Sammi says.

Ollie looks between us, then nods at me. “Maybe, but she’s more limber. Okay yeah, you could help,” he says to me. “But we must go now.”

“Okay,” I say, and then Ollie pushes open the window and hops out onto the ledge like he’s a superhero. We’re so high up, three tall stories, I instantly regret volunteering. Knowing Camila, Keondra, and Sammi are hoping for me to fail makes me swallow my fear and crawl onto the ledge. I try to stand, but I wobble and keel over. Ollie catches me and pulls me up by the seat of my pants, giving me the worst wedgie ever.

“Crazy bitch,” Camila says behind me.

I follow Ollie, dying to pick my underwear out but knowing everyone’s watching, as he makes his way to the first balcony. I try to mimic exactly what he’s doing, where he steps, what he grabs. It’s harder for me as he’s way taller with a longer stride, but I manage since I’m flexible enough to do the splits all three ways and heel stretches to my ear without holding. (Finally!)

We eventually reach the balcony of the lovers Charles and Myra. Hiding behind an Adirondak chair, we're still visible between the slats. I peek through the blinds to find the lovers near the front door, making out against the wall.

Charles, with tufts of dark hair yet none up front, pulls the hallway door open. But then Myra, with curly blonde hair and a flouncy black dress, pushes it closed with one hand and reaches around the front of his pants with the other.

"How the hell are we going to get in there?" I ask.

Ollie tries the sliding glass door near us, but it's locked. "No idea. We can't break this unless—" He grabs a metal watering pitcher nearby. "Maybe this'll work."

As he stands, the glass door slides open, and Charles walks out onto the balcony. Ollie ducks back down.

"Myra, you're really trying me here. They're going to worry."

Myra comes out and wraps her arms around Charles, whispering into his ear.

I pray they don't notice me and Ollie mere feet away squished behind the chair. The couple kiss again, and I stare at Ollie through my goggles, trying not to picture us doing that. I wonder if he's thinking that too, or if he's imagining Camila in his arms mere moments ago.

"This is so freaking weird," he whispers as the couple is in and out of their room, pressed against the window, then back to the balcony, then onto the bed. They leave the glass door open. Ollie whispers to follow him. He crawls toward the opening on the opposite side of the balcony.

I scurry after him, and as we make it behind an armchair inside, the couple end up on that very chair. Myra straddles Charles, pulling her dress top down now so her bra is showing.

"Oh shit," I whisper, and Ollie covers his masked mouth, his shoulders bobbing.

"Wait, Myra, seriously, let's continue later," Charles says, lifting her off him and standing. "I need Arthur's take on those new stocks to know if I should sell or continue another quarter. Let's go for appetizers, and then we'll find an excuse to leave."

"Fine, okay," Myra says, pouting while fixing her dress in the mirror. She applies lipstick and fluffs her hair. "I could use a drink."

"Great. Let's go. Honestly, I'm starved."

The couple leaves, and we search the entire room. I finally locate the coin in the heating vent near the ceiling above the toilet. Taking off my glove, I coax it out with my nails. Burning my fingers since it's red hot, I put it in my belly bag.

We walk toward the main door anxious to meet the others and conclude the round when it bursts open. "Oh, Myra! Screw the McKenzie's!"

Ollie and I dive behind the bed while the couple return to their doorway in a deep embrace, and then they're a tornado through the room again as their passion grows.

We wriggle under the boxspring so that we're flat on our stomachs, and as I turn my head toward Ollie, the mattress above us sags. We hear Charles and Myra escalate until I feel like I'm watching a porno, only thank God I can't see what's happening. The sounds alone are nauseating.

Ollie touches his fingertips to mine.

"Oh my God," I giggle, pushing my face into the carpet and stifling my screams of laughter, so incredulous we're trapped under here until they finish while our lives are at stake, ticking away while they do their thing. God, I hope Charles is quick about it.

Surprisingly, he's not, and as the action above gets increasingly frantic, Ollie grips my hand tighter and tighter, his touch ricocheting through my whole body. I yearn to feel his muscular chest against mine, to wade in the sea of his blue eyes behind his goggles, but then Mark-Bot reminds us that we only have seven minutes to get to the center of the map and put the firescope together.

"Fuck," I whisper. "We can't wait."

"No, we can't. Follow me."

Ollie crawls out and I go after him, with Charles and Myra still doing their thing. We slip out the door, and the lovers never notice, as far as we're aware.

We find the others, and all make it to the center as Mark-Bot is counting down thirty seconds, and then we put the fire kaleidoscope — firescope — together in order of coins, from the Azure Dragon to the Vermilion Bird, as Karyn-Bot instructs. The coins start to glow, the gold turning red-hot, and right before us, the stack of four coins elongates and thins into a solid scope perhaps twelve inches long by two inches in diameter.

"What the hell?" Camila asks.

Sammi grabs it, putting it to her eye, and says, "Guys, I got the location of the secret finish line and I'm ready for you. Are you ready for me? I'm winning this thing, no doubt about it." She slugs herself across the chest and shouts out some weird warrior call.

Behind our eyelids, the words "Arch Rock" appear in a flaming text font, and I sigh, unsure what the Vermilion Hour will entail. I remember the Game Rules saying that robbing, injuring, and killing another player is allowed, and I swallow hard, moving back ten paces with everyone else as Karyn-Bot instructs us to do.

"Reaching the desired circumference has been done," she reports. "The Vermilion Hour has now begun. Good luck, everyone!"

Sammi rushes forward and grabs the firescope first, but then Camila catches her and pulls down her pants, revealing green panties. The scope slips from Sammi's fingers. Camila snatches it and runs, but then Sammi tackles her, and they go back and forth while we follow.

"And they're off," Mark-Bot says in my ear. "Now, keep in mind, from the Clover Board, Luckster only has to get Camila, and then someone loses a limb for the next round — if they make it through this one."

Camila darts down the street, no longer concerned about the scope or claiming victory.

"Leprechaun chasing rainbows," I hear from nearby, and Luckster dashes after Camila, who whips around a corner and disappears.

I ask Mark-Bot for the map and find that Arch Rock is all the way on the eastern shore, past where Paige and I found the Azure Dragon at Skull Cave. Let them battle it out the whole way and then I'll try to get them at the end. If I even stand a chance. Sammi's damn tough, and Ollie is way stronger than me. Keondra, Camila, and I are about tied on physical fitness and ability. Jiro is small and weak, and Paige is about to die because she can't breathe and looks like she never ate anything except that maple fudge her aunt brought her that once.

It suddenly hits me that I'm where Davina usually is, second best, unable to overcome those much stronger than me, and my cheeks flush as shame pounds me over the head. I never knew what it felt like to not be best — until now. What a time for such a discovery.

Someone throws a rock. I glance over to find quiet Jiro picking up another and another, chucking them at Keondra and Sammi as they wrestle for the firescope. They're so stunned, they momentarily stop, and Jiro grabs the scope from Sammi. Then, they go after him, Ollie gets involved, and I sort of follow along on the periphery waiting for my moment.

I glance back, and Paige is resting by a wall, her hand on it, breathing hard. She can't even run, much less go against us. She has no chance at all in this game, and my heart goes out to her. But I can't solve her problem right now. I need to stay alive to even do that, which means, I need to win, or at least, we can't fail to complete the challenge and lose a random player. Because then, it could be Paige or Ollie — or me. I choke on the thought but press on, hoping to swoop in and somehow steal the firescope.

We approach Arch Rock, and it's breathtakingly beautiful, with a massive piece of limestone curved over an open space with icy waters beyond. Frosted greenery winds around the arch, and a snowy footbridge ascends to the top along the right side. It's so awesome that I momentarily forget about The Game.

A man appears under the curve of Arch Rock wearing brown bellbottoms and a cable-knit cardigan over a striped shirt. His pointy collar is partially hidden by a lion's mane of brown curly hair. He's the spitting image of Craig O'Grady. He waves, and Mark-Bot tells us he's the Game Master who will collect the firescope for "Craig's Challenge."

Ollie has the scope now, and right as he's about to hand it to the guy, he stops and his head swivels. He retreats from the man, staring at the ground like he's trying to retrace his steps. Sammi swoops in and grabs the firescope from Ollie, running toward the bellbottomed guy and slapping it into his hand. The Game Master nods and walks back the way he came, and then Mark-Bot declares Sammi the victor of the first round. She whoops and hollers, telling us all to bite it, she's going to win Vermilion. Mark-Bot also says that Luckster failed his mission in clovering each player in time, so he will suffer the consequences.

What in the world? As I see Keondra run toward Camila who hugs her, I rush over to Ollie and grasp his arm, calling his name, asking if he's okay and wondering what consequences Luckster will endure. I thought Luckster was one of them, out to get us. Is he really one of us, and they're out to get him? Could he really be Troy, reassembled and brought back to life?

I laugh at the silly thought, but then I realize nothing is too silly for this game. Like a Hollaphone making a smartphone from a hologram using 3-D printer techniques at lightening speeds, maybe Luckster is really Troy, the cute basketball player from Frankenmuth, regrown like a plucked hair and cast in a whole new role. Perhaps the Soldier-Bots and Med-Bots conspired and brought Troy back somehow. Wouldn't that be something?

Or maybe his disintegration was an Eye-Bot hallucination, and he never died. Who the hell knows?

I continue tugging at Ollie's arm.

"Yeah?" he asks.

"What happened to you?"

He gazes at Sammi then back at me. "With what?"

"You were so close."

Sammi tries to high-five Camila and Keondra. They flip her off and walk away. Sammi makes Jiro slap her hand by forcing his with her own. After, he looks at us and shrugs.

"So close with what?" Ollie rubs his temples. "I have a splitting headache." He attempts to take off his goggles.

I grasp his hands. "Don't do that. You don't want them to spin the Punishment Wheel."

"Huh?"

I tighten the strap around his head, pushing the goggles firmly against his eyes. "Remember the Vermilion Game Rules?"

He shrugs. "What? What are you talking about?"

"Is this your brain injury you were telling us about?"

"Did I do something?"

As we walk back toward the ferry, I explain to Ollie about Vermilion and what happened during the first round.

"Shit, really?" He sighs. "I remember it now, The Game at least. Not sure how I'm going to win this thing. I got the skill and physical ability and all, but —" His shoulders slump. "I don't want to win it if it means you won't anyway, you know?"

My stomach and heart switch places. "Yeah. I do." We walk in silence a few feet, and I kick the upsetting thoughts away by changing the subject. "So, can you believe how much that guy looked like Craig O'Grady, the one who collected the scope?"

He shrugs and points to his head. "TBI, remember. No clue."

"Yeah, right. Well, it was someone in a realistic mask, rather. It had to be fake because the real actor is much older now. Before, when I saw Karyn-Bot on the eyelid video, I thought maybe she was computer-generated, but this guy wasn't. He was like Craig in the later episodes, you know when he was older and had his bedroom in the basement, during his Donny Bravado days when he had that big afro."

Ollie shrugs. "Sorry, don't know the show at all. My mom watched it sometimes, but I was pretty much at the gym since I was four. Never really got into TV."

"Oh. Well, my parents are totally obsessed with it, run an O'Grady Kids fan site even, so it's always been on least one TV in our house since I was little." I lower my voice, regretting letting it slip, not sure yet I can trust Ollie even though most of me thinks I can.

We walk back, me still wondering about the Craig-masked guy and who he could possibly be. We gather Paige along the way who still struggles to breathe and Jiro to whom Ollie speaks Japanese, which freaks him out all over again. As we climb into Home Base, and enter Doorless Bay for Nap Time, the hour before we go to bed where we can unwind, I ask my new friends how any of us will ever beat Sammi the Destroyer.

"We'll get her," Ollie says. "We just have to be smarter next time."

My hair is in my face, annoying me as usual, and Paige says she knows how to French braid. Now I'm in her bed with her behind me working my crown. Ollie and Jiro are in their upper bunks already asleep, after bidding each other a *Oyasuminasai*, which I gather is "good night" in Japanese.

"Attention Vermilion Contestants!" Mark-Bot says as Paige tugs at a knot in my hair. "Good job evading Luckster this round and staying whole. Because you did, he won't! Look behind your eyelids."

I close my eyes, afraid of what I'll see, and I find Karyn-Bot staring at me from her spotlight on a darkened gameshow stage. She stands next to a large black pot full of shiny gold coins at the end of a fake rainbow forged from bleeding watercolors painted on an arch of cardstock. She waves her hand around all the gold coins, looking directly at me with a gleam in her eye, and then she chooses one, showing what it says on one side: Luckster.

Grinning wide, she flips it over to reveal that it says: Right Thumb.

A second spotlight shines next to hers, and a door opens. Through it, Marci and Robbie O'Grady escort Luckster, whose hands are cuffed behind him, to a chair at a desk. They force him to sit. Marci bends down and struggles to cuff each of his feet to the chair as Luckster kicks at her. Robbie unlocks Luckster's handcuffs momentarily, and he forces the leprechaun's green-gloved hands toward a large loop in front of him. Robbie cuffs Luckster's left wrist to the loop and then wrestles his right wrist to the table. He ties the leprechaun's hand down with a thick leather strap.

Karyn-Bot opens a drawer in the table and pulls out a silver cleaver that shines bright in the overhead light.

"What the hell?" Paige whispers.

"I don't know," I say. "But I don't want to watch the rest." Opening my eyes, I look back to find hers are now open too.

"Me neither," she says, but a scream in my ears makes me clamp my eyes shut in time to see Luckster's face contorting in pain. He holds a bloody hand while howling as Karyn-Bot stands over him with her cleaver.

Luckster howls like a girl.

The screen beside Karyn-Bot shows a close-up of the table in front of Luckster, where his thumb encased in a green glove still sits. Its severed end is a cut hot dog all raw and oozing.

The screen darkens with Luckster moaning and crying as Mark-Bot warns that Luckster will be even more determined in the next round to clover us all.

Great.

I gulp back the vomit in my throat and open my eyes, trying to imagine the pain Luckster must be in now and what it would feel like to lose a finger — or worse. I sure hope to never find out. "As awful as that was," I say to Paige, "we have to make sure he doesn't clover us all for the next round or that could be one of us."

"Who do you think he is?" Paige asks.

"I don't know, but I'm not even sure he's a 'he.' Sounded more like a 'she.'"

"Yeah. Maybe."

I tell Paige of my earlier suspicion that Luckster might even be Troy, new and reassembled, although if he's a she, I don't know anymore.

She shivers. "Wouldn't that be incredible? You think the bots are that advanced?"

I shrug. "Hard to say." I hear a sniffle, and I twist around. "You okay?"

She frowns, putting all my hair in one hand while wiping an eye with the other. "No."

"I know. Sorry. Is it about your inhaler?"

"Yeah, that's scary, but it's not just that. I'm super worried."

"About Luckster or not winning?" I ask.

"Both, but not really for me. I need to get out of here to save my little sister Kimmy."

"Yeah? How old is she?"

"She turned six in November," Paige says, "shortly before our parents died in a train derailment."

I turn again. "Train derailment? You mean, that huge one in Indiana a few months ago?"

Paige pulls at my hair. "Yep. It happened two days before Thanksgiving. It was all over the news for a week until there was another gay club shooting, and everyone promised to reform gun laws again and then forgot about both. My parents were going to visit my aunt in Indianapolis, and they decided to take a train to avoid icy roads and get some work done. They were criminal attorneys who just caught a big case."

"Yeah, I remember the conductor who lived said someone drove onto the tracks and then darted from their car right before the train reached it."

"That's right," Paige confirms. "He saw someone from the back with dark hair and a checkered gray flannel disappear into the forest. Could be anyone. Investigators found my parents in the dining car crushed to death by a huge fridge that rolled their way and pinned them in place."

She sobs behind me, and I turn toward her, rubbing her arm. "God, that's so awful. I'm so sorry. Are you staying with your aunt now?"

Paige looks at me, her eyebrows arching. "My aunt?"

"You mentioned some aunt who gave you fudge before. And your uncle, who went on the horse-drawn carriage ride, and this aunt in Indiana. Not sure if they're the same. "

"Oh, yeah, right, her." She turns my head back around and begins braiding again. "She couldn't take us. Like, she didn't qualify because she's been in and out of mental institutions for years. She and my uncle have a lot of domestic disturbance calls on record because she likes to dial 911 when she gets manic."

"Aw, that sucks."

"Yeah, so, now we're staying with the Shelleck's, our fosters, and they're awful. Like truly terrible people. We have been there only a month, and Kimmy told me like a week in that Mr. Shelleck was watching her when she woke up in the middle of the night to pee."

My face scrunches up. "Ew. No way."

"Yep. She was terrified, thinking he was the Boogey Man. So, I've been making her sleep with me. But one night, I woke up and he was there, watching both of us. Now, I can barely sleep, so worried for her and for me. And then I've seen Mrs. Shelleck hit her, even once with an electrical cord that left marks, and that witch even struck me once. She's abusive, but he's creepy, not sure which is worse. They made me quit school and told the social worker that I'm in virtual school, which I am but they never give me time to attend class or do homework, so I'm failing all my classes. They make me and Kimmy do everything around their restaurant, house, and small farm all the time like we're their slaves." She cries into her hands as my heart lurches, feeling so scared for her and especially her vulnerable little sister who's now alone with them, maybe indefinitely.

I tear up too. "God, that's so awful." Then, something doesn't compute for a second and my mind lassos it in. "Wait, I thought you went to Fitzgerald High?"

"Oh, yeah, I did at first, for like two weeks when I got there. When my parents were alive, I went to Walled Lake Western. The Shelleck's made me quit to become their slave." Paige finishes my hair and secures it with an elastic. "And now I'm someone else's slave. Just great. Anyway, I had an escape plan worked out. Stole some webcams from school before I stopped attending, and I set them up in the Shelleck's basement where they keep their restaurant money in a safe until they can get to the bank. I was trying to crack the combination by recording them twisting the numbers, and then we could get the hell out of there. Or, at least, that *was* the plan."

She sniffles, and her breathing becomes more labored. "I should have never gone on this stupid tour. I got a full scholarship based on my SAT scores, and I had to come to sign paperwork and meet the benefactors. They wouldn't let me do it online for some reason. I hoped to sneak Kimmy into my dorm room once I started."

“I’m so sorry. That’s the worst story I’ve ever heard.” I think of little Kimmy having to be so afraid that her foster father will do whatever to her, or that his wife will hit her as they force her to toil like Cinderella. Then, I wonder why Paige got a scholarship, but I didn’t with my perfect SAT score. I ask, and she says she took hers much earlier than me, and my offer should come soon.

“Yeah. I gotta’ get out of here somehow. I can’t let her …” Paige sighs. “Honestly, I have no chance of winning this game. I’m the least fit here. Even Jiro is more able than me. And I can’t brea…” Her voice trails off, and she slumps onto her pillow.

I hear Karyn-Bot announce that our naps will begin until the Prep Time of Round 2, Skeeter’s Challenge, before I fall over onto Paige.

## PART 5

## DAVINA'S SECRET MESSAGE

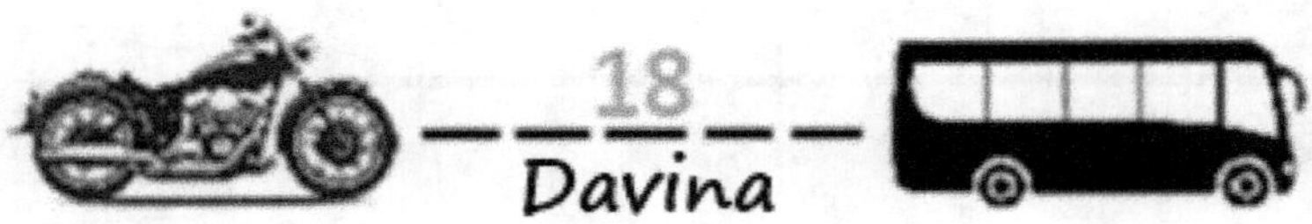


**Thursday, January 17, 2030**

I awaken on the Thursday after Mallory's kidnapping depressed as anything. I spent most of the night in the emergency room with my parents waiting for news on Zayde, worried about him even more now on top of my sister. Yesterday, Mom was visiting him after work at his stroke rehab and went to use the ladies room in the hallway while he was napping. When she returned, Zayde wasn't in his bed. She looked toward his private bathroom and saw his feet sticking out the door. She discovered him unconscious, his head bleeding on the floor. Now, he's in a coma, and they're not sure he'll recover. Mom is inconsolable, blaming herself because she thought he was asleep and didn't call an aide when she left him alone.

Dad sent me home in an Uber around two in the morning. After a mixture of nightmares about Mallory and Zayde, along with everyone else from the bus whose faces are now emblazoned in my mind, I awakened wondering if there's any hope of saving any of them. In addition to Zayde, should I somehow prepare to lose Mallory?

I wipe tears from my eyes, trying to steer my mind elsewhere, not ready yet — or ever — to be an only child. Even if Mallory and I don't get along too well and she makes me look bad all the time, I don't want something bad happening to her. She is my sister, after all, and besides, we've had some good times too. I start to think of a few, like the time she gave me half her ice cream cone because mine fell on the floor (albeit the second half after she'd slobbered all over it, but still). The pleasant thoughts are kicked out by a barrage of faces that parade in front of me.

The names and haunting faces of the Missing Tech Nine as they're now being called in the news are in my head as if I've known them my whole life: Sammi Grayson, Troy Mormont, Jiro Tanaka, Darla Higgins, Camila Rodriguez, Ollie Melson, Keondra Williams, Paige Tellison, and Mallory Rosenbaum. And they're being shown even more now on the

OuterNet and on TV as people think they were at Mackinac Island. Three girls in rainbow sweats, masks, goggles, and hats did a dance routine yesterday in front of a tour group at someplace called Crack-in-the-Island, which is trending now since everyone's wondering what the heck that is. They suspect it was Mallory, Keondra, and Camila.

I grab my Hollaphone from my nightstand. Opening Gaggle, I find a news article about the Missing Tech Nine. After skimming it, I find that the police were able to extract enough still shots from the dancers' video to compare it to the hostages' facial structures. They confirmed it was Mallory and the other two dancers even though their faces were covered in masks and goggles. Also, the hair poking out of their hats and skin colors matched. Mallory's reddish shade, Camila's pin-straight caramel hair with blonde highlights, and the heart-shaped braids on the sides of Keondra's head were unmistakable. We could see Keondra's braids when her hat fell off while doing back handsprings. Her mother said she got them done right before the tour.

What in the world? Mallory, dancing while kidnapped? With her dance enemies?

Meanwhile, the article said, others similarly dressed in rainbow solids with faces covered by masks and goggles took something out of Crack-in-the-Island. People filming zoomed in on them behind the tour guide. A little one and a big one helped some other super-buff one lower into the hole with rope. When the built one emerged, they put something shiny into their waist pack. Even after the police blew up and enhanced the video images, they could not determine what it was. They think the three were Ollie, Sammi, and Jiro, judging from their sizes compared to the rest of the Missing Tech Nine.

The whirling questions start another onslaught of tornado-like action, and I sigh. Swiping to another channel, I see a brunette reporter standing in front of a Mackinac Island sign saying that people are now calling the Missing Tech Nine the Rainbow Pranksters. There were sightings yesterday all over the island by cops, park rangers, shopkeepers, hotel staff, and a few SantaSeg drivers. The screen shows a large man with a crazy curlicue mustache complaining that one of them stole a purse from his store, and then her friend attacked a cop trying to arrest her with a snowball. He holds up the beaded clutch, and it reminds me of the one Bubbe made for Mom that Snake Riley stole.

Was it Mallory they're talking about, and she took it because it's so similar? Why is she shoplifting while kidnapped, and then dancing of all things? Reminds me of that Patty Hearst from the 1970's who I learned about in history class, who they say sympathized with her kidnappers — something called Stockholm Syndrome — and even robbed a bank with them. Is that what's going on here? Is Mallory stealing for her captors? And why does the purse look so much like Bubbe's that was stolen by Snake Riley?

The screen switches back to the reporter, who shows on her Hollaphone that someone is selling T-shirts online. The camera zooms in on a normal cotton tee with the new nickname of the Missing Tech Nine stylized as RainBO PranXterz, and it is printed above a tie-dyed hand sticking up a middle finger. "They sold out within ten minutes," the reporter says. "Now, everyone wants one, and the price keeps rising. Last we checked, maybe two hours ago on eBaymazon, they were going for $300 each, or two for $580."

I shake my head, eyeing the simple t-shirt that probably cost $5 to produce. It makes me so sick. Someone's profiting off Mallory and the others. Is it whoever took them? Is simple financial gain the motive here?

I wonder for the millionth time who has them and why, and whose theory — if any — is correct. Are any of the bus kids or someone they know a target, or is it like I thought, they were just the ones who signed up for the bogus Tech Tour, gathered for some sinister purpose? Is the connection between Mallory and the two dancers important, or the fact that my parents and that girl Paige's parents teach at the same university? The whole thing sends infinite chills rippling through me, and I wonder why they're in Mackinac Island of all places. It *is* on the way to Michigan Tech from Detroit, so maybe that's where they're heading after all. Should the cops be meeting them there? Should I?

I flip to a local news feed as a man in a suit chats with a female co-host in a purple dress. "The other thing everyone's watching," she says, "is Darla Higgins, a member of the Missing Tech Nine with curly brown hair dressed like the others in rainbow gear. She collapsed when a cop handcuffed her to his PoliceSeg." The camera switches to the male host, and the lighting changes. A grim expression overtakes his face. "What you are about to see may be very disturbing for some. Please shield children and anyone else for whom mature content is unsuitable."

The camera zeroes in on the screen behind the reporters showing a heavy figure in a mask, brown curls escaping from her hat. She struggles against a handcuff chaining her to the rail of a HoverSeg wrapped in khaki camouflage with some official-looking logo on it. Collapsing, her cuffed arm supports her from above while her other hand clutches her chest. Her body jerks and she writhes about, then goes completely slack. I wonder if gravity will pull her arm off, but before that could happen, her skin becomes all rippled. Then, she somehow *implodes*, becoming a pile of skin, hair, eyeballs, and teeth.

Chunks rise in my throat, and I hop out of bed, rushing toward the bathroom feeling totally sick but unable to take my eyes from my Hollaphone's screen. I watch as Darla gets sucked away by some invisible vacuum, even her rainbow clothes, until all that's left of her is the dangling handcuff with her severed hand still in it. I'm glad they somehow put a filter to blur the grossest parts, but it's still enough to make me wretch repeatedly — especially when I think that next, that hand could be Mallory's.

When I'm done and cleaned up, I return to my bed, horrified yet mesmerized. Now, they're back to the dancing RainBO PranXterz, replaying the three girls doing their hip-hop, and I know for sure the one in the middle is Mallory. She has a bad habit I recognize in her dancing, often snapping to the beat when she's not supposed to. I thought she'd overcome it, but she must be really nervous because she does it throughout. Plus, her unique wavy red-orange hair poking out from her knit cap is unmistakable, as is her infamous head spin. She is Twista' Sista', after all.

They return to Darla's story, now with a panel of scientific eggheads theorizing about where she could have gone.

One expert suggests Darla was smuggling baggies of drugs containing some sort of acid inside her body and they burst, the acid devouring her from within.

A girl on the panel who looks about my age laughs. The caption below identifies her as Darla's best friend. "That's absolutely ridiculous! Darla wasn't smuggling drugs. She was a National Honor Society student who started our school's engineering club."

Nothing makes any sense. I slide off my bed, throwing down my Hollaphone, my head pounding. Yet I'm determined to go to school. I haven't been all week, and I hate falling behind. Besides, I need distraction big time or I'm going to lose it. I can't keep sitting here and asking endless questions to my ceiling who hasn't answered even one.

Everyone will be staring and whispering, but hopefully, I can tune them out. I need math lectures, chem labs, and learning about random tribes in anthropology. I want to work on my animal rights club that I've been trying to start and figure out a strategy to recoup our title with the Nerd Bowl team. I need school now, right now, the more the better. I need *anything* so I don't think about Mallory and what she might be going through — if she's even still breathing.

I would think as her twin, I would feel it if she wasn't. That's the sliver of hope I have, if that whole twin thing is true. *God, I hope it's true.*

I picture Darla's hand in the cuff on the PoliceSeg and acid burns my chest. I return to the bathroom, sick all over again.

When I'm finally okay enough to leave the toilet, I get ready and then hop into our Jetta, now sadly all mine. I drive to school, checking messages on my Hollaphone along the way. The glimmer of hope that Mallory somehow got to a phone is dashed as I hear I have one message, and it's from my other Bubbe. She's Dad's mother, the one who lives in St. Paul. I sigh.

She keeps calling to check on me, acting all concerned, not knowing how much I hate her. More than once when she came into town to visit, she thought I was Mallory and said my parents were so puzzled how one twin could be so much better than the other. She confided that they think since Davina was born second, she didn't get as much oxygen to her brain. Why would she even tell Mallory that? I avoid her as much as possible. I certainly can't deal with her now.

As I roll into the student parking lot, I delete her message and block her, justified and satisfied. If it's ever brought up, I'll just play dumb. I park and walk into school serenaded by whispers, all eyes on me, and bustle about at my locker while Antonia and her friend Claire buzz in my ear.

"I heard they think the Missing Tech Nine may not even be in the country anymore," Claire says without a brain in her head. "They might have been shipped overseas somewhere, being forced to —"

I slam my locker door and turn to Claire, who I only tolerate because she's Antonia's BFF from childhood. Antonia confided she can't stand her anymore, but their moms are still besties and make them do everything together. “Thanks for the update,” I say tightly. “When I need more info, I’ll know just who to ask.”

Antonia pulls Claire away toward the bathroom saying she needs help adjusting her bra.

I grumble under my breath and open my locker again, realizing I never even grabbed my books. As I search an upper shelf for my Anthropology text, my fingers stop on something unfamiliar.

Running my hand all around some new object, I feel smooth and rounded pieces of some sort. Pulling it toward me, I discover the beautiful, beaded purse that my Bubbe made my mother shortly before she died. It’s the one Snake Riley stole when he robbed and disfigured my mom on Valentine’s Day.

My breath catches in my throat as I inspect it, running my hands over Bubbe’s beautiful beadwork. I never thought I’d see it again.

I pry it open to find several things. In the lining, there’s a tag with the quote, “Sorry sir, but you’re upside down” embroidered on it, a line from Mom and Bubbe’s favorite movie, *What’s Up Doc?* There’s a pearlescent compact and some bills kept together in the money clip Mom stole from Dad after she bought him one that he liked better. Then, there’s a rectangle of tissues, a silver-capped lipstick, and a roll of Breathsavers. Mom’s driver’s license and a debit card poke out of a side pocket. Behind them are two scuffed and wrinkled envelopes. One says, “Deer Davina, Plese Reed Sekund.” The other says, “Deer Proffesurs Rosenbaum and Davina, Plese Reed Furst.” They are printed in boxy boy writing slanting right.

My heart is in my throat as I inspect my locker. The metal near the handle is bent. Did Snake Riley break into my locker to put this here? I thought he was still in juvie. My parents did that whole video during the hearing, and it was so damning, I thought for sure they’d give him extra time, not let him go. But maybe his family finally got to his judge, so who knows?

I retrieve the envelope that says to read it first, the one addressed to my parents and me. As the warning bell sounds, I rush off to anthropology. While my teacher drones on about the burial customs of the Tawankawaniskaranthahanakawakaranchi Tribe of Southeast Asia, I take out the letter to me and my parents, dying to know what it is.

# 19
## Davina

I open the first letter, and a crumpled hundred-dollar bill falls out. Unsure what it's for, I tuck it into my pocket and start reading.

*Deer Proffesurs Rosenbaum and Davina,*

*My name is Jonah "Snake" Riley, the kid you think attakd you. Im sorree for hurtin you. I did not meen to run you both over and take yur nice purss. I culdnt tell the polis or the loiyers or anywon as you will see. But I need you to no wut rillee happined. I never ment this. Plese, you gotta beleev me.*

*The hole time I bin lockt up, I bin riting you, so I hope you reed it. As soon as I get sprung, Im gonna giv it to Davina at skool so you will have this lettur and know whut rillee happined that day, why I ran you both over and evreethin. I'm veery sorry it went down like that and will make up for it how you want.*

*Im not shure if you no but Davina savd my life back in the forth grade, and I oh her bigtiem. I didnt no how to thank her. I aint never thankt aneebodee B4. And then time passt, and I never did. So Davina, if yur reedin, I just wanna thank you for been so smart to get that dog off me and sav my lif. Thank you, and sorree I aint say nuthin B4.*

*Mabee this letter will ansser some of your queshtuns about wy things happined. If I can make up for it, I wanna no. You can reech me at (248) 555 -1242 or at snakebyte123@metaapplesoft.com.*

*So, a little abowt me and my familee, wich has to do with stuf. As you may no, my fathur is Duke Riley, Prezident of the Metro Detroit chaptur of the Rebel Demons Motersykel Club. He runs the west side wile this guy Hawk runs the east, with Woodward Avanew dividin theer teritoreez.*

*My older brothur Rocco's gonna be Prezident of the Rebel Demons soon. Hes onlee 23, but my dad is dyin from lung cansur since he smoks 3 paks a day, and hes gotta trust hoo takes over. Dad said hell no to the new nanerbot treetmints that be saving other cansur pashunts, sayin he wuld rathur die than have littel musheens in his bodee that can be hakkd and controld. The kemo and radiashun havent werkd, so he may go like soon. He just got his voiss box out, so now he smoks out of his nek bitween puffs of oxegen, which is rillee afull to see.*

*I hafta be in my familees motersykel klub even if I dont want to. I've been rayzd to be in it sinse the day I was born when they slapd a Harley-Davidson vest on me, gave me a skull-shapd passifyer, and stuck a tempararee tattoo of the Rebel Demons logo on my arm. When I was 4, Dad thot I was old enuff to rillee get it and laffd like crazee when I skreamd. Dad and Rocco are making me be the Rebel Demons VP in a fue yeers.*

*Last Valantin's Day, Dad sent me and Cody, a Rebel Demons prospek and best frend to me and my brother our hole lives, out to take care of club bizness. We new it was a test, and one we did not wanna flunk. Dad sent a coupla other guys too to make sure we aint mess up.*

*Me and Cody were suposta get monee from Hawk, a tall dude with a huge forhed and long noze, givin him his name. He leeds our Eastside divishun but Dads still in charge of him since he did prizin time for Zeke – hed of all the Midwest chapterz – when I was littel. So, Zeke gives Dad 60% wile Hawk only gets 40% of our total cut after club doos and paying everywon off. Hawk complanes all the time to anywon hoo will lissin.*

*Hawk hangs out at this biker bar down on 8 Mile kalld the Dirtee Devils Rodehowss. Dad said I betur not come home till I had Hawk's weeklee take.*

*Hawk copt an atitud sayin I had to wate until he finnishd his pool game to give me the cash. Cody got antsee and got me all mad, telling me I cudnt just let him treet us like krap. I tride to blow it off and keep my cool, and I did arite – until Shailene wokkd in.*

*She was my brother Roccos gurlfrend until the week B4. She made out with Hachet, Hawk's VP, rite on his trike in front of everywon at this biker ralee we went to, even Rocco who was in line for korndogs. Hachet got his name cuz wen he was 9, he saw his mom's jerk boyfrend rappin her and grabd the furst thing he culd find, a hachet, and put it threw the guy's skul.*

*At Dirtee Devils, Shailene wokkd up to Hachet in the korner playin darts, dragin her purpel fingernals along the tatts on his arm. Just as he grabd her for a kiss, she flickt her cigeret, whipt her blond poneetale arownd, and walkd rite by him, a totul diss.*

*Shailene went up to Hawk bent over the pool tabel and pusht him up wile he was in the midel of shootin. She hopt up on the metal edjj, spreddin her legs wide to show everybodee no underweer beneeth her lether miniskurt. Straddleen him, Shailene kist a very supprizd Hawk with tung I culd see from like ten feet away wile Hatchet curst and downd his beer, and the rest of the bar hootid and cheerd.*

*I wisperd to Cody how shockt I was over Shailene's sudin risin in the ranks of the Eastside Boyz now that she finisht with Rocco and the Westsidrz, and Shailene overhurd me. She lookt at me, her face pisst off, and took sumthin out from her large chest explodin out of her lether top. Throing it at me, she told me to give the cheep peess of tin bak to Rocco.*

*On the floor between me and Hawk was the skull nekliss with the rubee eyes that my mothur gave to Rocco when she was dyin. Dad gave it to her on theer wedin day and she never took it off unteel then. Mom told Rocco to give it to a nice gurl, and he thot that gurl was Shailene, wich was totalee redikulus even B4 she showd her troo colers.*

*My mom died too weeks B4 wen a Hummer hit her, nokkin her off Dad's bike when he went inside the Sitgo for some sigs. She was my best frend in the hole world bussides Lola, my ranbow retikulatd pythen I reskud from my seniel grandfathur who ignord her so much that she now has savere separashun anksietee. (That's wy I weer Lola all the time, and how I got my niknaam Snake.) Shailene throwin Mom's nekliss like that rillee hit me the rong way, espeshulee since Mom <u>juss</u> <u>died</u>.*

*B4 I culd get the nekliss, Hawk came over and stompt on it with his boot, gryndin it into the floor. He told me to send my brothur and fathur his reegards. Then, Hawk sed he wasnt givin me a diem, that he and his boys were defektin and formin theer own club. He ript the Rebel Demons flag off the wall and throo it down, stompin it while his idiet frends lafft and clapt. Then he ternd to his thurd-in-charg, this guy Brute, who handid him a peese of cloth. Hawk hung a new flag on the wall that sed "Eastside Boyz" over a litning bolt with a skul insied the ziggzag. Bloin a clowd of smoke in my fase, Hawk turnd back to Shailene, and they both laffd, then made out like they just won the loteree.*

*Everywon but them was watchin me, and Cody sed I culdnt just let Hawk and Shailene diss my brothur and my ded mothur, not to menshun my father and the Rebel Demons.*

*And Cody was rite. So, I grabd Hawk's shoulder and throo the furst punch. Then Hawk swung, the Eastside Boyz jumpt me and Cody, and it was a regulir brall. Speshully wen our bakup guys jumpt in.*

*At one point, Hawk chokt me agenst the jukbox. Digging my nales into his fingurs, I kikkt my nee weer the sun aint shine. Pushin him off me hard, I tryd to get away.*

*Hawk fell back and slipt on the pool ku on the grownd that he'd been shootin with B4 Shailene come up. Falling agenst the pool tabel, Hawk's bird-shapt hed made a wack on the metal edjj loud enuff to stop everywons punchin. They all turnd to gokk. Hawk went down like a sak of potatoz, and blood gusht onto the scracht-up floor all arownd his dented hed. His eyes froz on the ceeling full of swingin beer cans and spinnin fans.*

*Sumwon swore and then everywon lookt at Hawk and then at eech othur and then at me as Motlee Crews Kikstart My Hart blard in the backround. The perfikt timin of the song gave me chills like the jookbox sumhow new what wuld happin and had it all redee to go.*

*Hachet puncht his fist into his hand and glard at me sayin "Man yur ded" and then the hole Eastside Boyz club chasst me out of the bar and down the street.*

*That's wen I ran into you, Proffesors Rosenbaum, and nokkt you over. I didnt even see you unteel I was rite on top of you. And then, Mrs. Rosenbaum, I took yer mothur's purss bekuz I was afrade to explane to my fathur what happind, speshully without the monee Hawk ohd. It was a last-minit desishun Im sorry about. Im sorry about everythin that happined, incloodin the cop who saw everythin in the street and arested me.*

*I throo the purse into some bushes B4 he got me and found it theer wen I got out. I hatd to go to juvie, but at least I was safe theer. Now, hoo nos? The Eastside Boyz have a contrak out on me, wich is why Im now in hidin.*

*I've returnd the purse to Davina, and I onlee opined it to put this lettur insid, you have my wurd. You shuld have every sent you had B4 since I didnt tuch nuthin. I also gave you a hundrid dollers to pay for cleenin bekuz the back of the purse got dirtee on the grownd, but if it costs more, let me no and Ill giv you the rest.*

*I been wantin to return the purse to you sins that day, but as you know, I bin away. I hope you can see now wy this all happined, and I pray you rillee no how sorree I am. When I can, I want to pay you back for all the medikul bills for Mrs. Rosenbaum's sergerys and denist stuff, and Mr. Rosenbaum's sergery too. Pleese send them to 8274 Chicory Road Farmington, MI 48332 and I will pay em off.*

*You problee don't no, Mrs. Rosenbaum, but I asso have skars. In the 8th grad, I was tryin to make my mom a birthda diner of spugeti and meetballs to thank her for helpin me save Lola, my granddads snake who we got helthee agen after he forgot abowt her. Mom even made Lola littel housis in our motorsykel trunks with enuff holes for her to breeth so we culd aways have her with us.*

*I left the boilin spageti noodels to aksept a pakkig at the door. When I came bak, I didnt see the water all over the floor. I pikt up the huge pot, slipt back, and pord the hot likwid onto my fase and nek.*

*I was totalee bumd about the burns all over. Then Mom sed I should do what women who have there brests removed do hoo tattoo theer uglee skin after theer sergerys to hide theer skars with sumething pritty. Even tho I was terrefide and it hurt alot, I got a tattoo of Lola on me. Mom sed after Lola dyes, it will be a tribuut tattoo I can aways remembur her by.*

*I tell you this, Mrs. Rosenbaum, bekuz I undurstand what its like to have evrywon stare even if they try not too, and I cant even begin to tell you how soree I am for what I did to cawse your cuts on your fase. I hope the nanerbot teknoligees can fix it soon, and if you want, I can keep you updatd on it. I will find a way to pay you bak for any ekspenses and do aneethin I can to help.*

*I'm not shure yull ever forgiv me, but I hope you no now that I didnt meen to hurt anywon. Thank you for heering me out, and agen, Im rillee soree.*

*Sincirlee,*

*Jonah "Snake" Riley*

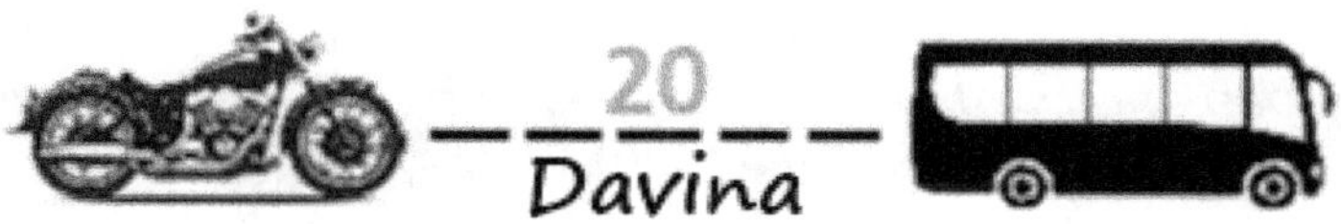


Rubbing my eyes from shock over what I read and how he could speak much more eloquently than I would have thought — yet spell so horribly — I rip open the second envelope. My heart hammers as my shaky fingers struggle to hold the note still.

*Deer Davina,*

*This is Jonah Riley agen. Pleese aksept my sinseerist apoligee for never thankin you for savin my life from that dog. I was stupid, and a tuff guy. I'm not sure wy, but I didnt, and it was rong. So, agen, thank you from the botum of my hart. It's bekuz of you that I'm alliev.*

*Now, I muss tell you too things:*

*As I sed, I'm in hidin, but I trust you will keep my lokashun sekret. Do not tell anywon, even yur parints. The fuer peepel hoo no wheer I am, the bettur.*

*I'm stayin at the Shooger Mapel Preeserv in the sittee of McAllister, wich is abowt haffwae beetween Canton and Ann Arbor, way out west of Oakland Countee were theer are horss farms. This preeserv, which you can put into yur GPS, has aways been lokkt. Some govermint peepel come by sumtiems. I broke in yeers ago bekuz its rite behind my grandpa's farm, and its buttiful with all kinds of wildlief pokin threw the leevs. I have heeted the laggoon for Lola, and thats were we spend most of our tiem.*

*Pleese come meet me theer as soon as you can, and I ask you to come alone. I meen it, but pleese, don't be afrade. Lola and I wuld never hert you. We oh you evreethin and want to help you and yur familee. I finlee have a way, a reel way to pay you back for wut I did. Pleese keep reedin.*

*I have informashun about Malleree and the missin bus kids. I overhurd my dad and brothur talkin abowt them wen I came home from juvie, and I want to help you reskew her. My dad and Rocco were invitid to partissipat in some top-sekrit live game calld "Vurmilleon" as VIPs.*

*There bettin on yur sistur and the other missin bus kids who have been forsst to be kontestints to deminstraat some super-improovd nanerbots to a bunch of krimnals. Yur sister and the othurs hav bin injektid with them and held hostij from within, threatind with torcher and even deth if they don't folo game rools.*

*I didnt hear everythin, but Ill tell you wut I did. The police cant no, and yur parints cant too, or thell mess everythin up and well lose Malleree and the others forever. <u>I have a plan for how to save yur sistur</u>, and Ill eksplan more wen were tagether. Plese come now, and dont tell anywon, so we can find them. We dont have alot of time. I'm 100% sereus.*

*Sincirlee,*

*Jonah "Snake" Riley*

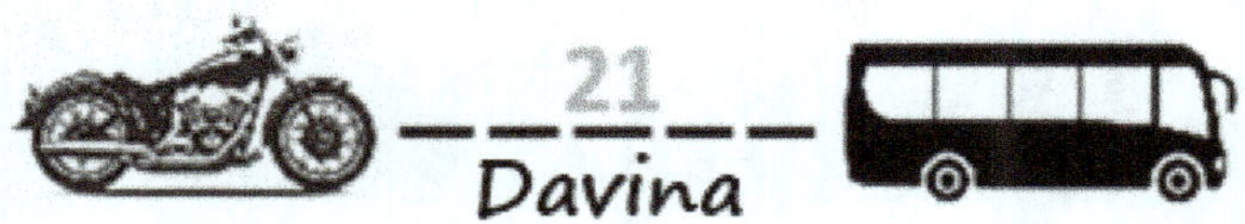


# 21 Davina

I duck out of school, texting my mom that I have bad cramps and need to leave so she can call the attendance office. I hop in the Jetta and type the Sugar Maple Preserve into my GPS, my heart beating in my ears. Peering in the mirror, I fix my hair which is all over the place. My cheeks are flushed, and I feel like I'm ready to jump off a cliff.

I need to go meet Snake, this guy I've hated for so long who suddenly wrote this sincere apology letter that totally made sense and even made me feel a bit sorry for him being trapped in his family's gang. I'd judged him about his head and neck tattoo, condemning him for marking himself up like that, having no idea that he got it to cover all his burns. What else did I have wrong about him?

A memory springs forth of him beating up a guy in eighth grade, wailing on him in the courtyard until some teachers pulled Snake off. He'd sworn up a storm, thrashing around with bloody fists and making threats that he'd sic his entire family on all involved as they dragged him away.

I'm not sure what to think of Snake, what to expect from this violent guy I've just ditched school — oops, crap, and a chem quiz — to meet. He insists he won't hurt me and wants to help save Mallory, but maybe he's one of the kidnappers and is luring me somewhere secluded with some bullshit story. As I drive, I obsess about this possibility, remembering how terrified I was on the bus when his family came looking for Krystall Nykkolls, thinking he was there to get me. A flashback to the trickle of fluid leading to the front of the bus slaps me, and I recall my suspicions that the Rebel Demons set the bus on fire. Do I want to be involved with any of them at all?

*Yes, if it's for Mallory,* my mind screams, and it surprises me in a way because of all the negative feelings her very existence has created for me. But none of that seems to matter anymore, and I know deep down that it's not her fault. Sure, Mallory can be rather unpleasant at times, and living in her shadow is quite stifling, but that doesn't mean she deserves to die.

Besides, it should have been me on that tour, not her, my mind dutifully reminds me. I need to do everything I can since it's all my fault.

I hit I-696 westbound and eventually merge onto I-275, going through the details of all that Snake wrote and trying to figure out what I'll say, wondering how I'll feel when I face this guy I hate.

It takes me about a half hour to reach the turnoff, and then I follow several long, winding dirt roads that seem like they go on forever until I spot a wooden sign that says, "Grandpa's Farm." Snake said the preserve was right behind his grandfather's property, so I follow the arrow. On a plot of land, there's a white farmhouse in the distance and a big red barn with pretty trees closer to me. Behind the barn, a tall fence stretches straight ahead and to my left walling off what looks like a preserve. I'm not sure where I'm to meet Snake exactly, or if he even knows if I'm coming now, or tomorrow, or never. I recall I have his number, but I'm not yet sure I want to make contact.

I park and cut my engine, getting out to a brisk wind. I'm in the middle of nowhere with some guy I've always thought was super violent until today when he wrote these letters to me and my parents – supposedly – and I wonder if I'm the biggest idiot ever. Everyone teases me about being naïve.

Just as I'm about to turn back to my car ready to flee, a shadow approaches. From a woodsy area, a slightly pudgy guy a head taller than me emerges. The first thing I notice — besides the shock of black hair that falls over his right eye and his black leather vest with silver studs and patches all over it — is the huge python around his neck that matches the one tattooed on the shaved half of his head.

I jump back, my heart pounding.

"Hey," he whispers. "It's okay. Don't be scared. Lola's just checking you out."

The rainbow snake he wears like a mink stole slithers up to me, her blue, purple, black, and yellow head bobbing while her forked tongue darts in and out.

"Oh, wow, she's totally into you," Snake says before grabbing Lola's head and kissing her on the mouth.

"Huh?"

"Oh, she's gotta' system for people. If she hates you, she'll diss you and only talk to me."

"Talk to you?"

"She slithers in my ear, telling me cool secrets."

"Yeah? Huh."

"If she likes you, she'll bob her head side-to-side. If she really likes you, thinks you're chill and we can hang, she'll also slither, but if she super likes you, she does what I call her Slither Smile, where she bobs her head and slithers while smiling."

"Are you serious?"

"Totally. Oh man. I don't believe this. She ain't did this with nobody except Grandpa and Mom and of course me. Not even my brother Rocco, who she Slither Smiles for all the time."

"What? What's she doing?" I gape at the bobbing and smiling snake.

"She's doing her Slither Smile, but now she's offering you her belly. See that? She wants you to pet her. Means she totally trusts you. She ain't hardly never did that with nobody."

I move a little closer and Lola comes right up to my face. Her tongue is out, and her curved mouth makes her appear happy. She rolls around so I can see her underside. I reach my hand forward, then pull back, chickening out.

"No, s'aright. She won't bite. She wants you to pet her."

"She does?" The overly friendly snake and me being here in the middle of nowhere chit-chatting with Snake Riley of all people makes me feel like I'm in a dream.

"Yeah, look.  On every website about this kind of snake — called a reticulated python for how she's all marked up — they say they ain't have no emotions, but them scientists never met the likes of her. She's totally offering herself to you."

He reaches for my hand and guides it to his snake.

I touch it a second and recoil, surprised. "It's weird. Looks like it would be wet, but it's dry and cool."

"Yep. That's what they feel like. All reptiles do cause of them scales. She also has separation anxiety bad because my senile grandaddy forgot about her, and now she's pregnant too. So maybe she's got them hormones goin' or somethin', but she's like *really* into you."

I laugh as Lola wraps around my arm and Slither Smiles at me. "Pregnant? Snakes get pregnant? I love animals, but I don't know much about reptiles."

Snake grins, and I notice he has a super cute smile, which I also don't expect. His interesting fang-like teeth make his face quite unique. A nicely groomed mustache and goatee frame his mouth, something else I don't recall from before. "Oh yeah. My brother Rocco watched her when I was up in juvie, and he thought he did good, never let her be with no other snakes, so he was all confused how she got knocked up."

"She did it on her own?"

Snake nods. "It's called 'parthenogenesis,' and sometimes girl pythons like her do this. She's gonna lay her eggs in April and then wrap around them, something called 'brooding,' another eight weeks to make their temperatures right."

"Wow. So, how many will she have?"

Snake shrugs. "Could be only like fifteen to twenty, but some have over a hundred. I'm giving them to the Detroit Zoo or Michigan State's Vet School. No way can I feed 'em all."

I know what snakes eat and don't inquire, but I pet her again, and she slithers along my shoulders until Snake pulls her back and puts her on his own. "She'll crush you. She's almost forty pounds."

"Geez, really?"

"Yeah. She's a little piggy girl." He kisses her again and she Slither Smiles at him. "Aren'cha, little Piggy Girl?"

I laugh, surprised by Snake and his adorable snake. But I'm not here to socialize. "So, what can you tell me about Mallory? What did you —"

Snake puts a finger to his lips as he looks around. "People could be listening," he whispers. "Wait." He nods to the preserve behind him.

"Who's listening?" I start to ask, but his eyes dart all about and his nervousness is making me even more anxious, wondering what he's thinking and who may be eavesdropping.

My eyes scan our surroundings, and there's a million places someone could hide, with rows of trees in every direction. My initial apprehension returns, thinking Snake's story in his letters may have been a way to lure me here for some reason, like that he's one of the kidnappers. Maybe he used AI to create that sordid tale about why he attacked my parents, and it's all crap.

He comes closer to me, and I think he's about to grab me or something. I jerk back, but he and Lola bend forward to whisper in my ear. "I'm hidin' out, and I've gotten kinda' paranoid. Them Eastside Boyz or Vermilion people could be anywhere. Sorry. It's just more private in the preserve."

I nod. "Okay." He's not the only one feeling paranoid. But I must play along in case he really does have news about Mallory, even if me being here and going with him into an even more secluded preserve may lead to the end of me.

We stare at each other awkwardly. I clear my throat, unsure what else to say. "You seem to know a lot about snakes," I blurt, realizing I'm putting off going into the preserve now even though I'm desperate to hear about my sister. Probably has to do with the whole dying thing, something I'm not trying to do.

Jonah grabs Lola's head and pets it while she Slither Smiles. "Aww, widdle Lola, you're such a beauty, aren'cha?" He talks like he's cajoling a baby in a crib, tickling her under the chin. "Widdle, widdle Lola Girl! So pretty, aren'cha?"

I laugh despite myself. "You babytalk your pregnant rainbow reticulated python with separation anxiety?"

"Totally." Jonah grins, revealing his cute fangs. "She gets excited when I do. Otherwise, she's all bummed and won't eat. This makes her happy as a pig in shit, just like her living on my shoulders."

I squint at Jonah, who is nothing at all like I believed, at least so far. It's so odd to discover something is nothing like you'd always assumed. I hope this isn't an act and it's actually true.

“Okay,” he says, clapping his hands suddenly, “let’s get to the preserve cause Lola wants to swim, and I need a freakin’ break. Piggy Girl’s getting heavier every second.”

“She swims in this cold?” I rub my palms together, wishing I’d brought gloves.

“I put heaters in the water so it’s a safe temperature and tested it to make sure it had the right pH. My mom helped me. I make sure she ain’t get too tired, which they can do if it’s too cold. I learned me so much about them snakes since I rescued her four years ago, I found out I could do this for reals, like take care of snakes as a job.”

“Oh yeah. That’s a specialty area. I’ve been checking into vet school too. It’s either that or studying math, but maybe both. I could combine the two and do biomedical engineering like my parents but do stuff to help improve animals’ lives and design surgery tools and stuff.”

“Yeah? That sounds cool too. You’d be in school forever though.”

I shrug. “Totally, but it wouldn’t bother me.”

He leads me toward the edge of the enclosure’s fence and pulls back the corner of the wire mesh. “I cut this forever ago with some tin snips. Took about three seconds. Lola and I been hanging in the preserve ever since. Watch them sharp edges.”

We crawl through without a scratch, and I stand, squinting up at an umbrella of beautiful, frosted trees. “What is this place?”

Snake shrugs. “Before Grandpa lost it, he tried to find out, and he saw some government dudes enter sometimes, do whatever, and leave, but he couldn’t get no answers. I was dying to see inside, and I was shocked as shit there’s this lagoon right in the middle.”

“Really?”

“Hell yeah. Come see.”

“Okay.” I hesitate a second, doubt tripping me up, but Snake turns and beckons me. With Mallory in mind, I start to, but then I trip for real on a root and stumble into him. Snake catches me, and I almost take him down, but a huge tree stops us.

“Oh, sorry,” I say. “Didn’t mean to tackle you.” As he helps me upright, I notice he smells amazing. Like, more than amazing. Like, the best thing I’ve ever smelled. “What the heck is that?” I ask.

“What?”

“Your cologne? Aftershave? Not sure, but it’s *incredible*.” I smell toward him, not even caring that I’m embarrassing myself.

He laughs, and a cross with a snake wrapped around it dangles from his ear, twinkling in the sunlight. “It’s called Drakkar Noir. It’s a regular cologne. Grandpa wore it and was always badass, so I started too. Then, it’s all he’d get me — until he forgot who I was.”

“That’s so sad. I’m sorry. My Bubbe got Alzheimer’s at age fifty.”

“Man, that’s young. Worst thing I can ever think, to forget like that. I hope that ain’t never happens to me or people I know. Wouldn’t wish that shit on my worst enemy.”

I nod. “Agreed. So, where is —”

We exit a woodsy path, and in the distance, there’s a flat rock at least ten feet long and five feet wide. Beyond it, a circle of water that’s maybe triple the rock’s length is flanked by a curved half-wall of odd-fitted boulders stacked four and five high. A stream trickles down them into the lagoon.

“That’s Lola’s Waterfall,” Snake says, beaming.

“Wow, it’s amazing,” I breathe, scoping the scene and making sure there’s no one in the shadows lurking.

“Well, not yet, but I’m working on it. Been watching some InstaTok videos. After I made the water okay for Lola and put in her heater and all that, I started stealing boulders to make this thing.”

So far, I don’t see any people, just beautiful shrubs, foliage, and random plants. “Yeah?”

“Before juvie and now this hiding, I used to hunt for them in Grandpa’s old pickup. I only built this so far, but I hope to make it much bigger. Lola and I hang out here all the time when it’s hotter. She’s happy as shit in the water, even more than on me, and I dig the peaceful vibe of the place. Helps me think.”

“This is the coolest place ever.”

He grins and takes my hand, leading me to the rock. Sitting, he pulls me down with him. Snake unwraps Lola from his neck, and she slithers into the water, swimming around and peeking out, her head bobbing and her tongue darting. She smiles even more like she's in total heaven. I can't believe I'm here watching her with my mortal enemy, who now suddenly —maybe — isn't.

"It's Lola's Lagoon," Snake says, "the best place ever. And now that I'm in hiding, I'm here all the time except when it's too cold. Then I go to Grandpa's house. I get to watch Lola all happy and healthy now and wishing one day, I could be a reptile veterinarian, not a VP of an MC." He sighs, blowing his bangs from his eye. "But hey, that's what life dealt me. I ain't talk good enough no how." He shrugs. "Ain't never spent much time on homework, ya know?"

I think of how my parents were pressuring Mallory to be an engineer when she wants to be a dancer, and I feel sorry for him in the same way, maybe even more. That's his whole life, and he's made to do bad stuff of which he hasn't elaborated, and I don't want to know. "Can't you just tell your dad?"

Snake shakes his head. "No way. Talking to Dad ain't gonna' help. He and everyone else expects me to be VP. It's my lot in life. You ain't say no to the Rebel Demons no matter who you are."

I consider arguing, but I don't really know what he's up against — his family and way of life — at all. I've just met him, again.

"Oh, hey, you're cold," he says.

I shrug. "Guess so."

He takes off his heavy black leather vest and hoodie below and offers them to me, revealing a thick plaid flannel beneath.

I smell that Drakkar Noir, the best scent I could ever imagine, and accept. After he warms me by wrapping it around me, he reaches into a side pocket. "Sorry," he says.

"What?"

"Oh, I just need —" He pulls something out. I think he's going to withdraw a cigarette and light up, and I brace myself, wondering if I'll have to be rude and move away because smoke is something I cannot tolerate. Instead, he puts a short tube to his mouth and puffs. I think he's vaping or huffing, maybe has a pen with weed in it like some kids I know sneak around at school, but then I realize it's an asthma inhaler.

Snake struggles to breathe, taking three puffs in a row.

"You okay?" I reach to pat his back but think better of it, pulling my hand away.

"Yeah. My chest just gets real tight in this cold."

I snuggle in his warm vest and hoodie that smells amazing and doesn't reek like cigarettes as I had assumed. "I honestly thought you'd be a smoker," I admit.

He nods. "Yeah, I'm pretty much the only person I know who *doesn't* smoke cigs or vape. My dad's dying from it, my brother hacks up a lung like every morning and he's only twenty-three, and Mom had a couple of things on her lung that were nothing in the end, but she had to get sliced open to get them. I ain't never liked smoke — hate it in fact — and it pretty much caused my reading and writing problems, ADHD, ear infections, and severe asthma."

"Really?"

"Oh yeah. It's proven. Mothers who smoke cigs while pregnant like mine have smaller babies who get reading, attention, breathing, and ear problems. I get bad infections all the time."

"I didn't know all that. Sorry. That's awful."

"Yeah, tell me about it. ADHD is the worst. My mind just wanders. Hard to stay focused. And, well, I'm having shit luck with something."

"What's that?"

"I dropped out of school since I'm in hiding, and I can't do club stuff neither. Dad said when this whole thing with the Eastside Boyz is over, I can't go back, that I gotta' start prepping to be VP. But for now, I secretly signed up for Michigan Online High School. Hope to at least knock out some credits toward my diploma."

"Really? That's great. Good for you."

"Ain't sure I can figure out college and vet school too, or how I'll do both and the club, but for now, I just wanna' graduate. But, well…" Jonah's face reddens, and he stares at his knee.

“What? You can tell me.”

“The math part’s seriously kicking my ass.”

“Yeah? Don’t be embarrassed. What are you in?”

“Trig. And it don’t make no freaking sense. It’s because I forgot all my algebra, which I learned forever ago and didn’t even get then.”

“Trig is all algebra. People don’t realize.”

“Yeah, well, I remember you being a little kiss-ass teacher’s pet with all them right answers, always with your hand up, ooh-ooh-oohing in the front row.”

I frown, but he grins and jiggles my arm. “That’s a good thing. I learned more from your questions than her teaching.”

“Yeah, she sucked. I remember. She didn’t even understand it herself, yet she was trying to explain it to us. I caught her making several mistakes.”

“Anyway, we ain’t here for this, but could you help me sometime? I could totally pay you and —"

“Oh, God, say no more! I could use a good distraction. And math is my favorite thing! In the meantime, there are some great websites. I’ll text you a few.”

“Great. Cool. Just let me know when you free. Now, about Mallory …”

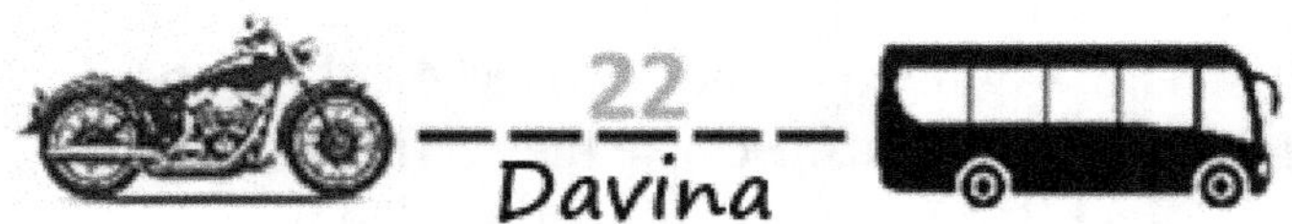


I stare at Snake in disbelief. "You want me to *what*?"

"Get my brother Rocco to take you to The Game."

I shake my head. "Me?"

"Yeah you. They're controlling your sister and the others with them nanerbots in this game Vermilion. They're even getting VIPs like my dad and brother to give the contestants glitches, which are kinda' like handicaps, I think. They also said there's this leprechaun or something that's gotta' tag them all with a clover during the round, and if he does, one of them loses a limb."

"What? Are you freaking serious?" I picture Mallory without a leg, unable to ever dance again, and tears pinch my eyes. Then I think of Darla's hand remaining in that cuff and fight the rising acid in my throat.

Snake winces and nods. "'fraid so. Look, this game is happening now, and we ain't know how long it's gonna' last. I saw them at Mackinac Island on the news too. God knows what else they be makin' 'em do."

"Only your brother and dad can go?"

He nods. "Yeah, and their old ladies. Problem is, don't know where the next round is. When Rocco and my dad went, they met them Vermilion people at the airport. They flew to Mackinac Island on Tuesday night in a private jet, and they ain't know where till they was there. They stayed in some big fancy Airbnb right on Lake Huron. They was offered girls, boys, drugs, booze, anything. Not sure how many VIPs there were, but seemed like a lot. Dad won't be able to go no more, he's too weak, and I ain't goin' for him, or the Eastside Boyz could find me. They might even be there." Snake exhales. "I ain't know where the next round's at, so we gotta' get Rocco to take you with him. Then, you tell me where, and I meet up with you. Then, we move onto Phase Two, the actual rescue."

"Why can't we just tell Rocco my sister is in the game, and we need to save her? Won't he help us if he knows? That would be so much easier."

Jonah shakes his head. "Nah, he ain't gonna' care. He don't know you, or your sister. The way my dad and brother be talking 'bout it, they thought making them kids do stuff because they's filled with them nanerbots was freaking hilarious. Couldn't believe the way they was talking, to be honest. And besides, since Zeke, this dude in charge of all Midwest Rebel Demons chapters, is having Dad go in his place as a favor, Rocco won't risk messing up The Game and getting us embarrassed. If we could get Rocco and Dad to help, it would be better, but I tell you straight up, they ain't gonna'. Dad's too sick now, so it'll just be Rocco and any girl he brings, but no one else. We need to make him bring you. Wish I could just take you myself, but it's risky as hell."

I gulp, the thought of it sending goosebumps down my arms. I think of the Rebel Demons who held a gun to my forehead, may have set my school bus on fire, and want to kill Krystall Nykkolls — or already did — and I raise my eyebrows at him. "So, that's your big plan? That I somehow convince your brother to take me?"

"Yep. Become his new old lady. Remember Shailene? He's fresh out. And he's been away on club business a lot since her, so he's still gonna' be tryina' get some."

"I know but, *me?* I know nothing about being in a motorcycle gang."

"Well, lucky you, because I do. And it's 'club.' Ain't no one say 'gang'. We's an 'MC', or 'motorcycle club.'"

"Okay, see, I didn't even know that. I've never even ridden on a motorcycle."

Snake regards me like I just sprouted wings. "Really? Well, come on!" He gets to his feet and offers me a hand.

I don't move. "No, um, sorry, but no thanks."

"Really? You ain't gonna' try?"

I shake my head. "I'm too afraid. It's all my mother's fault."

"Yeah?" Jonah squats down again.

"Mom's cousin used to ride for fun, not in a club or anything, but he got in a bad accident and needed several surgeries when I was little. Mom never, ever let us accept rides on motorcycles growing up, scared the daylights out of us so we'd never even try."

Snake nods. "Yeah, sure they dangerous, but also great. You just need to ride safe. I been takin' classes. I'm as good a driver as any. I won't let nothin' bad happen, I swear."

"It's not you I'm worried about. It's the other guy, like that Hummer who hit your mom."

Snake nods with his palms forward in surrender. "Hey, that's cool. I ain't gonna' force you. But you sure is missin' out."

Suddenly I remember my own parents and think they must be frantic by now if they've tried to reach me who's supposedly home with cramps. They don't need any more worry on top of Mallory and Zayde. "Excuse me," I say, checking my Hollaphone for messages. The glowing screen reveals several. "Gotta' call my parents. They're probably worried, with my sister gone and all —"

Snake raises a hand. "Ain't no problem. Want me to go away?" He points to some bench along the path.

"Oh, no. I just need to see what's up. There might be some word on Mallory."

I dial my mother, but it goes straight to voicemail. Hanging up, I try my dad.

He picks up on the first ring. "Oh, thank God, Davina! Where have you been?"

I start to respond, but he interrupts me. "Davina, come quick. Something's happened."

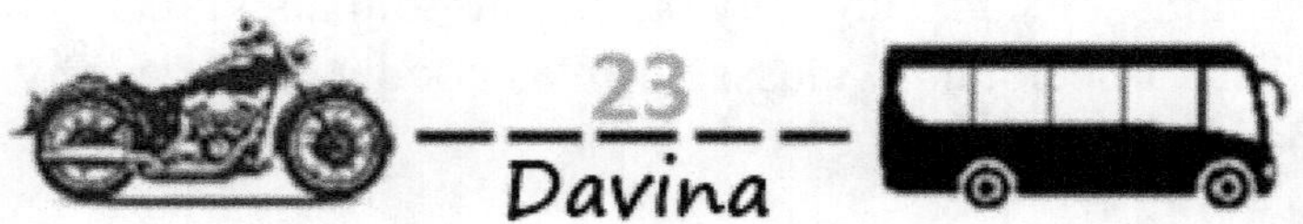

# 23 Davina

"What's up?" Snake's face contorts with concern as I shrink my Hollaphone into my wrist and jump to my feet.

"It's my mother."

"What?"

"Dad found her in the bathtub. There were sleeping pills. Wine. He got there just in time." Tears escape down my cheeks, and I wipe them as Snake's face twists with concern.

He touches my arm. "This on purpose?"

I shrug. "Sounds like, I don't know. Dad said Mom may have snapped. She forced my sister to go on this tour. I'm not sure if you know, but Mallory is a really accomplished dancer who is trying to get to Broadway, but my parents know she's brilliant and want her to — get this — become an engineer like them and pioneer new nanobot technologies."

Snake's pierced brow shoots up into Lola's forked tongue on his forehead. "No way. And now they be trapping her? Oh man, that's like iconic or something."

I bite my lip not to correct with "ironic," nodding instead. "Totally crazy. And then, there's my Zayde." I explain about Mom's guilt over what happened to him because she left to use the bathroom. "It's too much for her. Plus, all her work commitments, which have spun out of control. Dad thinks she needs a good mental rest for a while." I gulp. "They've admitted her to Beaumont Hospital's psychiatric ward on suicide watch."

"Oh man, I'm sorry. At least she's at the best joint in town."

"Hey, thanks for understanding. This is a tough time." I think about how he's trapped in this gang life that his whole family is in, and that he hates smoking and wants to be a reptile vet and must sneak to attend high school, plus he just lost his mother right before doing time for a crime that wasn't his fault. His father is dying instead of getting the nanobot treatments, foreseeing the reality of them being hacked just like what is happening to my sister. *And* Snake's in hiding with a contract out on his life, all for defending his family. "I know it's probably rough right now for you too."

Jonah smiles. "Yeah. Thanks. Well, let's get you to your mother. She and your dad probably gonna' wanna' see you now."

He stands and pulls a towel from a nearby tackle box. He summons his snake and lifts her gently from the water, then dries her off as she lounges around his neck. Then, he snuggles her snout, baby-talking her, assuring her that he loves her and she's a pretty girl.

I giggle despite everything, still marveling over who Jonah is, so different than I thought. Peering around, I still don't see anyone hiding and waiting to pounce, and I must keep reminding myself he's the same guy I thought I hated all this time. He seems to be legit, so far so good. In fact, better than expected.

Or he's a fabulous actor.

We return to the edge of the preserve, and I climb back through the hole in the fence to the outside, then hold it open for Jonah and Lola. "Well, thank you for telling me about Mallory and offering to help. I will start my research immediately."

"Watch the reboot of that show *Sons of Anarchy*," Snake instructs. "Also, check out that old *Mayans MC*, a spin-off. Not much different except they use some old school tech stuff."

"Yeah?"

"Yeah, like even flip phones. The shows ain't totally true about MC's like ours, but they'll give you an idea. Think about how they talk, act, and dress. Everything. You'll be going up against some other girls who wanna be Rocco's old lady too. Probably be a few."

"Oh, really? I was scared enough when I thought it would just be me. This is going to be like a Biker Cinderella, with us all competing for Prince Rocco, huh?"

Jonah flashes his interesting fangs. "Pretty much. Now, not sure when the next round of Vermilion is, but it's coming up. We gotta get you ready, and soon. They been through at least one of six rounds. Not sure we're gettin' invites to all, so visit your mom and don't say nothin' for now and —"

"Totally. I don't want to let them know about Mallory with what she's possibly going through and get their hopes up."

"Don't sound like your mom could handle it, and probably your dad can't neither."

"No way," I agree, getting into my Jetta. I jam the key into the ignition. After I tell Snake thanks again and we put our numbers into each other's Hollaphones, I twist the key.

The engine sputters, refusing to turn over.

"Ah crap." I try a few more times, but my car won't cooperate. Beating my steering wheel with my fists, I fight back tears.

Jonah opens my car door. "Just chill. You left your lights on. Battery's dead. I can take you though. It ain't no problem. But Grandpa's truck's got a flat. Can't get it to your car to jump. It's gotta' be on the bike."

"Oh, no. No way. No, I can't."

Snake crouches down to gaze into my eyes. "Hey, I know you're scared. I get it. But I'm a good driver. Never had no accident yet and I been ridin' a few years."

I sigh. "I know, but what if – "

"You can say what if about so many things."

My Hollaphone rings. It's Dad. I put up a finger to Snake. "Hi, Dad, what's up?"

"Just seeing where you are. Mom's asking for you."

"Oh God, sorry, I'm with a friend and my car died. I'm far out. I'll take an Uber. Be there as soon as I can."

"Okay, please try. It'll make her so happy to see your face. She really needs that right now."

I choke back a sob. "I will." We say goodbye and hang up.

"Wish I could jump your car with Grandpa's truck," Snake says, "but it's over behind the house, way too far. And an Uber from here's gonna' be a hundred bucks, easy. You got that? Cause I ain't. I'm strapped until Rocco stops by, and he ain't never say when."

I shake my head, searching for another solution. Suddenly, I remember the hundred dollars he'd given for purse cleaning that I'd jammed in my pocket. I ram my hands in each, but it's not there. It must've dropped out somewhere.

Shit.

"Look, I take you a few feet at a time 'round here on my bike so you can get your groove. Then, I'll drive all the back roads where there ain't no traffic and that way, we ain't gonna' get hit. We'll go slow, no freeways, I promise. Wha'cha think?"

I nod, desperate. "Yeah, I guess." My palms sweat, and I feel breathless.

Snake tells me he'll be back, and he disappears for a while, making me freak out in the middle of nowhere again. My mind starts to doubt everything I just learned about him, sure he's about to bring out whoever to do whatever to me as I initially believed when I hear a revving in the distance. Soon, Snake emerges pushing a wine-colored motorcycle that says Harley-Davidson in silver cursive along the side. The motor's louder than I would have imagined. A circular headlight blinds me, and my heart revs along with the engine.

Pulling a helmet from the side, he puts it on me, fastening it tightly with a strap below my jaw. He slips another on himself.

"Oh my God, I can't do this," I say, but he doesn't hear me under the roar. He yells directions for how to get on.

Realizing how much a rider must trust their driver and that I have no other choice if I want to see Mom anytime soon, I go to Jonah's left side and step with my left foot onto the metal pedal. Problem is, I'm not sure how much I trust him, but I don't have a choice if he can maybe help me, both with Mom and with Mallory. Hoisting myself up, I throw my right leg over the seat and all caution to the wind until I'm straddling him. Settling back, I find it surprisingly comfortable wedged between Jonah's solid body and a trunk with a padded backrest behind me.

"Where's Lola?" I shout to him over the bike, and he yells that she's in the trunk. I remember he said his mother made a little house for her there and wonder what it looks like.

We ride a bit, and it's kind of scary, especially on a dirt road caked with snow where we jerk up and down and slip all around, but it's also kind of thrilling, the chill in my face and wind tangling my hair and the odd, unexpected motion jostling me about. I clutch Snake even harder as the bike revs below me purring like a satisfied cougar. We go a little further, then some more, and I gain confidence like it's not so bad. I finally tell him yes, let's go for real, get on those backroads and get to Royal Oak where the hospital is. He says it'll take around an hour.

As we ride, it feels like the strong winds could tip us like a cow or we might slip on an ice patch, and I'm rightfully terrified. But with my cheek pressed against Snake's soft flannel as I grip him tight, I'm practically hypnotized by his amazing scent. Jonah, the guy I hated, loves his mother and Lola, and knows about snakes and lots of other stuff, more than I would have ever guessed. He also hasn't done anything bad like I expected, and as far as I know, there was no one there waiting to hurt me. I focus on all that instead of the fear, and it gets me there.

As we arrive at the hospital and I thank God for being in one piece, Jonah offers to come in with me. I politely refuse, knowing my parents still hate him. They have no idea he may be a good guy. And it's not the time to tell them. I have to be 100% sure myself, and it's too soon to say. Instead, I hug him goodbye, a quick little gesture that popped out of me, begrudgingly return his vest and hoodie, and make my way into the Emergency Room entrance. As I head toward my mother's room, I'm floating on a Drakkar Noir wave that I cannot believe, asking myself what the hell is wrong with me.

I visit with Mom and Dad a while. Mom's spacey and murmuring nonsensical stuff while occasionally smiling and rubbing my face. It's really disturbing. After she dozes, Dad puts me in a Lyft home telling me to get some sleep, and admittedly, I'm relieved. Seeing Mom like that did a number on me.

I'm all wired when I get to our house, not sure what to do with myself. I'm tempted to call Niyah or Antonia, but I'm not sure I can keep what happened today a secret. And from what Jonah told me, it needs to be, and I agree.

After texting with Jonah who sent a few messages expressing concern about my mother, I go up to my bedroom, take out a fresh notebook from my desk drawer, and queue up the reboot of that *Sons of Anarchy* show that Jonah recommended. I watch a few episodes and take careful notes, promising Mallory I will do everything I can to help her. Even if she and I don't always get along, and she beats me in everything, she's still my sister and maybe for the first time ever, needs me. I fall asleep picturing my parents' reaction when they find out I've saved my sister. Will they finally be proud of me, or will they only be glad I've returned their favorite daughter, their beloved Mallory?

# PART 6

## ROUND 2: SKEETER'S CHALLENGE

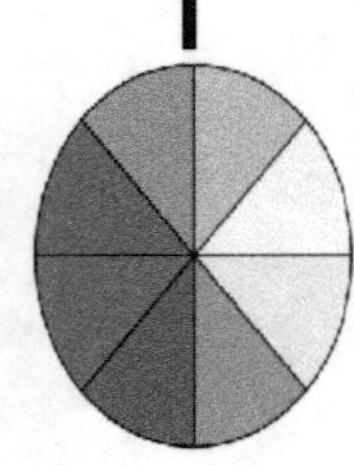

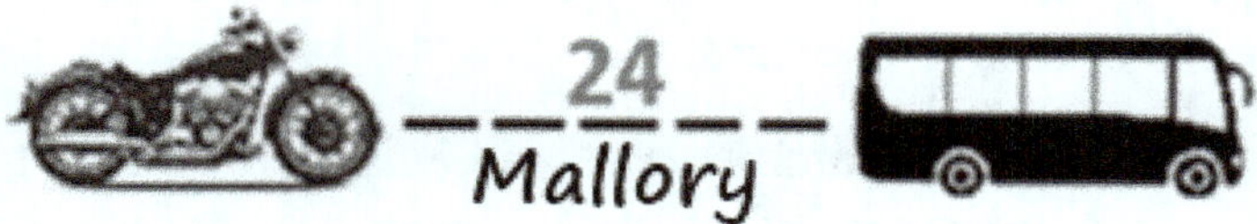

# 24 Mallory

**Friday, January 18, 2030**

I wake up in my bed and look across at Paige sleeping. That's where I fell out too, when the Med-Bots delivered our sleeping potion as we were talking about her little sister Kimmy and the danger she's in with their foster parents.

I sit up and brush cooties from my skin, so creeped out that someone I don't know has touched me again to carry me into my own bed. It makes me feel a mixture of helpless and pissed off, a strange blend. I want to do something so bad but can't. The way the game is designed, where they're always monitoring us and controlling our insides, I can't change my circumstance, unless I want to be killed and disintegrated or play Vermilion and try to win. Those are my only options besides suicide, but that won't help anything.

Sammi is working out again, grunting as she does deep squats. How can I possibly beat her, much less Ollie? I don't want to defeat him because that means if he dies, I'll know it's my fault. I don't want that for anyone, really, even Jiro whom I don't know at all or the dancers who hate me and vice versa. I don't want any of us to disintegrate like poor Darla and Troy, even if Camila sabotaged me with her cup of ice water at the

WRIF Dance-Off and Keondra laughed. I still don't want them to suffer and become specks of dust in the wind.

I should get ready like Sammi, so I stand, raising my palms toward the ceiling, getting a good stretch of my back, and start one of my dance warmup routines. I try to reclaim my flexibility, which if not often used and maintained, can be lost. After my upper body is sufficiently warmed, I slide sideways into a split and grab both ankles, pressing my chest to the ground and focusing on my breathing.

"Hey, you," I hear someone say, and Ollie slides sideways into the same position as me. Our heads touch with our split legs parallel to each other, forming an uppercase "H."

My eyebrows shoot up. "Shit, that's hard for a guy."

He winces and presses his chest further to the floor, pointing his toes even better than me, and grabs his heels. "Tell me about it," he grunts. "But I do it at least once a day so that I don't lose it."

"That's good. You need to, for sure."

"I don't work out for cheerleading nearly as hard as I did when I was trying to be an Olympian, but I do still like to maintain as much strength and flexibility as I can." He frowns. "At least, there's that."

"That must've been so hard to have to leave what you love. I'm sorry." I think of my parents and their wishes for me. They'd expected me to enroll at Michigan Tech because I'd suddenly discover I loved it and ignore that street a few states away called Broadway. No way would I have been able to stand that, even if they did somehow talk me into college first, to know it was there and I wasn't. I can't even contemplate having to deal with not being able to do what I love, although even that would be better than my current situation.

How do my parents feel now since they forced me to be here with all that's happened? I think of Zayde, and how Mom is taking his condition especially hard. Tears spill from my eyes like someone just turned on a faucet as worry for her and him pour out of me.

I can tell that she's not doing as well as she pretends. I hope Dad sees it too. Why didn't I make sure he knew of my concern? Why didn't I speak up, send even a short text, to alert him? I sigh, kicking myself. I'd been all about me and my dancing.

“Are you okay?” Ollie asks, and suddenly he’s there next to me as I sit up and cross my legs. His finger catches one of the tears on my chin. He wipes it away, stroking my jawline with his thumb.

“Yeah, just thinking of my family.” I share a little with him about Zayde and how it has been so hard on everyone, especially my mom, and wonder for the millionth time how my parents and Davina are coping with me missing on top of it. “I’m so worried for all of them. I don’t know how they’ll be.”

“Yeah, sorry. I get it. I’m quite concerned about mine as well, and I’m sure they also are for me.” Ollie sighs. “They only have me now, so they must be very scared. I just turned eighteen, so I am working on adopting them all, but it’s slow-going. Lots of hoops to jump through.”

“Them all? How many siblings do you have? And where are your parents?”

Paige stirs in her bed. Ollie crawls up into my bunk, motioning for me to join him. I do, and he curls naturally around me and covers me with the blanket, talking softly in my ear. “My mother died a few months ago from pneumonia, right when it started to get cold in October.”

I turn toward him, and his ocean eyes are cloudy. “Oh, I’m so sorry to hear that. Didn’t know people died from pneumonia nowadays, though. I thought it was highly treatable.”

“It is if you actually treat it and aren’t scrubbing toilets and making fancy dinners and cleaning huge windows and shining chandeliers on high ladders instead.”

“What’s that mean?”

Ollie sighs. “My mother was a maid who basically worked herself to death. She ignored her needs to support us after my father, a successful patent attorney, died suddenly in a car crash. He left her with me and my six siblings and no money because he happened to have a secret addiction to online poker and bet away everything we had, including our house.”

“Shit. This really happened?”

He winces. “It was right around the time I fell off the high bar and ruined my gymnastics career when I was a freshman in high school, which is just as well since we wouldn’t have been able to afford my coaching after Dad left us with nothing.”

I shake my head, so saddened for him and his family.

"When the Sherriff evicted us from the only home we'd ever known, making us grab what we could and literally kicking us to the curb, we had nowhere to go. My mother, a trophy wife with a 'Mrs.' degree and no experience couldn't command more than a minimum wage job anywhere. It wasn't close to being enough even with food stamps, social security, and Medicaid."

"How awful."

"It was. So, Mom's best friend, a wealthy socialite named Celia Darby, whose family *and* her husband's family were old money and had an estate fit for royalty, offered for my mother and her seven children to upkeep their house for a small salary, food, and a place to stay. They fired their regular staff and suddenly, we were it."

"Oh, how uncomfortable."

"It was. My mother and siblings and I got to stay in their fancy but small two-room pool house with one bathroom while we did everything around their mansion. We shined the floors and silver, vacuumed all the rugs, and scrubbed every bathtub – there were nineteen – every single day."

"Nineteen?"

Ollie nods. "Most were never used, but we still had to clean them. Celia, the bitch, did random checks, and if anything was remotely dirty, Mom's meager pay was docked, and we weren't given as much food. Meanwhile, we cooked every gourmet meal — none of which we were ever allowed to eat — and threw all their fancy parties. And boy, there were a ton, at least two a week."

My eyebrows shoot up. "Wow. That's a lot of partying."

"It was. Celia pretended Mom was still her friend in ways, gossiping like they always had about social stuff that Mom used to care about, Celia wanting to keep her in the loop and all. But Celia was aware — as was my mother — that although she was speaking with Mom about their common friend Danika and her latest shenanigans around East Hampton like they were still best buds, they both knew Mom had just scrubbed her toilet, changed her soiled bed linens, and washed her underwear."

"Ugh, that's so awkward. And now?"

"We're still there working for the Darby's while the legal stuff is being sorted after Mom's funeral, which the Darby's paid for but said I owe them when I can. I still need to figure out how to financially support everyone, and I'm not even sure about college, even though Michigan Tech offered me a full ride. I can't exactly leave them, and I never should have for this stupid tour. I just needed to get away to figure things out. At least the Darby's didn't kick us out on the street, yet, and they pay for some stuff like medical or whatever to make up for what insurance doesn't cover. I worry so much because all my siblings, well, they have issues, and now I'm not there, so…." Ollie blows through his puffed lips.

"Oh Jeez, like what?" I'm afraid to hear, his heart-breaking story rivaling Paige's, and I start to feel less sorry for myself and my family.

"Well, the oldest is Meg, who's thirteen, and has fallen in with the wrong crowd. She and some of her friends were recently arrested for breaking into a house and stealing some jewelry, and now we have a court date and legal fees. I have no idea where I'm going to get the money for them without having to beg off Celia, which I'd rather die than do. She'll make me polish all her thousand-dollar shoes, again. She has more than Imelda Marcos, I swear."

"Oh man, that's awful. What'll you do?"

Ollie shrugs. "Who knows? I'm here. And then there's Weaver, who's eleven, and he always wants to take care of everyone, which is great, but he's super controlling, getting so stressed trying to make everyone do everything his way. He has little tantrums all the time, and it takes a while to calm him."

"Aw, poor kid."

"Yeah, and I saw some marks on him and think he's been cutting himself. I need to find him professional help before it gets worse."

"God, Ollie," I say, sitting up and turning toward him, "I'm so sorry for you and for them." I feel like crying again; I'm super emotional today, and his story is as sad as Paige's.

"Thanks. Then there are the twins, Dobby and Darcy, who are nine. They've always been very withdrawn and quiet, painfully shy, and now their teachers at school want them to do all kinds of expensive testing. They're both quite delayed in their speech and reading. The only one who they ever respond to for some reason is Candace, who is seven. She's just trying to have a normal childhood, play with her dolls and read and all that, but we have so many chores to do on top of school and everything to earn our keep, she doesn't get much of a chance. She feels she must constantly watch over the twins because they only listen to her. It's a lot on a little girl's shoulders."

"I'd say."

"The youngest is Mandy. She's four and follows Candace everywhere. Candace hates it and begs everyone to help. So, we all juggle little Mandy around because she's a ton of work."

I think of how he and all his siblings try to care for each other whereas me and my twin sister can't stand each other and barely talk. Years' worth of pent-up frustration and guilt spill out of me, and I burst into tears again.

Ollie embraces me and I sob into his chest, so embarrassed after what he just told me. I begin to apologize, and he runs a finger along my cheek and down my neck. "Oh, Mallory…" He winds a hand through my hair and pulls me to him, his lips parting.

I close my eyes, anxious to feel them on mine as a fire ignites within and spreads to my limbs, when we hear, "Hey guys. Wha'cha up to?"

Paige peers into our bunk, her mouth agape as we bounce apart.

"Nothing," I say, at the same time Paige says, "Oh shit, sorry."

Blake's face floats through my mind, but I kick it away and smile at Paige like nothing happened. "Hey, what's up?"

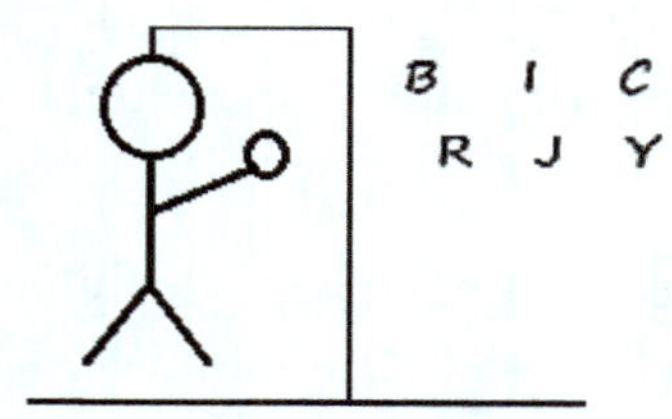


# THE HANGMAN PHASE

When our captors release us from Home Base, I notice it's now wrapped in an ad for Nosingarettes — the new healthy cigarettes that expel vitamins, minerals, and other nutrients instead of harmful toxins and blow turquoise smoke. Behind me, Keondra says, "Oh wow, I can't believe this, but we're like home!"

I peer up at a sign that says, "The Detroit Zoo." In a city called Royal Oak, the Zoo is not too far from most of our hometowns.

"Don't matter," Sammi says. "No one can save us."

Keondra sighs. "Yeah, I know." She kicks at the ground. "Sucks."

"Well, let's get in now and go to our regions," Paige says. "Mark-Bot is already counting down our time."

We find more money in our belly bags now, enough to buy admission tickets and a few incidentals. Once inside, we discover almost everyone is dressed just like us, all in rainbow separates, while some wear T-shirts that say RainBO PranXterz with a tie-dyed hand flipping the bird. Is that what they're calling us? We blend in and no one notices us, which is just as well. We all agree it's hysterical that people are trying to dress like us now that they saw us on the OuterNet, the very people the police are probably searching for, making it even harder. They'll never find us for sure. And if they do, we'll be considered "detained" and will be permanently eliminated from The Game. It's a lose-lose situation all around.

When we're well into The Hangman Phase, Keondra and Camila in the east region attempting to get the Azure Dragon coin so far have collected the following letters for their puzzle: G__ __ A __ __ E __ N C __ __ N __ __ R

Sammi and Jiro and Paige are in the north region trying to find the Black Tortoise, and they've gotten these letters: __ I __ E __ H __ __ __ T A __.

This time, Ollie and I have been designated the White Tiger coin collectors, so we go to the western region. We split up, and I run all around, finding letter clues in the Artic Café, near the chimpanzee area, one in a Dippin' Dots kiosk, and another under a bench near some building with anteaters and bush dogs, whatever those are. During that time, Keondra, Camila, and Jiro all report that Luckster clovered them. I stop a minute winded and notice a young boy nearby, maybe aged seven or eight, breathing heftily from an asthma inhaler.

"Huey, honey, calm down and you'll be okay," the woman with him says as she rubs his back. "Just take it easy, nice and slow. Mommy's here."

Shit. I need that inhaler for Paige, but I can't take it from a kid who's actively using it, can I?

His mother can get him a new one, I reason. She can go right to a pharmacy and order it, call the doctor, or go to a hospital if necessary. Beaumont Hospital is literally a few miles down Woodward Avenue from us. We can't do anything for Paige without violating Game Rules if she needs one, which she will. She needs a new inhaler pronto.

The woman coaches her son to calm himself so the medicine can work.

I can't take it from him right when he needs it. No way. That's *so wrong.*

"How you doing, Mal?" Ollie asks through a Walkie-Bot in my ear.

"Okay, but I have a situation." I walk away from the mother helping her son and whisper to Ollie what's going on. Ollie says he thinks we should take it, kid be damned. They can call an ambulance if needed, and he also mentions our proximity to the hospital. If the boy needs help, he will probably get it in time, whereas once Paige needs it again, which could be at any moment, she won't.

"Can't we just wait to see how he is? Like, take it when he's better?" I glance over, and the struggling kid puffs on his inhaler again.

"We're running out of time, and we only have a few letters so far. It's now or never, and you might lose him. He and Mom might leave."

Closing my eyes, I see our progress: __ __ __ A __ B __ __ R __ R__ __ N

I exhale. "Shit, you're right."

Ollie walks toward me. "Go distract Mom, and I'll run over and take it."

"Seriously?"

"We have no choice. We've got to get the White Tiger coin still, and times a-wasting."

I take a deep breath and try to think of what to say as I walk toward the mother and her son. "Oh, hi, excuse me, but where did you get those boots? Oh my God, they're so cute!"

The mother frowns at me. "This isn't a good time."

"Oh, I'm sorry, I didn't mean to — but, oh! Those are just amazing! I love the little tassels and the suede on the bottom. I've been looking everywhere for a pair just like that. Do you happen to know where you got them?"

The mother rubs the kid's shoulders, not answering.

I continue gushing, sitting down beside the mother and pretending to study her feet, ignoring the kid there unable to breathe. Meanwhile, I'm in goggles and a mask, dressed like a rainbow. What she must think of me.

The mother inches away. "Miss, I'm sorry, but can't you see that —"

Ollie runs by and grabs the inhaler from the kid's mouth. The boy's mother jumps up to chase him. I apologize to Huey before darting away.

Ollie and I find each other by some place called Exploration Station, and I put the inhaler in my belly bag. "We're going to hell for sure," I say. Glancing through the trees at the kid still fighting to breathe while his mother shouts into her Hollaphone, I pray they get Huey help in time.

Ollie claps me on the shoulder. "Agreed. Now, let's keep on keeping on because I have no clue yet where the coin is."

We go different ways, coming back together after several minutes with more letters:

P __ L A __ B __ A R __ R A __ N.

I can see an ambulance cart approaching Huey through the trees and breathe a sigh of relief as they slap an oxygen mask on his face.

"We just got the Azure Dragon!" Keondra tells everyone in our ears. "Our clue was GIRAFFE ENCOUNTER, and our coin was in the vat of lettuce leaves that the woman sells you so you can feed the giraffes. She's not very happy with us right now since Camila practically attacked her, bitching about paying four bucks for lettuce and making the poor woman drop her basket, but we got the coin!"

"Awesome!" Sammi says. "We just got the Black Tortoise in the Tiger Habitat. We got chased by Zoo cops because me and Jiro had to go in to distract the tigers in there, but we found it in some leaves near where the tigers were sleeping in their den. Then, Jiro stepped on a twig, and they all woke up. You shoulda' seen how fast he ran!" Sammi cracks up. "Probably pissed his pants!" She cracks up again.

"Um, okay," Ollie says. "Well, good job, everyone. Glad you got them. We need help though, so please come now."

"Why, where are you?" Camila asks.

"We're at the Arctic Ring of Life. I'm pretty sure our clue says POLAR BEAR DRAIN."

"What's that mean?" Keondra asks.

"Well, from what I can see since I'm now in a glass tunnel under the huge polar bear tank," Ollie responds, "the coin is in some sort of drain in the actual tank."

"Oh shit, there it is," I say, coming up beside him. "Right in the floor grate way at the bottom."

"Oh God," Camila groans. "Please tell us there are no actual polar bears in there."

"Okay, but then I'd be lying," Ollie says.

# 25
## Mallory

Ollie and I are standing near the back door to the polar bear enclosure waiting for the others when a zoo worker walks out. In the middle of Ollie talking about his cheerleading team and how intensely they've been preparing for Nationals, he lunges for the guy. Ollie hits him on the back of the head with the heel of his hand and knocks him out.

"What the hell?"

"Saw it in a movie once," Ollie says, dragging the zoo worker into some bushes and grabbing the keys off his belt. I stare at Ollie, realizing I don't know him at all or what he's capable of. He stands there all casual, twirling the keyring around his thumb like he didn't just make someone go unconscious. When the others arrive, Ollies lets us all into the enclosure where we find other workers feeding fish to two huge polar bears in the water.

The White Tiger coin glimmers in the drain way below them. After I hand a hard-breathing Paige the new inhaler which she thanks me for with a huge hug, I jump into the freezing water. Everyone else does too except her, and the workers shout at us. We ignore them, playing Monkey in the Middle with the polar bears and their fish. The workers call for help on their Hollaphones.

"Keep them busy!" I yell at my bus mates. Taking a huge breath, I dive toward the coin in the drain at the very bottom of the ginormous tank.

Pretending I'm in swim class freshman year getting pennies from the deep end for my midterm grade, I try my best to ignore the two angry polar bears above me. As I head toward the bottom, trying not to think about how it's becoming more and more difficult to hold my breath, I see green out of the corner of my eye. I turn to find Luckster swimming toward me with a clover.

I try to get away, but he catches my foot. Kicking at him, I connect with his jaw, and he floats back, holding it with a stunned look. But he comes at me again and again, more determined each time, his jeering face taunting. I notice his thumb missing and the glove he wears stitched up there. He finally surges forward, holding onto some rope around him, and stabs his clover through my calf.

I scream underwater, bending to yank the spike out as a thin stream of blood escapes.

The evil Leprechaun climbs toward the surface on his rope, his kicking limbs in green tights making him look frog-like. It's weird that he has a rope. I'm sure it may mean something, but I can't breathe or think. All I can say is good riddance.

I try to ignore the pain in my calf and the weirdness of the situation and focus on the task at hand, hoping to get the coin as fast as possible since my lungs can no longer expand. But when I glance back, I've lost all sense of direction. I look up which is down, and right which seems left, and then I don't know where the coin is anymore, the sight of it jumbled in my panicked mind. I thrash about like the polar bears above me, trying to figure it out and getting tons of water in my nose and lungs as the glass tunnel nearby fills with pointing people.

Sputtering under water makes it worse, and I finally stop and let whatever happens happen. I have no fight left. In this game, I am not the best. It hits again like a ton of bricks that my sister must feel the same way when I always do better than her, and the guilt impales me like a harpoon. But that hardly compares with what might happen to me very soon.

A polar bear charges toward me with his snarling mouth full of razor-sharp teeth, and I try to swim away, but I make little progress since I'm so weak. The bear reaches for me, his sharp black claws connecting with my leg —

I scream, getting water into my bursting lungs. Bracing for unimaginable pain, I wonder what it will feel like as my flesh is pierced.

Someone yanks me by the waist.

The next thing I know, I'm spitting out water and Ollie is hunched over me, concern all over his face.

"What happened?" I ask, trying to prop up on an elbow. My head swoons, and I fall back down. On the way, I notice two bleeding puncture wounds on my thigh and grasp it, applying pressure.

"You flaked out underwater and I had to go get the coin while Ollie saved your ass," Camila snarls, holding up a gold coin with a white tiger on it.

I peer through a flurry of stars to see we're in some bathroom. Everyone is there, soaking wet and shivering, running their clothing under the hand dryers. A pile of masks and goggles is at their feet. "The Leprechaun was there," I tell her, taking turns between holding my aching head, gripping my bleeding thigh, and squeezing my sore calf where I was clovered. I wonder again if Luckster is Troy resurrected by the Rover-Bots, and he was given a new job in The Game. "And thanks," I say to Ollie, grabbing his hand and squeezing it.

"Of course," he says, squeezing mine back.

Hearing a commotion, I twist around to see the stall door behind me burst open. For just a second until it slams closed again, I see Luckster there sitting on a toilet with his arms behind him and his mouth bound by some cloth.

Only as the door slams shut, I realize his mask is off.

"What the hell?" I ask as the door bounces open again and I get a glimpse before it swings shut. "You captured him?"

"Yeah, and it was easy to do," Sammi says, catching the stall door. "He was tethered in the pool with a long rope, like he couldn't swim without it. I just pulled it as he was trying to escape, and I got his mask too."

She holds it up and then opens the door, and I see Luckster wriggling around on his toilet throne, trying to say something through the gag in his mouth.

"Everybody watching the polar bears got pictures of the unmasked Luckster on their Hollaphones, so I'm sure that'll be all over the OuterNet too," Keondra says. "Someone will recognize her."

I hear loud and clear Keondra said 'her' instead of 'him.' Blinking through the water spilling down from my wet hair into my eyes, I find the missing drug dealer Krystall Nykkolls there in Luckster gear, struggling against her restraints.

What in the world? My mind protests what I am seeing. It's not Troy after all. My heart sinks to realize he's really gone. "Krystall? Is that you?"

Everyone looks at me.

"You *know* her?" Camila asks.

I nod, grabbing Ollie's outstretched hand and letting him pull me to my feet. "Yeah, I do." I approach her, my head swimming.

She shrinks away, her eyes circles of fear.

"Damn, I thought Luckster was a dude," Keondra says.

"She goes to my school, but she's been missing ever since —" I picture the Rebel Demons chasing her through our yard and then think of my parents again and my suspicions that this whole kidnapping somehow has to do with them. Suddenly, I need to know what she has to say more than anything. "Krystall, it's me, Mallory Rosenbaum. I'm Liza's best friend. Why are you here?" I reach around and remove her gag.

"Help me!" she pleads, her eyes watering. "Let me go! The Rebel Demons got me and gave me to these people. They'll kill me if they see you captured me." She wriggles against her restraints, her eyes wild.

"Who are they?" I ask, my heart soaring with hope for more information, but she shakes her head.

"I don't know! Please, please, please, Mallory, just let me go!"

I think a second and reach for her, ready to untie her, but someone pulls me back.

I turn to find Camila and Keondra there, glaring at me.

"What, are you crazy?" Camila asks. "She'll just clover the rest of us and —"

"I won't! I promise!" Krystall pleads. "I'll leave and lose another finger or whatever. I won't try to clover you anymore. Just let me go and —"

Mark-Bot reminds us of the dwindling time in our ears.

"Just leave her here," Sammi says, slamming the door. "We gotta' go!"

I'm frozen with indecision, pro's and con's listing in my mind, but as Sammi turns to leave, Krystall explodes out of her stall, evil twisting her face which now, somehow, is covered in a new mask identical to the one in Sammi's hand. She holds a stack of clovers, and she tags Jiro, Camila, and Ollie in a row before anyone knows what hit them. "Leprechaun chasing rainbows!" we hear before she tears out of there.

Gawking after her, we help our teammates remove the clover spikes from their skin as we lament that she'll be back for one of our limbs.

"But how did she even break free?" Camila asks. She shoots me a dirty look and mumbles, "And you was gonna let her go, stupid-assed Mallory."

"She must be shot up with the bots too, and the Med-Bots and Soldier-Bots gave her extra strength and adrenaline," Paige suggests. She picks up a rope that Krystall had been tied with to show the end is frayed like it just snapped.

"But how did she get a new mask and clovers?" Keondra asks. "She didn't have any when we captured her from the tank."

"Anything seems possible in this game," Sammi says. "Maybe the Med-Bots shot shit out of her pores and made those clovers and new mask. Who knows? What I do know is we only have fifteen minutes, and we don't even have the Vermilion Bird. We gotta go." Sammi whips open the door.

We all follow her, sprinting toward the south region on our maps, my head feeling like I just got off a loop-de-loop roller coaster. The Vermilion Bird coin is waiting, as is The Vermilion Hour, and I've got to fight like hell now or I may never fight again.

# THE VERMILION BIRD

We quickly collect letter clues in the south region and spell:

A T __ P __ M __ H __ B __ __ I __ __ E.

As I chase some kid on a skateboard with a vermilion tag sticking out of his rear pocket, Keondra says in my ear that she knows where the Vermilion Bird is. “Everyone, meet me at ‘Amphibiville’!”

“What’s that?” Paige asks.

“I guess where they have amphibians,” Camila says. “I agree. I think the first word is ‘atop.’”

“Good thinking, guys,” Sammi says. “It’s the only location that fits.”

We rush there to find a two-story rounded structure with a steel framework on the upper circular roof, angled like a tall silver can cut on the diagonal with spokes pointing outward like the Statue of Liberty’s crown. There’s another part with just a regular V-shaped roof upside down.

“Dancer girls, I need you,” Ollie says.

We gather and he suggests trying to use a cheerleading mount to get one of us on the lower pointy roof.

“Oh, not me,” Keondra says, taking out a cigarette and lighter. “I don’t do heights.”

Paige moves away, poised with her inhaler.

Camila scoffs. “Really, girl? You gonna’ be like that?”

"Let's not argue it," I say, going over to Ollie who crouches down with his legs spread wide. I rush toward him and step into his cupped hands, and he props me up so that my ankles are even with his shoulders. I lock my legs, shoot my arms up, and try keeping my core tight to balance. I fall backward anyway, my efforts for shit, and soon, I'm staring into someone's masked face.

"Thanks," I breathe, the wind knocked from me, realizing the arms I'm in must be Sammi's. She's the only one strong enough besides Ollie.

"Don't mention it," Sammi says. She sets me upright.

"I can do it," Camila says, and she jumps up. Ollie hoists her high enough so she's standing on his massive hands, and she pulls herself onto the roof of the lower structure.

Camila runs around the sloped rooftop, the pom-pom on her knit cap bobbing as she goes up and down. "Shit!" she screams. "Where is it? There's nothing up here but roof! There are no coins. Are we sure the puzzle is right?"

"I'm sure of it," Sammi says. "Are there any pipes or drains or vents or anything mechanical? It could be in something like that."

"Or it could be on that other rooftop!" Keondra says, and she points to the one that's another story up, the circular one with the metal spokes.

"Oh no, you're right!" Camila moans, and then we all know Ollie needs to somehow get up there to get her up to the next level or climb up there himself.

Ollie jumps on a low wall and propels off it to catch the roofline, then pulls himself up so that his belly is even. Kicking forward and back, he presses a wide split up to a handstand, then does a front walkover so he's on the rooftop. Impressive. He runs over to Camila and hoists her up on his hands again.

Ollie eventually gets her up to the top, but Mark-Bot counts down the time from thirty seconds in our ears. As he gets closer and closer to zero, I know there's no way that we are going to be able to get the coins together to complete the firescope, even if she finds the last one now.

"Five, four, three…"

I close my eyes only to see a ticking clock behind my eyelids. There's no escape from the reality of our fate.

When the clock strikes zero and Camila is still scrambling about the high roof of Amphibiville hunting for the Vermilion Bird coin, Mark-Bot says: "Round two, Skeeter's Challenge, failed. Get ready for the random elimination of one player."

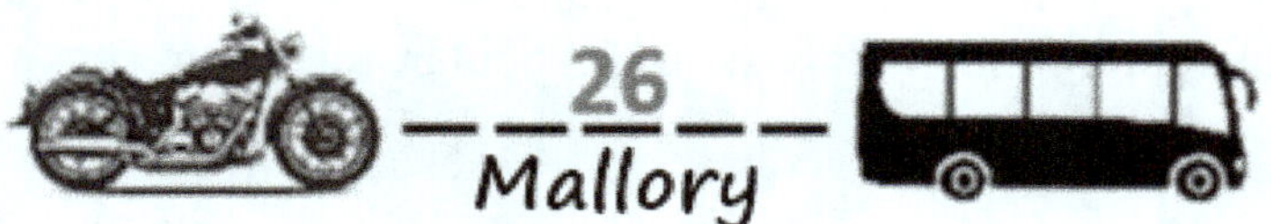

# 26

## Mallory

Camila comes down with Ollie, and she clings to him. He holds her the way he held me. No one says a word, but my mind is screaming that one of us is about to die, and another will lose a limb. I fight myself not to make the calculation, but I do anyway, realizing that I have 2/7 of a chance that I will be one of them. That's almost 30%. My throat is tight as we find someplace away from other zoo patrons in a woodsy area filled with wandering peacocks. We stand in a circle holding hands, all of us one, but about to be one less. Bowing my head, my eyes fill with tears as my knees knock together.

I'm terrified, for myself and for all of them. Every single one of my new family I care about, even if we're supposed to kill each other or hurt one another or something else to try to win. I don't want anyone else to die.

But the Player Wheel is already spinning.

"Karyn-Bot here. I wish we were meeting under better circumstances." She tries to comfort even though she's really part of who captured us.

The wheel stops so the pointer lands on Ollie, then Keondra, Camila … and me.

My heart plunges, and I exhale. I'm the eliminated player. *I'm the eliminated player.* It's me. Oh, dear God, it's me! I clamp my eyes shut and brace myself, waiting for my heart to cease, hoping I'm fully dead before disintegrating.

Behind my eyelids, I see the wheel move just a bit more so that the dangling yellow triangle points at someone else's name.

My eyes pop open and breath escapes me as Sammi drops to her knees. She presses her hands together in prayer, begging to be spared, all her bravado from her Junior ROTC accomplishments gone. As she suffers her last breath and collapses clutching her chest, then disintegrates before us, I try to turn away, to close my eyes, to shut it all out, but I'm shown on my eyelid screen anyway.

Sammi, who was nice and pretty and very fit and quite determined in general and determined not to die in particular, turns into nothing right before me.

A young guy looking just like Skeeter O'Grady with curly brown hair and a dreamy smile comes and brushes away Sammi's remains with a kick of his penny loafer. He nods at us before disappearing into a dark sedan that speeds away.

We stare after him and then turn back to where Sammi had stood to pay tribute to a great player, and probably a wonderful girl. Goodbye, Sammi Grayson. I'm so very, very sorry. And I'm relieved that it was her instead of me, which it almost was. Feeling awful for thinking that and wondering if Davina feels that way about me since she's supposed to be here instead, I follow the others toward Home Base. I vaguely notice it's now covered in advertisements for the new low-sugar gluten-free blue-raspberry-flavored Kid Beer, a junior alcohol product. My tears flow freely for Darla, Troy, and my family, who must be so worried about me now on top of Zayde.

Now I must add one more name to the death list. It was almost me but instead was Sammi. Talk about feeling guilty.

We hold a little vigil for Sammi, Darla, and Troy during Nap Time. Even Camila, Keondra, and Jiro say nice things they remembered about each as we sit together in Doorless Bay in a circle holding hands.

"Sammi was coloring or something under her blanket at Nap Time after the first challenge," Camila says, a tear streaming down her cheek. "When she went to pee, I peeked. You'll never guess what she was drawing."

We all look at each other.

"Porno stuff?" Ollie guesses.

Camila shoots him a look. "Hardly."

"Monsters," Paige says. "Like aliens and stuff. She's a sci-fi freak."

Camila makes a buzzer sound, then shakes her head. "It was like fashion models with different dresses and skirts and stuff. It was really good. At least I thought that they were models at first, but upon closer inspection, I realized that she was always drawing the same girl — Barbie."

"Barbie?" Ollie asks, and our brows scrunch as we try to imagine the masculine ROTC girl who always talked about military stuff and working out caring at all about the fashion of dolls.

"We didn't know her well," I admit. "Nor Darla." A pang of guilt for how unfriendly I'd been to an enthusiastic Darla on the bus before all this started stabs me, and I realize besides that, I didn't know much about her either. No one else really does, and we all admit it's not the best time for proper social etiquette.

Camila and Keondra recite some Biblical prayers, and they sing a few hymns as Paige and Ollie join in. I hum along since I don't know any of the words.

"So, when do you think we'll find out about the other thing?" Paige asks as we're getting up to disperse to our bunks.

"What other thing?" Ollie asks.

"Who's going to lose a limb?" Paige swallows and her shoulders jerk. She wraps her arms around herself as fear glistens in her eyes.

I suck in a breath. "No way to tell. Either they'll warn us beforehand, or it'll just happen." I can't figure out which is worse and try to put it out of my mind for now. My bathroom time comes earlier than usual since Sammi, Player #2, was eliminated, and I'm relieved to leave the conversation for the Land of Denial where such things like losing a limb — or your life — are not possible.

I go into the restroom and do my thing, then decide to take a quick shower, unsure of the last time I bathed. I reek like fish and my skin is slimy. No wonder I was almost a polar bear's lunch.

I think about Krystall Nykkolls as the water pricks at my skin like a bunch of pins. She's in the game in a different way, shot up with Bots but having to get us or be gotten herself. I'm not sure which is worse, her place or ours, but no matter how bad I feel for her or for me, I want to stay the hell away from her.

Then, I realize that by her being in the game and telling us the Rebel Demons put her there, she confirmed it was them on the VIP screen. That means this all does have to do with my parents. The bikers are punishing them by taking me since my parents took away their precious Snake. Is it really just tit for tat? Does this whole Vermilion thing really come down to that?

On my way out of the tiny stall, water still in my eyes mixed with tears over having to say goodbye to Sammi, I trip over something. Wiping my face with a towel, I discover that I've toppled the little wastebasket. As I'm replacing everything in the bin, I spot an asthma inhaler in the pile. It must be Paige's old one.

Squinting at the small text on the label, the typed name says Lara Campbell, not Paige Tellison.

Is that the mother of the little boy Huey from whom I stole it? I shake it to find it's empty. No, the one I took today seemed full. This is the original, with another girl's name.

After I emerge from the bathroom, as we're all getting ready to sleep until the next challenge, I ask Paige why her inhaler has Lara's name on it.

"Oh, uh, my foster mother wouldn't get me one. My girlfriend got her doctor to prescribe her one, and she gave it to me."

"Oh," I say, "but does she have asthma?"

"No," Paige says. "But she's in drama club, so she's a great actress. Very convincing."

As she rolls over to rest while the Med-Bots do their thing, I wonder if it's possible for someone, even a talented actress, to fake asthma and fool a trained doctor into prescribing an inhaler like that. I don't know, but before I can put any more thought into it, the sleepy drugs reach me, and I drift into the darkness with a million questions burning my tongue.

# PART 7

## DAVINA, HER AMINALS, AND TWO SNAKES

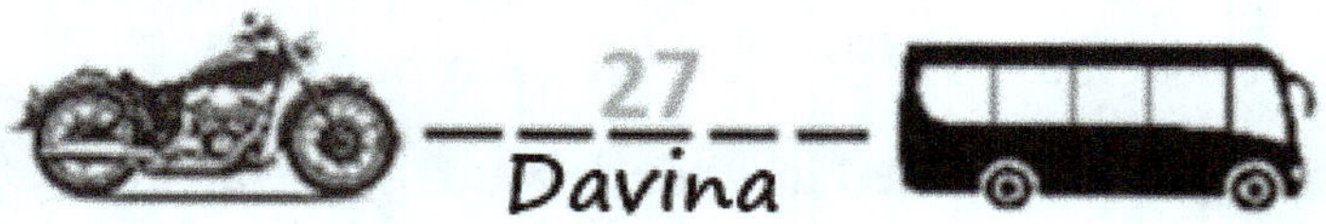


**Friday, January 18, 2030**

As the sun inches upward bringing a new day, I lay on my bed with my doggie Archie, named for my favorite mathematician Archimedes. Archie is a clingy rat terrier Chihuahua, black and brown and about twelve pounds, who must always be in my lap unless Mom's around. Then, I don't exist. He's sad because he knows Mom is sick, that she's totally out of sorts, and he's needier than ever, groaning as he nestles into the crook of my arm. I rub him between his eyes like he loves and then pet our big black Lab named Brian. The sweetest dog who ever lived, Brian is named for the talking dog in the cartoon Family Guy because instead of being all white with a little black, he's all black with a little white. He's a Reverso Brian, really.

Archie goes over and starts humping Brian who's at least five times his size. He does that when he's stressed and because when Brian was a puppy, they were the same height. I pull Archie away and comfort both dogs. They can feel Mom's absence now, her pain. I don't even want to go near my parents' bathroom where Dad found Mom who had just slipped under the water.

I try not to think about how she was so sad about Mallory and Zayde that she just went in with some sleeping pills and a bottle of wine and perhaps a hope, a wish, that she'd maybe slide under and be free from the torment that was getting the better of her. Purposefully leaving me and Dad upsets me to no end, and I can't help feeling a little angry at her too. And I wonder if she'd be so upset if it was me missing as it was supposed to be. Would she rather have Mallory? But then guilt for such a thought chases the anger away, but then anger over the entire circumstance overtakes the guilt until I'm not even sure what I'm feeling anymore. Everything and nothing all at the same time.

Dad says he's not even sure if taking a bath with the wine and pills was a conscious thing, but he's never seen Mom in this shape. She's almost catatonic, staring into the distance and then crying suddenly, then staring some more, sometimes mumbling to herself stuff that makes no sense. Dad is at her side as much as they'll allow him.

Knowing Mom is locked in a psych ward under suicide watch because she can't handle everything that's gone on makes me feel like joining her, but Mallory is counting on me. She doesn't know it of course, probably has no faith in me like usual, but Snake — my mortal enemy who hurt our parents but probably really didn't mean it at all, who seems to be nice and sincerely sorry — is connected to one of the VIPs in this weird game Mallory is being forced to play. Snake, who says he feels he owes our family and wants to help, might have a way to help for real, something the police couldn't even do. They don't have an in to the gang the way Snake does. It almost seems like that whole thing with Snake hurting my parents happened for a reason, or he may not be so motivated to assist me in saving my sister.

The thought sends a chill to my shoulders as I wonder about God, if there is one, and his divine plan. Is this somehow part of it? I've heard everything happens for a reason, and now I'm starting to ponder if that's possibly true, or if this is all really something else about which I haven't a clue.

Jonah thinks Mallory dancing on TV at Mackinac Island while kidnapped has something to do with that game they're being forced to play. She's been threatened by those bots and whoever's controlling them, making her act strangely. Jonah says it had something to do with the others getting whatever they pulled out of the Crack-in-the-Island, that it must be part of The Game. He thought he heard his dad and brother talking about the contestants having to collect some coins.

I need to be okay, even though mostly I feel like joining Mom, because I don't know if Mallory can win without my help. That Sammi Grayson girl is huge, strong, and fast, I'm sure, judging from what I've learned about her from the cops and on TV, which I'm now trying not to even watch. Then that Ollie guy is like a gymnast and cheerleader, so he's super fit and strong, and the basketball player Troy looks pretty built also from his pictures. Those other two dancer girls, they're as in shape as Mallory, just as capable, so who knows if she even has a prayer of beating any of them?

According to Snake's brother, only one in Vermilion can win, and all the others will be killed. Sure, Mallory defeated forty-nine other dancers for her spot at Miss Sylvia's, a huge accomplishment, but that's dancing, not playing some violent game to the death. Mallory has some real competition in Vermilion. For once, she's not the best. And I don't feel good about that at all.

But she's also got me and Snake, and he's willing to help me because he feels he owes us — or he has something else up his sleeve. Snake wants to help me to become a biker chick to convince his brother to take us to The Game. Or so he says.

I gulp, thinking of what I watched on *Sons of Anarchy* so far. There's no way in hell I can pull off such a thing. I'm such a prude, it's not even funny. Antonia and my other best friend Niyah always tease me. And they're prudes themselves, neither really having a boyfriend yet but each kissing two boys whereas I've only ever kissed one. And I don't think Isaac even counts.

"Is she okay?" Holly, my Hollaphone's virtual assistant, suddenly asks. I jump about a mile and Archie stops humping Brian, looking all around. I forgot I turned the phone's narration on in case Dad called about Mom.

Jonah's name appears on the screen, and my heart soars before I can ask it what its problem is or try to contain it. "Not really," I say, and my Hollaphone texts that to him.

"Man, that sucks. Wish there was something I could do. You okay? You need something? I can bring you food or pick you some wildflowers. They got some real pretty ones here at Lola's Lagoon."

My heart lurches again, surprising me into sitting up more. He's so sweet, I can't believe it, and I feel like crying. "No, I'm okay. That's nice, but my cats will eat the flowers and they're maybe toxic, so thanks, but no thanks."

He calls and I answer. "Hey, you're on speaker. I'm feeding Lola now. Yeah, no, I don't want to poison no little kitties."

"That's all I need," I laugh.

"Yeah, right. Well, not sure if you're into school today, but if not, I could come over and we could hang. Eat something. I make a mean egg frittata."

"Thanks, but I'm vegan."

"Oh, well, I could make you oatmeal with some cinnamon sugar and raisins and fruit, if you're into it. I'm basic, but I got oatmeal down by now. And we can talk on how to get Rocco to take you to The Game, and what to do when he does. Like I said, the next round could go down anytime. There be six rounds and they done one at least, so we gotta' move soon or we'll be shit outta' luck."

"Yeah, I know we do. I'm going to have to somehow become…" I sigh. "Well, I watched three episodes of *Sons of Anarchy*, and I just don't know if I can do it."

"Course you can. Cause I'm here. Also, just thinking, but I should meet you once we find where they're gonna be. Then, we gotta' plan other stuff, like how to take 'em down. You shouldn't be alone then, or right now."

Like he knows me? Only, weirdly, he seems to. "Yeah, I feel odd. I haven't even told Antonia or Niyah about anything." My closest friends have no clue what's going on with Mallory, my mother, or Snake, who they think I hate.

"I remember that Antonia girl," Snake says. "She always seemed nice to everyone. She smiled at me once or twice, and even said hi and that she liked my Kiss shirt. Ain't no one ever done that 'cept her."

"Yeah. I love her. She's my favorite person, pretty much, except my other friend Niyah." I tell him about them. It feels good to be thinking about something more than Mom, Mallory, and Zayde, and how Dad might just drive off a bridge soon with the pressure he's under. "Hey, I'm not into school today," I decide. "I'll break down crying. I could use some distraction. How 'bout we do a fun trig lesson — please tell me you're doing proofs because that's my jam — and then you can teach me how to be a biker slut."

"I am doing proofs, and I ain't gotta clue, and also, they ain't all sluts."

"Oh really?" I say it with sincerity because I thought they were all trashy girls who wear too much make-up and too-tight clothes, all from broken homes and poor families, who swear a lot and smoke all the time and drink beer like it's going out of style. They do drugs and have babies too young and who knows what else.

"No. Not true. My buddy Cody's old lady Corrinne, yeah, she dresses like a slut, but she also works out all the time and looks good in her clothes. Makes her feel good for all that hard work. And she'd never cheat on Cody. She ain't no slut. They been together since ninth grade. Corinne's totally devoted, like makes his lunch all the time for work and dinners from scratch. She's a great cook too, always bringing cookies and casseroles to everyone and making nice cards and stuff. She ain't just remember everyone's birthday, but they's kids' birthdays too. She cuts Cody's hair and even shaves his back and —"

"Ew."

"It's surprising too, because he's got a whole mess of light hair, but, I guess, well, it grows there a lot. I seen it. It ain't pretty."

I giggle. "This conversation has turned weird."

Jonah laughs. "I know. Anyway, oh, your car. I was able to fix the tire this morning on my grandpa's truck. Found some video online that showed me how to make a patch from some gooey crap I had in the shed. I got his truck to your car and jumped it, so you good to go. Want me to come and pick you up in it?"

"Aren't you supposed to be in hiding? And you don't have the keys. How'd you even —"

"I have my ways. And don'cha worry, I gotta' disguise. Got me just the thing."

"Okay," I agree. When we hang up, I find myself smiling despite everything, and that surprises the hell out of me. I pick up my shirt from last night and inhale that Drakkar Noir cologne before – and a few times during – and after – getting ready, until he arrives. Thinking about how thoughtful and sweet he seems is doing all kinds of strange things to my mind and other parts of me, confusing indeed. Especially when a small part of me still thinks he's a great actor and I'm super naïve.

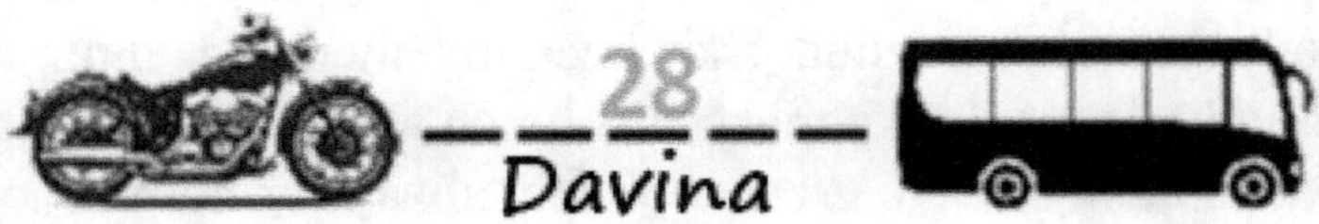


"Oh, wow, I'm just not even sure what to say," I stammer.

Jonah stands on my porch sporting a huge cowboy hat and a big mustache over his regular one with giant mirrored sunglasses. He wears jeans and a camel color suede coat with light stitching. "Howdy, ma'am." He tips his brim at me, keeping a straight face. He hands me a bag of pastry, telling me he found a vegan bakery on the way and got a few things I might like to tide me over until he could make me oatmeal at his place.

I thank him while cracking up at how silly he looks and grabbing my stuff to leave. I check all the pets are in the house and latch all the doors. As I do, Jonah ducks in and compliments our home, meeting all the pets who sniff him and seem to approve. No one graces him with a Slither Smile like Lola gave me, but Archie does hump his leg. We go out to my blue Jetta where he opens my door for me and offers a hand, helping me into the seat.

"Thanks." I buckle my seatbelt as he walks around to the driver's side.

He starts the car. "Thought on the way to my place, we could get you some new threads."

I peer at my blue button-down and jeans, light green cardigan, and brown loafers. "Yeah? You mean, these won't do?"

He chuckles and turns up the music. Some guy sings about someone named "Mr. Brownstone."

I kind of like it. "Who is this?"

"Gun's 'N Roses, one of my two favorite bands. Motley Crüe's my other."

"Yeah? Really? My dad loves Gun's 'N Roses' Nightrain song. Always talks about the Night Train house at Michigan Tech where he and my mom would attend parties. They would play Nightrain every third song, and when they did, you had to drink Night Train wine. I didn't think I liked this band that much, but this is decent."

"Wait until you hear this." He turns on a song called "Think About You."

As I listen, I agree the guy singing is damn good. "He sounds different than the last song."

"Axyl Rose has a big range, like low to real high, all in the same song. Here, listen to this one…" and then we hear, "My Michelle", which I love the best.

"Huh, I had no idea. I've always been into No Ice Cream for Ian and The Drunken Heads. They're my absolute favorites. I think they're more mainstream, bordering on punk, with some techno opera and rap thrown in."

"Yeah. I know some of their stuff."

A bus in the distance pulls off to the shoulder, and I'm reminded of my lovely bus trip from school this past December when Jonah's family almost blew me up. And then I think about Krystall Nykkolls and that the Rebel Demons were there for her, not me. I ask Jonah about it, if he knows anything.

He winces, looking uncomfortable. "Was still in juvie then. This is the first I'm hearing of it."

"So, do you know if they ever got to Krystall?"

Snake shrugs. "No clue. Like I said, I ain't know anything 'bout her 'til now."

He stares straight ahead, his face stone, and I wonder if he's telling the truth. And then I realize even though he's being nice about wanting to help Mallory to clear his conscience, I still don't know him. Not well enough to trust him.

Yet I'm letting him drive me somewhere.

"We gotta' get you cooler clothes," Snake says, "and we need a cover story. Like, who are you and how do I know you? Hey, got any cash?"

I peek into my wallet. "Not much. Like thirty bucks."

"Well, I can put in fifty. So, let's go to this thrift store I know of where Cody's old lady Corrinne shops. Get you some better clothes."

"Okay, good idea. I guess you'll help me, because, well, I'm a bit fashion challenged." I glance down again.

Jonah bites his lip. "You said it."

We go for a long while, me picking things out and Jonah putting them back and picking better stuff. I do a little fashion show for him, feeling self-conscious, but he seems to like what he sees, applauding and whistling and complimenting me, so I feel a little more comfortable. I end up with two jean skirts, a black leather mini, a pair of black leather-like pants, shredded jeans, and several bustiers or tank tops, mostly in animal prints. Snake had me get a few t-shirts ripped with beaded fringe sporting sayings like "Bad Gurl Says Whut?" and "Kiss These" and "Biker Babes Rule the Road." He also makes me get a pair of black combat boots, which he says we'll spray with Lysol because we're running out of funds, and my loafers just won't cut it. At the register, he grabs a few pairs of fishnet stockings.

When we leave, Snake shows me on his Hollaphone some hairstyles that are more suitable, and I tell him I'll work on mimicking them. He says I need to rough it up, my hair is too prim and proper. He tells me to go buy stiff hairspray and shows me with his fingers how to rat my bangs and other parts to make them have a wild texture.

"It's weird to be taking fashion tips from you, just so you know," I say as I sit in the passenger seat.

Jonah peers down at me over his mirrored frames, his elbow resting on top of the door. "I dig the way you look now, just so you know, but we gotta change it all." He slides his fingers into my hair and messes it all up.

"Hey!" I clear it from my eyes, and he pulls down the visor mirror.

"Look," he says. "Like that. Messy. Rough. Hot. You got the hot, but like we need more in your face, *sleazy* hot. You're too girl-next-door hot."

*He* thought *I* was hot. Me? I laugh. *Me?* "Okay, okay!" I giggle, and he closes my door and comes around.

"Now, let's go get Lola before she freaks, and then, please, I need help so bad. What the hell is a trigonometry proof, and why would I — as a maybe future reptile vet or bike club VP — ever freaking need to do one?"

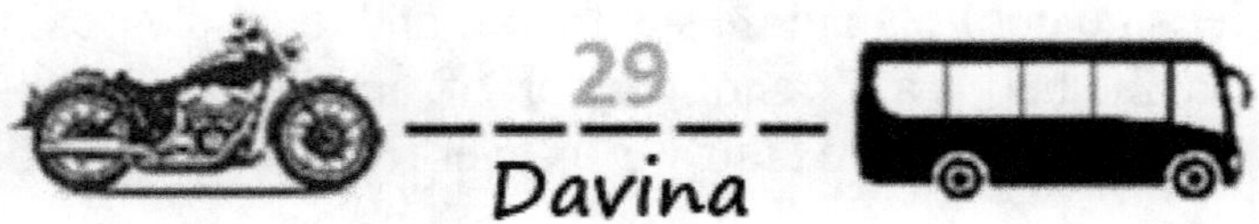


"Davina, your name is cool and all, but we gonna' need to change it too. It ain't screamin' biker chick," Snake says as I follow him to Lola's Lagoon. The afternoon sun shining through the square fence links waffles the grass, framing clusters of dandelions. "What's it mean, anyway?"

"Mom said Davina is Scottish and Hebrew and means 'beloved,' a feminine variation of David. What does yours mean, Jonah?"

Jonah stops and squints at me, grinning with his cute fangs. "You know, you's the only one besides my mother who ever used my real name."

"Really?"

"Yeah. Course, my teachers knew too. Wrote it on detention slips 'nuff times. My dad and brother just call me 'Kid' or 'Hey You' or 'Dude', and since I got Lola, everyone else just calls me Snake."

"Is that bad?"

"No, but I like that you said my real name, like you be knowin' who I really am."

I smile. "I'm starting to realize you're nothing like I thought." At least I hope so.

Jonah beams. "Thanks. Cool of you to say." He slides Lola into the heated water where she splashes about and bops her head out, slithering and smiling and rolling around.

"She's so happy. I love to see that." I laugh and tap at my Hollaphone screen, searching for his name's meaning. "So, Jonah is a masculine Hebrew name that shares ties with a prophet Jonah, whom legend says was swallowed by a whale, only to reappear on land days later unharmed."

"Oh, ain't there some movie 'bout that?"

I nod. "I think more than one. So, in terms of my new biker girl persona, who am I? What's my story?"

We bat some ideas around, but they're all way too complicated.

"Let's just say I go to school with you," I suggest, "or you know me from school — I'm your friend's kid sister — and I saw Rocco at some biker rally or wherever you all hang out and wanted an introduction because I thought he was hot. That's believable, right?"

"You know, it might work. Cut the friend though. Too much to keep straight. Just, we know each other at school. You saw Rocco where?" He thinks. "Yeah, he mentioned they was at a rally like three weeks ago. A big one over in Hell."

"In Hell?"

"Yeah. Hell, Michigan, near Ann Arbor. There was a Hell Fire Rally three weeks ago." He punches it up on his Hollaphone. "Yeah, that's the one they was at. I'm sure of it." He shows me the website for the event, which flaming letters announce has already passed.

"Okay, sounds good. I went with some friends, friends who also ride. So, what's my name then?"

Jonah finds a list of female biker names on Gaggle, and we try many, but none of them seem fitting.

"Wait, I got it!" Jonah says. "I have the perfect name, cuz of one of my favorite shows, and cuz of your hair."

"My hair *and* your favorite show?"

"I dig that old *I Love Lucy* show all in black and white. Me and Mom used to watch them reruns all the time. She did with her ma' too. With your fiery hair, I say we call you Lucy."

"Lucy?" I peer into my Hollaphone camera on reverse, where my red hair is still all mussed. "Lucy, huh?" I try to imagine myself as this biker girl, but even with trashy clothes, big hair, and a new name, I just can't see it yet. I keep it to myself, giving Snake a thumbs-up and as much of a smile as I can muster.

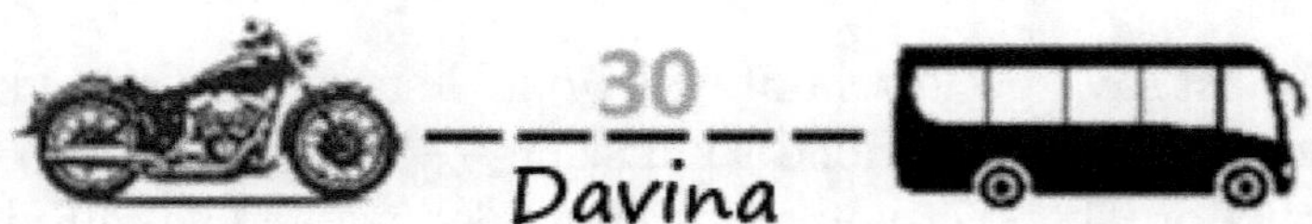


"Why the hell would anyone ever do a trig proof?" Snake complains as we sit at his kitchen table in Grandpa's old house sipping Cokes and munching on tortilla chips. I've shown him a few examples, and he struggled, not really getting the concept that sometimes you must work backward to work forward.

"It's kind of like with Mallory," I say. "We know the endgame, at least, the one we want, which is for her to win Vermilion so she can live. Now, I must figure out with whatever and whomever I have at my disposal, how I'm going to get to her and save her." Unfortunately, that includes Rocco Riley, Jonah's older brother, who may be the only one with the power to bring me to Mallory.

Jonah frowns at his paper.

I pat Lola's head as she eyes me from her perch on Jonah's shoulder. "When a sick python like Lola comes into your clinic, can you ask it what's wrong?"

Jonah levels a look at me. "Course not. They ain't know how to answer."

"So, what will you do?"

Jonah shrugs. "I dunno. I guess I'd see if they're moving, ask their owner if they've been eating, pooping, or swimming. See if they's pregnant."

"Okay, so those are good clues. What if the owner doesn't know or you find the snake and there's no one to ask?"

"Good point. I guess I gotta' do tests to rule stuff in or out."

"Are you going to just shoot in the dark and hope you come up with an answer, or will you have a systematic checklist to make sure you address everything it could be?"

"Uh, yeah, that. A systematic way."

"And that's why you need to do proofs!"

Jonah's brow furrows. "I don't get it."

"See, you have all these clues from Lola or another snake, lizard, or iguana. Whatever you're treating. And you must rule things out, one by one, be complete, have a method to your madness, all that, so you don't overlook something it could be. You want to think of everything and fast to prevent this poor animal from suffering or even dying. And that's what doing things like trig proofs and other complicated math procedures helps you to do. It trains your brain to think of all sorts of things at once, to prioritize them and work with the given information to find a solution. You only have certain medicines and tests to use, right?"

"Yeah, I s'pose."

"Well, in trig, you have these fundamental 'trig identities' or relationships to help you, and that's all you have." I point to his list. "They're the only meds, or tools, you can use, and you somehow must get from the start, or what's on the left side, and transform it using these identities to look like the right side. You cannot use anything else except these basic relationships and regular rules of Algebra, which we'll review again. These identities are your medicines to transform from sick pet on the left side to healthy pet on the right side of your equation."

"That kinda' makes sense," Jonah says. "So, even if I ain't never hafta' do a proof in real life, by learning how, I can reason shit better and figure out more complicated stuff? Totally get that now. Why ain't no one else ever put it like that?" Jonah grins, staring at his computer screen with new eyes. "I get why I gotta' be tortured, but it still kills my head. A lot." He removes his reading glasses and massages the bridge of his nose. Locating a bottle of pain reliever, he twists off the cap and pops a few tablets into his mouth.

"Yeah. I have trouble sometimes too, but I like a good puzzle, and that's all math is. I love math because usually there *is* an answer. When in life, sometimes other answers are so difficult and not obvious, I know I can come home and do a math problem and check the back of the book to see if it's correct, feeling good that I at least did *something* right. It's my strange coping mechanism. I do math problems to relax because often, they're the only ones I can solve."

Jonah's eyes crinkle as he gazes at me with his chin in his hand, exposing his fangs. "You sure is a weirdo, Davina Rosenbaum. I mean good shit when I say that though. It's cool that you make me think, and even better that you do all the time and stuff. That's really kinda'—"

Jonah's Hollaphone rings, playing "Merry-Go-Round" by Motley Crüe, his favorite song. He glances at the screen. "Sorry, it's Rocco." Putting the phone to his ear, he listens with a few uh-huh's and then clicks off, turning toward me.

"What? Is it important?"

"He wants me at Blades Cave to talk club business."

"Blades Cave? What's that?"

"Rebel Demons hangout. Come on now, Lucy. Get yourself dressed. It's showtime."

I gulp. "Already?"

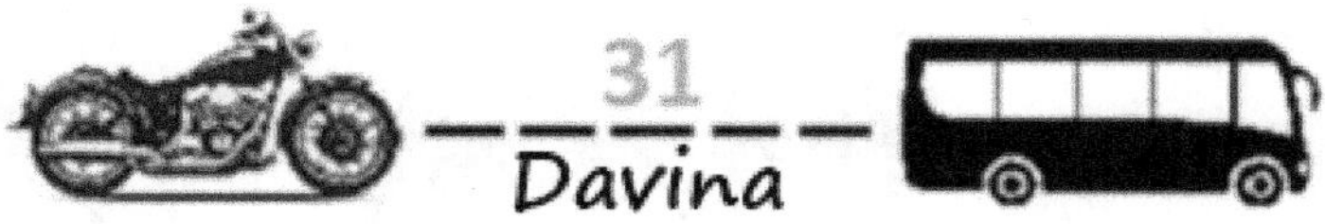

# 31
## Davina

Grabbing a black leather miniskirt and a tight zebra tank top that goes over one shoulder and makes my boobs look huge, I run and change. I slide on a pair of fishnet stockings, then pull on my skirt. Wearing two pairs of socks underneath the new used boots, I try not to think of how disgusted I am. I've never worn other people's stuff before and didn't think we'd be going so fast that I hadn't a chance to wash any of it or spray Lysol to kill germs. Just as well. I'm supposed to be a dirty girl who wears used clothes, I guess, so this is legit authentic.

I leave my hair down and it hangs below my shoulders now, needing a trim badly. I put a ton of mousse and spray in it, bending over at the waist and ratting it like Jonah showed me. I flip back up, and it looks full, although most of it falls in a second. I put on a ton more make-up than usual, copying a picture of a biker babe I found on Gaggle, and finally emerge from the bathroom.

Snake's eyebrows shoot up, and he whistles. "Wow. Total knockout."

"Yeah?" I turn around in the hall mirror. "I feel so self-conscious." I smush my boobs inside my top.

"You look hot. Way hot. Perfect. Now, push those back out, and don't stand so straight up. Slouch a little. Have attitude. You're badass. You own the room." Snake puts thumbs through his belt loops and struts before me. "You know you got it, and every eye is on you. Go with that. Make Rocco *beg* to talk to you."

"Yeah?" I try to imagine having such a demeanor and can't. Jonah keeps strutting, and I bite my lip so hard not to laugh, I taste blood.

"Think of all them girls on *Sons of Anarchy* and how they be lookin' and actin'. Be like them."

"Okay, I'll try. So, what should I say? What type of things should I talk about with Rocco when I meet him? Let's practice on the way."

"No, well, we can talk 'til we get to my bike, but you know we ain't hearin' nothin' on no Harley."

"We have my car, your grandpa's truck, why would we —"

"We gotta' look the part. We ain't showin' up in your Jetta or the truck. So, come on, cuz it's far."

I swallow and brace myself, trying to get lost in our conversation the whole way to Snake's motorcycle, but I'm still terrified of it, even though I rode once. He said he won't be going slow this time because we must get to Blades Cave pronto. Rocco has called, and you don't keep him waiting.

It's more crowded now, more cars on the road since it's rush hour, which I point out. Jonah reaches behind and squeezes my knee. "Don't worry, Davina — er, um, Lucy — I'm ain't gonna' let nothin' bad happen. Trust me."

I try to believe him, to trust him, but I'm smart enough to know it doesn't always matter what his intentions are, others are idiots or careless and could hit us. And that whole trust thing with him… Still not entirely sure what the real situation is yet. He's like too nice maybe, too good to be true. A total three-sixty from the guy I thought I knew.

After we put Lola in her home inside a baby's playpen with all kinds of grass and rocks and branches for her to crawl on and a big screen cover that Snake secures with bungee cords, we go outside and get on his bike.

I pray the whole way, wrapped in Jonah's Drakkar Noir cloud with my cheek pressed to his back and my arms tucked in his vest feeling his jiggly belly. When we get to Blades Cave in one piece, I feel like crossing myself, I'm so relieved. I don't because I'm Jewish and am not sure if it's rude. I don't even know if we have something equivalent.

The clubhouse of the Rebel Demons is in a real house that they own, a two-story with a high peaked roof. Snake says his dad and brother live together upstairs now since they both lost their old ladies.

"Will I meet your dad too?" I ask as Jonah straps our helmets to his side saddle, the thought making me even more nervous as I fluff my flattened hair in his mirror.

Jonah shakes his head. “Nah. He ain’t doing too good. You ain’t want to anyway since he’s smoking outta’ his neck. I can’t barely even look at him, it’s so pitiful. He says, hell, why try to quit now? He’s dying and just lost his wife, ya’ know? Says he’s ready to go.”

I shudder, attempting to imagine that and contemplate losing both parents in a short time, and I can’t. Then I think about Mallory and Zayde, and realize I’m in the same boat, only with them. I squeeze his shoulder. “I’m sorry.”

He shrugs and studies his boots for a second. “Thanks. Okay, now, when we go in, just be cool. No math talk. No school talk. You hate school. You don’t give a shit about them classes. All you care about is getting with guys and listening to metal and drinking and just being a biker babe. That’s what you talk about.”

I shoot him a look.

“Okay, don’t talk much. Use your body to do the talking.”

I shoot him another.

“Okay, just watch some them other girls and do what they be doin’. Act just like ‘em. Say, *hey baby* or *hey sugar*. Be sexy, like you want ‘em to want your body, and you got the goods.” He eyes me up and down. “Yeah, you got it. Now, show that shit off.”

I crack up without meaning to. “Me?”

“Yeah, you.” Jonah isn’t laughing. “You’re sexy as hell. I say that as a friend, but I’m also a guy. Now, sell it to Rocco. He’s cute. You gonna think so. All them girls do.”

“Okay. I’ll try.”

Snake knocks on the front door. A small window slides open, and someone peeks out.

“Hey, it’s me,” Snake says.

“Password, asshole.”

“Buzzkill420.”

The door opens, and Snake bumps fists with whoever is behind it. He mutters a name I don’t quite hear.

I smile and say, “Hey.”

The guy gives me the once over and then whistles low. "Hey yourself, little lady."

The long room we enter has a bar along the left side with a huge TV over a Rebel Demons flag, and then on the right, there are more TV's suspended from the ceiling. High tables with stools and leather sofas with coffee tables line the perimeter. The walls are decorated with all kinds of daggers, knives, and swords, fitting for a place named Blades Cave. Beyond, there's a large, covered porch out back. Several biker guys and their girls — or "old ladies" as they're known — are seated in each area, and as Snake introduces me around, I try to catch all their names. There are so many at once, it's all a blur. So far, everyone seems much friendlier than I would have expected, all saying welcome and it's nice to meet me.

I notice people outside with cigarettes and realize it's not smoky in here at all like I would've expected. I ask Jonah about it, and he says people smoke only outside because they know it bothers him so much. "You'd be surprised, but we got each other's backs. It's like that in a club like this. We do potlucks a lot and all them old ladies be makin' tons of grub and plan all kinds of family stuff. All us kids be friends since birth too. We's like one big happy family, straight up."

"Really?"

"Oh yeah. Motorcycle clubs like ours get a bad rap, but they ain't all bad."

A guy with a blond ponytail, scruffy mustache, and long goatee with red rubber bands sectioning it off approaches. A shorter girl with blonde spiky hair with purple tips follows. The guy claps Snake on the back while shaking his hand.

"Lucy, this here's my buddy Cody and his old lady Corrinne," Snake says.

I remember Cody's the best friend of Snake's and Rocco's and a prospect of the club while Corrinne is his devoted girlfriend who's a great cook and shaves his back. Jonah said a prospect is like a fraternity pledge, taking shit and doing all the grunt work until he proves himself and they trust him enough to let him join.

Cody grins and welcomes me to Blades Cave with a warm hug while Corrinne smiles at me and squeezes my arm. She's beautiful, with a figure so killer that you can tell she does something a lot — Pilates, yoga, running, Crossfit — something. Her petite yet muscular form is highlighted in a leopard bustier and a black leather mini, with fishnets just like mine and combat boots like I notice everyone is wearing. Snake said it's because on the bike, you don't want the heat from the engine to burn you while riding, so it's good to wear thick boots to protect you. Seems odd with a miniskirt, but that's the norm here.

"Hey girl. How ya' doing?" Corrinne asks, her dimples plunging.

"Hey, good. I love your necklace," I say, admiring the silver heart locket with a C+C on the lid, which I suppose is for their first names.

"Oh, thanks." She fingers it, showing me. "Cody got it for me for our seven-year anniversary a few months back. It has our baby pictures in it." She opens it and beams as I study the little images.

"Seventh? Wow, that's a long-assed time," I say, trying to sound rough.

She nods. "Yep. Been together since freshman year in high school when me and Cody flunked Algebra together."

"Yeah?" I'm about to ask why they failed, to give helpful advice if they want to learn it better, but then I stop myself and kick nerdy Davina to the curb. "Yeah, math sucks," I say, practically choking on my words.

"Totally," Cody and Corrinne agree, laughing. "There's like no reason to know it. I swear, they just force that shit on everyone as a rite of passage, and then you never, ever use it again."

I agree, biting my tongue so hard I taste blood again.

"Hey girl, come on out after ya'll get your drinks, and we'll hang some, maybe dance a few. Band's killer tonight." Corrinne takes her drink and waves. "See ya'll soon!" She and Cody go out to the porch area where I can hear an electric guitar wailing while someone screams and drums beat, leaving me alone with Snake.

He congratulates me.

"That was rough," I admit. "But I didn't geek out."

He laughs, clapping me on the back. "Ya' did good, Kid."

Some guys enter the front door. I peer past Snake to them, and my jaw hits the floor. The tall one in front has a huge Swastika tattooed on the side of his bald head. As everyone greets him and his similarly marked friends, he takes off his black leather jacket to reveal a tattoo of Adolf Hitler on his arm. Chunks rise in my throat as my face bursts into flames.

Snake turns. "Shit, I forgot to warn you about Breaker."

"Breaker? *Breaker*? That's his name? I thought it would be Stupid Idiot."

"Yeah. Some guys in the club are just like that."

I spin to Snake, my nostrils flaring. "Like that? *Like that?* Like they celebrate a man who killed so many innocents — Jews, gays, and others? Like they pay reverence to him and his people, Hitler and his Nazis, who hated pretty much *everyone*? Like that he has such a hard-on for the guy that he tattoos *freaking Adolph Hitler* on his body?"

My head is ready to explode, but before I can confront Swastika Dude or leave, Snake hooks his arm through mine, pulling me to him. "Where you goin', Lucy?"

Tears fill my eyes. "I can't do this! I gotta' get out of here. I'm no biker girl. I can't —"

"But what about Mallory? The Game? Rocco?"

"I know, but I can't. I'm not mixing with a guy like that. Him or any of his stupid friends." I eye the others with their Swastikas adorning parts of their exposed skin and clothing.

"No one's asking you to. Just say hello once. Be polite. It's all you gotta' do." Jonah nods like it's so easy.

"I don't even think I could."

Swastika Dude and his friends come toward the bar where we are, and we move down, still waiting for our drinks. The imbecile points his Hitler-inked arm toward the TV above. "Damn 'nother queer club all shot up, and good riddance. They make it easy, all together gaying out to their music and whatnot." He pounds his fist on the bar. "Don't be Jewing me out of no vodka," he says, and the bartender pours more into his glass. He slams it back like water, then smacks the granite again, demanding another.

Swastika Dude looks at another TV, saying some Black man being beaten to death by a few police officers the other day was hilarious and justified. Then, he knocks Jews again, saying they've taken over all the banks and Hollyweird and the OuterNet. Then he attacks Hispanics, accusing them of being lazy and always wanting a handout. "Man, what's this world coming to? That's why we need to rise up." He pumps a fist into the air. "Take our country back. Let the Great White Man rule again!" He raises his arm to his ear, fingers together and outstretched. "Seig Heil."

His wannabe Nazi friends cheer his "wonderful" speech with their own silly Nazi salutes while the bartender laughs and shakes his head.

Our drinks arrive, and Snake drags me out to the porch area away from Swastika Dude. Luckily Cody and Corrinne are on the dance floor, because I can't even fake friendliness right now. I can't calm down. I feel like crying over someone so ignorant and stupid who believes his own lies and the people around him agree. I just had the pleasure of witnessing such a person, who lives in my same society and has influence over others, at least his friends, spreading his vicious hateful bullshit while paying tribute to a mass murderer.

"No, I gotta' go say something," I tell Jonah, heading back inside.

Jonah pulls me to him and puts his arms around my waist, whispering in my ear. "Think of Mallory, Lucy. Keep your eye on the prize. Don't blow your cover. Ain't no biker girl gonna have a problem with Breaker and his buddies. Or at least, they ain't gonna' say so. If you do right now, you ain't never getting in good with Rocco. Then we not getting to the next round, and then what about your sister?"

"But who am I if I just let that go? I'm kind of Jewish, you know?"

"It's part of the culture. You'll see it on *Sons of Anarchy* and *Mayans MC* too, you just wait. It ain't everybody, but some."

My face twists in disgust. "That's what you do, your family? You think like that too?" I push away from him, suddenly realizing I don't know Snake at all. "You're *okay* with *that*?"

"No. Hell no. I ain't about hate. But that's how a lot of them is." He shrugs.

"What, they believe stuff that isn't even true? He says 'Jewed down' to imply cheapness, but all Jews aren't cheap! Some are quite generous while others spend money like water. No one group of people is all one way! He obviously doesn't know enough Jews to realize that, but I do."

“You gotta’ understand. Breaker, he’s been raised to think this. His daddy was like that, and his daddy’s daddy too. He’s been taught all this nonsense like it’s real by everyone he knows his whole life. How’s he supposed to believe something different? Just like you been taught ‘bout being fair and giving people a chance, he and his buddies all been taught the exact opposite since day one. They’s practically bred like that.”

“Can’t they just open their eyes and *see*? I mean, not every Black person or Asian person look alike. Not all Jews have big noses. Mine is tiny. Everyone is totally different in appearance and how they act and what they believe. Not all —”

“We know that, but someone like Breaker, he ain’t gotta’ clue ‘bout another way to think. It’s all a conspiracy against the Great White Man. He been taught this whole time he needs to do something ‘bout it. He be doing what he thinks is right, even if we know it’s flat out wrong.”

I shake my head. “So stupid. My best friend Niyah, she’s a wonderful person, a Black girl I’ve known since I was little. One of the coolest people ever. And brilliant. I’ve heard people say Black people can’t do math, but she can way better than me or anyone I know our age. She already goes to college, for God’s sake, and has a high A in Calculus III. She’s maybe even smarter than Mallory. And then there’s Antonia, who is Brazilian, so Hispanic, and not a lazy bone in her body. She works hard at school and on her piano, which she practices every day, and she often helps her parents with their little produce store, which they work around the clock to maintain. What he said is just flat-out *wrong*. I could provide several counterexamples for his stupid hypotheses that he treats like fact.”

“Lotsa’ people got blinders on, so they ain’t see what’s obvious,” Snake says. “They use them stupid stereotypes to be hurtin’ others.”

“Yeah, I know. Makes me sad, and mad. But at the same time —” I lower my eyes, unsure I want to share the next part.

“What’s that?”

“Well, part of me thinks, who am I to even say anything? At least, about defending Jews. I mean, like maybe I don’t even deserve to.”

Snake’s pierced brow arches. “What’chu mean?”

“Well, I’m not a very observant Jew. I didn’t have a Bat Mitzvah. I don’t go to synagogue or celebrate the weekly Shabbat. My family is just not very religious. My parents are agnostic like me, unsure but with hope, we say. We have celebrated many of the Jewish holidays through the years — Pesach (or Passover), Yom Kippur, Rosh Hashanah, Chanukah — and have eaten a lot of the traditional foods, although we're vegan so we make our own variation, but that's about it. I don't even really know much about being a Jew, like even basic bible stories, except what I learned at the Jewish camp I've attended since sixth grade. So, who am I to defend Jews when I'm not even a good one myself?"

"Search me. I ain't sure. Maybe it ain't matter if you are a good one, just you know the shit he says is wrong. You ain't even hafta' be Jewish to defend a Jewish person."

I eye the cross with a snake wrapped around it dangling from Snake's ear. "Are you very religious, and what kind of Christian are you?"

"We're Protestant, but barely." He shrugs. "I ain't too sure the differences between all them types, to be honest wit'chu."

"But your earring."

He catches it on his fingers. "I just wear it cuz I dig snakes. Obviously." He rubs the Lola on his head. "I guess it means something though. Ma said it was called a Serpent Cross. Ain't sure what that's all about."

"Did you ever think you wanted to know more?" I ask.

Jonah shrugs. "Sometimes, I think maybe. Like it could help. Them people who are into they faith have this kinda' peace I ain't got. So that's something. Not sure it's reason enough though. It's like selfish maybe."

"My Zayde — that's grandfather in Yiddish — told me once that I owed it to myself to discover my Judaism, and I asked him why, why should I just because I was born into it and not explore other religions? I mean, just because I'm born a Jew, does that mean I have to subscribe to all they believe? Because I do have some issue about a few things I've read. I'm just a bit confused about the whole thing. So is my sister Mallory. She says she's 'open to suggestion,' willing to learn and not commit to a particular ideology until she's sure."

"When this whole mess is over, we should go to different types of churches and stuff. Ask questions."

“Synagogues and mosques too.”

Snake nods. “Yeah, those. We learn what they all is and how they different, then we decide what makes sense. Maybe none ‘em will. But we gotta’ try first.”

“I think that sounds great. A worthwhile thing to do. I’d totally explore different religions with you.”

Snake fist bumps me just as the music stops. Cody and Corrinne approach, out of breath from dancing, each downing their drinks at a nearby table.

As I’m about to tell Corrinne that she’s a good dancer, some guys burst out the doors from the bar room. They signal to the band to stop playing. “Hey, listen up. Rocco’s called for backup. Says he’s over in Sterling Heights on John R and Maple, and the Eastside Boyz have cornered him. We gotta get there *now*.”

All the guys except Snake grab guns from some room behind the bar and file out. Soon, a cacophony of Harleys roars from outside.

“Oh God,” I say, a new realization pouring over me. “I never thought Rocco might be in danger from this war with those guys. What if he —” I leave the words hanging like a cloud of smoke. As Jonah and I sit listening to Corrinne chatter on about something, I think, if Rocco dies or is captured otherwise, I’ll never get to The Game. And then what will happen to Mallory?

# PART 8

## ROUND 3: ROBBIE'S CHALLENGE

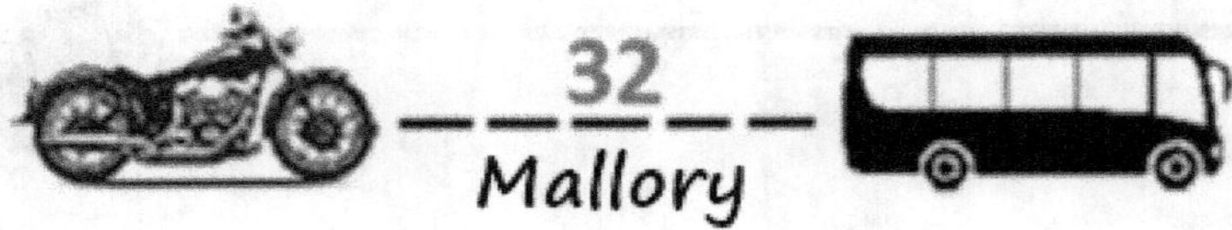

# 32
## Mallory

**Saturday, January 19, 2030**

I wake up to screaming. It's frantic and terrified, like that time Jonah Riley was almost mauled by that huge dog in fourth grade. I bolt upright in my bed, sweat pouring from my forehead, to see Paige across the way sliding out from under her covers.

"Who's that?" I ask, my eyes sweeping the beds above.

"I think it's Keondra," Ollie says, hopping down from his bunk and landing between me and Paige. He runs around the bathroom into Door Bay, and we follow.

Camila hugs Keondra, trying to force her still as she writhes all around on the lower bunk, her face ashen and eyes wide, gripping her left arm at the shoulder — or rather, where her arm *used* to be.

I can see through her fingers a bloody bandage is wrapped around her stump, and she keeps crying out for her mother as Camila and Ollie hug her and try to quiet her. They do a pretty good job until Keondra discovers her severed limb next to her in her covers.

She screams and jumps from her bed, running toward the door, trying to open it with her remaining hand. Camila and Ollie embrace her, stopping her from trying to escape, knowing if she does what will be her fate.

"Please, Karyn-Bot," Camila begs. "Get this poor girl some drugs or something. She can't take the shock and pain. Please give her something — anything — so she can keep playing your stupid game."

Keondra continues crying so tragically, I have tears in my eyes, and even her friends' comfort isn't helping, but after a short while, she stops and exhales. "Whew. That's better," she says, relief overtaking her face. "Them Soldier-Bots just been by with some real good shit." Her eyes roll around, and she smiles with half-closed lids, slumping toward Ollie.

He catches her while Camila shakes her awake. "Don't go sleeping on us, girl. We need you for this round."

"So, was Luckster here?" Ollie asks, motioning to a groggy Keondra and eyeing the door.

"Maybe," Paige says, examining it. "Hard to tell. I wonder if the bots somehow did that, like chopped off her arm from the inside. I mean, if they can destroy bone and implode people and all. That would mean he, or excuse me, she, didn't have to show up to do the deed."

"Could be," Ollie agrees with a scowl on his face. "Although I would think they who are running things would derive great joy in making Luckster do that too." He glances around. "They seem to enjoy making us squirm."

"That's the understatement of the year," I say.

Karyn-Bot announces we're almost at our destination, and Keondra's eyes pop open. She breaks away from Camila and Ollie, standing, her jaw steeled in determination. "Let's do this shit," she says, clapping her hands together. But since one's missing, the other hits air, spinning her around. She crashes into a bunk and falls to the floor, looking drunk.

"Girl, get yourself together and go change," Camila says, handing her a plastic white bag with her rainbow gear. "We're almost there."

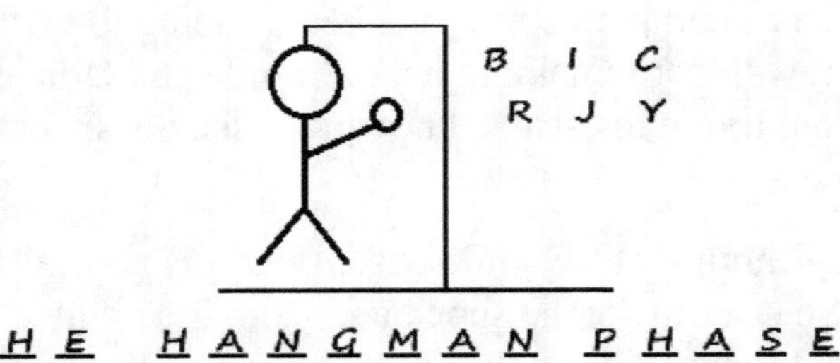


## THE HANGMAN PHASE

When we're freed from Home Base this time, which is now clad in an advertisement for the long-awaited summer concert tour of No Ice Cream for Ian, we find a huge pyramid with the words "Long Live Rock" in tall red block letters in front of it.

Keondra shakes her head. "Can't believe this shit," she slurs. "We like at the Rock & Roll Hall of Fame in freaking *Cleveland*." She leans heavily on a nearby garbage can. "I was supposta' visit next month fer my sista's wedding here." Her hand slips inside the can's opening, and her good arm disappears. "Didn't plan on coming so early."

I gulp as Camila pulls her friend from the garbage. "We're not in Michigan anymore." I feel like Dorothy in the Wizard of Oz.

"Wow, they've taken us across state lines," Ollie says. "This is even more serious now."

"Why?" Camila asks, brushing debris from Keondra's empty sleeve as she holds her up.

"Just that, if they're ever caught, they took you minors out of state against your will, a more substantial charge."

"That's a big IF," I say. "I hate to admit it, but I don't think they'll ever be —"

"Keep that shit to yourself!" Camila warns. "They'll be caught. I know it."

I shake my head, sure that she cannot really be certain. But it's not worth arguing with her and dispelling any hope she has left. "Well guys, time's a-wasting. See you at the Vermilion Bird."

Mark-Bot tells us that in this challenge, instead of the four quadrants, we'll be separated into four floors. Camila pulls a collapsing Keondra toward the Azure Dragon on the second, Ollie and Jiro go to the White Tiger on the fourth, and Paige and I head to the Black Tortoise on the third. The Vermilion Bird will be on the fifth.

I try not to notice all the cool stuff everywhere I look, even though I've been dying to come here forever. As a dancer and singer, I'm also a huge lover of all types of music except country. I scan everything only searching for clues, ignoring all the great stuff about Madonna, The Rolling Stones, Whitney Houston, Prince, Pat Benatar, Elvis, and many others. The black letter cards for the Black Tortoise clues are hard to see in the dimmed hall, but at least they're shiny, which helps.

As Paige and I walk around, I notice practically every single person, from older men to girls my age to children, all wearing solids of different colors or RainBO PranXterz t-shirts, and I just cannot believe how fast the trend of us has spread. Some are even wearing knit hats with pom-poms, Covid-28 masks, and goggles just like us. So stupid.

We collect several clues, and after a while, we get:

E ___ ___ N ___ ___ ___ R ___ ___ A ___ ___ H ___ R ___ E E ___ ___ H.

Paige whips out her new inhaler and tucks it under her mask, and I suddenly remember my thoughts about her other one that I found in the bathroom with someone else's name on it. I want to ask her how her friend fooled a trained doctor, but I don't know how to say it without it sounding accusatory. I see a girl with a black card sticking out of her bag, and I start to follow her when I notice Paige across the way sitting on a bench. Her hands cover her goggles and her shoulders bob.

I rush over. "What happened? Are you okay?"

Paige tells me through sniffles that she saw a little girl that had the same pink coat with the gold unicorn horn on the hood as her little sister Kimmy. "I'm just so worried for her. I've *got* to help her somehow."

"I know," I say, searching for a way to comfort her. There's nothing I can really do, and I hate false promises telling her it'll be okay when I don't know as Camila tried with me. That doesn't help at all.

"Please, Mallory, promise me that if you win, you'll somehow get Kimmy. Rescue her from the Shelleck's. Bring her to live with you, or at least get her out of there. Here's their address." She hands me a slip of paper.

"I will. I promise." I tuck it into my belly bag and cry too, realizing how much of a long shot it would be for me to win against Ollie and Camila and Keondra, who are all as fit if not more and just as smart and daring. What if neither Paige nor I win? Then, what will happen to Kimmy? I hug my new friend. "I will do everything in my power to help her if I can, and we'll recruit Ollie too. I'm sure he'd also do it for you. Maybe we can even talk to the others tonight at Nap Time and give them all the address. At least, whoever's left."

She squeezes me back, thanking me.

"Goddamn it," Camila says through our Walkie-Bots. "You guys won't believe this."

"What?" Ollie asks.

"Karyn-Bot whispered a secret to me this morning, saying our coin would be in a guy's guitar."

"Whose?" I ask.

"She didn't say, but she said a *guy*."

"Yeah, and?"

"We're at this Garage exhibit, which is super cool, where they let you play all the instruments of famous bands and stuff. Well, we've been looking in all the guys' guitars, but also collecting clues, and here are our letters. See behind your eyelids."

I close my eyes and the letters appear: __ N __ L __ __ D __ E S __ U __ T A __.

I shake my head, confused. "Yeah? What's the problem?"

"I think it says: IN BLONDIES GUITAR."

"Oh. Not a guy."

“Right. That Karyn-Bot be lying,” Keondra slurs. “We after it now, but we taking longer because of that. Wastin’ our time and shit. Don’t go trustin’ that Karyn-Bot bitch.”

“Thanks for the tip,” I say.

“I got it!” Paige says, coming over. “I know our clue. It says EMINEM FRIDAY THIRTEENTH.”

I study it for a second. “Shit, you’re right. But what’s that?”

Paige shrugs.

We walk around until we find the Eminem exhibit.

Paige leans forward, studying a plaque. “He was inducted in 2022, it says. He grew up in Detroit, you know.”

“Of course. Shit, it is that?” I point. “There’s a Friday the Thirteenth outfit of Jason with his mask. Says Eminem wore it on tour to promote his ‘The Marshall Mathers LP.’ So, where’s the coin?”

“There!” Paige says, standing to the side. “I see it behind Jason’s mask. But how are we going to get it?”

A security guard is in the distance, not looking at us but easily able to any second. “Go distract that guard,” I tell Paige. “Have an asthma attack and get him to help.”

“Okay,” Paige says and heads toward him.

When the guard bends to help Paige, I slip past the barricade to the display and carefully pry the coin from the mask.

Just as it comes loose, the guard with Paige sees me. “Hey! You can’t be back there!”

I skip over the short barricade and duck into the shadows, finding an exit stairway and practically flying down the stairs. A couple floors below, I hide in the crowd, blending in with all the rainbow idiots. The guard emerges from the stairwell, searches the crowd for a bit, and somehow his eyes land directly on me. Everyone around me looks just like me, all of us in rainbow separates, but we all have different colors. He must have remembered my exact outfit.

He starts toward me, and my instincts kick in. I shove two rainbow idiots toward him, and they trip forward while he stumbles over them. I book out of there, and gain the attention of another guard, who comes after me alongside the first who has now recovered. My heart drills concrete, sure that any minute, they'll detain me, and then I'll be eliminated and disintegrated.

The haunting images of Troy's and Sammi's demises play in my mind, which makes me run faster and faster. I finally reach an emergency exit and burst through it, instantly hearing a blaring alarm. I know if I take the stairs and try to escape onto another floor, they'll catch up to me. But if I go the quick way…

I channel Ollie and dive over the side of the banister. Catching onto the rungs of some railing on a lower floor, my legs swing wildly. I hold on for dear life, then vault over the side with the momentum, sheer adrenaline and fear fueling me like when that Krystall Nykkolls who couldn't swim sprung out of our pool. I run toward the door and yank it open to find myself on another floor. Blending in with others colorfully dressed by the time the guards emerge from the stairwell, I'm safe as they scan the crowd, especially when I duck behind a guy much taller than me. After a long while, they give up and leave the way they came.

Unbelievable, but the rainbow idiots have kept me going in this game.

It takes me several seconds to breathe again as I replay what I just did and marvel that I didn't end up splattered on the basement floor. When I summon Paige through a Walkie-Bot to tell her I got our coin, she says they're ready to get the Vermilion Bird and to meet at the Foster Theater on the fifth level.

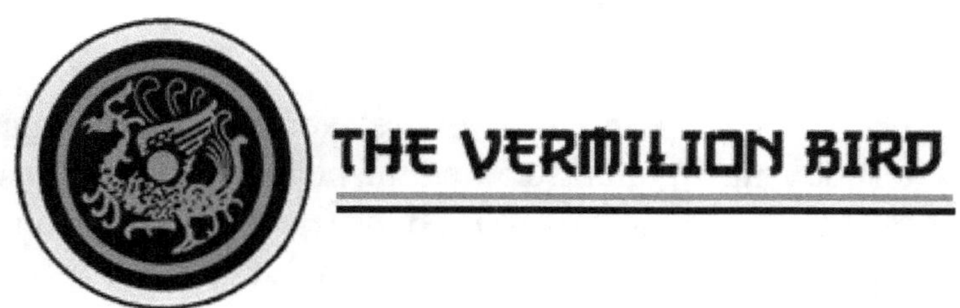

# THE VERMILION BIRD

I had to go on stage during some big awards presentation," Ollie says to everyone as I arrive. "The White Tiger coin was in the goddamn podium if you can believe it."

"Oh my God," Camila laughs. "How'd you manage to get it?"

"It was so funny," Jiro says, giggling.

I do a double take because it's the most words I've heard from him since the first day when they held a gun to his head, and he said he wanted to be a chemical engineer.

"What was?" Paige asks.

"Ollie accept award."

"No!" Camila cackles.

"Yes! They call up Mick Jagger from Rolling Stones to give lifetime achievement award, and he get up, but he take while to get out of row, and then, Ollie —" Jiro points and laughs some more. "He go on stage, pretend he Mick, and give speech while Mr. Mick stand there in aisle scratching head."

Everyone cracks up as Ollie holds up his coin. "Thankfully, we got away. Now, let's get this done so no one else dies today."

We all split up, hunting for clues, and after a while, we have:

P __ I __ C __ B __ U E __ N __ E L.

"I got it!" Camila says. "I think it says: PRINCE BLUE ANGEL."

"What's that though?" Ollie wonders. No one knows, so we disperse again, studying the exhibits all around us.

"Here!" Camila says. "Come around to the back part of the hall. I'm at a Prince tribute display."

Finding her there propping up a very relaxed Keondra, we gather around Prince's Blue Angel guitar. Reading the plaque, we learn that Prince, one of my favorite singers ever, used his Cloud 2 electric blue guitar on his Purple Rain, Parade, Sign o' the Times, and Lovesexy tours. It sold for over a half million at auction, and the new owner generously lent it to the Museum.

And of course, the guitar is locked behind a glass display case.

"Shit. We need the key," Ollie says.

"Can't we break in?" Camila asks. "Like in the back? Cut the wall or something?"

"With what? And what if that sets off an alarm?" Paige asks.

"Hey, that Karyn-Bot bitch wasn't lying!" Keondra says, pointing to the guitar and laughing. "Coin *was* in a guy's guitar! Why'd she give us a real clue but like a fake one too?"

"Just to trip us up. Who knows? Doesn't matter now," Camila says. "How do we get it?"

"Let's just break the case, grab the coin, and get out of here," Ollie says. He snatches some woman's cane from next to where she's sitting on a bench and swings with all his might toward the case.

The cane bounces off the glass, and he spins the other way, almost taking out a couple who luckily have the great reflexes to duck in time. They start to yell at him, but he darts away, leaving us to figure out how to get into the case.

"What about one of those keys?" I say, noticing a guard with a huge cluster on his hip. "He's gotta' have it on there, don't you think?"

"Yeah, probably," Camila says. "Let me take care of him while you all work on getting behind there to see how to get into that box."

"Okay," we say, and she shoves Keondra at me, who almost takes me to the ground with her dead weight. I lower her to a bench nearby and pace in front keeping a watchful eye on her and everything else while Jiro and Paige work on the box. Camila goes and starts flirting with the guard. Things are going fine, and she backs him up into a corner, practically giving the stunned guy a standing lap dance like she's a stripper. But then she's too bold and lunges for the keys at his hip. The guy yells, "Hey!" as she breaks away, running for the stairs.

"Go! Get keys and back here!" Jiro yells, and I take off, chasing them. We end up on the third floor where Camila runs all around with the guy after her, and now another two guards have appeared. She tosses the keys to Ollie who happens to be there, who then throws them at me, and I race out the exit again, feeling someone behind me. Darting up to the fourth floor, I run all around, weaving through different groups. I duck behind a huge display and peer out, only to see someone heading my way.

I keep running in and out of rooms, losing whomever it is after a while, because the next time I stop and peek, no one is following me.

Except Luckster, a.k.a. Krystall Nykkolls, who calls to me from above, then jumps down from some display and tackles me to the ground, clovering me with a spike in my chest.

Screaming while plucking it out, I hear "Leprechaun chasing rainbows," as Krystall / Luckster runs off, her evil laugh shuddering down my spine. I wonder if that's really the way she sounds since I don't recall ever actually talking to her, or they're programming our Ear-Bots to hear her like that. Probably why we thought she was a guy the whole time.

Mark-Bot announces my clovering as I hold back my tears and try to catch my breath. When I can talk again, I summon Jiro through a Walkie-Bot.

"I still at Blue Angel," he says.

I rush back there, and we go through every single key, finally landing on the right one. As soon as we open the case, a blaring alarm sounds.

"Get the coin!" I shout.

Jiro coaxes it out from inside the guitar and throws it at me. I completely miss and chase it as it lands and rolls away. Unsure why he didn't just keep it, I dive for it, sliding through someone's legs…but not quit making it. Bowling them over, I catch the coin just before it disappears under a curtain, and then turn onto my side, tucking it into my belly bag. Just as I do, someone picks me up and puts me on my feet.

“Miss, come with us,” a guard says, and he pulls me along with him.

Mark-Bot announces my fifteen seconds countdown has started, elimination in my near future, but then Ollie comes out of nowhere and kicks the guard’s shin, pulling me the other way and almost wrenching my arm from its socket.

“Thanks,” I breathe, and he nods.

We run to another floor and all around like maniacs, going in different directions and to other levels. When we finally meet outside at the center spot for the Vermilion Hour, everyone’s there, even a drugged Keondra, and I look at Camila her true friend still propping her up with new eyes. As Mark-Bot starts counting down our time, we put the four coins together and form our firescope with ten luxurious seconds to spare. We all thank God this time that we don’t need to face another random elimination as I ponder his existence and if he’s really helping us. But then, why are we in this predicament in the first place?

Our secret destination to complete the round is the Whiskey Island Marina, which is a mile east of the Museum according to our maps. Camila grabs the firescope first and starts running toward a huge clock that strikes noon, getting a decent head start. Suddenly, she throws the scope into traffic and drops to the ground, rolling onto her side with her hands on her ears, screaming, "Ahhh! The polka music! Make it stop!"

An auditory hallucination. She's out for a minute.

Ollie darts after the firescope, but after he gets it, he trips on a grate in the street and the scope flies out of his hands, skittering to the sidewalk.

Keondra flies out of nowhere and pounces on it.

She takes off running toward Whiskey Island, her adrenaline likely knocking her out of her stupor, and we all follow, except Camila. She's still writhing on the ground with her hands over her ears, begging for the obnoxious music to stop. Keondra crosses an intersection, cutting off a cab driver who slams on his brakes. She suddenly throws the scope behind her and takes off in a different direction, screaming that she's being chased by a swarm of bees.

I catch it and turn to run. Ollie swoops in and grabs it from me before I have a good grip, and he breaks away. Jiro comes out of nowhere and trips him, attacking him and yanking the scope from his fingers. Paige darts in front of me, and she stabs a stick through Jiro's calf, hobbling him. She snatches the scope.

Ollie goes after her and easily wrestles it away, shoving her aside. She stumbles over a low wall into a snowdrift.

I chase Ollie, unsure I really want to catch him, if I want him or me to be victorious because I know if I am, it'll be hard to lose him. But my survivor instincts kick in, and I race after him. He's way faster than me when he gets his momentum, and I slow after a while because I have no chance.

Sighing in defeat, my sister Davina's face flashes before me, and I identify with her again, realizing how she must have felt each time I left her in the dust.

But then Ollie keels over and goes down, holding his hands over his goggles. I'm not sure if he got a glitch or it's his TBI, but I rush forward and take the scope now. With Keondra and Camila in my periphery, I race toward the finish line. Just as I'm about to hand it to a guy who resembles Robbie O'Grady with short flipped brown hair and freckles standing in front of Whiskey Island Marina, Keondra and Camila tackle me.

My knee cracks against the ground and I keel forward. As my hands hit the pavement, I see something orange in my fingers. Holding it up, I realize I just somehow pulled off someone's Covid-28 mask. Glancing back, I find it was Camila's, and her goggles are askew so that most of her face is revealed. Cursing, she snatches the mask from me while Keondra and I struggle for the scope.

Keondra gets it, but I wrestle it from her one hand, using my feet and teeth and nails, giving it everything I've got. She's unable to fight me off with her other hand since it's missing. I grab the thin gold cylindrical scope and give it to the Robbie O'Grady imposter, who nods and walks away with it. As he disappears into the marina, Mark-Bot announces that I am the winner of Round 3, Robbie's Challenge, as Keondra's and Camila's cursing fill my ears.

My dance enemies let everyone know the whole way back to Home Base that it was bullshit that I won, that I just got lucky because Ollie flaked out again, just like when Sammy claimed the first round. They bitch up a storm, demanding they be granted a do-over. They don't acknowledge that I beat them both in the end, like at the tryouts for the job at Miss Sylvia's.

They help Jiro along, who's limping since Paige stabbed him. He'll be healed during Nap Time by the Soldier-Bots, but now winces and sucks air between his teeth like he's in great pain. Camila requests meds from Karyn-Bot again, but she's either busy or ignoring Camila. Paige walks behind them with her head bowed, muttering she's sorry and she hopes Jiro can forgive her.

Did Ollie's TBI resurface again, or did he have a glitch like Camila and Keondra did? I try to ask him, but he seems dazed like before, like he doesn't know anything about The Game or what just happened.

When we reach Home Base, this time wrapped with an ad for the newest model Hollaphone, this one with a super-singing mode, Paige gets into bed and rolls over with her back to me, and then so does Ollie. Even when I try to ask if he's okay, he waves me off, grumbling he's tired and just wants to sleep.

I stew about it in bed for a while, feeling like everyone is mad at me for winning.

Karyn-Bot interrupts me feeling sorry for myself, announcing that Luckster failed in his mission to clover us all, and this time she chops his left hand off. When he screams like a girl, I know it's because he's really Krystall Nykkolls, another captive, forced to come after us to save her own life, and I have mixed feelings as I listen to her wailing.

My mind goes back and forth from my teammates angry with me to Krystall now suffering, but then when I'm half asleep, waiting for the Med-Bots to deliver their drugs, I feel someone curl around me. A second later, I realize Ollie's muscular form is wrapped about me like we're lovers.

"Hey!" I jump up and twist around, pushing him away.

He catches my hand and laces his fingers through mine. "Sorry, didn't mean to scare you. Just wanted to let you know I'm better. Didn't mean to blow you off before. You were trying to talk to me, right?"

I nod, and Blake flashes through my mind. I withdraw my hand from Ollie's. "I wanted to check if you're okay. TBI again?"

He shakes his head. "I don't think so. No, this was like bright lights everywhere, so blinding I didn't know which way to go. I'm not sure that was my head injury or a visual hallucination one of the VIPs gave me, because I never had anything like *that* before."

Did the VIPs think I'm a weaker one and didn't bother giving me a glitch? Now that I'm technically the leader since only Sammi had a win and she's eliminated, I expect they're going to come at me full force. Luckily, they can only do two glitches per game, but I need to be ready. "How long did it last?"

He shrugs. "Hard to say."

"You're okay now though?"

He nods and smiles. "Totally. More than okay." He puts his arm around me and pulls me to him, nestling my head under his chin so that I'm resting on his massive chest.

“Uh, okay,” I say, momentarily enjoying the closeness, but then I push him away again. “Um, I have a boyfriend.”

“Yeah? What’s his name?”

I bite my lip. “I’d rather not talk about him. But just letting you know —”

Ollie grabs my hand and squeezes it. “Look, I understand that you do, and I have someone too, but we may never see them again. All I know is the thought of losing you to this game if I win…” He closes his eyes, and when he opens them again, they’re wet. “It’s very confusing. Part of me wants to let you win.” He lifts my hand to his lips and kisses my fingers. “It’s crazy talk, I know, but I also know how I feel right here with you.” He sighs with contentment, his chest rising and falling.

I do too, which is why I pull away again. I can’t let myself care, only to maybe lose him very soon. The thought brings tears to my eyes, and he pulls me to him again, stroking my hair as I let go and cry into his chest, all my emotion since this whole thing started catching up with me, but then I realize by me leaning on Ollie, I’m leading him on. I push away and move to the side of the bed, wiping my eyes. “I’m sorry, but let’s just keep it professional. We’re opponents in The Game. Let’s keep it to that, and only that. It’s for the best.”

Ollie pouts. “Okay, but please promise me this. If you should win, will you get a message to my siblings from me? Tell them I love them, and I have stolen some money from the Darby’s for them. It’s about twenty-five thousand dollars. I need you to tell Meg, the oldest, where it is, and she’ll know what to do. Make sure to tell Weaver too or Meg might squander it with her buddies.”

“I thought you didn’t have enough for Meg’s legal fees.”

He scrunches his face at me. “Huh?”

“You said Meg fell in with the wrong crowd and stole some jewelry.”

"Oh, right. That. Well, the fees could be more than that, and I'd rather have the money to support us, so I'll figure that out after. Them escaping before the Darby's put them all in foster care is more important. Tell Meg I said that."

I think of Paige's little sister Kimmy at the mercy of her foster parents right now and agree.

Ollie tells me that Celia has been hiding money in a secret panel behind her mirrored shoe carousel, which he found when cleaning all her heels. He put it all in a tacklebox in the farthest shed, the one with the green roof, behind some old paint no one ever uses, days before the tour.

"But Meg is only thirteen, right? How can she take care of everyone?"

"She's already doing it. And Weaver and Candace too. It'll be better than now, where they're slaves to the Darby's. They're better together than apart."

"I guess. Well, of course I'll get them the message if I win and watch out for them. Whatever I can do." Right then, I want Ollie to win, so he can help them. But then what about Paige's sister Kimmy? Or Davina and my parents? How will they be if I die in addition to whatever happens with Zayde?

I remind myself that only one in Vermilion can win. Glancing over at Paige asleep in her bed, I know I care about her too and don't want her to die. And I don't even know who Camila, Keondra, and Jiro are leaving behind. My heart aches with the agony of each win and what it will mean for everyone else and the people who love them.

Ollie leans over. "I'll get you the address tomorrow. Thank you, Mallory. You're a good friend." He kisses me softly on the lips before slipping away and climbing up to his bunk.

I close my eyes thinking of how wonderful his kiss felt for that brief instant and allow myself just a little bit of happiness for the first time in a long while, shooing reality away for a spell. I revel in Ollie's wonderfully masculine scent left all over my blanket and pillow until the Soldier-Bots deliver my sleepy drugs.

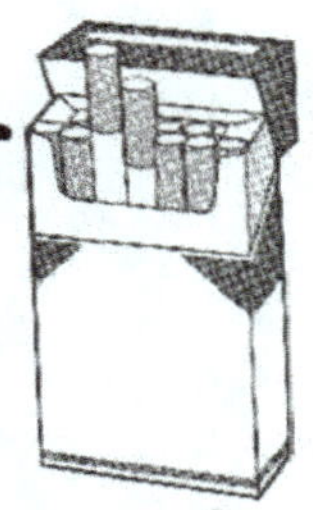

# PART 9

## DAVINA GETS A KISS TOO

**Saturday, January 19, 2030**

Niyah and Antonia come over early Saturday morning to bring me breakfast and catch up. I yawn, tired from being up so late last night with Snake. It took the Rebel Demons a while to let us know everything was okay, that they outnumbered the Eastside Boyz two to one when they showed, and those guys took off. Rocco texted Snake late to say they'd meet the next day, and I didn't get home until after midnight, nor did I meet him.

"Hey," Niyah says, "I don't know if you have been watching the news, but — "

I hold up my hand. "No, on purpose. It's just really getting out of hand with all that RainBO PranXterz stuff and the conspiracy theories and everything. People are using their situation as an excuse to pull pranks all over. It's ridiculous, all those copycats. Just sickening."

"So, then you didn't hear about the latest twist?" Niyah asks.

"What? There are so many, I can't keep it straight."

"Well, they were last spotted at the Detroit Zoo people think, and after stealing some kid's asthma inhaler, and mugging some zoo worker and knocking him out, they dove into the polar bear tank."

I scrunch my brow. "What?" I play dumb, knowing it all has to do with The Game and getting those coins that Snake told me about. And I had been at Beaumont Hospital, maybe two miles away from the Zoo where Mallory was! She was that close to me, and I had no idea.

Maybe that whole twin thing isn't true after all. My heart sinks, and I sigh, my glimmer of hope extinguished.

"And then this dude dressed like a leprechaun tries to attack one of them under the water, coming out of nowhere. All these spectators caught shots of the struggle from the glass tunnel under the tank, and then others saw them unmask the leprechaun — who looks like that one on the box of Luckster Gems — and you'll never believe who it was."

I shake my head. "No clue. Don't make me guess. Who?"

"Luckster the Leprechaun was none other than Krystall Nykkolls."

My jaw practically falls off as my mind tries to piece it together, wondering how she fits in. The Rebel Demons are VIPs in The Game, and they were after her. Did they get her and donate her to those running The Game, or are they the ones behind everything? Is Snake's story of innocence and recruiting me to seduce his brother somehow part of this too? My head swarms with questions all contradicting everything I thought I knew until I don't know what to do. "What the hell?"

"Everyone is shocked," Antonia says. "They've been talking about it nonstop ever since. No one knows how she's involved, but now the police have been knocking on the Rebel Demons' door again since they were after her. They're still playing dumb."

"And yesterday," Niyah adds, "the Missing Tech Nine were spotted at the Rock & Roll Hall of Fame, or at least, people think it was them."

I scrunch my brow. "In Ohio?"

Antonia nods. "Yeah. Some people there dressed in rainbow clothes made the security guards chase them all around the museum and were messing with displays and exhibits and stuff, but it could've been copycats. Everybody's dressing like them now and doing weird shit. One of them even gave an acceptance speech for Mick Jagger from the Rolling Stones at some awards show. People are posting the pranks they've done on a new InstaTok RainBO PranXterz channel, like it's become a copycat pranksters contest. And now someone's even advertising a First Annual RainBO PranXterz Fest."

"You serious?" I ask, shaking my head. "That's crazy. People are freaking nuts."

"Agreed. And get this," Antonia says. "I even saw ads on TV to get your 'RainBO PranXterz Separates' at New Navy and Hallister and several other stores. Everyone's trying to make a buck off them."

I attempt to take the news in stride in addition to the new involvement by Krystall Nykkolls, wondering where they're going next. I need to meet Rocco sooner rather than later and somehow get him interested in me. I must get to that next round to save my sister and hopefully the others too, now maybe even Krystall, unless she's somehow in on whoever took Mallory and the others. Jonah and I haven't quite figured out how we'll rescue them once we get there, but we'll have to come up with something. I can feel it in my bones, a sudden inferno raging through me, anger and determination like never before. It could all be bullshit, part of something I don't yet understand, but I must take a chance. What are the alternatives?

I consider telling my friends the truth. But then I'd also have to share with them about the whole Eastside Boyz thing and Snake's letter, and what if Antonia says something to her cousin Carlos who works at a biker bar? Who knows what could happen? No, I can't say a thing yet, if ever. It wouldn't help, and why involve them? I don't want to get Snake killed or have anything bad happen to them for knowing about The Game.

Antonia and Niyah fill me in on stuff from school and I get lost in the normalcy of it all, a welcome reprieve. Then, I tell them about my mom a little, finding out from Dad that she's more coherent now, but very sad and worried. They're still going to keep her awhile for therapy and to make sure she's stable enough to release.

"I'm so sorry for everything," Niyah says. "The news is just insane with all their theories. I think it's better you don't watch it. We'll keep you up on anything important, okay?"

"I haven't been. And yeah, thanks. That would be great."

"Well ladies, it's been real," Niyah says, getting up and discarding her paper plate. "I got a huge Calc exam on Monday and must meet my study group. Text ya' later, k?" She bends over to kiss us both on our cheeks and grabs her bookbag, slinging it over her shoulder.

Antonia and I say goodbye to her and go up to my room, laying with the dogs on my bed while I play some No Ice Cream for Ian, who Antonia loves even more than me. We discuss other things about school, especially Nerd Bowl which Niyah isn't on.

"Oh, Isaac's been asking about you. Says he texted a few times and you haven't responded."

I sigh. "Yeah. I'm just not sure what to do about him, and he's messaging more than ever now, way more than a few times, acting like my concerned 'boyfriend.'" I air quote and grimace. "I've answered minimally, letting him know I'm busy with family things, but he's just not getting the message. He's still after me."

We dissect the situation, both on our stomachs with our knees bent and feet up, and the suggestions of what to do to get him to stop asking me out get sillier and sillier until I'm practically crying. I've never been in such a situation, and I know I'm handling it badly, and that I should just be more up-front. But when I think of doing that, I worry about his hurt expression and that he'll end up hating me. I know that's selfish, but I'm chicken. And then what about Nerd Bowl?

"Oh, come on!" I giggle after Antonia says we should make up a girl online and catfish him to lure his attention elsewhere. "Now, that's just wrong. We can't do that!"

"Is it though?" she laughs. "I mean, you said being with him was like kissing wet clay. That's reason enough."

We come up with more ideas, even worse than that, and it feels so good for the first time in a week to smile, to let loose. Antonia rolls over and looks at me, and I'm about to move away and sit up when she kisses me. Like, full on with tongue and everything. She rolls on top of me and pins me down.

I wriggle out from under and push her away. "I'm sorry, but I'm not —"

Antonia's face turns beet red as she slides from the bed and pops up to her feet, adjusting her shirt while staring at her shoes. "Sorry." She grabs her bag and rushes out the door.

"Wait, Antonia! Don't go. Please. Let's talk about this! Don't leave!"

The front door slams.

By the time I get down to the foyer, she's starting her car. I whip open the front door to find her backing down the driveway. "Antonia!"

What just happened? I watch her car disappear around the corner, then close the door, back into the living room, my heart thudding in my ears. I had no idea she felt that way about me, or about girls in general. I plop on the couch sighing. As I struck Archie on my lap, I try to process it. Antonia always talked about liking various guys at school, especially Trystan who she pined away for since he moved here in seventh grade. Of all my friends, she was the most boy crazy. Was it all fake? Or is it just me she's attracted to? How do I handle it? I wish I could ask Mallory. She'd know what to do.

God, I miss my sister so much, I realize, which is such a surprise. I stare at our family picture on the wall, with Zayde standing behind Mallory at Mom's insistence, not wanting him to be alone his first Chanukah without Bubbe last year. I practically drown in the tears that spew from nowhere.

Suddenly, Jonah is at my door in his cowboy disguise, saying he was in the neighborhood, which is so not true since Grandpa's Farm is a good forty minutes away without traffic. After I reprimand him because he's supposed to be hiding, have him put his bike in the garage, and invite him in before anyone can see, he offers me a bandana from his pocket. "It's clean. You okay?"

I realize he's the only one whom I have right now besides Niyah, whom I can't tell about everything. Or maybe I can, I don't know. It's a lot to put on her though, and I won't share with her about Antonia, her friend too, and betray Antonia's confidence like that. Now things are weird with Antonia, and I'm not sure if I should text her or what. I fill Snake in on what happened, and he cringes. "Man, that sucks. You ain't had a clue?"

I shake my head. "No way. Super shocked over here. I didn't mean to hurt her, and now she's all embarrassed."

"Maybe just tell her the truth, that you love her, but you ain't gay. Let her know you all acceptin' and shit. She'll be cool. I'm sure of it."

"And I am. I just hope it doesn't make things different between us. She's been one of my closest friends since second grade when she moved here."

"I hope it don't."

We talk some more, and then Jonah suggests we watch some more *Sons of Anarchy* while getting ready for tonight.

"Tonight. Why? What's going on?"

"Oh, you're gonna' meet Rocco at Blades Cave. It's Potluck Night. We need to bring some grub. Know how to cook?"

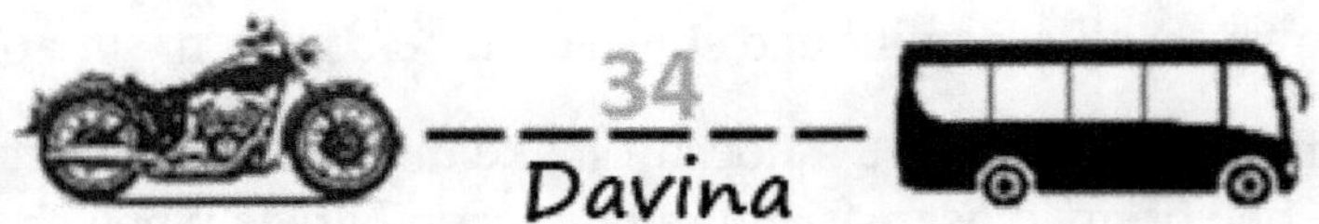


We make vegan lasagna by following directions we find online, and it turns out decent, although a bit runny and jiggly. While I'm wrapping it in foil, Jonah tells me how the police keep coming by, questioning Rocco about that Krystall Nykkolls, who is somehow part of whatever's going on with those RainBO PranXterz, a.k.a, Missing Tech Nine, if it was really them at the zoo.

"I overheard Rocco tell Dad he didn't want to go anymore. Said they're getting too much heat about Krystall."

My stomach crashes as this new possibility dawns on me, that the whole Krystall situation may affect Rocco's participation, which could also stop me from rescuing Mallory. "So, now he's not going?" I look down the lasagna. "Why'd we make this?"

"No, Dad set him straight. Reminded him that he's gotta' represent and make Zeke look good. He can't wuss out."

"Your dad's a smart man," I say, and then I wonder if he's the one who came up with the whole plan to kidnap my sister and the others. And if they are running things, does Jonah know or not?

"Okay, so come on. We gotta' get on the road."

I run and change, dressing this time in my ripped jeans and one of my cut and beaded t-shirts, this one saying "Beautiful Badass" surrounded in a frame of roses and daggers.

Jonah gives me the once over and grins. "Perfect. But slouch more. Hold them belt loops with your thumbs. You're too straight up. Oh hey, I picked these up. Do you think you can try one? They'll make you look way more legit." He pulls out a pack of those Nosingarettes, the new healthy cigarettes that deliver vitamins and nutrients instead of toxic chemicals.

I back away. "Ew, no, I don't think I could. I might throw up. And besides, they blow turquoise smoke, so everyone will know."

"Not these. They're new. They look just like regular cigs."

"Don't they smell different?"

"Yeah, but it'll be so smoky, he ain't gonna tell. Try one."

I sigh. "I don't know. I think I might die." We go outside where the sun is setting, and I take one from his pack. Putting it to my lips, I try to stop them from quivering.

"Hold still." He attempts to light the tip, but it moves too much.

I steady it with my other hand. After a few tries, he gets it lit. Of course, I hack up a lung the first time, and the second, but I keep Mallory in my mind, and her doing who knows what at the Rock and Roll Hall of Fame, forced to play some deadly game. Eventually, Jonah says I'm passable by taking little puffs without inhaling.

"Hold it more than smoke it, cool? A'right, let's go."

I attempt to follow Snake into the house, but suddenly my head is a helium balloon, and I fall forward.

Jonah catches me before I wipe out. "Slow down, Lucy girl. Nosingarettes get you light-headed at first."

I roll my eyes. "A little warning might have been nice."

Snake bares his adorable fangs. "Sorry. I ain't never taught nobody how to smoke before."

Suddenly, I notice all the beautiful colors on his snake tattoo since I'm so close. "Wow, Lola is sure pretty. I never really looked. Did it hurt?" Noticing the raised and uneven scars in the middle of the brilliant colors of purple, yellow, blue, and black, I reach forward, but then stop, suddenly self-conscious.

Jonah catches my fingers and guides them gently to his brow. "Yeah, hurt like hell. Mom got me all high and drunk, making me pot brownies and giving me a few beers. Said I ain't allowed to do none of that again until I'm thirty. Helped though. Why? You gettin' one?"

"Oh, no way. I couldn't. I can't even get up the guts to get my ears pierced. I'm terrified of needles."

"Yeah? I ain't too thrilled with them neither. Got my Rebel Demons tattoo when I was four. Hurt like hell.."

I touch his forehead where Lola's tongue spikes into his brow. "Wow, this part must've really killed."

He sucks in a breath. "Yeah, it did. But you get through it. And now look. I got me pretty girl Lola and her Slither Smile with me for the resta' my life."

Suddenly the ugliness of Snake's tattoo transforms into the most beautiful thing I've ever seen, and it makes me grin and remember when I was so down on him for it. Things are surely different when you can see them up close and know their truth. I trace around the various markings that reticulate his beloved python, stroking his pierced brow. "It's really spectacular."

Jonah takes my hand in his. "Thanks. And now, we gotta go." He still has his arm around me from my little meltdown, his other hand holding mine, and makes no move to change position. I peer into his beautiful dark eyes and lick my lips, our mouths an inch apart.

He drops his arms and steps away, his cheeks reddening as he avoids my gaze. "Uh, yeah, we gotta' focus on Rocco. You and *Rocco*."

"Right," I say, looking at my shoes. I wipe my eyes. "I'm just emotional. It's been a lot."

"I gotcha', and I'm here. I owe you big time."

"No, you don't. I totally understand and forgive you, for the record. I never told you that. I know you didn't mean to hurt my parents, and when Mom's home a bit and up to it, I will give them the letters and convince them how sincere you are, and they'll forgive you too. I'm sure of it." And I mostly mean it, although a little part of my mind still harbors doubt, holding onto my past feelings about him and his family.

He smiles. "Thanks. That would be cool. We'll talk about that after saving your sister. Let's focus on that." He moves further away from me, shoving his hands into his pockets. "And *only* that."

I get his meaning with a full-on blush and follow him out to his bike. The whole way to Blades Cave, as I hug Snake, pressing my cheek to his leather and inhaling his Drakkar Noir, I tell myself that it's awful instead of unbelievably great and try to convince myself he's not the nice, sweet, caring, and smart guy I've just discovered, that he's really a talented actor playing a part in a play whose plot I don't yet know.

Is this all payback to my parents for putting Snake in juvie? I force myself to think about that instead. By the time we arrive, I realize I was so distracted attempting to ignore or discredit Jonah that I haven't a clue what to do about Rocco. And now it's showtime, and I'm on.

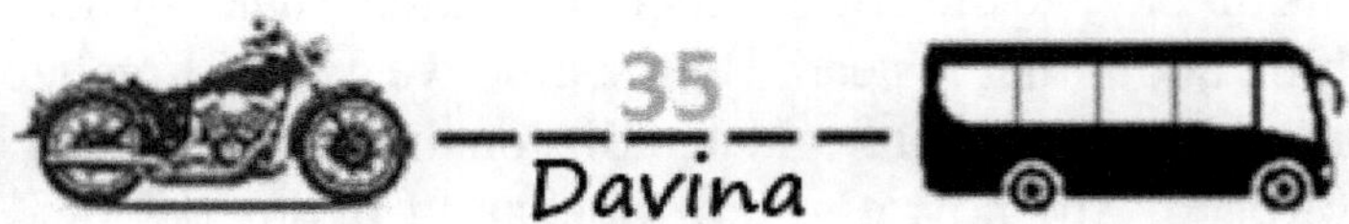


The music's kicking when we enter Blades Cave. I see Swastika Dude first, his stupid Hitler tattoo prominent on his beefy arm. He wears his leather vest without a shirt underneath in the middle of winter just to show it off. I look away, my cheeks on fire, my tongue burning to say something but knowing, like Snake said, it wouldn't make a difference to someone like him and would out me as a non-biker chick. I need to focus on Rocco, who I still haven't met. Mallory's life depends on it.

When we emerge onto the porch with our drinks, Jonah points out Rocco. Squinting through the dim light as day becomes night, I do find him attractive, but not nearly as much as his younger brother.

I mentally slap myself for the natural comparison and try to appreciate Rocco's good qualities. He's taller and thinner than Jonah, more muscular, but they have the same features, the same cute fangs. Rocco's face is more mature with gaunter cheeks and curlier hair, slicked back with lots of product. He has a scruffy beard and a skull dangling from his ear. Thick silver rings on his fingers remind me of brass knuckles gangsters wear in the movies.

Rocco sits at a stool at the outdoor bar, cigarette in hand, surrounded by three girls in getups like what I'm wearing but with way bigger boobs. Each tries to edge the others aside, vying for Rocco's attention, each swaying her hips to the music as they chat with him. They flick their cigarettes, swig their beers, and fluff their hair as they laugh and flirt and touch his shirt, feeling his arms and his chest and giving him little kisses every chance they get.

Shit.

"How the heck am I going to compete with *that*?" I hiss in Snake's ear.

"Man, they be swarming more than I thought. Word's been out awhile now about Shailene dumping him, but he's been away on club business a lot until now." He offers me a Nosingarette. I take it, and he lights it for me. "Well, I can break in and introduce you, but then you gotta' keep him interested. Ask him to dance."

I snort. "Seriously? That's the plan?"

"Yeah. Why, ain't you no good?"

"Have you seen me dance?"

"No, but ain't your twin sister a dancer?"

"Yeah. But we think she's adopted, even Mom. We have no idea why she can dance. The rest of us have three left feet."

Jonah laughs and points behind me. "Well, do what that girl is doing. Just bop your hips like her, side to side. You think you can do that shit?"

I look, and she doesn't seem too advanced. I could try to copy that. I shrug. "Okay. But what do I say?"

"Just get on his good side. Say what others say, but like different. Your own way."

"Okay. You're not allowed to leave though. Help me if I choke."

Jonah grins. "Okay. Let's go before more girls squeeze in. Look at them chicks in the corner about to pounce. Porch is a-hoppin'."

My skin prickles with nerves as Snake parts the sea of hovering biker girls to introduce me, the biggest fake ever.

There's no way I can pull this off.

Snake leans in and does some sort of macho handshake with his brother, and then he whispers something in Rocco's ear and turns to me.

Rocco's eyes roam up and down me unabashedly, his long lashes on his cheeks as he checks out my lower half. He grins with Jonah's same teeth. "Hey, Lucy. How you doin'?"

"Fine, Sugar," I say, and it sounds so ridiculous, Rocco laughs.

I nearly gag from his smoke breath, but I cover it with the sexiest grin I can muster.

"So, you saw me at the Hell Fire Rally, huh?"

I lean close, under the nose of another girl who is trying to nudge her way in, drowning in his smoky stench. "You were by far the hottest guy there. How'd you get so much cuter than your brother?"

He squints at me, a slow smile breaking across his lips. "Are you for real?"

I nod. "Totally, I – "

"Hey, Baby. Been waiting for me?" Some girl swoops in out of nowhere and grabs Rocco around the neck with her long red claws, dragging him onto the dance floor. "It's our song!"

I turn to find one of the most beautiful girls I've ever seen dancing with Rocco way better than I could ever dream. Her chest is huge, bursting out of her leather bustier, and she shakes her hips and grinds into him, her spiked heel boots making her jeaned legs seem miles long. Her face itself, heavily made up under the wide brim of a cowboy hat, is so attractive, you know it looks that good even without all that gunk. She smiles with the self-assurance of a girl who knows that she's hands down the most attractive woman in the room and always is.

"Wow," is all I can say, totally mesmerized. "Who the heck is *that*?"

"Oh, that's Trish. I thought she was Hazzard's old lady, but guess they broke up." He glances to the side. "Yep, he's over there in the corner near Breaker and Cody shooting them the stink-eye."

I turn to find the one with the name badge saying Hazzard glaring at them. "Trish? What planet did she descend from? She's like hot enough to be on the cover of Biker Babes Magazine. Is there such a publication?"

Snake shrugs. "Not sure. Yeah, she's hot and knows it. So, do like her, only better."

"Sure, I could try, but she's like the real deal, and clearly has his eye."

Another girl thinner than Trish even, wearing a shiny black bodysuit with cutouts all over, comes up shaking herself against Rocco's side, and suddenly he turns and dances with her. Then, another girl pulls him in another direction, and then it's like he's on a crazy biker girl merry-go-round. All sorts of women come out of the woodwork to pull him over to dance.

"Shit, this is way serious. I didn't think I'd have *this* much competition."

Jonah bites his lip. "Yeah, I ain't neither. We need do something better."

I peer down at peeling deck boards. "I can teach them all about trig proofs, I guess."

"Oh, Davina, ain't no offense. Believe me." Jonah comes close and whispers in my ear. "To me, you're the coolest girl here. We just gotta get Rocco seein' that, but how he likes."

Tingles overtake my body, and I gaze into Jonah's dreamy eyes, my breath suddenly gone. Picturing Mallory and reminding myself of my goal, I force my gaze away. "I hear you, but what can I possibly do?"

Jonah shrugs. "Ain't sure. Don't know you that well, but you're all like into school and stuff. No offense."

"None taken. It's true. You don't have to beat around the bush. I'm the least likely person to fit into such a group. I wish it could be my sister Mallory. She could be all sexy and dance and stuff. I can do math. That's it. And she kicks my ass in that too. Mallory always does better than me, pretty much in everything I do, and now, she's not the only one."

Jonah tips up my chin and smiles. "It ain't no competition, between you and her. You're your own cool chick with your own shit. I'm sure of it. And I be sure you much more than that too, just knowin' 'bout math, and that ain't nothing to sneeze at no how. But Rocco, yeah, he's more into stupid stuff. Superficial."

"I see that. Okay, I'll have to think about how to be more about stupid stuff."

Suddenly, the music changes. The jukebox kicks up while the band walks off for a break, and some people leave the dance floor while others enter. Everyone remaining forms into a grid. That old Hustle song comes on, and suddenly Swastika Dude gets into the front of the room and leads the group. Although the people behind him are pretty good, each adding a little flair here and there to the line dance, Swastika Dude is way better than any of them, and after a while, people clear a circle, and he freestyles in between everyone.

"Go Breaker! Go Breaker!" Several clap along while others pump their fists.

Swastika Dude does some breakdancing in the middle, eventually performing a backspin into a twisted sideways backbend while people cheer and whistle.

"What the hell?" I blink, thinking I must be hallucinating. "Swastika Dude can *breakdance*? That's unexpected."

"Yeah," Jonah says. "That's why he's called Breaker. Dude does this every time too. Kinda his thing. He even teaches country line dancing here twice a week. Many them old ladies come, but some of the guys too."

"How odd. Really? I thought his name was Breaker because he beat people up." I look at him again, still seeing red, but it adds another unexpected layer to him. As he moves effortlessly across the floor, whirling each girl around and catching onto the next, I realize even though I hate his guts and everything he stands for, he's a fabulous dancer. I must give him props at least for that. I wonder what Mallory would think. And it makes me realize no one is all bad and no one is all good, or at least, he has one redeeming quality despite everything else I know about him that I despise.

And then I glance over at Jonah. Every time I do, it takes my breath away. I never thought I'd be attracted to someone who looks like *that*, with a huge tattoo all over his neck and head and part of his face. I had misjudged him so completely, saying I could never understand why anyone would ever mark themselves up like that and thinking he was so awful for so many things. He had a good excuse for almost all of them and a great reason to tattoo his beloved Lola onto his scarred skin.

He apologized for never thanking me for saving him, and I liked that he also promised my parents to pay them back for the surgeries and stuff. He has been so sincere and just different in every way than I assumed by looking at him. I know that old saying about never judging a book by its cover, and I realized I did judge him the way Swastika Dude judges incorrectly about everyone, and it was wrong of me in the very same way. I discriminated against Snake in my mind because I thought I knew who he was the way Swastika Dude thinks he knows who everyone is. *I'm just as guilty.*

And then I realize as I catch Jonah looking my way and smiling that he can't be lying in some ploy to fool me. He really is who he seems, someone I just can't believe.

But I need to focus on Rocco and Mallory. I hate that I must keep reminding myself. Jonah's an unexpected distraction along with the unanticipated major competition I have for Rocco's attention, especially that gorgeous girl Trish. After the music changes and more girls drag Rocco back into the fray, Trish pushes him onto a chair in the middle and gives him a lap dance. I wrack my brain trying to think of any single thing in the whole world that will get his attention more than *that*.

Every girl around me has several prominent tattoos, and suddenly, I tell Snake we need to go and swig back the rest of my drink in one gulp.

"Where? Why?"

"How much money do you have?"

He checks his wallet and says he has forty bucks.

"Good. I have sixty. Will that be enough?"

Snake shrugs, following me. "Enough for what?"

"If I ever want to fit in here, I need a tattoo. You think we can score any vegan pot brownies?"

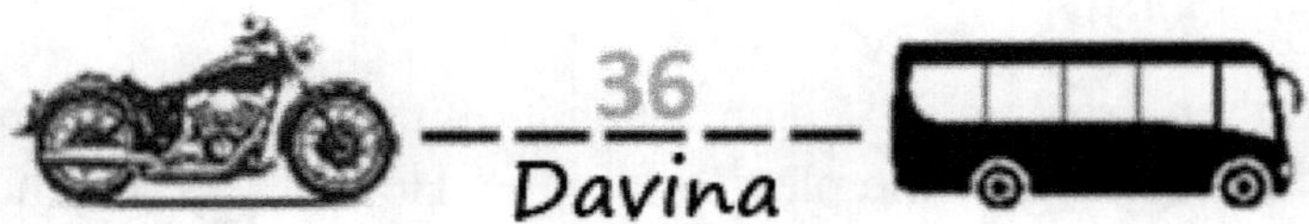

# 36
## Davina

After flipping through the tattoo book for so long the artist is starting to pace, I decide on a pretty rose whose thorny vine spells out Bubbe's initials, BSL, Bethany Sarah Levine.

"What if they start and I can't take it? Will they stop?"

"Of course," Snake says. "But it ain't that bad. You get used to it. I did. Mine took over twenty hours. I went four times."

"Wow, really?" I study his ink more, but the alcohol has started to kick in and I'm seeing double.

"Whoa, you be feeling it, huh?" Snake grins at me, grasping my hands as I start to sway.

I sit down hard on a stool nearby. "Let's get thissso'er wit'," I slur. "How many drinksssid I have?"

"Like two. Man, you's a lightweight. Probably them vegan THC gummies be doin' it too."

"Yeah," I say, and then the tattoo artist comes over and starts, and when he applies his needle to my upper left arm the first time, I feel I'm going to jump out of my skin. My fear of needles from the youngest of ages when I had to get blood tests and vaccines makes me want to run from the room screaming.

As tears prick my eyes, Jonah squeezes my hand hard, then smiles at me and tells me I'm doing great. Every time I wince and look at the door wanting to bolt, he guides my eyes to his with light fingers on my jaw. I stare deep into them like a snake being hypnotized by a Snake.

We stay like that a long while, just taking each other in, while the tattoo artist puts Bubbe's initials forever on my arm. The whole time, I know I may have to return to put Zayde's initials with my grandmother's, but I pray I'll never need to return to put Mallory's too because I'm going to get Rocco's attention somehow, no matter what I need to do. I will get to The Game and save my sister. (The rest of me can't stop imagining what Jonah might look like without his shirt.)

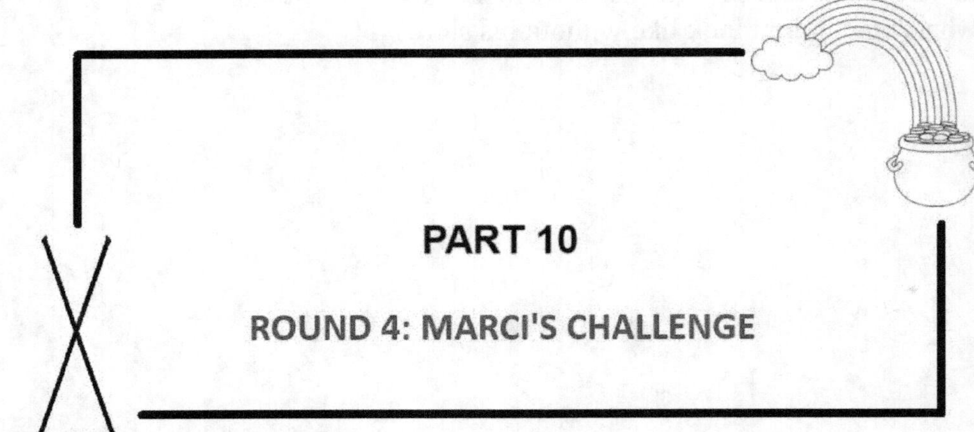

# PART 10

## ROUND 4: MARCI'S CHALLENGE

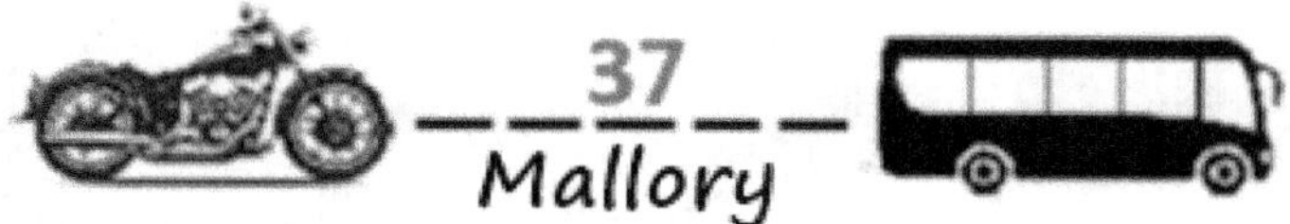


**Monday January 21, 2030**

Mark-Bot wakes us with a loud bell in our ears, saying we have a situation. “Someone has violated Game Warning #1, and their family member will be subject to the Punishment Wheel.”

I peer across at Paige, and she shrugs. Ollie peeks down at me and he shakes his head.

“The person who violated Game Warning #1 was Camila Rodriguez. She lost her mask and goggles during the last challenge and revealed her identity, and now, the one who will pay the price will be someone in her family.”

“But that bitch Mallory tore them off me!” Camila yells in my ear through her Walkie-Bot. “I didn’t mean to show my face!”

“It’s your responsibility,” Mark-Bot warns. “Now, look behind your eyelids as Karyn-Bot spins the Punishment Wheel.”

A wheel with several colored partitions rotates so fast that I can't read the words. It finally stops on "Bone Break" and then Mark-Bot tells us to watch behind our eyelids.

I close my eyes again, my fists tight, afraid of what I will see, especially when the video I'm watching on Karyn-Bot's white screen focuses on a little boy riding his bike.

"No, Paulo! No!" Camila screams from Door Bay.

Ollie hops from his bed and runs over to her.

I close my eyes again, my stomach spewing acid into my throat as Paulo stops at a crosswalk. When the light turns green, he rides ahead slowly, gaining speed, and out of nowhere, a black sedan with dark-tinted windows speeds up and hits him. It swerves around his bent bike and takes off as I hear Camila scream again from Door Bay. "Oh my God! Paulo! Someone please! Please help him!"

I run over to find her in Ollie's arms crying into his chest as he strokes her hair and whispers into her ear. Keondra hugs her from the other side, sobbing into Camila's shoulder, and I realize she has both arms now, somehow rebuilt through the night by the ever-collaborating Soldier-Bots and Med-Bots. Like how Luckster/Krystall had those clovers and new mask suddenly in the bathroom at the Zoo.

"You don't understand! I raised that boy. My parents are always at work. He's like my kid. He can't be —" Camila chokes, unable to continue.

"I'm so sorry, Camila. I really am," I tell her, but she continues crying all over Ollie.

I close my eyes again to find several people including the crossing guard tending to Paulo as he screams in pain. As someone nearby directs a 911 dispatcher from her Hollaphone, I'm reminded of my father in the same situation in his sledding accident in college when he and Mom met.

"He'll be okay," I say, glad so many are there tending to him.

Camila glares at me. "Bitch, what do you know?"

"I'm sorry. Please believe me, I'm so sorry. I hope he'll be okay. I never meant for this to happen." I burst into tears.

"You can fake it all you want. I know what you did, and I'm going to make sure my whole family does too when I beat your ass and win this thing." Camila lunges at me, but Ollie pulls her back, folding her into his arms and trying to comfort her.

"Hey guys, sorry to interrupt," Paige says, coming into Door Bay, "but time is running out, and we need to plan today." She stands next to me. "This time, who knows where we'll be? We should decide who does what and think strategy."

Camila points to me, glaring. "Don't put me with that bitch, and I'm good. Me and Ollie will get the White Tiger."

"Fine," Paige says.

Keondra stands and backs away, crossing her arms and staring at the wall.

"How about me and Keondra do Azure Dragon together?" Paige asks. "That okay with you?"

Keondra nods at her, a green smile touching her lips. "Yeah girl, we gonna' rock it." She high-fives Paige and stands near her.

My stomach churns with the slight, like Paige is suddenly mad at me, or keeping her distance even though I secretly vowed to ignore her and Ollie to focus on winning. But now that they're with others and I'm left with Jiro who barely talks, I'm feeling a bit sorry I thought such a thing. I wonder if Paige is sore at me for winning the last round like everyone else seems to be. I didn't do anything to her, so I'm not sure what her deal is, but as Jiro and I stand near each other and I force a smile, I wonder how we'll work together when he's practically mute.

Ollie says Jiro talks his ear off now that he knows Ollie speaks Japanese, but he doesn't speak much with us, embarrassed at his broken English. Jiro told Ollie he grew up on a rural farm and did homeschool until about a year ago, when his family suddenly moved to the US to help his uncle with his business. Jiro never really talked with English-speaking people, only learned with books and videos.

"So, any ideas for today?" I manage.

He stares at the wall.

I wonder if they'll make me speak Japanese next and pause, waiting for magic words to come forth. They don't. When I can't take the awkward silence between us any longer, I say, “I think we should split up and figure out different paths so that we don’t retrace each other’s steps. We should check in every five minutes and see if we can solve the puzzle. What do you think?”

Jiro doesn’t respond, and I am about to ask if he understood me when Mark-Bot announces the round is beginning.

Home Base stops, and the door whips open. Camila and Keondra step out first, and I hear them saying, “What the hell are we doing *here*?”

Ollie gets out and then Paige and Jiro, and I hear, “This is so weird. I wonder what’s going on tonight?”

“What? Where are we?” And then as I emerge from Home Base into the darkness, surprised it’s not morning like usual, I see some big stadium with a neon lit sign saying Little Caesar’s Arena. “Yeah, so? What is this place?”

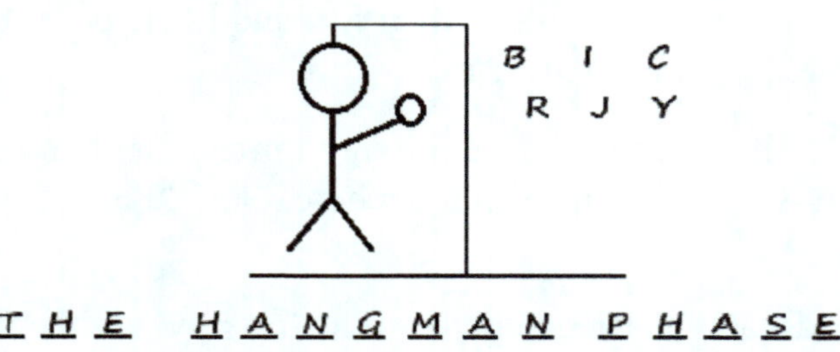


Everyone looks at me.

I shrug, clueless. "What? Is this someplace important?"

"Uh, this is like where the Red Wings and Pistons play," Keondra says like she's explaining two plus two.

"Oh," I say, my cheeks burning. I've never paid attention to sports, nor have anyone in my family, even my dad. He'll watch football when his father or neighbor friends come over just to be polite, but he never does on his own. "So, we have to collect coins in there?" It seems so massive from where we stand, stretching far to our right and left.

"It's gotta be Red Wings since it's January – at least I think it still is," Keondra says, kicking a clump of snow on the ground. "Wonder who they're playing?"

We approach the entrance and Keondra cups her hands, peering through the glass door. "Ooh, the Colorado Avalanche. They're *huge* rivals. It's going to be a big game with lots of fighting players and rowdy fans. My mom is a Wings superfan, always talking smack about the Avalanche and the Blackhawks. She even named my brothers and our pets after her favorite Wings players, and my dad got her a diamond Red Wing necklace for their twentieth anniversary last year. The only way you can get her to stop criticizing and bossing you and be halfway nice is to watch a Red Wings game with her and let her explain it all to you as she records the stats." Keondra laughs. "Let's just say I'm an expert by now."

"Let's get in there," Paige says, whipping open the door to the stadium and approaching the ticket booth. We follow, buy general admission tickets with the money in our belly bags, and then go to our assigned regions.

The seats are mostly filled when Jiro and I find our northern section to locate the Black Tortoise.

"Okay, I'll search rows one through thirteen, and you do fourteen through twenty-six, and then we'll meet here, okay? Find as many clues as you can!"

Jiro nods, and he tries to get into the top row, but the two guys there are out of their seats shouting at the action on the ice, and they don't notice him.

"Edge your way through!" I call. "Make yourself known!"

Jiro just stands there, his head swiveling from me to them and back again.

"Just barge through, like this," I say, running up the steps to him and ramming my shoulder into the guys' bellies like I'm a linebacker. I get by and pull Jiro with me, and we muscle through the next group, and the next and the next, yelling "Excuse me!" while looking everywhere for clues.

"I got one!" Jiro says, holding up a shiny black card.

"Good," I say. "Look at it so it goes into the puzzle board."

We get through the row and collect another clue, and when we reach the aisle, I ask Jiro if he can do the next alone.

He shrugs and tries, but he bounces back as a woman leans forward to reach into her bag.

"Show 'em you mean business!" I push Jiro back and he tries, but no one will let him in.

I finally come along with him again, and it's slow going. After two more rows, we have collected the following letters: G __ __ S __ __ S __ __ __ D __ __ B

"No idea. You?"

Jiro shakes his head. "We look in hall?" He points behind me toward where we entered the section.

"You go, and I'll continue here. There are more clues in these seats, I know it."

"Okay. Ten minutes. Meet there."

I rush off to the front and start in the first row, which is easier because there's extra leg room. But as the game on the ice gets more heated, with countless players hitting the glass and sticks being flung and fists thrown, the more people in the stands yell and stomp and shout. They fight the horrible Avalanche from their seats with their own air punches while I duck below, looking around each one to the seat behind them.

"Excuse me!" An indignant woman scowls at me as I feel around her for a clue, which I locate and snatch up.

"Trying to find my purse," I yell as I rush away. I repeat this more and more as people notice me weaving through their areas as they're yelling for the Red Wings to score.

After about five rows of groping Red Wings fans, I take a breather in the aisle. Jiro approaches. "I know where is. Look."

I close my eyes and see: G __ O S __ I S __ A __ D P __ B.

I shrug. "Not sure."

"Come." He pulls my hand.

We exit into the main hall where there are all types of restaurants, bathrooms, and beer stands. "There!" He points to a sign that says "Goose Island Pub."

I check the puzzle again and grin. "That's it!" I hug Jiro, so thrilled not to have to fight the fans down in the arena anymore. "But *where* in the pub?"

Jiro shrugs. "Don't know. But we go. Time low."

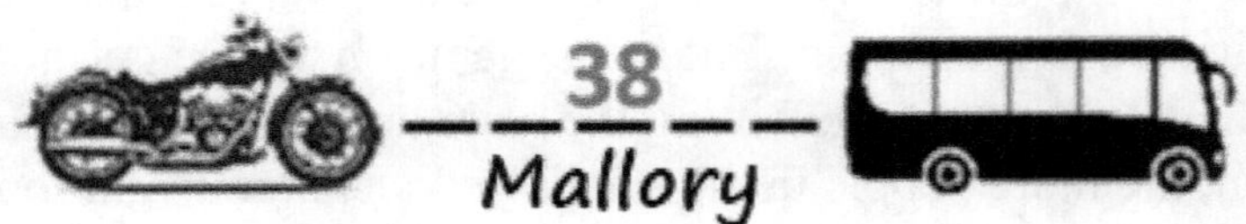

# 38
## Mallory

There's a line to get in, and we try to bypass it, claiming a bathroom emergency. The hostess says only one of us can enter, so I rush inside while Jir waits at the end of the line. I head to the back where she indicated the bathroom is, but when she gets busy with a customer, I bend down, pretending to tie my shoe, and look low, underneath a bar area. I don't see any coins. There are seve tables around, some high, some regular height with chairs, and others situated between padded booth seats. There's also a kitchen area. Oy, this is going to be tough. The coin could be anywhere in only a million places I can see just from this vantage point.

I try the "I lost my earring" excuse this time, which allows me under people's tables and even chairs.

I'm under the third table in a row, trying to find my coin, or rather, "earring," when I hear, "Miss, can I help you?" Glancing up, I find a man in a s with graying temples scowling at me.

"Oh, I was in here earlier, and I lost my good earring. My mother will ki me!" I try to muster tears, but then remember I'm wearing goggles anyway. I plead with him to let me continue searching. How odd they must think I am, dressed like a rainbow and crawling under them while they eat. I'm not sure if I want to crack up or cry.

"Miss, we can't have you crawling around under people while they are trying to eat their meals. Perhaps you can look after the guests clear out, but before then —"

He offers me a hand to help me up. I ignore it but stand as he wants.

"But you no understand!" Jiro says, coming up suddenly. "She need to give mother earring back! Her mother dying. Need earring to be happy. Hand down whole set to daughter. You see?"

The manager shakes his head. "I'm sorry for your mother, but I cannot have you —" He reaches over and touches my shoulder to guide me away from the guests who are all gawking.

I scoot away from him. “Don’t you touch me. I’m going.” I walk several feet with the manager behind me, but suddenly, I break to the side and run away from him. Shoving through the swinging doors to the kitchen, I allow myself a brief smile as they crash back into the manager behind me, eliciting a satisfying “oomph.”

The tantalizing aroma of oven-fresh garlic bread and baked pasta practically knocks me off my feet, my aching hunger almost bringing me to my knees. Those protein bars I’ve been living on just aren’t cutting it.

Several people in white immersed in various stages of food prep glance at me as my eyes sweep the scene for the Black Tortoise coin.

“Miss, you can’t be back here,” one of them says, turning to block me.

I vault across the stainless-steel center prep bench, sliding all the way to the other end and sending a bunch of dishes in every direction. A turkey flies across the aisle but doesn’t quite make it to the other counter, thudding to the floor instead. An approaching chef trips over it and crashes to the ground, throwing the knives he was carrying all around.

As everyone ducks, I skid from the island and spring off the downed chef like he’s a trampoline. The bounciness from his large stomach and my adrenaline propels me up onto the sink. Kicking dishes to the floor, I run my hand over every surface I can, above cupboards and under oven vents, burning my fingers more than once.. Jumping down to the ground, I duck low and peer under tables and counter ledges and anything else I can find as the manager and others keep after me, telling me to leave or they’ll call security.

I eye a walk-in freezer in the back that someone just exited, and I lunge forward to catch the door before it closes. Slipping inside, I paw through frozen fries, chicken fingers, and bags of bread, the image of Sammi clutching her chest and dropping to her knees in my head. I try to be thorough, going through each layer, the horror of what Sammi and Troy and Darla suffered making my heart beat a jillion miles per second as I hear a ticking clock in my ears.

The manager comes in after me, telling me he’s just alerted security and they’re on their way. I ignore him, tearing through all kinds of bags of stuff and flinging them behind me once I see they’re coin-free. The manager fends them off and charges toward me just as I feel the coin inside a pile of hot dog buns. Grabbing it, I stuff it into my pouch as his beefy hand clamps around my wrist.

“Miss, please, leave now so we won’t —"

I yank my arm away as Mike-Bot starts warning about my upcoming demise. "Well, why didn't you ask so nicely like that before?" I leave the freezer with the manager at my heels only to find Luckster there, grinning at me.

"Leprechaun chasing rainbows," she says, lunging at me with her clover.

I sidestep her, and she tags the manager instead.

"Yow!" he howls as a clover spike stabs him in the neck.

I push through a gaggle of gaping kitchen workers and try to get out of there, but something pulls me back.

"Not so fast," one of the chefs says as he grips the collar of my sweatshir Another employee latches onto me, and Mark-Bot gets wind of it and starts counting in my ears again.

I buck and kick like a wild stallion newly mounted, but the chefs who have me are pissed and strong, one bitching about the turkey he'd been cooking all morning becoming airborne. When Mark-Bot reaches five, my life starts flashing before my eyes.

At three, I realize what a bad sister I've been, all the times I'd shown Davina up and gloated whipping through my brain, the realization of my insensitivity such a surprise. At two, I decide I deserve to die.

At one, everything goes white, and I hold my breath, wondering if this sudden white haze is how I start death.

"Come!" someone says and pulls my hand.

The white dissipates as we push through the door, and then I see Jiro is leading me with one hand and holding a red fire extinguisher with his other.

Looking down at my skin covered with white fluff, I realize Jiro just sav my ass, spraying everyone with that stuff.

"I got the coin!" I tell him, and he nods. We rush off, clutching each othe and laughing as the white-sprayed and clovered manager yells for security.

"Oh, that was awful!" I say, peeking behind us as the manager points us out to a few guards.

Jiro nods. "I never go back there."

"Agreed." As we run, I keep cracking up until I can barely see as I recall all the startled expressions of the strangers I just groped or crawled underneath, innocently trying to enjoy their meals or watch hockey.

Suddenly, Keondra's in our ears. "Guys, we need you, especially Mallory. We need more cheerleading maneuvers, and you know I ain't about heights. Get here now." She tells us she's in the south region and they're ready for the Vermilion Bird.

"Already?"

"Yeah. Me and Paige got our coin in a row of screaming fans in this one section under someone's seat, and then Ollie and Camila got theirs from someone's box suite. They pretended to be guests, and no one knew they weren't for long enough to find the coin, which was in the lining under a leather couch in there. They're hiding them coins good this round."

"Yeah. Ours was just in the walk-in freezer of some restaurant, in a bag of hot dog buns," I report.

"That's great. Tell us later. Get here now."

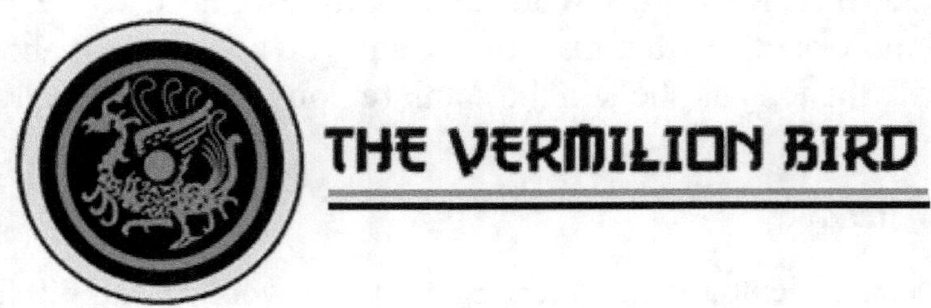


In the south region, we collect clues in the stands of screaming fans again to discover that the Vermilion Bird coin is somewhere in the huge jumbotron above the ice.

"Are you freaking serious?" I look past a guard to the game below and then up to the ginormous digital display above it. "How the hell are we supposed to get all the way up there?" I eye a few cables that lead up to it from each area, connected to the wall somehow but high up.

Camila steps toward Ollie, whose fingers she laces through hers. "We'll go after it," she says, pulling Ollie with her. He shrugs and follows. Suddenly, she's all over him, kissing him through her mask, and he embraces her back, the two of them tornadoes all over the place like Charles and Myra at the Grand Hotel on Mackinac Island.

Ollie and Camila bump into the guard there who is taking tickets for this upper section. The woman pushes them away and tells them they're acting inappropriately. She demands their tickets. They ignore her, Ollie groping Camila in a way that makes me need to turn around. The guard tells them to stop, or she'll call security and have them escorted out of the arena. I turn back as the woman double taps her Hollaphone and it sings "Holla' for your Hollaphone!" and solidifies. Camila breaks apart from Ollie and snatches it. After throwing it into the crowd, she takes off running.

The guard chases her. Meanwhile, Ollie waves us through. We follow him inside that section and around to the back behind all the fans in the stands. He hops onto a railing and extends his hand. I take it, and he pulls me up like I weigh nothing. I glance back, and Keondra, Paige, and Jiro all peer up at us, Paige's hands pressed together in prayer.

"Guess it's just us," Ollie says to me.

"No, I'm here too." Camila climbs up to us, her chest heaving as she attempts to catch her breath. "Let's get out of here before that guard returns. I think I lost her for now."

Ollie lifts me up on his hands, and I climb up onto one of the thick cables that leads to the jumbotron. Clinging to it, I inch upward toward the center with Camila and Ollie now behind me, all of us upside down hanging like sloths.

When we're almost there, I notice-people in the stands pointing toward us. Then, an image of us appears on the jumbotron's screen.

"This is Officer Jeffries of the Detroit Police Department," a voice overhead booms. "Will the RainBO PranXterz wannabe's get down this instant! If you do not return at once, you will be arrested."

Fear freezes me in place, but Camila shouts to keep going. She eggs me on with insults and threats until I reach the square box of vertical screens above the rink. I glance down at the ice, and it seems a million miles away. Everything stretches and bends, appearing like an ink drawing on white paper, all the distances and angles exaggerated and the black wavy lines jumping all around until I'm dizzy as anything.

Camila crawls toward me with huge eyes, sharp teeth, and big lips that spittle when she talks, strange because she's supposed to be in goggles and a mask. She overtakes me, hissing more insults in my ear, as I cling to my cable. Camila's foot connects with my head like I'm a steppingstone, and she moves toward another part I can't quite see, while all sorts of lines wiggle around like I'm in an alternative world all drawn in 3D.

"Mallory, are you okay?" Ollie calls behind me.

"Visual hallucination glitch. Go on ahead!" He climbs over me, stepping on my fingers and kicking me a little, but he gets by, and somehow, I'm still holding on. Ollie moves past Camila, going up to a higher part and leaning over, calling to her and pulling her up while I try to manage my breathing and not think about how dire my situation is. Either a whole slew of cops will arrest me, and I'll be eliminated and disintegrated, or I will slip and splatter to the ice. Not sure which is worse, but those look like my two alternatives. I hug the cable with every ounce of strength I have left, trying to ride out my minute of visual weirdness as Camila and Ollie scramble to find the Vermilion Bird coin in time.

“Do you see anything?” Ollie yells. He’s now climbing onto a center beam while Camila goes in another direction. I clamp my eyes shut, but I still see all the strangely exaggerated distances and weird-looking people with crazy-big features shouting at me from the stands. I wait for it to subside, trying not to freak out from how scary everything appears. When my hallucination finally fades, I climb higher with tired limbs that feel like they’ll give out any second, trying to join Ollie and Camila so I can help.

“Stay back, bitch,” Camila growls. “You’re no help no how. Just get back over there and —”

Ollie jumps down to a group of intertwining steel bars, then hangs from his knees to get lower. “I see it!” he calls.

Camila tries to lower herself to get closer to him.

“He’s in the middle!” the announcer calls, and I can see on the inner screens now a close-up of Ollie as he’s hanging on a bar from one leg, reaching for a coin on the top of a canister light below. He’s still too far.

I peek down again. The hockey players have stopped playing and are staring up at us along with everyone in the stands while the group of cops at the end of the cable on the upper mezzanine wait to arrest us.

“Let me help!” Camila demands.

Ollie sits up and grabs the bar, then changes position so that he can support her. Camila crawls over his head and extends her body straight out so she can reach. She balances on a rail nearby, and her other hand just barely touches the Vermilion Bird. She coaxes it forward as the audience cheers, and she finally grabs it. Ollie helps her upright, and she tucks it in her waist pack as I breathe a sigh of relief.

I go back the way I came, anxious to get off this cable, when I hit something solid. Looking at my feet which are pointed back toward the stands, I find Luckster there, her mask half off and much of her sprayed white from the fire extinguisher. She’s clutching the cable grinning at me, holding on with her good hand and the stump of her other one which is wrapped in a bloody bandage.

“Leprechaun chasing rainbows,” she says, reaching toward my foot with her clover.

I kick at her, and she recoils, gripping the cable with terrified eyes as she struggles to hold on with her phantom hand.

But she is determined, and she comes at me again as the announcer reminds us that the Detroit Police are waiting to arrest us.

The crowd boos. Then, someone starts chanting "Go, RainBO, go! Go, RainBO, go!" and everyone follows suit.

I scoot away, my limbs and hands burning and ready to give out.

Krystall swipes her clover at me again and misses. "Please, Mallory," she hisses. "Let me get you! If I fail, they'll cut —" She gulps and holds up her missing hand and then indicates on the other her absentee thumb. "If I get you, you may still be okay, you may not get picked to lose a limb, but if I don't clover everyone…"

I scramble away, not willing to give up my bus mates' limbs, and especially not my own.

"Please, Mallory, I'm begging you! Let me clover you!" She lunges at me.

My foot connects with her jaw like I'm playing kickball, and when I look back, I see her fall.

My hand thrusts back on instinct, hoping to catch her, but she's too far gone.

I'm not sure which of us screams louder.

Krystall doesn't hit the ice like I expect. Her body lands on the plexiglass guard on the edge of the rink like she's a stick of butter thrown against a sharp knife. Half of Luckster the Leprechaun, really Krystall Nykkolls, lands in the lap of a Red Wings player in the penalty box while her top half streaks down the plexiglass and lands face up.

The crowd gasps. The jumbotron shows it again in slow-motion before someone can fix the auto-replay and change the screen's video.

My scream runs out of steam as Mark-Bot announces that we only have ten minutes left. Turning my attention away from Krystall, her dual personality now a physical one as well, I glance back at the cable behind me. A few police officers are now sloths, inching toward me on the cable at alarming speed.

The one in front grabs my sneaker. “You’re under arrest,” he says, pulling me toward him.

“Attention Contestants,” Mark-Bot starts. “Player #4, Mallory Rosenbaum, has been detained —”

I swing my other leg around like a huge reverse fan kick and connect with the officer’s jaw. He releases my foot, but my tired fingers give out, and I start to fall.

I feel a chill on my chest and abdomen as my sweatshirt slides up over my face, and I go up and down like a yo-yo, bouncing in place.

“Mallory! I got you!” Ollie says. “Climb up me!”

Blinded by the red sweatshirt’s material all around me and deafened by the crowd cheering from below, I’m fully aware that the entire arena is currently viewing me practically topless. I grasp Ollie’s muscular arm and sink my nails into him, pulling myself higher and higher until I can grasp the cable. Grabbing onto it, I feel Ollie’s hand on my knee as he helps me get my feet and the cable to meet. When I can, I pull my shirt down so I can see again — and find I’m face-to-face with the angry cop.

He lunges for me and grabs my collar.

Without hands or feet available to push him off, them being reserved for holding the cable and all, I use the next best thing at my disposal. Opening wide, I bite him through my Covid-28 mask.

The officer howls, releasing my collar, and I scurry over him, kicking him again and again, trying to get away so he can’t detain me. I climb over the other two cops behind him, stepping on faces and hands and other parts I don’t want to know, then slide downhill the rest of the way.

A throng of cops catch me, pulling me off the cable. One twists my arms behind my back.

Fueled by images of Sammy, Troy, and Darla disintegrating, I stomp someone’s foot as hard as I can, then elbow one’s gut and another’s jaw. Breaking away, I run for my life, mowing people down, ducking into groups, trying to lose myself in the rainbowed and Red Winged crowd.

A while later, I sneak a peek behind me. No one seems to be following me anymore. As I exhale a huge sigh of relief, someone grabs my arm.

"Miss, you're under arrest. Please come with us now." I twist away from whoever it is, so used to this whole situation already, and keep running, finding an exit door and skipping down the stairs three and four at a time. Bursting outside, I race down the street and duck behind a white box truck in a parking lot. Gasping for air, I peer out to see who's after me.

No one is there. Whoever it was is gone, probably giving up when I left the arena. I struggle for air, incredulous that only moments before, I had been hanging in the rafters above the Red Wings game seconds away from arrest and death, and now I'm here standing on the street like a normal person.

It's the first time that I can process the fact that Krystall Nykkolls, a girl I went to school with and who is the cousin of Liza's boyfriend, is now dead. And it's my fault. She was desperate to clover me to avoid losing another limb, already suffering two amputations. Should I have let her? She was right that I may not have been the one picked to lose a limb, the odds were in my favor, but I didn't want any of my bus mates to suffer either.

I was not wrong to save myself over her, but as I relive her gruesome demise in my mind, all the protein bars I've eaten today come up onto the asphalt. I kicked her to her death. I killed her. It's because of me that she's no longer breathing. I wretch until my stomach muscles hurt, crying for her, myself, and all the others involved with this twisted game.

Who the hell is doing this to us and why? My eyes give a good cry. I don't want any more of us to die.

"Mallory? Where's your sorry ass?" Keondra barks in my ear.

I rush back to the group at the front of Little Caesar's Arena. Ollie and Camila are there along with the others, somehow also escaping the guards. We put the coins together to form the firescope right as Mark-Bot calls time.

The secret location is the Detroit Institute of Arts, which the map behind our eyelids says is a little over a mile away.

Ollie is the first to get the firescope, and he runs northwest along Woodward Avenue as we all chase him.

Keondra and Camila are in the lead behind him, running much faster than me. Jiro and I are about equally matched in speed, and Paige trails in the distance. I stop after a while, knowing this round is beyond me and I have no chance of catching the others.

Ollie has the scope and is in the lead, but then he dives into the snow, swatting and protecting his face from nothing I can see. Camila snatches it up and takes off.

Keondra's on her heels as Camila approaches the Art Institute, but then suddenly, Camila darts out into traffic and nearly gets hit. Jiro comes out of nowhere and pushes her out of the way, getting hit himself as a driver screeches to a stop. Jiro goes down for a second, but then pops up and says he's okay to several who have slammed on their brakes, while Camila crosses the street much easier now.

I dart after her, taking advantage, but just as I reach her, a girl who is the spitting image of Marci O'Grady with waist-length, ironed blonde hair and a purple A-shaped dress walks out from behind a thick column at the top of the steps.

I dive for Camila's legs, digging my nails into her calf. She screams and we thrash around on the steps, me feeling my head hitting the concrete until I can barely see straight, but suddenly, through the haze, huge teeth emerge from Camila's mouth, and she transforms before my eyes into an angry leopard ready to pounce. Even though I'm aware it's just a visual hallucination given by a VIP, which I expected since I have the most wins with one, I still drop the scope and take off because it's so realistic, it's hard not to.

As I run for my life from absolutely nothing except images put into my mind by an Eye-Bot, Mark-Bot congratulates Camila for winning

Round 4. I glance back and the Marci O'Grady imposter disappears through the museum door.

I rush to follow her, ignoring my fast-approaching leopard who hasn't gotten me even though I'm now walking, but I don't have any money to enter, all I had spent on the hockey tickets. "Marci" disappears into a hallway beyond the guards at the front. I can't get to her to see who she really is or where she might be going. As she stops to study a Diego Rivera mural in the first hall, I consider breaking past the guard and confronting her.

"Mallory, we're waiting for you," Paige says. She tells me to meet them at the corner.

Realizing I don't have the luxury of time or money to chase Marci now, I begrudgingly join my group and head toward Home Base parked nearby. Camila walks with her arm around Ollie like they're best buds or more while Keondra trails behind talking to Paige like they're new BFF's. Jiro and I fall into line, not talking at all. I have nothing to say to him or anyone else, heartbroken about Krystall and what happened. What I caused. First Sammi and now her, both dying because of me. God, I just want to win this thing and go home already.

I try not to watch as Camila's arm drops to Ollie's waist, and then his to hers, as they walk in an embrace the whole way to Home Base. I attempt not to think about how Ollie made out with her before, even though it was through their masks. I make myself think about dance, about a routine that I was making up to surprise Santos with for our next competition, to block it all out, but the whole Camila and Ollie thing seeps in no matter what.

After we get inside and the door is locked until our next challenge, Ollie leaves Camila behind and comes to me in my bunk. She whips off her goggles and mask, looking as surprised as I am, turning on her heel in a huff and disappearing into Door Bay. And although Blake is also on my mind, I can't help but grin inwardly, happy to see Ollie and more importantly, to see him diss Camila for me.

Ollie removes his goggles, mask and hat, then tosses them onto his upper bunk. "I missed you all day," he says, batting his eyelashes and grasping for my hand, which he kisses.

"You seemed to be enjoying yourself," I say, pulling it away.

He pouts. "That was all an act. Couldn't you tell?"

I shake my head. "Not a bit. And the best actor Oscar goes to …"

I pretend to hand him a golden statue and he grasps my hand again. "Well, it was. I only have eyes for you." He gazes down at me with his amazing blue eyes and smiles, and I see a little boy there with the world on his shoulders, having to support a whole family when he's practically a kid himself.

Then, I remember his girlfriend, or boyfriend, or whoever he had before The Game, and pull away again. "What about your someone special on the outside?"

He scrunches his brow.

"I told you I have a boyfriend, and you said you had someone too."

He grins. "Did I? Well, I don't. I said so because you told me you had someone. I didn't want to seem like a loser with no one."

“Those without anyone aren’t losers, nor are those who tell the truth.”

He tips an imaginary hat toward me. “Touché. So, can we cuddle just a bit before bed, to unwind from the day? I love being close to you.”

I start to move away, but he’s so damn irresistible, I let myself just this once, pulling the covers over us and snuggling with him. He’s a perfect gentleman, keeping his hands where I can see them, and I rest my head on his shoulder as he strokes my hair, trying to forget all the weirdness and upsetting things that happened today.

At least now I won’t have to worry about Luckster and losing a limb, I tell myself, but the words are hardly comforting and just make me feel worse.

“So, how was working with Jiro? It was weird you weren’t with Paige.”

“I know. She chose Keondra. But Jiro was surprisingly a good partner,” I admit. I recount how although he was a huge wimp at first, unable to look in the stands for clues, he came through in the end, saving me with that fire extinguisher from the manager and Luckster.

“Yeah, he’s a cool guy. Just very shy, especially because of his limited English.”

We talk some more, but I’m so sad about Krystall, I can barely form words.

I cry while he holds me, assuring me that I had no other choice. He rubs my back, and I eventually calm, falling into step with his breathing rhythm. He kisses me on the forehead, saying the sleepy drugs are starting to take hold, and goes up to his own bed. As I watch him and try to focus on his form as he wrestles with his blanket trying to get comfy, Karyn-Bot chimes in my ears.

“Attention Vermilion Contestants! Congratulations on completing Round 4: Marci’s Challenge. As you can see from the Leader Board, Sammi has one win but was eliminated, so hers doesn’t count, and no one claimed victory in Round 2, so we have one win for Mallory and one for

Camila, with two more rounds to go. And now I'm going to tell you all something you'll really want to know."

I fight off the meds that are threatening to make me fall out, straining to hear.

"In Vermilion," Karyn-Bot whispers, "there is something called the Second Survivor Secret. If someone manages to win Vermilion, which is not a guarantee, they can choose one other contestant to live — if they both survive until the end." As my eyes go wide, she tells us to have a good night, and she'll see us for Round 5.

As I process the news, I eye Paige asleep across from me and think of her little sister Kimmy who is in dire need of her older sister to rescue her, and then I peer up at Ollie, who has six kids counting on him. If I somehow win, how could I possibly pick between them?

Ollie's shampoo smell surrounds me from his just being here, and I reprimand myself, knowing it wouldn't be fair to let my attraction to him cloud my judgement. Plus, he'd been all over Camila today, which he said was an act, but maybe he's using me. Or her. It's hard to say. And then, Paige kind of ignored me since the last challenge. But maybe she's upset I won because Ollie flaked. Perhaps she agrees with Camila and Keondra who were pissed about it. I'm not sure. And then there's her inhaler and her story about her friend fooling a doctor with fake asthma, which doesn't make sense.

As my eyes give way to the meds coursing through my veins and begin to close, I wonder if I'll get far enough in The Game for a choice to even be an issue. I'll only be able to select someone to live if I win, and I must do that first. With two rounds to go, I know by now that *anything* can happen. I'm not going to count my chickens too early.

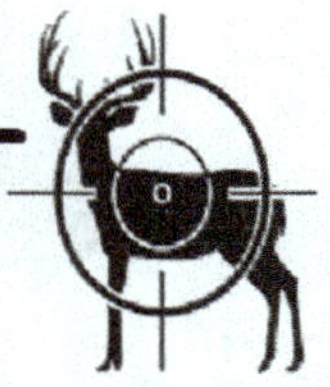

# PART 11

## DAVINA AND THE FUN BUNDT HUNT

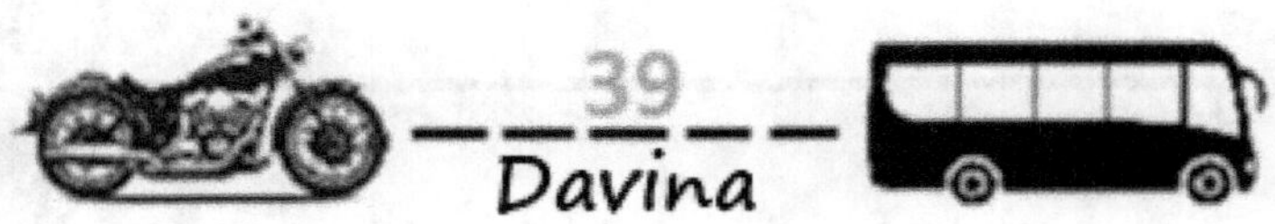


**Wednesday, January 23, 2030**

I've been forcing myself to try to get back to "normal", or as normal as things can be right now, by returning to school all week as I brace myself for news.

Antonia's avoiding me, suddenly BFFs with Claire again, and won't even return my texts. I know she feels awkward about kissing me and being rejected, but my sister is kidnapped, my mother is in a mental hospital, and my Zayde is in a coma. She's more concerned with her embarrassment or whatever than supporting me, which is selfish, hurtful, and surprising.

I'm just not sure what to do about Antonia and can't focus on her right now, but it's hard to see her in the halls and at lunch purposely ignoring me and laughing it up with Claire, who she can't stand. Feels like a constant slap in the face from which I keep trying to turn away, but I can feel it from every angle anyway.

And now, Niyah has a new guy she's been seeing since Sunday, someone from her history class who kissed her during their study date, so she's all wrapped up in him now and doesn't even notice Antonia and I aren't talking. She hasn't asked me about my sister or mother or Zayde in days or filled me in about anything in the news as she promised, and I doubt it's because nothing newsworthy has happened. Every sentence from her lately has the word Jeremy in it, I swear.

People I barely know, or some I don't at all, are still asking me stuff in the halls and during class or telling me they're sorry about my sister. And everyone's now also talking about Krystall Nykkolls, who I guess got cut in half at a Red Wings game after a RainBO PranXter kicked her off a cable leading to the Jumbotron when she attacked with a four-leaf clover. People are saying that it was Mallory judging from the hair coming out of the cap, unless it was a copycat. I try not to think about what Mallory must be going through, each thing crazier than the last, but that one takes the cake. Krystall being cut in half was way worse than I thought the Rebel Demons would do to her. I wonder what she did to them.

When two of the RainBO PranXterz got something from inside the jumbotron, experts were able to blow it up and enhance it enough to see a gold coin with something called a Vermilion Bird on it, so now everyone is wondering what that is. Some people near me in the library looked it up and read it has something to do with the Chinese constellations, some mythological fiery red bird that looks like a phoenix and flies into the sky when it sees flames. They said it represents the god of the south and worship of the sun. No one knows what that coin has to do with anything — except me and Snake, who know about the Vermilion game.

I'm horrified about Krystall, as everyone else is, and no one knows how she's connected, although I probably know more than most. I hear way more than what I want everywhere, but I've just thrown myself into my studies and catching up with what I missed in between watching *Sons of Anarchy* and visiting Zayde and Mom. I'm trying to block it all out by being a good student again while waiting for Jonah to have some news.

I've been avoiding Isaac who keeps sending concerned texts and finding me in the halls, and I make excuses to duck away and answer his messages minimally and noncommittally, yet he still doesn't get the hint or respect my space. I told Radesh, our Nerd Bowl captain, that I'm going to take a break from the team. It's because of Antonia and Isaac really, but he thinks it has to do with Mallory. Of course, that's true too, because I can only focus on Rocco and getting to The Game to save her. Radesh said he understood, and I'm welcome back anytime.

Jonah and I have texted here and there as he's been checking on me and my mom, which is nice, but nothing has happened with Rocco or The Game or anything the past few days.

Dad had them transfer Zayde to Beaumont Hospital where Mom is so she can visit him, and now Dad practically lives there before and after work. He usually crashes next to Zayde on a cot and visits Mom first thing, only coming home to shower and grab more clothes.

I've visited with Mom several times, and she still seems spacey, sad, and fragile like I've never seen. I'm not sure what will happen to her unless Mallory comes walking through the door soon and Zayde miraculously opens his eyes.

I'm dying to tell Mom about Jonah and his letter, but I'm not sure if it would bring back too many unpleasant memories, which she doesn't need right now. It's been so hard to keep in what I know about Mallory and the Vermilion game from my parents, but I just don't want to complicate things further and fear that it would. They'd call the police or do something equally as dangerous, plus I don't want to get their hopes up. I'm not even sure what my chances are that Snake's plan will work; it seems low at best. Especially because even if we manage to save Mallory, someone can still control her with the bots in her. And then what? Will they like make her go assassinate the President or something?

Jonah calls me after school on Wednesday, his face appearing on a video chat.

I accept, thrilled to see him.

"So, I got me some good news and some bad news."

"Oy, which do I want first?"

"Shit, I don't know. Pick one."

"Just out with it."

Jonah's face twists with discomfort. "Okay, so, there's this hunting trip this weekend."

"*Hunting*? That's gotta' be the bad news."

"Yeah. It's a Rebel Demons tradition, ever since they let us hunt again for just this last weekend in January. Season ended in December. This weekend's our fifth annual Fun Bundt Hunt."

"Fun Bundt Hunt? What's that?"

"The old ladies plan lots of activities and food around the hunting, including a competition for who makes the best Bundt cakes. Everyone stuffs they faces all weekend on Bundt cakes for judging purposes, and then they vote. They also play softball in the yard, where you get extra points for bunting the ball. It's a whole big weekend with families and bands we look forward to all year. Always a good time."

"Ugh, really? No offense, but God no. You know I'm vegan and an animal rights advocate, don't you? I can't go *deer hunting*." I gag as I imagine biting into venison stew.

“Yeah. Of course. That’s why that be the bad news. Good news is, Rocco specifically asked for you.”

My eyebrows jump off my face. “No way. And no way. I mean it both ways. No freaking way. Seriously?”

“Yes, and I get ya. I already know what you gonna’ say. It’s cool Rocco remembered you with all them other girls there, but you can’t go based on morality or whatnot.”

I think of attending for a second, maybe even participating, and a shudder travels my whole body that feels like it’ll never stop. I’d rather get locked in a morgue alone in the dark all weekend or swim in shark-infested waters with a cut on my arm or even jump from a plane with a Swiss Cheese parachute than go hunting. “Oh, I couldn’t. There’s just no way.”

“Are you sure? I mean, I just gotta’ say, which is worse, dead deer or dead – “

“Don’t say it. Fuck.”

Jonah bursts out laughing.

“What? What’s so funny?”

“You swore!”

“I swear, gosh darn it!”

Jonah laughs even harder.

“Fuck this shit. Is that better?”

Now, he’s howling.

“Need to call me back?”

“Yeah,” he gasps and hangs up.

A few minutes later, he rings back. “Thanks. I needed that.”

“I’m not *that* much of a goody-goody, I’ll have you know.”

“Just by saying that, I know you are.”

“Okay, but I’m learning. So, back to hunting. I just can’t. Do you like personally kill deer and stuff?” I never realized he might, and that’s something that may make him *not* my ideal guy after all.

"Yes and no."

"What does that mean? That's like being sort of pregnant."

"I killed a deer twice cause my dad made me. I had me some nightmares 'bout it ever since. I freakin' hate hunting, but it's huge in the club. They go all the time, and we got tons of cabins all over the Midwest and the South. I go and just sort of deal with it, but I ain't do nothing but hang out with Lola and go ridin' and explorin,' play softball sometimes. Imma' good bunter."

"Do you eat it?"

"Hell no. I don't do venison or squirrel or rabbit. Yuck."

"But you eat meat."

"Yes and no."

"Again, sort of pregnant. You do or you don't. I mean, you want to be a veterinarian and help animals, but then you kill and eat them too?"

"I do," Jonah says, "but ain't much and only cause I gotta have protein. Sounds like an excuse, I know, but I ain't eat most things. And what I do is bad for me too. I seriously only like bread, cheese, onions, green peppers, and fries. Sometimes I force myself to eat some beef or chicken for protein, but I usually ditch it after a few bites. I tried to go vegetarian three times, but I got too sick cause I ain't eatin' enough good stuff."

"I get you. I've grown up vegan, so I know a lot about how to cook things to make them taste good and give you enough nutrients so that you don't get sick. If I could teach you, would you give it a try?"

"Yeah, totally. I just need enough to eat without the meat. Kinda' hard when I can only stand two vegetables. Can I like have grilled cheese and fries for every meal? I'd be down with that. Oh, and waffles. They're bread-like. That would be heaven. Oh, and donuts. Definitely donuts."

"Uh, no." I laugh. "You'll be big as a house with diabetes and coronary artery disease by the time you're twenty. But I hear you. It can be challenging, but there are more and more restaurants around with at least vegetarian options, if not vegan. Especially in Metro Detroit with the large Arabic community that give us a lot of great Middle Eastern places, many of which have vegetarian and vegan options that are incredible. You're lucky you live here because we have a wide variety of food compared to other areas. And then there's also Mexican, which has a lot of the ingredients you like, and Chinese, Thai, Indian, and other international cuisines. I can show you some easy recipes and we can experiment and see what appeals to you."

"That would be very cool. I need help big time."

"Then I'm your girl."

He chuckles, his dark eyes brightening. "Oh yeah?"

I clear my throat. "For cooking vegan, I mean. Yeah, for that. So, is there any way for me to go on this hunting trip and not see anything icky or dead?"

"Probably not but just don't be lookin'. And bring your own food. Just don't advertise, because biker girls mostly ain't vegans. Them girls we know all hunt and fish on the regular. So, keep them views to yourself. Cool?"

"Totally. I'll bring stuff. If anyone asks, I'll just say I'm watching my figure with some healthier food. I can have you try some things, like panko-fried eggplant with spicy marinara and pesto or lentils with onions. You'll love them."

Jonah sucks in a breath. "Ooh, I ain't know about all that."

"You like onions. Wait until I have you try Mujadara, a Lebanese dish with lentils, grilled onions, and rice."

"That ain't sound half bad. I never ate no lentil before though. What the hell's a lentil?"

I think of Mallory and wonder if she's even being fed, and then I picture the deer — perhaps more than one — whom I might witness being killed if I attend this Fun Bundt Hunt all weekend, but I realize I need to put the welfare of my sister above the deer like Jonah said. I tell him I'll go on the hunting trip if he tries my Mujadara.

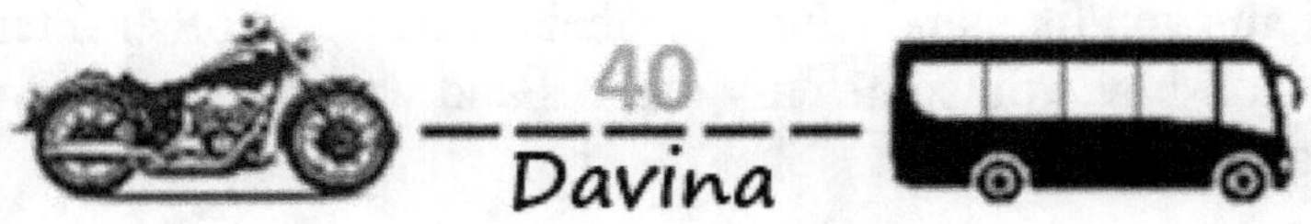


**Friday, January 25, 2030**

The first person I see Friday morning when I enter Blades Cave is Trish. She hoists a backpack over her shoulder, then eyes me holding my bags with a contemptuous look. “Who invited *you*?”

Snake comes out to greet me with Lola on his shoulders, and she Slither Smiles while offering me her belly. “I did, Trish. This here’s my friend Lucy. Rocco wanted me to bring her.”

She eyes me up and down in my “Bad Gurl Says Whut?” t-shirt, ripped jeans, and combat boots with a sneer. “Really? Why?”

“Bitch. Step off,” I say, putting a hand to my hip. Eying her up and down, I sneer back at her.

She laughs at me and walks away, flipping me off behind her. Rocco comes in then, and Trish throws herself at him like a wound-up baseball, me completely forgotten.

Snake raises his eyebrow at me.

I shrug. “Saw it on *Mayans MC* the other day.”

Snake laughs and low-fives me. “Keep doin’ it, and don’t be lettin’ her get to ya’. Rocco invited some other girls too, but just keep telling him he’s all that and being sexy as you can. Copy Trish if you gotta’. And use them more.” He looks at my chest. I blush and so does he. “Sorry, but do it.”

I salute him. “Aye aye, Captain. Will use boobs more. Yessir!”

Snake bops me on the head and grabs my bags to put in the car.

The Rebel Demons and their friends and family ride up to a hunting cabin near a city called Cadillac in several SUVs since there is so much gear. They tow a fleet of toy trailers carrying everyone's Harleys so they can joyride through the backroads.

I'm in the back of an SUV next to Snake with Rocco driving and Trish in the passenger seat. Most of the time, we listen to heavy metal or country music, whatever Rocco puts on. When we hit a patch with no reception, Trish starts talking about herself and her job as a life insurance agent, saying how she really wants to be a singer and is being stifled by such a boring career. When the music comes back on, she sings along to it, and she's awful. Beyond awful really, as bad a singer as I am a dancer. While Rocco strains to keep a straight face in the rearview mirror, Snake grabs my hand and squeezes. I hide my face in my palm and glance over to find him doing the same, which makes us both laugh even harder.

Jonah doesn't let go of my hand, nor do I pull away until I see Rocco checking me out in the mirror. I retract my hand from Jonah even though I don't want to, and I nudge my chin forward when he glances my way. Jonah blinks and nods, gazing out his window with his hands stroking Lola's head instead.

After we arrive at a beautiful log cabin with a massive stone fireplace and a huge great room with a rustic yet modern kitchen, we divvy up the bedrooms. I get my own, a small one near the pantry. Some of the guys and their old ladies and kids settle into the many campers parked around the huge woodsy property. After everyone throws their stuff down, they vote to go snowmobiling.

Trish falls toward Rocco with outstretched arms to claim him as her partner, but Rocco ducks away and comes over to me standing near Jonah, leaving Trish grasping air and gaping after him.

"Hey Lucy," Rocco says, flashing Jonah's same cute fang smile. He offers me his hand. "Let's go have some fun."

# 41

## Davina

Rocco leads me to a shiny red snowmobile while Trish climbs on another with some guy, scowling at us like we killed her dog. She's so damn pretty, she even looks good doing that.

Rocco helps me on the back of his and then gets in front, pulling my thighs so I scoot closer to him.

"Cool. Thanks," I say, and he leaves his hands on my legs, squeezing them higher and higher until his hands are practically in my back pockets.

He leans back so that his head is on my shoulder. "Ever been snowmobiling, Lucy?"

"Nope. I'm a sheltered gal."

Rocco laughs. "You seem like it."

"Thanks?"

"Oh, no offense. I mean, you're just younger than most girls I hang with."

"Yeah. I'm seventeen," I admit, unsure what Jonah told him. I'd never pass for older; people always tell me I look young for my age.

"That's cool. I'm six years older. Ain't too bad, is it?"

"Not at all. I'm down."

"All right, then." Rocco grins Jonah's smile at me and straightens up, revving the engine, and I grab him around the waist, pressing against him even more so I'm practically melded into him, doing what Trish would do.

"Hey baby," I say in his ear using my sexiest voice. "I'm ready. Let's do it." As we take off, I fight from cracking up at how odd I sounded, like I'm a ventriloquist's dummy and someone's talking for me.

As we ride, I see Jonah driving another snowmobile with just Lola, and I wish I was with him instead. I try to concentrate on Rocco as he tells me all about different deer they've killed and other things they hunt at various times of the year. He describes how great their game stew is when they put leftover meats in it and let it simmer for a whole day until it all falls off the bone. I'm glad I can only half-hear, ready to throw up all over him. Suddenly, he slows to a stop and turns to me. "Hey Lucy, you ever shot a deer? Snake didn't say."

I shake my head, knowing I could never even lie about doing so, and he grins. "Well, tomorrow's gonna' be your lucky day then! I'll walk you through it. It's life-changing, your first kill, I swear. You'll love it! In the meantime, you ever fire a rifle?"

"No," I manage around the huge lump suddenly in my throat.

Rocco hops off his seat and walks behind me to open the trunk. "Why don't I teach you then, so you'll be ready for tomorrow?"

I get off the snowmobile as he grabs two pieces of a huge rifle from the trunk, puts it together, and hands it to me. "I, uh —" I search for Jonah, hoping he'll magically appear and bail me out, but everyone's so far ahead now, I don't even hear them anymore.

"Don't be scared. I'll show you." Rocco pushes his gun toward me.

Terrified, I slide back. Rocco steps forward, and my mind churns, thinking of how I can get out of it. I don't want to fire a gun, or even hold one. Ever. Not if I don't have to. I consider clutching my side, thinking I might fake food poisoning, but I'm not sure I'd be convincing enough, and that will hardly be a turn-on. Unfortunately, that's my goal. I need to turn Rocco on enough to become his old lady and get invited to The Game.

So, I go with Plan B and push the rifle slowly toward him, then stand on my tip toes and kiss him right on the mouth. I wince with the taste of smoke but cover it with a sexy look I've been practicing in the mirror. "I'd rather do other things, wouldn't you?"

His eyebrows shoot up, and he grins. "Oh." He leans the rifle against the snowmobile and puts his arms around me, pulling me in for another kiss. "So, this is how you like to get to know new people then?"

"Only ones who look like you," I say, licking his ear.

Rocco kisses me like I've never been kissed, his tongue practically touching my tonsils, and he's *way* better than Isaac. But then I realize I'm picturing Jonah. As Rocco backs me up so I'm sitting on the snowmobile and sinks to his knees to reach me better, I imagine he is his brother. I'm so unbelievably turned on, I finally push him away, afraid I'll lose control.

"Oh, Lucy," he groans, coming at me for more.

I kiss him again, tentatively, worried things will progress beyond where I'm comfortable as he slides his hands all over me, working their way up beneath my sweater and under my bra. He presses himself between my legs until I can feel his arousal. "Look what you do to me," he growls, pulling my legs up to straddle him and leaning forward so he's on top of me.

Some snowmobiles approach, their engines slowing, and we find most of the group gawking at us. They break into cheers and whistles as Trish glares at us while Snake studies his dash.

Rocco withdraws his hand from my shirt, sets me upright, and stands. He replaces the rifle in the trunk before jumping on the front of the snowmobile. "Last one to the cabin does dishes tonight!"

I get behind him, and he takes off while I clutch him for dear life and silently thank everyone for interrupting us.

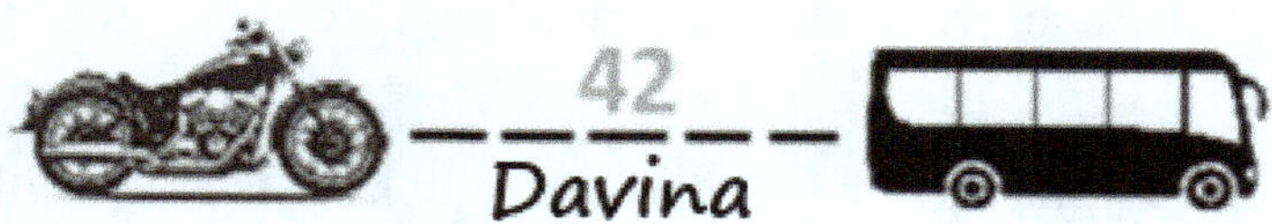

# 42
## Davina

Other girls on the hunting trip are there for Rocco by his request, and the evening becomes another Biker Cinderella competition for Prince Charming. Candy sits in his lap for a while, then Ginger steals him away to go outside and rock on the porch swing with her, then Tawny takes him out somewhere in the forest to "look at the stars" on a totally clear night.

A country band shows up, and everyone goes out back. They all know various line dances that I don't. I sit with Snake watching, knowing I could never catch on and be as mesmerizing as Trish and Candy and another girl named Tamilee as they each show off their boot-scooting skills with their mega-tight jeans, cowboy boots, and come-hither smiles.

As I get another drink, hoping to numb myself to the fact that I might have to witness innocent animals being slaughtered tomorrow, Rocco comes in with Trish, his arm around her, announcing their goodnights. "See y'all bright and early at six for the first outing of the Fifth Annual Fun Bundt Hunt!" he says with a wave.

I think of Mallory and what she must be going through. I'm so stupid to think that I could possibly get Rocco to choose me just because I got a few articles of trashy clothes and a tattoo and smoked some Nosingarettes. There's no way I could possibly compete with Trish or any of the other girls.

I burst out the back door into the night, desperate to sort things out as my head swirls with mounting panic.

Jonah comes after me. "Lucy, you okay?"

I stop and spin around. "I'm not freaking Lucy! I'll never be her. Rocco will *never* choose me. I'm not the type of girl he wants. Even though we like freaking *made out* today, he still went home with *her*."

"It don't mean you can't win him over tomorrow," Jonah says. "If he only wanted Trish, he wouldn't be flirtin' with you and all them others when she's right there. He ain't declared her his old lady yet. He's just ridin' this thing out long as he can, getting all them girls competin' over him. And who the hell wouldn't if they got the chance? We need something better than just bein' pretty and sexy. He got 'nuff of that with all them girls."

"You're right, but what? I don't want to have to sleep with him to get him, you know? And that wouldn't even do it. I'm sure Trish has done it plenty of times, is currently as we speak, and who knows how many others he's been with, while I —" I look down at my boots, biting my lip. "Well, I haven't done it yet."

"Yeah, not me neither. Ain't nothin' wrong with that."

I look up at him. "Really?"

He smiles. "Why? You thought I did?"

I shrug. "I figured you must have. Anyway, I don't want Rocco to be my first, but I guess I'd do it to save Mallory. But, well, I wouldn't even know what I was doing, and I'd probably turn him off. He'd be able to tell I've only ever kissed one other guy besides him like literally once, and it was beyond awful. I'd just embarrass myself, or probably chicken out."

"Come on with me." Jonah grabs my hand and leads me across the yard, not answering when I ask where we're going. He pulls me into the woods and stops suddenly so that I crash into him. Turning, he slides his arms around me, baring his adorable fangs as he gazes down at me. "You know, we *could* practice. Ain't I suposta' be teachin' you how to be a biker slut?"

I grin, a warmth descending upon me as I stare into his eyes. "Totally. And I'm not slutty at all. I need *a lot* of practice."

Pulling me closer, Jonah nuzzles his face into my hair, breathing into my ear as he nibbles my lobe. I get lost in his unbelievable scent as we sway to the music made between us and the chirping sounds of nature all around.

Brushing my hair aside, Jonah kisses my neck, and I moan, a roaring fire blazing through me. He winds his hands through my hair and pulls my face toward his, but just then, we hear a tinkle of laughter and bounce apart. A second later, Cody and Corrinne approach from a path deeper in the woods.

"Hey guys, what's up?" Cody claps Snake on the back.

"Oh, just looking at them owls," Snake says, pointing at nothing in the trees.

I giggle. "Yeah, owls."

"Great. Well, meet us inside and we'll get a game of Texas Hold 'Em going around the fire, okay?" Corrinne squeezes my shoulder with a grin. "Maybe we'll make s'mores, and I'll whip up some yummy cocoa with hot milk and mini marshmallows."

"That would be nice," I say, not sure how I'll get out of eating the honey graham crackers, marshmallows, milk, and chocolate — none of which are vegan — without being rude. Something else to worry about.

When they leave, Jonah smiles at me, taking my hands into his and kissing them. "I totally wanna' practice with you, but we can't."

I exhale, blowing through sad lips. "Yeah, I know."

"We need to focus on getting Rocco but also, ain't no one can catch us together and blow our cover. Remember, you's supposta' have the hots for my brother, not me."

I snap an aw-shucks. "Yeah, right. I am, aren't I?" I press a button on my Hollaphone, recording. "Note to self. Use boobs more. Stop crushing on wrong brother." I tap at the screen. "Note saved. Reminders set." I reach up and kiss Jonah's cheek as he bares his fangs, then turn back toward the cabin.

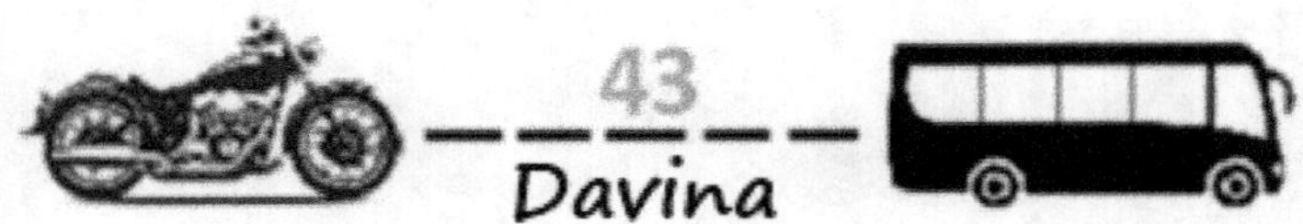

# 43

## Davina

The next morning, Rocco knocks on my bedroom door as I'm changing after my shower and tells me to be out front soon because he wants to show me how to shoot a rifle. I rush around to get ready, my heart thumping wildly, dreading the day and wondering what I can do to minimize how terrible it'll be.

As I go outside with Rocco and find Trish, Corrinne, Tamilee, and some of the other girls standing with rifles in their hands aiming at targets in the distance, I try to figure out how I can get out of having to fire a gun and God forbid killing anything.

Jonah is there, Lola bobbing on his shoulder, and he brings me off to the side to show me, but Rocco comes and takes over. As I line up my first shot, feeling like I might have a coronary right there, I wonder how far I'll have to go to impress Rocco. What can I do that the others wouldn't be willing to do? As I notice them all eyeing him practically salivating, I realize not much. When I shoot at a bullseye in the distance, not even coming close to hitting it, I wince at the kickback which almost knocks me off my feet. Rocco catches me, laughing and telling me to try again.

I make several shots with his help, and after a while, I improve, but I keep getting jarred by the sound and the kickback, much to Rocco's delight. He smacks me on the butt and tells me good job after I hit the bullseye on Candy's target two away from mine. He finally moves on to help Tamilee.

Snake comes over. "You okay?"

"I feel like I'm gonna' puke," I say, eyeing some of the guys in the distance loading up the jeeps with guns and supplies for our day's hunting trip.

"I know. Just remember Mallory and do what'cha gotta'."

I swallow. "I'll try."

About an hour later, as we duck into some shrubbery to watch a huge buck in the distance, Rocco comes behind me and whispers in my ear. "I'd like him to be your first. Your virgin buck!" He yanks me over to a closer bush. "Okay, line up your shot like we practiced before." Rocco hands me a rifle.

"What? Now?" I grasp it with sweaty palms, worrying I might drop it and shoot myself in the face.

"Yes now, before he takes off." Rocco helps me to position the rifle while I shake like crazy.

"Hold still," he says, trying to steady the butt on my shoulder.

"I'm just nervous," I manage and clamp my eyes shut.

Rocco explodes with laughter.

I peek at him. "What?"

"How're you gonna get it with your eyes closed?"

I shrug. "Luck?"

He cackles, then shushes himself, repositioning the rifle in my hands. "Okay, come on. He's lookin' antsy like he's gonna bolt."

I peer through the little eyehole atop the rifle, and even though I'm maybe a hundred feet away, I can see the deer's eyes as he notices us. There's no way I can do it, even when I think of Mallory and saving her. "Ooh!" I groan, clutching my stomach with one arm while lowering the rifle with the other.

"What's wrong?"

I keel over, breathing hard. "I think I got food poisoning or something. Oooohhh…"

"He's getting away!" Rocco takes the rifle.

Before he can aim, a shot rings out. "What the —?"

We look over to see Trish with a smoking rifle aimed at the deer. She fires again.

The buck drops along with my heart.

She flashes us a satisfied grin.

“Now, that’s how you do it!” Rocco says, high-fiving Trish.

“Woo-hoo, Motherfucka’!” she says, pumping her fist in the air. She and Rocco skip toward their prize while I puke into a nearby bush.

Jonah tries to comfort me, his hand on my back, but I whip around and glare at him. “I told you I couldn’t do this! And now, he’s off with her. She won, fair and square. She’s willing to do what I’m not.” I glance over to find Rocco and Trish kicking at the poor animal who’s down but still moving, poking it with a stick while it suffers, and they laugh. Rocco hugs Trish to his side, pausing here and there to kiss her for half-killing the poor thing. My stomach turns inside out, and I barf again into the brush.

“I’m sorry, Davina. I know this sucks,” Snake whispers.

I wipe my mouth on my sleeve, then think of the deer maybe understanding his imminent fate when he saw me aiming my rifle and wretch again and again until there’s nothing left. I finally stand on shaky legs, and Snake steadies me with his arm around my waist.

“Trish won, plain and simple,” I tell him through my tears. “I can’t win against a girl like her willing to do *anything* to get him. I couldn’t do it. I choked. I have no chance, and neither does Mallory. Even if we can get to her, she’s full of bots anyway. Whoever is doing this thing can still kill her or control her, and God knows what they’ll make her do, including killing one of us, or all of us. What the hell can we even do to stop that even if we do manage to get to The Game?”

“I ain’t know yet. We ain’t get that far. But what you sayin’ ain’t right. There’s still hope.” Jonah puts a hand on each of my shoulders. “You upset right now, and I get it. We just need to like think a different way about —"

I pull away from him. “Look, I don’t need any more false hope that I can do anything to save my sister, so stop filling my head with bullshit. Thanks, but no thanks. I’m done.” I stumble away, blinded by tears, being honest with myself for the first time, knowing there’s no way in hell Rocco would invite me as his old lady to any round. He’ll take Trish or one of the other hundred sexy, smoking girls who would have no problem shooting and eating a deer, having sex with him, and whatever else to keep his interest. I can’t top that, and I’m certain of it even if Jonah isn’t. He doesn’t know me as well as I do.

And then the guilt that I didn't do eveything it took to save Mallory starts rivaling my guilt over her being there because of me, and I realize right then that I'm the worst sibling who ever lived, useless at helping her the one time she needed me. Tears bowl me over.

Jonah catches up with me, rubbing my back again. "You want me to get you home?"

"Yes. Please. The sooner the better. I can't be on this trip anymore."

"I gotcha'. I'm real sorry."

We go into the cabin to get our things, me praying no one notices my red-rimmed eyes, and just then, Rocco and Trish emerge from a back room with bags over their shoulders. "Hey dude," Rocco says to Jonah, fist-bumping him and petting Lola who Slither Smiles at him. "Just got called up for this thing me and Dad got invited to, this game. Tell you more about it later. I'm taking Trish. Back in a day or two. Mack's in charge. See ya soon." They rush out while I gawk after them, shaking my head as more tears stream down my cheeks.

Jonah puts me into a fancy black Jeep and gets my stuff, then comes to drive me, telling me he explained to everyone that I had food poisoning and was going home to recuperate. They all wished for me to feel better and sent a pot of venison stew for me to enjoy when I was better.

The thought of it makes me sick all over again, and I open the window, desperate for air.

As we get close to a town, I ask Jonah to pull over at a gas station. I want to throw the disgusting stew away, the smell making me want to hurl again. On the way to the trash, I notice a homeless man sitting on the side of the building and give it to him instead. I rush into the station, grab a plastic fork and some napkins, buy a few juices and water, and bring them to him.

"God bless you," he says, removing the foil from the bowl.

"God bless you," I return, glad the deer's life sacrificed for that stew wasn't a total waste.

On the way home, Jonah makes the mistake of flipping on the radio. Before he can change it, we hear about the Missing Tech Nine, or people pretending to be them, climbing up to the jumbotron at the Red Wings game. The reporters discuss how Krystall Nykkolls dressed as Luckster the Leprechaun was kicked off a high cable leading to the jumbotron that some of the RainBO PranXterz were on, meeting her end in a very horrific way. Many witnesses say they will have nightmares for the rest of their lives over what they saw.

"They're back in Detroit?" Jonah asks.

"They were. God knows where they'll be next. They're somehow traveling around, although no one has reported any suspicious bus like they were on. They're in something else, but it could be any type of vehicle."

"Probably a big SUV, at least."

"Yeah, right, but that leaves lots of possibilities," I say.

We're quiet the rest of the way, me lost in my doom-and-gloom thoughts, thinking about Krystall and Mallory especially, while Johnah's playlist rotates between Motley Crüe, Guns 'N Roses, and Metallica. When he pulls into my driveway, I thank him for trying to help.

"It ain't over," he says. "We gotta' think of other stuff, be systematic like you taught me, test one thing at a time until something works. We still gotta' chance. The Game's still goin' on. We maybe in Round 4, but there's six total. We ain't done."

"I am. I have no chance of saving Mallory. And I don't want to get my hopes up anymore. I'm going to have to figure out how to let her go." I sigh, feeling so shaky inside like any second I might explode with endless tears.

"Hey, let's sleep on it, okay? Let's – "

"Thanks. I gotta' go. Be well."

I rush out of the Jeep and into my house, not looking back, not wanting to see Jonah's disappointed face. I just need to be free of his false hope and crazy ideas and all that he is and move on somehow. Move on as maybe an only child with no real friends and absentee parents, alone to start over, I guess. How did everything get so screwed up so fast?

At least I have my pets. They're always loyal and loving. Closing my front door behind me and locking it, I greet them all in the foyer while trying to stuff away such awful thoughts, but they keep popping up to torment me like a bunch of Whack-a-Moles.

Sitting on the wood planked floor with Archie in my lap, I pet him with one hand and Brian with the other. Our three Siamese cats Buggles, Bruce, Bowie, and our black cat Blue surround me. Dad's gerbil, Henry VIII, peers out of his glass aquarium at us, his little nose twitching.

The cats and dogs take turns rubbing against me to claim me as their territory. I focus on each, finding all their favorite places to scratch, and when I hear Archie's satisfied groan or Brian puts a paw on my shoulder like we're buds or a purring Blue kneads my thigh, I get sidetracked for a little while from my torturous thoughts, a welcome reprieve. I try to be there for our lonely pets who have no one lately besides me.

The pink and blue rhinestones on my watch light up, signaling I have a voicemail. Opening my Hollaphone, I see it's from an unfamiliar number. I play it back and hear a woman's voice. "Hello. This is Nurse Davies from Beaumont Hospital in Royal Oak calling for Davina Rosenbaum. Your father Seth Rosenbaum was brought in by ambulance after calling 911 because he couldn't breathe. He's tested positive for Covid-28, Strain Q, and he's been placed on a ventilator in our ICU. I wanted to let you know. You can reach me at (248) 555-7890 or come to the front desk in our ER with any questions, but you cannot personally visit him for at least two weeks while he's being quarantined. Please see our website for directions and our Covid-28 policies and procedures."

Tears fill my eyes. "Oh, Daddy," I cry. He's now in danger too. I don't know how much more I can take. I click on the callback number on the message. Just as it starts ringing, someone knocks on my front door.

Jumping a mile, I rush to peer out the peephole as Archie and Brian start barking, hoping Jonah came back, especially with what I just learned about my dad. I find myself needing him again, an odd feeling when we're practically strangers. I really have no one except him now.

Instead, I see Isaac on my porch with a huge bouquet of red roses. He smooths his eyebrows and huffs into his palm to smell his breath.

Ah shit. Not now.

After a millisecond debate, I duck down hoping he didn't see my shadow through the frosted front windows. Scooting into the kitchen, I hang up my call to the hospital so that it doesn't make any noise. I peer around the corner into the front hall, hoping he'll give up and go away.

Isaac knocks again. "Davina? It's me, Isaac. Just wanted to check on you."

As Brian and Archie scratch at the front door growling, I hold my breath, arguing with myself, not sure what to do. I need to go see about my dad, not deal with Isaac and his unrealistic expectations of me.

The blue rhinestones on my watch base light up signaling I have a new text. I see it's from Isaac: *I know you're in there because I just saw you come home twelve minutes ago. Please answer because I need to talk to you. I have information about Mallory.*

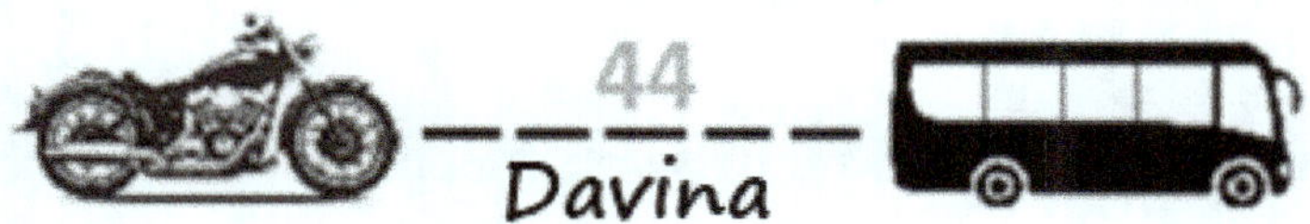

# 44
## Davina

I walk out and open the front door. Isaac steps into the foyer and thrusts his bouquet of roses at me.

I take them, pricking my finger on a thorn. “Thanks,” I mumble, sucking the blood, wondering what Isaac could possibly know about Mallory’s situation. They’re not exactly pals at school. Mallory wouldn’t even know who he was.

Archie sniffs him and starts barking again. Then, Brian does too. My dogs never do that with anyone once they see and smell them, but they act like they want to kill Isaac. Super-sweet Brian even bares his huge teeth.

All the hair on my arms stands up. I pull the dogs into the family room and close the French doors that separate it from the kitchen a bit begrudgingly.

I spin around to face Isaac. “So, hey, what’s up? What do you know about my sister?”

Isaac folds his arms across his chest and shakes his head, frowning at me. “So, wow, really? You were going to do me like that? What kind of person are you, anyway?”

“What? Do you like what? What did you hear about Mallory?”

“You weren’t going to let me in until I said I knew something about her.” Isaac locks the door behind him.

Brian and Archie bang the door in the family room as if they sense danger even though they can’t see, and I wish it wasn’t so secure and they could break through.

“What? Why’d you – “

“You were pretending not to be home, weren’t you? Hiding from me like the coward you are.”

“Wait, what? You don’t know something about Mallory?” Chills overtake my arms.

Isaac smirks. “I only said it so you’d let me in.”

Brian’s growling intensifies and I hope his strength is enough to break through the thick wood panel separating him from us.

I back away. “What the hell? Why? What did you need to – “

Isaac comes toward me, thrusting his Hollaphone at me. “Have you read *any* of the texts I’ve sent? I’ve been trying to be a good boyfriend all this time, and you’ve barely answered, blowing me off like I’m nothing.”

He peers at his phone, swiping the screen. “Yep, I texted you last Wednesday in the morning. No answer. Then at lunch. Said you were making up a quiz. After school, you texted you were visiting your mom. Nothing else. Never a question about me. Next day, messaged you twice. Nothing. Nada. Zilch. Not even the courtesy of an ‘I’m busy’ or a ‘text you later’ or any of your other bullshit. Then, yesterday, four times I texted. Four times! And you wrote back a total of once. Once! What, do I not count? Do you not see how much I care? Why’re you being such a bitch to me when I’ve only been trying to help?”

Isaac backs me into a couch in the living room and I almost flip over its arm. He catches me, pulling me to him and lunging to kiss me. I push away from him and run toward the back door, but he tackles me to the ground. My head hits something hard and everything goes black.

# PART 12

## ROUND 5: JANICE'S CHALLENGE

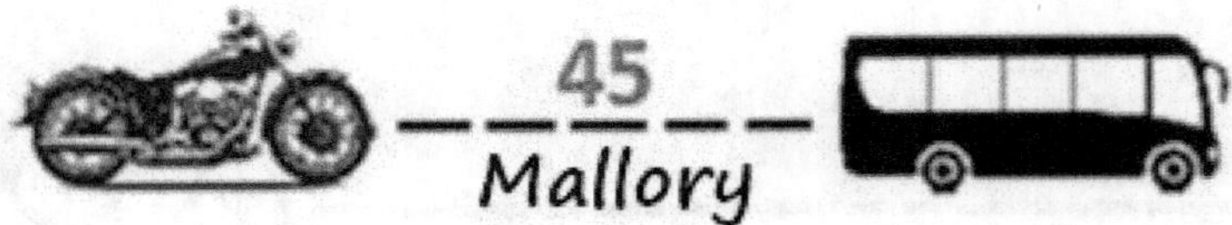

# 45

# Mallory

**Thursday, January 24, 2030**

My first thought when I awaken is that there will be a second survivor, and the winner gets to choose who it will be. We have two more rounds, and I've won one and so has Camila, so it could be one of us, but anything can happen. If I am victorious, I will have to choose between Ollie and Paige, who both have terrible circumstances with kids who need their help. I hope it doesn't come to that, but at the same time I do, because that will mean I won. But then one of them lives and the other dies, and I will have to choose who it will be. I can't imagine having to make such a decision, but I hope I get to at the same time. It's all very confusing and upsetting, especially knowing all three of us could die. We have no idea how long any of us has left. Troy, Darla, and Sammi all perished quickly, none knowing their fate until the last few seconds.

And then my mind goes to Krystall Nykkolls, and I well up with tears, thinking of the desperation in her eyes and what it felt like to kick her to her death, me picking myself and the others over her. I picture her half-white, terrified face as she fell screaming, her arms and legs wild, and especially the way her open mouth remained in a shocked "o" as the top half of her slid down the plexiglass partition onto the ice.

Paige puts something into my bag at the foot of my bed, thankfully distracting me.

"Hey. Is that for me?"

She glances over, her face reddening. "Oh. Didn't know you were up. Yeah. It's just a little note."

"Oh. Should I read it?" I sit up and reach toward the bag.

She plucks it out and crumples it up. "No, it's stupid." She reddens further and waves her hand. "Just really wanted to apologize and stuff."

"Apologize? For what?"

"Just the last round. Me picking Keondra over you to do the Hangman Phase. And I kind of brushed you off one night because I was beyond tired. I thought you might think I was mad at you or something."

I shrug. "Oh, no. I didn't notice."

"Well, I'm sorry. I just felt bad for Keondra when Camila didn't pick her, and then I realized when I volunteered to work with her, I dissed you, but it was too late. I should have told you earlier."

"Oh, that's okay. I understand. Jiro was a good partner, surprisingly."

"Really? How?"

"Oh, we just had to get crazy in this pub trying to find the coin, and he played along very well, much to my surprise. Then, he saved my ass from getting arrested and clovered with a fire extinguisher. It was great."

"Well, that's nice. Anyway, are we good? I didn't want any hard feelings."

I tell her of course and accept her hug, but when she rushes off to her bathroom time, I wonder if we didn't just learn of the Second Survivor Secret and I didn't have a win under my belt, would she be so sweet and apologetic?

Before I can ponder it further, Ollie comes into my bunk to hug me good morning and ask how I am. He's very complimentary about my performance in the last challenge, telling me I held on well even with my visual hallucination and did a great job escaping Luckster and those cops on the cable trying to arrest me.

Tears find my eyes again and stream down my cheeks, and I tell Ollie how badly I'm feeling about Krystall. "She was my best friend's boyfriend's cousin. I sort of knew her. Didn't really like her, but she didn't deserve…" My voice trails off and I relive her final moments, the ones I caused, and I fight the acid rising in my chest by holding my breath.

"You did what you had to do. Stop beating yourself up for it. You were great. I don't even know how you got away." Ollie's full of praise until he has his bathroom time, and then I'm left wondering if he's sincere, or if he, like Paige, recognizes I'm one of the two frontrunners for winning The Game and he should align with me in case I'm victorious and can choose a second survivor. He knows his TBI has affected him, so he probably doesn't have as good of a chance, even though he's so fit, like he said.

Then we all get together for a strategy session, both Ollie and Paige say they want to be my partner in the challenge at the same time, but I pick Paige and the Black Tortoise, telling Ollie he should do the White Tiger with Jiro because he's the strongest and most agile. Ollie pouts until I whisper to him that I'll make it up to him at Nap Time, and then he grins and tells me he won't forget despite his TBI. He writes a note to himself with black pen on his arm that says, "Nap Time = Ollie + Mallory" and hides it under his sleeve.

This time when they release us from Home Base, it's wrapped in an ad for Human-Flavored Lay's, their newest potato chip "For Your Inner Cannibal™." We step out to find a huge sign saying Mall of America.

"Where the hell is that?" Camila asks.

"Oh my God," I say. "I can't believe it. We're in Bloomington, Minnesota. My grandparents live right next door in St. Paul. I came here years ago when I was twelve to visit them. This is the biggest mall in the United States and there's a huge amusement park right in the middle that's called Nickelodeon Universe, if it's still there."

"Minnesota? Shit, where the hell are they taking us next?" Keondra wonders.

"I don't know, but let's get inside," Paige says. "Mark-Bot already started our time."

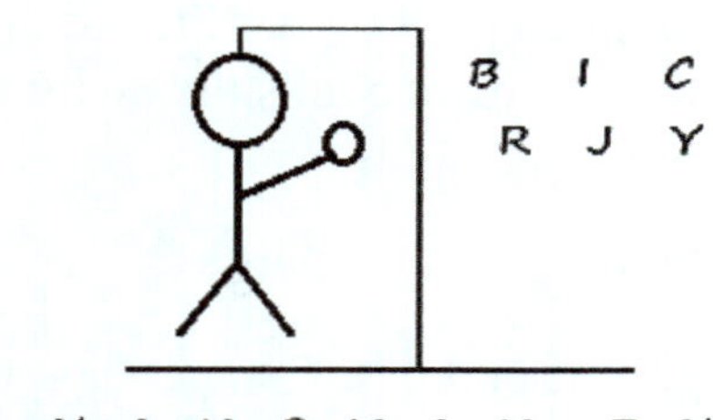


# THE HANGMAN PHASE

As we enter the huge mall teeming with shoppers, Karyn-Bot says in our ears that the Azure Dragon is on the first floor, the Black Tortoise is on the second, and the White Tiger is on the third. The Vermilion Bird will be somewhere in the Nickelodeon Universe theme park. Paige and I rush to the second floor, and we find ourselves in front of Nordstrom's.

"Gosh, so many places for clues and coins," I marvel, eyeing all the shops.

"Let's divide and conquer, like usual. You go right, I'll go left, and we'll meet directly across at that Urban Planet store."

"Sounds like a plan. See you on the other side." I take off toward the right, finding a clue in a Minnesota Twins cap at the Nike store, another in a basket of cookies at a Starbucks, then a third in the jean pocket of the mannequin in the front display window at an American Eagle. Another letter clue is in a stack of rolled t-shirts at a Guess store, and then one is tucked into a coat sleeve at Eddie Bauer.

By the time Paige and I reach each other, we have the entire puzzle except two letters. It says: IN MODELS PURSE.

Paige and I immediately know what that means. In the area between Nordstrom's and Macy's, there's a long runway stage with a curtained doorway in the middle of a lattice wall laced with flowers and greenery. Around the stage, several rows of folding chairs are filled with chatting people as upbeat music plays and overhead lights shine in different colors. Photographers crouch at the end of the stage, poised with their cameras at the ready.

"Oh God, not there," Paige says before I can, and we approach to find a girl about our age emerge from behind the paint-spattered curtain. She wears a bright orange sweater dress under a lime green suede vest with purple thigh-high boots. She has a yellow purse strung across her body and a necklace of red roses. The girl, with curly red and blue hair teased into an afro, walks with an exaggerated pout on her black-painted mouth as photographers snap photos. An emcee tells the audience all about what and whom she's wearing.

"Is the coin in her purse?" I ask Paige.

The model poses at the end of the stage, then pivots and walks back as another girl struts out in a red jumpsuit with high-top fuchsia sneakers, a green tank top, and a cream and orange checkered scarf over her shoulders. She's carrying a blue clutch in her hands.

"Or is it in hers?" Paige asks.

"Shit, who knows?"

"We need to," Paige says. "We've got to get in that show."

"In the show?"

"Yes. As models. How else are we going to get close enough?"

I groan. "I was afraid you'd say that. We can't though, not without giving up our identities."

Paige pulls me with her. "Just follow my lead. Act as if you belong. But no matter what, keep your mask and goggles on."

We sneak backstage to find a line of half-naked girls waiting for others to put clothes on them. Paige slides up beside them and pulls me next to her, taking her top off and throwing it to the side.

I do the same, and a woman with a measuring tape walks up, stretches it out, and wraps it around my bust. "Should be fine. Here, this." A woman thrusts a hanger of clothes at me, and I take it into a corner and change. I pull on a skirt full of different colored stars, a sweater with various stripes of sequins, and tights with the American flag on them. I'm given one black boot and one green, orange socks, and a purple purse. I feel inside of it, but no coin. Paige checks hers but finds nothing either. I leave on my goggles, face mask, and hat so I don't reveal my identity, the weirdest-looking model ever seen.

"Check out whomever you're on stage with," Paige whispers behind her as we are shoved into line with some other models.

I emerge onto the runway, my knees shaky as I face a whole audience peering at me. I imagine I'm in a Broadway musical and this is just part of the show. I see Paige ahead grab the model behind her and try to force her to Tango, but the girl shoves her aside and keeps walking.

A model at the end of the catwalk turns toward me, looking through me with squinted eyes, and I get next to her, throwing an arm around her, then start bumping her hip against mine like we're best pals. She tries to disentangle me, but I encircle her waist and grab her hand, attempting to twirl her, but she won't participate at all, pulling away from me and rushing toward the backstage area.

I follow her, my eyes on her khaki purse, and as she turns to confront me, I grab it even though the strap is still strung across her.

"Sorry, but I might have left my license in there," I say. "Can I see inside?"

She pushes me away, pulling the purse back. "Step off. Jeez. Let me change. Then, you can have it all you want."

One of the assistants gives the model some other clothes, and she ducks behind a curtain, then emerges in the new outfit. I rush into the stall after she leaves, checking her purse, but it's empty.

Shit, this is not working.

Paige goes up on the stage after another wardrobe change, but instead of trying to follow, I stay back where the models are exiting and collect their discarded clothes.

I get two models' change of wardrobe, namely their purses, both of which are void of the Black Tortoise coin. I turn, and one of the assistants inquires who I am. "Did Diane send you over?"

"Oh, yes, Diane," I say with a nod. "Yep. She told me to come by and see if you all needed a hand."

"Good. Hang all these up, and then these," the woman says. She throws heaps of clothes at me. As Paige goes after each model on stage until they're all ready to kill her, I get their outfits after they change, and luckily, I'm able to check their purses. Yet so far, none has the coin.

"Uh, excuse me, miss," the assistant says, coming over. "Diane says she never sent anyone over. Who are you, now?"

The color drains from my face, and my first instinct is to run, but I stick to my guns and stay where I am, "Hey, I left my license in one of these purses and need to find it or I can't go on my cruise tomorrow. Let me just search until I do, and then I'll be on my way."

"I don't know who you are, but you can't be back here — "

I push the woman into the changing room, and she stumbles, tripping into the wall. I come at her again and her eyes widen as I take a stretchy pair of tights and fasten her to a metal railing. Stuffing a pair of socks into her mouth, I tell her if she tries to leave, I'll have my "associate" come in. I shove a gloved finger in her terrified face. "And you don't want to meet him, trust me." I configure my fingers like a gun and put them to her forehead, then pretend to shoot, even adding a sound effect. "That's a good girl. Keep quiet, and my associate won't come pay you a visit."

She nods with wide eyes, and then I stand outside the curtained area and collect each model's wardrobe as they discard them. I still cannot find the coin, but suddenly, I hear Mark-Bot in my ear: "Attention, Vermilion Contestants! Player #1, Paige Tellison, has been detained! She has fifteen seconds to escape or will be permanently eliminated from The Game."

I leave my post guarding the poorly tied assistant and rush onto the stage to see Paige with a red and black purse in her hand struggling with a mall security guard. I hurry toward him from behind and pull a Myra to his Charles, reaching in front of his pants and grabbing whatever's there.

"Oh!" the guard says. His hands go to his groin, releasing Paige.

"Run!" I shout, and she darts away, jumping off the stage.

I push the guard hard and race in the opposite direction, merging into a crowd of mallgoers.

The guard gives chase, and he's surprisingly fast, so I glom on to some other people, who instantly notice me and shoot me strange looks. I leave them for another group, and then another, and another, with the guard still scanning for me. I trade my current group for a large indoor tree and duck down behind it, scoping things out. The mall guard passes, thankfully not noticing me behind the greenery. I breathe a sigh of relief, but just as I'm about to check in with Paige, I hear a familiar voice beside me.

"Did you call Seth to see how Barb is today?"

I peer over at the next table, and my Bubbe and Zayde, my father's parents, are sitting at a table sipping coffee, a large pretzel between them. My heart lurches, and my eyes prick with tears.

My Bubbe shakes her head. "No, not yet. He usually visits Barb at the hospital before work. I'll try to catch him during his office hours after his first class. I keep trying Davina, but she hasn't returned my call at all. Seth says she's too upset."

What? Why is my mother in the hospital?

"She's more stable now, right?" Zayde asks.

"Seth says she's better, but she's still not quite herself yet."

What are they talking about?

"Mallory, are you there?" It's Paige through a Walkie-Bot in my ear.

"Yeah, I'm here. Hold on a sec." My Bubbe glances in my direction, and I can't tell if she recognized my voice. I wish I could let her know it's me, but then Karyn-Bot will spin the Punishment Wheel because I've outed myself and violated a Game Rule and will probably punish her. Saying a silent goodbye to my grandparents whom I desperately want to hug but can't, I walk in a different direction than when I last saw the mall cop. My heart feels much heavier than before. Slipping a finger under my goggles, I wipe my eyes.

"Mallory?" Paige asks through a Walkie-Bot.

"Yeah, I'm here."

"Thank you!" Paige says. "You saved my ass! I don't know how to repay you."

"Oh, it's no problem. You hit that cop at Mackinac Island with a snowball. We're even. Glad we both got out of there. Too bad we still don't have the coin though."

"Speak for yourself," Paige says, coming around the corner. She holds it up and models her newest purse, this one green denim with gold zippers. I don't mention seeing my grandparents, still shaken up. I hug her instead. "What a relief!"

"Tell me about it," Paige agrees. "Okay, let's go see if they need our help with the White Tiger."

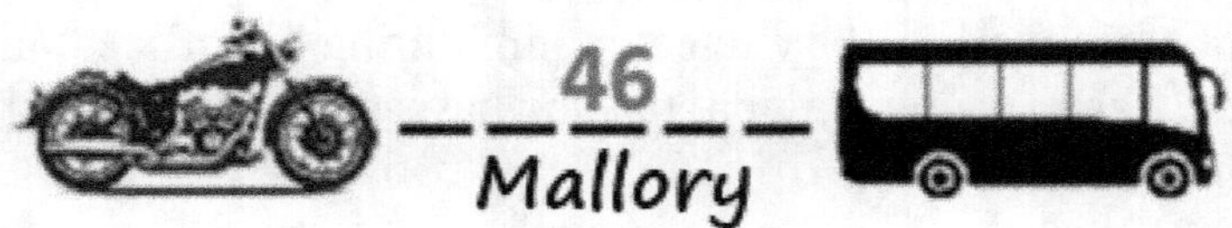


We get to the fourth floor, and Ollie tells us that their clues spell out: MOOSE MOUNTAIN HOLE.

"What's that?" I ask.

"Look right in front of you," Ollie says. "See that huge putt-putt golf place?"

A sign says, "Moose Mountain Adventure Golf," and I groan. "Great. It's ginormous. How many freaking holes are there?"

"Eighteen," Ollie says. "Me and Jiro have looked through ten, but people are getting pissed off, and we need your help to do the rest. The coin might not even be in a putt-putt hole but in one of the million other holes there are in each of eighteen different areas."

"Say no more," Paige says, coming up beside me. "We'll split up the remaining holes while you and Jiro look elsewhere."

"Where are the other girls?" I ask.

"We're here," Camila says, coming up with Keondra out of breath. "Our coin took longer than expected, but we got it. It was in a damn pair of blue suede boots at Famous Footwear, with all the millions of other shoes in that store. Had to fight some woman who wanted to buy them right as we saw the coin was in there, but we got it after Keondra pulled her coat over her head and ran out of the store with the boots."

We divvy up the remaining holes between us four girls, and then we all pay the entrance fee, taking most of our money. I use my lost earring excuse, saying I might have dropped it in each hole, and it works well … except none of my holes have a coin. I help the others with theirs, but we come up empty.

"We just have to keep looking around," Paige says. "Our time is quickly counting down."

We spread out, searching high and low, but there are so many different features and crevices, the coin could be anywhere. And then I realize since it's a harder coin to find, it's got to be in a tough place. A place that's hard to reach, not some simple hole in the ground.

I call Ollie over and tell him my theory, and he agrees. We scope out each area searching for décor or features that are high up or inaccessible.

"It could be in that structure," I say, referring to a course where some people are taking turns shooting their balls through the blades of a windmill. "Their ball must go through that dark area and come out the other side. The coin could be in there."

"Shit, you're right," Ollie says. "I'll go distract them, and you duck in and check it out."

"Ew. Okay." I cringe, but then I realize it can't be worse than Skull Cave at Mackinac Island. Hopefully there are no skulls in there.

Ollie walks up to the family shooting at Hole #4, and he asks if they'd be interested in trying his new restaurant on the third floor. He tells them he will give them coupons when they arrive for their six o'clock seating.

As the couple with two small children ask about what food they have and if his restaurant can accommodate their son's gluten allergy, I duck under the windmill into the base structure, feeling around in the dark. I touch what feels like gum, then maybe gravel, something wet, and then something sticky. My shaky fingers continue probing every surface in pitch black until I remember I can ask Karyn-Bot for night vision. I do, and then I can see that there's not a single damn coin in there and my fingertips are now hairy.

Ollie and I do the same thing for several more tunnels and caves, him promising the world coupons to his nonexistent Ollie's Neighborhood Steakhouse, but we come up empty.

"Where the hell is it?" Camila asks us through our Walkie-Bots. "We've looked everywhere."

I walk along peering above us, and I notice a plane suspended from the ceiling and a train on an elevated track. Both are just for display and aren't moving, but they're still up high and have all sorts of holes.

I call Ollie over, and he agrees the coin could be in one of them. We summon the rest of the group and tell them to distract everyone so Ollie and I can get up to the train and the plane. We tackle the train first since it's easier. Ollie climbs the wall like it's nothing and holds out a hand. I grab it, and he pulls me up with one arm.

We maneuver our way to different ends of the train filled with shiny wrapped presents, me at the front and him at the back. Out of the corner of my eye, I see a mall security guard pointing at me. He starts toward me while talking into his Hollaphone.

"Ollie, work fast. They're onto us."

I slide my fingers into every crevice I can find, but I don't feel anything coinlike as I'd hoped. And now, three mall police are headed toward the miniature golf range.

"Where the hell is it?" Ollie asks, coming toward me and checking every surface along the way.

"Not here. It must be in the plane." I glance back, wondering how the hell we're going to get up so high, especially with mall security soon coming by.

"Or there," Ollie says, pointing.

"Hey! You can't be up there!" a mall guard says. "Come down at once."

"Where?" I follow Ollie's finger to see he's indicating some tube at the front of the conductor car, right above the front grill. Perhaps it's a whistle or an exhaust pipe. Before I can wonder, Ollie jumps up there, stretching to reach. He dips his arm into the tube and pulls out the coin.

The mall security is no match for us, who are so used to breaking free of all types of police by now. We easily get away with mild foot-stomping and rib-elbowing, letting them off easily.

My glee over finally locating the stupid coin is cut short when Mark-Bot announces we only have twenty-six minutes to get the Vermilion Bird, or one player will be eliminated.

The Nickelodeon Universe amusement park on the ground floor in the middle of the mall is huge, with at least twenty rides that I can see. We split up, each going different ways, looking for clues.

We check in at five minutes, and so far, we have:

S __ __ N __ __ __ O __ __ O __ K __ __ T __ O __

After we find more, we fill in a few more letters to get:

S P __ N __ E __ O B __ O C __ __ __ T __ O M

Now, we only have fifteen minutes.

Our heads swivel as we study our surroundings.

"I think I know it!" Keondra says. "Look!" She points up high to a huge loop-de-loop roller coaster where the people on it are presently screaming their heads off. The sign says: SpongeBob Rock Bottom Plunge.

"I think you're right," I say. "But where?"

"I don't know, but we only have less than fourteen minutes to figure it out."

"Let's not repeat what happened on that rooftop with no coin," Camila warns.

An image of Sammi falling and disintegrating at the Detroit Zoo after we choked at Amphibiville flashes before me, and I nod, hoping to never experience that again. But then I realize that if I ever want to win this thing, I'll have to. In fact, that's the goal, to be the one standing at the end.

"It could be in one of the passenger cars," Ollie says. "I'm going to get a ticket and get on."

"We all should," I say, "so we can check more than one passenger compartment. It looks like there's four of them on that car."

"I don't do heights," Keondra says, stepping away.

The rest of us get in line.

"Go do something useful with yourself," Camila instructs, pushing Keondra toward another part of the ride.

When it's finally our turn, Mark-Bot tells us we only have twelve minutes left. We get on and strap in, and I clench my teeth, already terrified even though the ride hasn't started. Although I don't mind heights, I'm not a big fan of falling. After we all check the space at our feet, we verify that there is no coin in any passenger seat, but now we're all stuck on the ride.

I grin and bear it, feeling more and more like I might throw up with every twist and turn. Wracking my brain, I try to think of where it could be.

"I see it!" Ollie says, pointing.

As the ride continues, I strain to hear through my Walkie-Bots.

"It's on that huge blue tower. I saw it on the very top as we passed it."

After we get off the ride, I steady myself on a fence post because I'm so dizzy. Ollie says he's going for the coin, and the rest of us just need to keep the guards busy.

As Ollie rushes toward the tower, Camila comes at me swinging. "You bitch!" She clocks me in the jaw, and I go down.

"What the hell?" I scurry away as she comes at me again. Climbing a trash can which tips over, I try to run away, but she tackles me. I stumble forward, catching onto some people and tearing a lady's bag from her shoulder.

Camila jumps on top of me and tries to strangle me, her claws digging into my neck, but I grab something from the garbage, a half-eaten sandwich, and shove it in her face. She recoils for a second but tries to choke me again.

"Get off her!" Paige screams. She rushes toward Camila and attempts to pull her away from me, but Camila shoves Paige into a table of diners.

I scramble away, but Camila keeps coming at me, yelling at me about her brother Paulo, telling me it's all my fault that the brother she raised is hurt. I apologize again, but her continued attempts to throttle me lets me know my words are meaningless. I get free and sprint away at top speed, but Camila is fast, and she chases me down, diving at my feet and tripping me. I fly right into a mall security woman's arms, who tries to twist mine behind me. "You girls will have to come with me. There's no fighting allowed in the mall."

I stomp her foot and yank away, taking off.

She and other mall security guards chase me and Camila all over.

"What the hell's your problem, Camila?" I demand through our Walkie-Bots.

"Ollie said to keep the guards busy, so I am."

"Guys, do something!" I beg everyone. "Help us before we're detained."

Across the way, a guard rushes toward me. As he reaches for me, Keondra trips him and he flies forward. I duck out of the way, and he lands in some guy's lap who's reclining on a leather massage chair. We take off running again, but there is so much security now, it's like they've called the entire fleet.

Paige, Jiro, Keondra, Camila, and I keep them all busy as Ollie struggles to get to the top of the tower. It takes a while before anyone notices he's up there, but when they do, they shut the ride down and tell him through the loudspeaker he must stop climbing and return to the ground.

He ignores their directions and goes higher.

Ollie tells us through our Walkie-Bots he got the coin, and when he climbs down, several guards are waiting for him. But he's too fast and gets away. At least right then. But as we all rush to the front of the mall to start The Vermilion Hour, several mall cops are waiting for us.

“You have one minute left to form your firescope or elimination time will begin,” Mark-Bot warns.

“Here, give them all to me!” Ollie waves. He jumps up onto a metal beam above the door and pulls himself up so that he’s sitting on it. “Let me get higher so I can put the coins together.” We all hand ours over.

As the guards chase us around the parking lot of the Mall of America, Ollie climbs even higher onto the metal flag grid so he can’t be reached. “I’m freaking done!” he says just as Mark-Bot says, “Three, two, one.”

“Congratulations!” Karyn-Bot says. “Now, it seems everyone except Ollie has the required ten feet from the firescope. We can’t start unless —”

Ollie throws the firescope down into some bushes below and Karyn-Bot shuts up.

“Okay then,” Mark-Bot says. “The required circumference has been done. The Vermilion Hour has begun. Good luck, everyone!”

Keondra retrieves the firescope from the bushes first, and she peers into the hole.

I close my eyes in the bright afternoon light to see the fire text says: Great Wolf Lodge Water Park. Opening them, I find Keondra running with a few mall cops still in pursuit. Hiding behind a van, I ask Mark-Bot for the map and see it's a mile away.

The mall cops give up on a very fast Keondra, huffing hard as they head back.

I duck behind various shrubs to escape their view, and then book after Keondra who is way down the street.

Ollie is on her like a tiger, and he wrestles the scope from her, pushing her to the side. She falls momentarily but practically bounces to her feet and goes after him. Jiro trails closely, moving faster than I would have ever guessed with his short legs.

I follow along with Camila and Paige as the others take turns shoving and hitting each other, trying to get the scope. Just as I'm about to sprint forward, surprise everyone, and make my move, someone pushes me.

The next thing I know, I'm in traffic with a huge bus heading right for me.

Afraid to dive left or right in the heavy onslaught of cars, instead I lay down flat and pray the bus's undercarriage doesn't peel me like a carrot. As the bus barrels toward me, I hold my breath, my nose feeling metal as it roars over me. When I'm clear, I don't even take a second to breathe. I pop up and dart away before the next car can hit me, but another car screeches trying to stop and swerves into a bike rider on the side.

I rush over, checking on the rider who's stunned and upset about his bent wheel but seems okay.

"Sorry," I call, running back toward Paige and Camila a half-block down the street by now. I consider tackling Camila to get her back, but I really need to try to get the scope, not get even with her.

I barrel ahead of them, catching up to the other group, and I reach into Ollie's drawstring sweatpants and give him a huge wedgie, paying him back for the one he gave me at Mackinac Island.

"What the —?" he says, dropping the scope to pick out his underwear.

The scope bounces and I catch it, racing away, determined to reach the water park and claim a second victory. I chug and chug, imagining myself as a speeding bullet or a superhero like The Flash, but then I fall forward.

Did I trip? I don't think so, but I taste concrete anyway, my legs giving out and sinking me to the ground. I attempt to get up, but my legs won't listen to my brain, just hanging there like dead weight. I attempt to crawl, but as Keondra, Ollie, Jiro, and the others speed further away and turn down another street, I know it's useless. I've been hobbled. I expected at least one glitch by now, so here it is. At least it doesn't hurt, but it sure feels weird when nothing works.

I pray everyone else gets glitches too as I sit there in the middle of the sidewalk with HoverSegs hopping by, watching the action of the others.

Camila goes down ahead, sitting on the ground shouting she can't see anything, and I realize since she has a win also, it makes sense someone would give her a glitch now too. So, it's left to the others, both of us frontrunners now waylaid with glitches.

Jiro has the scope, and he climbs onto some raised wall trying to get away from the others.

Keondra rushes him and pushes him off his perch. A second later, several voices scream, and someone pleads for anyone to call 911. Keondra darts around the wall and right into the melee of people huddled around an unmoving Jiro. She reappears with the scope, racing down the street.

Ollie goes after her, and Paige is still expending effort, surprisingly not out of breath like usual although she's quite slow. Maybe her new inhaler is helping her.

I lose sight of them, and after a minute, Mark-Bot announces Keondra the winner of Round 5.

Ollie groans through his Walkie-Bot, "Damn bitch kicked me in the nuts."

"She also killed Jiro," Paige reports. "I'm near where the ambulance is, and they just put a white sheet over his face. He cracked his head on the pavement after she pushed him. There's a lot of blood."

"Oh God, I didn't mean to kill him!" Keondra cries.

"Stupid bitch shoulda' let me win," Camila growls. "If I had two wins, I'd have probably won Vermilion and could've saved your ass as my second survivor. Now, it's anyone's game."

I think for a second. We have one more round to go, so Ollie or Paige could still claim a victory, theoretically, and then we'd hopefully go to a tiebreaker. Then any of us could win except the one without a victory. She's right. It is still anyone's game.

Up ahead of where I'm still on the sidewalk, the feeling trickling back to my legs, Camila storms away from Keondra. A second later, Keondra follows all apologizing, but Camila yells at her and stomps off.

My heart lurches as I think about Jiro and the little that I knew about him. He saved my life with that fire extinguisher in that pub's kitchen at the hockey game, and when we raced away, he'd said, "I never go back there," which just made me hysterical. I remember my shock at hearing him finally talk that time when he told the funny story about Ollie giving Mick Jagger's acceptance speech. Oh, and what Ollie said about him being self-conscious about his broken English because he'd only been in the US a year. I wish I knew more about Jiro, and I feel awful because of this sick game, he lost his life too.

I find Ollie sitting on a bench looking down, hands over his groin, his mask puffing in and out as he breathes hard.

"You okay?"

He shakes his head. "Not really. Because now, I have no chance."

"Don't say that. There's still one more round. Wonder what happens if you or Paige win it. Will they go into overtime or just kill us all?"

Ollie shrugs. "They never said. It isn't in the Game Rules. I just checked."

"Oh, don't worry," Karyn-Bot, the eavesdropper, says. "If there is no winner after the sixth round, we'll go into the seventh, and by then, a victor shall be crowned, or it's over for everyone."

As I walk with Paige and Ollie toward Home Base, I agonize again over who I'd choose if I had to. No decision will be easy, but it's better than having none, because that means someone else has won.

When Ollie comes into my bed and snuggles up to me, I don't even fight him this time, desperate for any moment we can spend together before who knows what will happen. We share a little more about ourselves. Ollie tells me he loves programming computers in his free time and aspires to be a doctor, maybe go into sports medicine, which surprises me. I share my views on being a vegan and how my parents want me to be an engineer instead of a dancer. I realize I feel more connected to him in the short time I've known him than I ever did with Blake, even when he was so supportive after my Zayde had his stroke. Maybe it's because Ollie and I are in the same life or death situation and something like that brings people together or —

Ollie's lips are on mine, and I welcome them, groaning as his tongue probes mine and his huge hands caress me everywhere. "Oh God, Mallory, I've wanted to kiss you so bad, you have no idea," he confides in my ear, then pulls aside my shirt collar, his lips hot on my neck and shoulder.

"You're not playing fair!"

"Huh?"

Paige is there, hands on her hips, glaring down at us. "Shame on you, Ollie, using her like that. You know you're just after her to save you. You're despicable!"

Ollie scoffs. "Hardly. Mallory knows how I feel, and that's all that matters. Why don't you kiss her ass some more and then talk about who's playing fair?"

"I can't do what you're doing to win her over. I don't have a penis. But Mallory, come on, open your eyes. He's using you to win! You gotta know that. He was just all over Camila the other day. He wants you both to pick him!"

I stare at my two friends who glare at each other, and I am relieved when Mark-Bot says there's free bathroom time. I escape the situation and look in the bathroom mirror, my face bright red, wondering if there's any truth in what Paige said. Ollie seemed sincere, but he also appeared totally into Camila that time, then said it was all fake. He could just be trying to win me over or to just get some because he's horny. Or Paige could be saying it to put doubt in my head, which wasn't there until she butted in.

I finally emerge, and Ollie is waiting in my bed for me. Paige is in hers, glaring at us over her crossed arms.

"Well, that's a mood killer if there ever was one," I whisper to Ollie.

He pouts. "Finally got you right where I want you…"

"Poor baby."

Ollie kisses my cheek. "Welp, Med-Bots are doing their sleepy dance anyway. I can feel it. I'm going up to bed, k? Can't stand the evil stare of that witch over there. You know nothing she's saying is true, don't you?"

I look into Ollie's sea-blue eyes, and they seem so sincere. I squeeze his hands in mine. "I do. I know you by now." He's not Asshole Red Car Guy like I thought.

"You do." Ollie brushes the hair from my forehead and kisses it, then my nose, then my lips. "Well, nighty night. I have a hot three seconds to think about now, so thanks for that."

I laugh. "Yeah. It was a nice three seconds, wasn't it?"

Ollie flashes his Colgate smile. "The best."

As the Med-Bots do their thing, I think about how many times Paige and I have saved each other. I think we're about even. I don't owe her. But as I inhale the scent of Ollie all around me, I realize my judgement is clouded, and I'm not being fair to Paige, who like she said can't do for me what Ollie can. And she's right, but does that mean she should lose her life? As the questions go round and round, the drugs abound, and I'm done before I can answer even one.

# PART 13

## DAVINA'S DISCOVERY

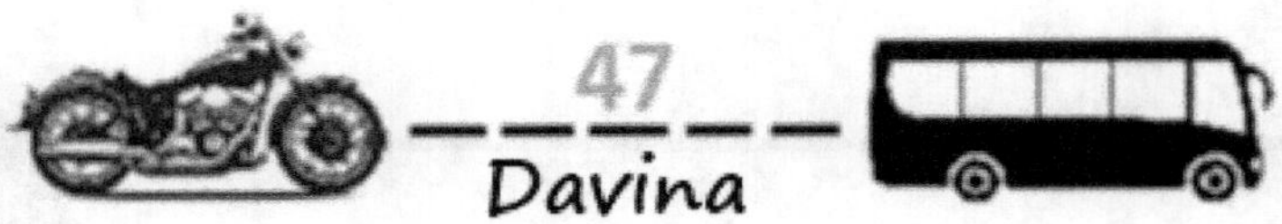


**Sunday, January 27, 2030**

I awaken to some old song blaring from an unfamiliar Hollaphone nearby, telling me I'm so vain, I probably think the song is about me.

Peering down, I find I'm tied to one of our kitchen chairs, rope binding my wrists and ankles to the wood so tight, I can't feel any of them and wonder how long before they fall off.

Isaac stands above me scowling while cutting a Granny Smith apple with a sharp knife.

I scream, but the music is so loud, there's no way anyone can hear me. Our neighbors' houses are too far. I hear Archie and Brian making a racket in the other room, but the singer's voice drowns them out.

"What the hell, Isaac! What are you doing?" I wriggle, but the chair threatens to topple, so I stop, not wanting to hit my head again. I blink through blinding pain over my brow as the first guy I ever kissed lifts the knife to his mouth, biting an apple slice right off the blade.

While chewing, he asks when I became a compulsive liar, his sour spittle landing in my eye.

I blink several times. It stings so bad, but I can't wipe it. Is this really happening? Struggling against the rope at my wrists, I wonder what Isaac hopes to accomplish. With all the horrible images that fill my brain, my breathing quickens, and I'm desperate to get away.

"Snake Riley. You told us all that he 'mugged' your parents. But that wasn't true, was it?"

I scrunch my brow, not sure why he's bringing Snake up. Then I realize he must have seen Snake bring me home. Shit. "Oh, it was true. He did. He even went to juvie for it. It's a matter of public record. You can check online."

Isaac smacks the kitchen table, making me jump in my seat. "Then *WHY IN THE HELL* did I just see him dropping you off? What, you get off on hanging out with guys who attack your parents?"

He comes toward me still holding his apple and knife, cutting another slice, offering it to me with the blade an inch from my face. I back away as much as I can in my chair, but he comes closer, shoving it in my mouth with the knife so I have no choice but to chew it.

"Be careful before you tell me another damn lie." He brings the knife to my neck now, dragging the tip along my skin and then poking it in until I wince.

I jerk away. "He really did attack them," I say around the apple in my mouth. I swallow a huge chunk sideways, and it scrapes down my dry throat. "Everything I said was true. I swear it!" I choke, coughing so much my face feels like it'll fall off.

He waits for me to breathe again. "Then why were you with him? And don't bother telling me you weren't. I was waiting for you. I saw you both with my own eyes. You were in his big fancy SUV bought with nice drug money. How does it feel, hanging out with a guy like that?"

I shudder thinking of Isaac waiting for me for who knew how long. Thank God I was upset and didn't hug Jonah before exiting the SUV. My mind tries to fabricate something new to tell Isaac, but it's so worn out trying to be Lucy, I can't even conjure another lie. I decide the truth is easiest and tell him about Snake's letter, leaving out the parts about what happened with Hawk and that Jonah is in hiding.

"That's bullshit!" Isaac spits on the floor beside my foot. "Another freaking lie. It never happened. Snake never mugged your parents. You just said it all to get attention, to make people feel sorry for you. And now you're seeing *him* when you're supposed to be *MY GIRLFRIEND*! Does he know the lies you've told everyone about him? Should I tell him?" He pokes me in the neck again with the tip of his knife, and this time, he pushes it a little farther until I cry out. He drags it down until he slices me like the apple. Pulling the blade away, he shows me the red tip. "Every time you lie, I get another slice. Maybe apple, maybe you, we'll see. So, better start telling the truth to me."

I spit at him. "You're crazy! That's the truth."

Isaac's nostrils flare and he backhands me across the face.

I shrink away, but there's nowhere to go. He slaps me again and again, yelling at me and telling me he's the best boyfriend I'll ever have, that I blew it, and I'll pay for what I did.

I look around, my mind wild, desperate for a way out of this.

Isaac comes at me again, and I brace myself for the next hit.

It never comes. Instead, there's a crashing sound, and my head whips around. A rock has just landed in the kitchen near me. Beyond that, one of the three tall kitchen windows has a huge hole in it, and suddenly a black boot kicks away the glass.

My heart soars as I think maybe my neighbors were walking their dog out back and saw us through the window.

Someone dives at Isaac and knocks him to the floor, then wrestles around with him a second before I see the Rebel Demons patch on the back of his black leather vest and realize Jonah is there straddling Isaac and punching him in the face.

"Jonah, stop! You'll kill him!"

Jonah ignores me, hitting with his left, then right, then left again, wailing on the insane guy I kissed a total of once who thinks he's my boyfriend.

"Jonah, it's not worth it! I'm fine. He didn't hurt me. Get a hold of yourself and stop right now!"

Jonah slugs Isaac one last time before pushing off of him and standing. He rushes over to me as Isaac lies bloody on the ground, rolling side to side while holding his nose.

Jonah unties my hands and feet, helping me up. "Aw man, you okay?" He grabs a towel off the counter and presses it to my neck.

I hug him, my eyes spilling tears. "Yes. Thank God you're here."

"Just a sec," he says, propping me on a bar stool at the kitchen counter. He goes back to Isaac and bends over him, grabbing him by his collar, and getting right in Isaac's face with his fist. "Now, you listen up asshole, and you listen good. You ever talk to her, text her, or come near her again, and I will sic the entire Rebel Demons Motorcycle Club on you and your whole family, and your family's family too. You hear me? That's a freaking promise. You don't even *look* at her in the halls. No contact at all. You got it?"

Isaac nods with wide eyes as Jonah pulls his arm and yanks him to his feet. He shoves Isaac toward the front door. "Now, get the hell out of here and don't never come back. I'll be watching you. I remember right where you live too, in that red pointy house on Sycamore and Fourth right next to my buddy from middle school."

Isaac mutters sorry before rushing toward the door and leaving.

How did life get so f-ed up so fast? My family members are all on the brink of death or who knows what, my two best girlfriends haven't been there for me at all for their own selfish reasons, and now this crazy guy from school… Thoughts of what might have just happened attack me and I collapse into Jonah bawling as he holds me to his chest, rubbing my back.

"Shhh," he soothes, "It's okay. I'm here. I shoulda' never left you alone, and I ain't gonna' again. You got my word. I'll be wit'chu always."

I look up at him through my tears and see he truly is the guy of my dreams, the one I always hoped to meet. I had no idea I already knew him — but I never really did. I hug Jonah, whispering in his ear. "Thank you for being my friend. I sure need one right now." I burrow my face into his shoulder, and he wraps me in his arms, holding me for a long time like that. I revel in the safety of his embrace, wishing he'd never let me go.

My father's face appears in my mind, and I push Jonah away. "Shit, my dad." I tell him about the call from the hospital, and Jonah rushes me out to the SUV, promising to take me to him.

On the way, I ask Jonah why he came back to my house.

"You said you forgave me for your parents, which I appreciate and all, but I still owe you bigtime. You saved my ass in fourth grade. And I hurt especially your moms. Even if I ain't mean it, it still happened. So, I owe you and your dad, but mostly your moms, and the only way I know how to make it right is to get Rocco to give you an invite. We gotta' save Mallory. I ain't know how yet, but I ain't no quitter, and you ain't neither. So, let's figure this out. We need to for Mallory. I ain't letting you give up, see, or I can't repay your family."

"I don't care what reason you came back, honestly. I'm just glad you did. And not just because you saved my life or want to help my sister.

It's because I love being with you. By the way, I guess we're even now. We've saved each other's lives."

"We cool then. And I love being with you too. Now please, let me repay your family. Let's figure out how we gonna' save Mallory."

After visiting the ER and finding out that my father is on a ventilator, unconscious so I can't even say hi through the window, I decide to go to Grandpa's Farm with Jonah for a few days. I'm terrified now to be alone with crazy Isaac lurking about, maybe plotting revenge. I hope Snake's threat scared him enough, but God knows how a mind like his works. We bring the dogs and Henry VIII, leaving lots of food and water for the cats, vowing to check on them in a day.

We spend two days bingeing on Sons of Anarchy and working on trigonometry, me doing schoolwork my teachers emailed to me and us making trips out to visit Mom, Zayde and the cats. Jonah waits outside when I see Mom, us both knowing she's not ready for him. They let me into Dad's ward, and I watched him in the distance unconscious and hooked up to a bunch of machines, which shreds my heart to strings.

To get my mind off things, I make Mujadara and eggplant parmigiana and some other vegan dishes for Jonah to try. He doesn't like any of them.

"Okay, we'll attempt something else next time," I say as he flips grilled cheese on the stovetop. "There are a million recipes out there, even websites on how to like different foods. They say you should try something ten times before you decide how you feel."

"Sorry. Told ya' I was super picky. Thanks for tryin' though."

"It's funny that me who's so limited even eats more of a variety than you."

"It's sad, but it's true."

Tuesday evening as we're deep into a trigonometry lesson, Jonah gets a call, and a few seconds later, his face falls. "When?" As he listens, he sinks down into a chair. After he hangs up, he studies his socks.

"What? Are you okay?"

Snake shakes his head and pets Lola, who snuggles him around the neck. "I always wondered how I'd feel when I found out, but this is way worse. It's so final."

"What happened?"

"Rocco found Dad this morning. He passed in the night." Jonah's lip quivers, and his eyes moisten. I go over and hug him to me. He sobs into my stomach as I realize that he's now an orphan, losing both parents within the year, and just like that, Rocco is the official President of the Metro Detroit chapter of the Rebel Demons.

Jonah lifts his head and smooths my shirt, then wipes his eyes. "Davina, you can stay here, of course, and help yourself to anything in the fridge or pantry. I'll have a couple guys bring your car and watch over you, but I need to go hang with Rocco at Blades Cave awhile. Decide arrangements and all that. Dad wanted to be cremated, but we'll do a service at some point, and there's some club matters we gotta' discuss. You'll come to the service and be with us?"

"Of course. Yes, whatever you need. Please, go be with your brother. I'll call my friend Niyah and see if I can stay with her right now. I don't want anyone to have to babysit me."

I go rediscover my friend Niyah for the rest of the week and get to learn more about Jeremy than his own mother knows. I'm dying to tell her everything, but I'm still fearful and don't want to involve her if it could be dangerous. I return to school, and I don't hear much from Jonah since he's busy with family stuff. I send him a few texts, but try not to overdo it, not wanting to be creepy like Isaac.

I see Isaac in the halls a few times, and luckily, he doesn't try to talk to me, nor has he texted once, thankfully. Antonia acts like I don't exist. I can't believe how wrong I was about her, and I'm pissed as anything that she and Isaac have ruined Nerd Bowl for me.

On Friday, Jonah texts me while I'm in Calculus, and I glance at my Hollaphone under the desk: *Gud news. Trish has Covid-28. Not bad like yer dad tho. How is he? And yer mom? Barn partee at Grandpa's Farm. Selbrate dad tonit. You shuld come, Lucy.*

I try to focus on the integral problem on the page before me or at least what I'm going to do to win over Rocco tonight now that Trish won't be a factor. Instead, I think about how Jonah's lips felt on my neck that time in the woods and fantasize about feeling them again everywhere.

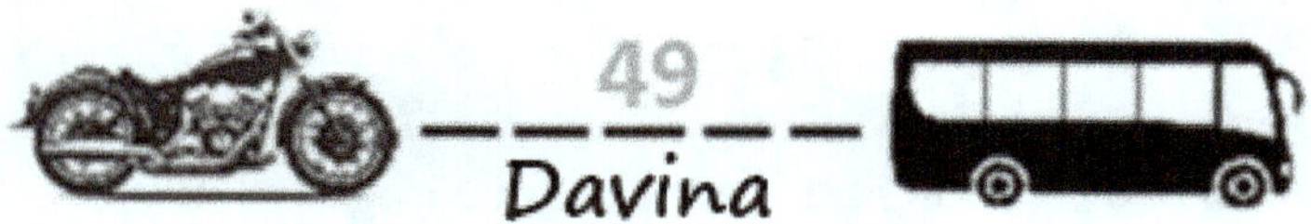

# 49
## Davina

After school, I rush home and biker-slut out, ratting my hair and changing into my skimpiest skirt and tightest bustier under a black leather jacket I steal from Mallory's closet. I feel bad taking it since she's not here, but I think she'd approve of my reasons.

The barn at Grandpa's Farm is hopping when I get there, a heavy metal band blaring from a stage, and there's a blown-up poster on an easel with Snake's father's face on it. Underneath, text reads: *The biggest badass of them all. Rebel Demons 'til the end. RIP, Brother Duke.* Next to it is a silver urn encrusted with skulls and daggers with the Rebel Demons logo burned into it. The demonic face inside a clenched fist even has rubies for the eyes just like Snake's mother's necklace.

As Snake comes with Lola to greet me, Rocco also approaches and grabs my hand, pulling me in for a kiss. "Hey, Lucy."

His smoke breath is super strong, and I feel chunks rise. Holding my nose, I pull him down for another. He pushes me up against the barn door, diving for my neck as I wind my fingers through his hair and look past him to Jonah, who stares at a rock.

"You're so good at saying hi, Lucy," Rocco whispers in my ear, and I lead him inside by the silver chains around his neck, asking him for a drink. He goes off to fetch one while Jonah approaches with a sheepish look.

"This is the epitome of awkward," I say.

"Nah. It's fine. It's what you're here for. I just had me a thought though. Tonight, you gotta' tell Rocco you're a virgin and you want him to be your first. *That's* something none them other girls can offer. *That's* your edge, your way in. Not sure why I ain't think of it before." He smacks the Lola tattooed on his forehead, then kisses the real Lola around his neck.

I raise my eyebrows at him as my heart twists. "But I don't want *him* to be my first. I want —"

"I know." He blows through his lips, shaking his head. "Me too, you ain't got no idea. But that'll get him, and it is way more important. Mallory is more important. Most guys would *kill* to be with a virgin, and he likes that you're so young and inexperienced. Makes him feel like a big man who can show you stuff. He ain't never had that, far as I know, being with no virgin. Play it up, and act even more clueless with him."

I sigh, knowing he's right but not liking it one bit. Especially because I really want *Jonah* to be my first (and second, and third), not his brother who frankly, I can't stand. I'll just have to pretend he's Jonah, which is so weird and despicable, but it might just be the only way to get through it — if I even have the guts.

Rocco returns with drinks, and just as I take a sip, Corrinne comes and drags me onto the dancefloor.

I feel Rocco's and Jonah's eyes on me as I try to channel Mallory, thinking of what she would do, how she would move. I try to mimic her, but it doesn't go well. I stop before I can do something worse.

"What's wrong, Sugar?" Corrinne asks. "Don'cha like this song?"

"No, it's not that."

"Good, because no one doesn't like Metallica! Woo-hoo!" She pumps her fist in the air.

"Oh, I do. They totally rock."

"Hell yeah, they do! So, why'd you stop dancing?" Corrinne bops around me, shuffling her feet and wiggling her hips.

"Because I can't. Like, at all."

"Oh, yeah you can, girl. Go on now. Show me what you can do."

I shy away, but she keeps at me until I attempt a few moves.

Her face twists with concern, and she puts up a hand to stop me. "Ooh, yeah now, don't do all that. I don't even know what that was. Here, try this."

As Corrinne demonstrates how to dance, Rocco, Jonah, and Cody watch us with amused expressions as my cheeks grow redder and redder. This is so not the image I want to convey, so I break away from Corrinne and grab Rocco's chains again, telling him to show me how a bad boy dances.

Instead of trying what Corrinne taught me, I grind against Rocco the way Trish did, feeling like my dog Archie humping his leg, and he backs me up so I'm sitting on a stool against the bar, pulling my legs up so they're straddling him. As we make out, him all Russian hands and Roman fingers, I feel Jonah's eyes burning into me. I finally break away and peek over Rocco's shoulder, but Jonah's not even there.

My heart sinks, which is so messed up. I scan the barn, studying every guy dressed similarly to Jonah in a black leather vest and jeans with a thick silver chain dangling from their hips, but I don't see him anywhere.

"Let's go," Rocco says, standing and holding his hand out to me.

"Where to?"

"There's a private room up in the loft where we can be alone and say hi some more."

He leads me toward the stairs as all kinds of thoughts of Snake snake through my mind, wondering at what point I should share with Rocco that I'm a virgin. When we're halfway up to the loft, right as I open my mouth to tell him, the music stops.

Every guy in the place draws their gun.

Following where they point, I see a woman in the doorway with a torn jean miniskirt, black rhinestone top, and the longest legs ever. Her blonde hair is pulled tight into a ponytail, and huge silver hoops dangle from her ears.

Rocco pounds the wooden railing. "What the fuck, Shailene! Why're you here?"

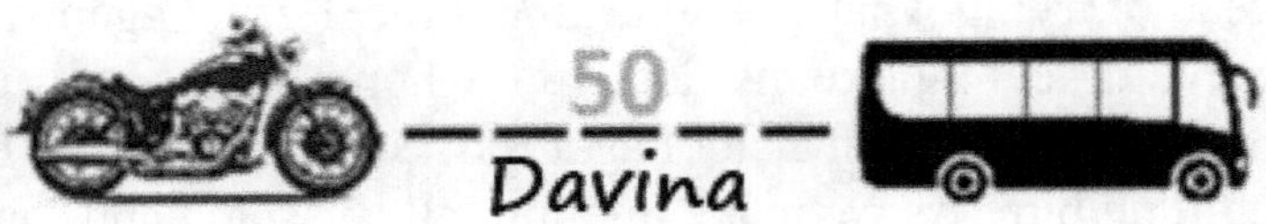


# 50

## Davina

Rocco tells everyone to lower their weapons. One of the guys pats Shailene down, finds she's clean, and then Rocco says he'll see what she wants.

I worry she saw Snake and is going to report back to Hatchet and the Eastside Boyz that he's there. How did she even know where Rocco would be?

I'm left with a million questions as Rocco takes Shailene up to the loft area, me completely forgotten. They go into the room where we were just headed and close the door.

After the band resumes, I wait through several songs, waving off Corrinne who keeps asking me to work on my dance technique. She's annoying after a while, and as time ticks by and I don't see Rocco reappear, my hopes for landing him tonight disappear. I just had him right there in the palm of my hand about to deliver my edge, the secret — or maybe not-so-secret — truth of my virginity, until that unexpected new complication named Shailene walked through the door. She screwed up Snake's life and he's in hiding, and now she's messing with mine, and Mallory's, and she doesn't even know us or what she's done. I can't really hold tonight against her, but I still hate her, even more than Trish.

"Hey, come on, girl! That's my jam!" Corrinne grabs my hand and tries to drag me out to dance again as the band starts playing a song that welcomes us to the jungle for fun and games. "Man, that Axyl Rose's voice makes me so hot," Corinne says, fanning herself.

"No, sorry. I gotta find Snake, make sure he's okay."

She pouts, saying Cody disappeared and now she has no one to dance with, but I leave anyway, wondering if Cody went off with Snake somewhere. I cross Grandpa's property, walking down the way to the preserve. As expected, Snake is there on his rock at Lola's Lagoon, staring at his waterfall as Lola swims around. Cody isn't with him.

Jonah stands when I approach, shoving his hands into his pockets. "Ain't expectin' to see you so soon."

"I'm sorry. I know it's uncomfortable. I get why you had to leave."

He shakes his head. "I left because I saw Shailene. She can't know I'm here."

"Oh," I say, disappointed. "Yeah, she kinda' shot a hole through my plans. She's with Rocco now instead of Trish, and instead of me. Yet another hurdle I didn't see, and time's dwindling."

Jonah extends a hand and pulls me down to the rock with him, where we sit watching Lola as she puts on a show. "No way Rocco will forgive her, especially after she threw Mom's necklace and dissed him in front of everyone."

"I dunno. He took her up to his loft, where he was about to bring me. I never even got to tell him I'm a virgin."

"Man, that sucks. Didn't see *her* coming back into the picture to mess things up."

"Yeah, I know." I exhale. "I'm kind of relieved though."

"Relieved?"

"I don't know if I could have gone through with it," I confess. "Not sure if it would've been better or worse than killing that deer."

"Looked like you was into it. Had 'em practically eatin' out of your hand and shit."

"Me?" I laugh. "Nah, I don't think so. Maybe a little nibble because he was desperate without Trish or any of the others, bored since none of them were around. He'd have done anyone."

Snake eyes me, shaking his head and laughing to himself. "It's like you ain't even know."

"Don't know? What don't I know?"

"Just how goddamn sexy and smart and amazing you are. Course I freakin' left cause I couldn't watch y'all together." Snake pulls me to him in the moonlight, kissing me long and deep and hard until I can barely breathe, his lips hungry as they devour me. He groans into my ear while I stroke the Lola drawn on his head and neck. The real Lola spies from her lagoon, Slither Smiling her approval.

I push away for a second, gasping for air. "Thank you, the feeling is *very* mutual like I cannot believe. And just so you know, every time I kiss Rocco, in my mind, I'm really kissing you, and I'm so turned on, I'm afraid I'll lose control. Is that messed up or what?"

"Yes, and no," he says, and his lips find mine again. His tongue circles with mine, making me tingle all over while my heart races and my cheeks burn. He pulls away and his eyes glisten as they stare into mine. "So, how's the real thing compare with what you imagined?"

I return his smile. "I never thought I could feel like this, especially with you," I say as he laces his fingers through mine. I think of how I felt about him until I read the letter, like I would've been happy never seeing him again, and now? The total opposite. I hope I never *not* see him. The flip-flop gives me the chills, like my life was a pancake that just got tossed on its belly. "No one in my family would believe we were together right now. They'd be floored."

"You so right 'bout that. And you have my permission to lose control *anytime*." He flashes his cute fangs and gently lowers me down so I'm lying on the rock, his arm cushioning my head, and he strokes my cheek, gazing into my eyes and licking his lips. As I pull him to me, the heat between us ignites the chill in the air. The trickling from the waterfall and my heartbeat are all I can hear.

I try to block out the whooshing water sounds and focus on Jonah and the amazing way he smells and how great he feels in my arms, but my bladder has other ideas. I try to ignore it, crossing my legs inconspicuously, trying not to focus on it, but when I can't take it anymore, I push away, apologizing and sitting up.

Jonah sits up too, his face concerned. "What, did I do something? Did I bite you or —"

"Oh no, it's not that. God, no, it's great. It's just that, uh, well…"

I get to my feet, but a wave of pressure overtakes me, and I cross my legs, practically keeling over.

"You okay?" Jonah's brow furrows and he gets to his feet.

"Oh, no. Sorry, but I just like – God, this is so embarrassing, but I really, really gotta' pee. Damn waterfall."

Jonah laughs. "Is that all?"

I nod.

He points. “Go in the shrub over there. I ain’t gonna’ look.” He turns around.

I peer over where he pointed. “Ooh, no, I can’t. I’m not good with going outdoors.”

Snake turns back and grins, a little laugh escaping him. “Really? Okay, well if you can make it to Grandpa’s house, the side door is unlocked. Remember it’s the second door on the right in the hallway past the kitchen. You gotta’ go yourself though cause Shailene’s around.”

“It’s okay. Back in a few.” I rush out of the preserve, darting past the barn to Grandpa’s house as fast as I can manage without losing it on the way. The band is loud, rivaling the revving of various motorcycles as more Rebel Demons show up.

I enter Grandpa’s house, and it’s dark. Rushing past the kitchen, I find two hallways, not just one, and they both have doors in them. I’m not sure which way to go.

Did he say second on the left or third on the right? Suddenly, I can’t recall, but my bladder just picks a door for me, and I yank it open.

Flicking on the light, I pull my pants down, expecting a toilet. Instead, Rocco’s there sitting in a chair, a euphoric smile on his face. Someone kneels between his legs, their blonde ponytail bobbing up and down.

As I realize that Shailene already got her claws into Rocco in the few seconds she’s been back, he jumps up. “Oh shit, Lucy! I, uh, I — what’re you doing here?“ He pulls up his pants and zips his fly, stumbling backwards over his chair.

Shailene gets up and turns around, only, it’s not Shailene at all, but Cody.

# 51

## Davina

I race down the hall with my pants around my knees whipping open different doors until I find the bathroom and finally relieve myself, wondering if I was just hallucinating. After I wash up, I rush out of there.

Rocco is waiting, hands shoved in his pockets, a sheepish look on his face. “Lucy, I can explain.”

Unsure what to say, I push past him and burst out the kitchen door, running through Grandpa’s farm, past the barn, and toward Snake in the preserve. As I stumble along in the darkness, I try to grasp what I just saw, wondering where the heck Shailene went and how Cody got involved.

I had no idea Rocco liked guys, just like I didn’t know Antonia liked girls, or at least me. I guess my gaydar is broken. But all the other girls’ gaydar isn’t working either, because Trish and the other Biker Cinderellas didn’t seem to know either. Maybe Shailene did and that’s why she suddenly dumped Rocco. I’m not sure Snake is aware. Should I say something?

No, if Snake knew, he wouldn’t have pushed me on Rocco to get him to take me to The Game. He would have known it was impossible for Rocco to pick anyone as his old lady if he batted for the other team, but he did date and live with Shailene. He gave her his mother’s necklace. And he did make out with Trish and Ginger and Candy and Tamilee and anyone else willing and pretty enough. He even made out with me.

So, he’s bisexual. Big deal. Good for him. It’s shocking, because I had no idea, but I don’t have any issue with him for it. Now, Cody on the other hand, cheating on super-devoted Corrinne, well, that’s a whole different matter. And Rocco’s screwing her over too by them being together, so that’s not cool.

As I lift the fence and slip into the nature preserve to find Snake again, I decide I can’t tell him about his brother. It’s not my place to, just like I haven’t told Niyah about Antonia kissing me.

I try to ignore this startling turn of events and resume my make-out session with Snake, but after a minute, he pulls away and squints at me. "Did something happen while you were gone?"

"No, why?"

"You just seem different, distracted. I thought maybe – "

"Oh God, I'm the worst." I blurt out what happened, unable to contain it any longer, but then I kick myself, knowing it was wrong and I'm just a weak gossip.

Jonah shrugs. "I figured as much."

"*What?* You *knew*?"

"Not for sure, but I suspected stuff over the years."

"That Rocco was with Cody or that he liked guys?"

"He and Cody. Other guys, I don't know. But he and Cody disappear together a lot. And they play video games, so they always up late at night in one of them's rooms, door shut. I ain't know for sure, but I ain't that surprised neither. I say, hey, good for them."

"Me too, totally, but I don't get it. You were trying to get me to seduce Rocco to become his old lady. Why would you do that if you knew he didn't even like ladies?"

"Oh, he does. That ain't no act. He loved Shailene. Talked about having kids with her. Gave her mom's necklace. And he must have an old lady, to look right with the club. That's how it works. Biker guys have old *ladies*, not old *men*."

"How long do you think it's been going on with them?"

"Who knows? Probably a while. We be knowin' Cody and his family since birth. Cody's maybe even his true love. But they can't never be out. They'd both be kicked out and made to black out their Rebel Demons tattoos and be totally disassociated. Blackballed. Alienated. Cody's just a prospect, so ain't that big a deal, but Rocco is President now. Huge deal."

"I thought the Rebel Demons weren't all like Swastika Dude."

"Oh, the guys ain't all racists and Jew-haters like him, but they're all anti-gay pretty much. Being gay just ain't very accepted in the biker community, with some exceptions. Just depends. Not here though, not by a longshot. Rocco can't let nobody know, which is why he's got this whole Prince Charming at the ball thing going on with all them hot girls. It's all for show. He'll eventually settle on one of them as his old lady, probably Trish."

"You think Shailene knew?"

"Maybe. Or she just likes to move up the ranks of biker clubs. There be girls like that, who sleep around and keep risin' up. Rocco probably told her to get stuffed after everything the bitch did. She'll probably move on to the Mayans next, then the Hell's Angels, maybe the Outlaws, because Rocco ain't never taking her back."

"Rocco will probably bring Trish to the next round," I say. "My virgin story won't be so enticing when he has such variety, between her and Cody."

Snake's face lights up. "Actually, it's perfect. This shit all happened for a reason. "

I raise my eyebrows. "Perfect? What's perfect?"

Snake grabs me into a huge bear hug. "We got our in."

"What are you talking about?"

"We gotta' use it against him."

I choke on my shock. "What, use Rocco's bisexuality against him?" I shake my head as Snake nods, a gleam in his eye. "Nuh-uh. No way. That's terrible. It's not his fault that it's how he feels. It's wrong that they're screwing over Corrinne, and we should probably tell her or force them to, but other than that, I see no problem with their relationship. If they must sneak around like that, which is super sad, at least they can be happy sometimes with each other."

"You see that movie about Winston Churchill's decision 'bout Coventry in World War II?"

"No. What? How is that relevant?"

Snake puts up a hand. "Just hear me a sec. Churchill found out that the Nazis was gonna' bomb some British city called Coventry, and they had enough time to warn people so they could split. But Churchill ain't do it cuz then them Nazi's woulda' known about that math dude's solving that Enigma Code. That's how they found out 'bout the bombing in the first place."

"You mean Alan Turing?"

"Yeah, that's the dude," Jonah confirms.

"Yeah. I don't get —"

"Like 600 innocent people died. Churchill said — I'll never forget this — you gotta' sacrifice a few for the good of the many, something like that. That code that math dude discovered helped them win the war and save way more than 600 people."

I shake my head. "Why are you telling me all this?"

"If we blackmail Rocco and Cody, yes, really shitty. Totally agree. But we gotta pull a Churchill and sacrifice a few for the good of the many. Threaten to out them and force Rocco to bring you — and maybe hate me — to save Mallory."

I exhale, thinking it through. After a ten-round wrestling match against myself and all the things I believe, I decide that my sister's life is more important. I'll sacrifice Rocco being mad at me and even his brother in exchange for her life any day, and hopefully, some of the others if we can rescue them too. I don't want Rocco to end up hating Jonah, but I guess sometimes you must do a wrong to do a right, a lesson I'm learning that I really, really don't like.

"Shit, okay. I guess," I tell Snake, and we start discussing our plan.

## PART 14

## ROUND 6: SANDY'S CHALLENGE

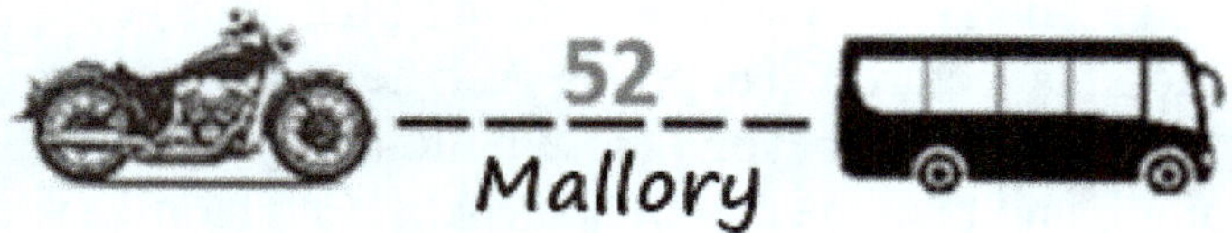


**Saturday, February 2, 2030**

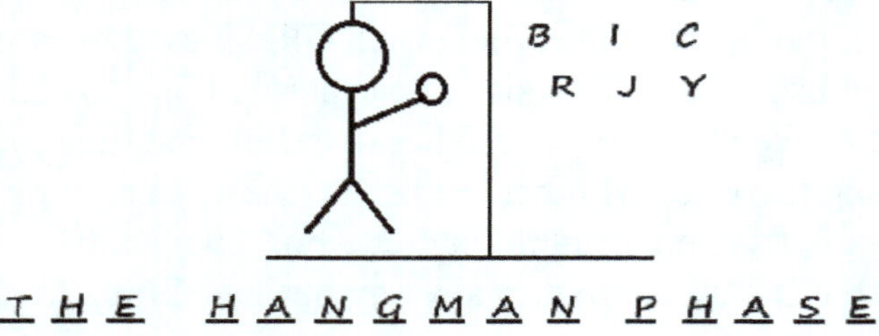


Everyone's nervous as we open the door to Home Base for maybe our last round. It's down to me, Camila, and Keondra now who each have a victory and can score another to win the whole thing. But we could end up going into an extra round, as Karyn-Bot said, if Ollie or Paige somehow win today. I don't know if I can take much more of this, but it looks like I don't have a choice besides giving up and dying.

At least now, we don't have to worry about losing our limbs, I think, and the image of Krystall's face right before she was split in two flashes before me. I fight the rising bile in my throat as guilt embraces me like an annoying best friend.

"God, now where the hell are we?" Camila asks, coming out of Home Base and standing next to me. I'm blinking from the brightness of the morning but also shock. As Home Base takes off and we stare at all the buildings around us and huge ice sculptures everywhere, I see a black, gold, and white banner in the distance that says: "Welcome to the 2030 Michigan Tech Winter Carnival!"

"What the hell?" Paige asks. "We're right where we were supposed to be going all along?"

“Yeah,” Ollie says. “We’re at freaking Michigan Tech! I recognize the campus from its pictures.” He points past me, and I turn around. “If I’m not mistaken, if you go beyond those buildings, you’ll find Portage Lake to the north and then the city of Hancock, Houghton’s sister city.” He points to his left, which is west. “And I believe over that way is the Houghton-Hancock Bridge that connects the two, right past downtown Houghton.”

I peer at students all around. Some are in Tech and Greek gear, but many are dressed like us, the original RainBO PranXterz. I shake my head, incredulous that even people up here in the middle of nowhere look like us.

“Let’s get to our regions,” I say, and I grab Paige. I felt so funny about our weird confrontation earlier when Ollie kissed me and then Paige accused him of using me, so I chose to partner with her for our final round instead of Ollie, even though I chose her over him last time too and seem like I’m playing favorites with her. But she thinks I’m playing favorites with him. I guess I seem partial no matter who I choose. It’s weird to be in this position, but it may not matter anyway because I may freaking lose.

Paige and I are to find the Black Tortoise in the North, while Keondra alone will try for the Azure Dragon in the East. She killed Jiro and Camila is no longer talking to her since Keondra won the last round, so I guess that’s her punishment. Ollie and Camila are together again for the White Tiger, which I’m not thrilled about, but I did choose Paige, so it’s my fault. If Camila wins, she’ll probably pick Ollie now.

As Paige and I rush over to the north region, I ask what day it is.

“It’s hard to know when they knock us out for undetermined amounts of time each round,” Paige says. “If you think about it, this could be like a year later. Who knows how long they keep us unconscious? Those Med-Bots can turn our urine into nourishment, so we could be like Sleeping Beauty. Why do you ask?”

“I just wonder if there are classes going on right now or what because there’s an awful lot of students outside.”

She peers around and agrees. “They seem pretty frantic too.”

We stop in front of an ice sculpture of a huge ship that’s half sunken below the surface, the part above ground tilted at a sixty-degree angle. I don’t even know how it’s standing up like that, defying all laws of physics. Several girls and a few guys tend to different parts of it.

"I think it's the Titanic," Paige says.

A girl nearby with a clothes iron in her hand attached to a long extension cord runs the metal face over something made of ice near her so that it becomes shinier. I realize as she steps away to examine her work that her sculpture is a dingy on the ground with someone on it peering at the ship a few feet away. Someone else in the "water" — really snow — holds onto the raft with an outstretched hand, their head visible above the surface.

"Oh my God, I think that's Rose in the little boat and Jack in the water," I say. "From the Titanic movie. It's Kate Winslet and Leonardo DiCaprio!"

"Yeah, wow, totally," Paige agrees. "Man, I cry every damn time at the end of that movie. I'm choked up even now." She sniffles and turns away.

"It's incredible. They should win," I say, closing my eyes to view a map of our surroundings behind my eyelids. "Okay, we're at the Pelt Library right now. You go left, I'll go right, and let's meet at that Dow Environmental Sciences Building as soon as we can with as many clues as we can find."

"Okay."

I stay where I am as she runs off, and I approach where several students are working on their Titanic sculpture. In the upper of two smokestacks sticking out of the ship, I see a black card poking out, much higher than I can reach.

A girl in a KTZ sweatshirt approaches. "Hey, did they send you over to help?"

"Yeah," I say, playing along.

"Good. Go take that hose there and make more ice blocks in those square forms. Pack snow first, then the water, then snow again. I need some pieces to make this suitcase in the water. And hurry up. The judges are coming within the hour!"

I nod and go to where she pointed. When she turns away, I walk past the hose, bucket, and wooden square forms, and I approach where the card is in the stack. I can't get it as it's way too high, but there is a ladder in the distance. As I start toward it, I hear a voice behind me.

"Hey you, Pledge Girl. I told you to make me some blocks. Why're you disobeying me?"

The sorority girl's face scowls and her hand is on her hip. I don't have time to fool with her. I rush over and grab the ladder, bring it to where I need, and climb to the top as she demands to know why I'm ignoring a direct order by a full sister of the Kappa Tau Zeta sorority.

I stretch to reach the clue as she starts talking into her Hollaphone.

"Yeah, and she won't even listen to me! Who the hell is this girl? Kick her ass out or give her ten demerits at least. Make her scrub all the toilets for a month. Bitch."

I finally get the card, inching it out of the smokestack so it doesn't drop further inside, and rush down the ladder and away, glancing at it briefly so it'll be entered into the puzzle board.

I hurry toward the Electrical Energy Resources Center, which is locked, but I find a clue in some bushes near the front entrance. I discover another half under a trash can in front of Dillman Hall.

Slip-sliding around on the hard-packed snow and ice, I grab clues as I see them, trying not to stop and study the amazing ice sculptures everywhere. I pass a montage of scenes from Alice in Wonderland, another of Humpty Dumpty and all his stages of falling off the castle wall in five separate sculptures with king's horses and king's men in each. I slide past another of Dr. Seuss Land, complete with Cat in the Hat, several odd-shaped mushroom-topped houses with crooked windows, and of course, Thing 1 and Thing 2.

Grabbing for a tree, I stop for a minute, totally winded, and sit on a stone wall outside the Walker Arts and Humanities Center. I stretch my arms, so tired of all this, and as I bring them down, I elbow someone.

"Hey! Watch it!" A girl I didn't even notice twists around to shoot me a dirty look, then scoots over and turns back to her Hollaphone which is blown up large enough on her wrist so that I can even read it.

"Sorry. Didn't see you." I peer over her shoulder at her Hollaphone, missing my own, desperate to just grab it and call my mother, but I know what'll happen if I use technology. My eyes focus on MetaApplesoft's main screen, and there's a reel of news stories. Curious if I can learn what they're saying about us, if they know of us at least from Mackinac Island, I lean a little closer, straining to see.

I can finally make out a headline. It says: *Paige Tellison, Missing Tech Nine Captee, and Entire Family Received Top Awards Right Before She Disappeared.* Below it, I see Paige there holding a gold trophy that says, "Lawrence Technological University Creative Writing Award – First Place – January 8, 2030." She's standing next to a woman with a gray bob, a balding man with a bushy mustache, and a tall guy a little older than her with almost white hair who has the same face.

"Jeez, do you mind?" The girl whose Hollaphone I'm spying on gets up and walks away, flinging her scarf and sprinkling snow at me.

Paige asks how we're doing in my ear. We agree we don't have enough letters yet. We only have: M __ __ __ B __ __ L __ __ __ __G __ __ D __

"Okay, check-in within ten minutes," she says.

"Fine," I mumble as I get up and start wandering around with my eyes peeled for clues. What the hell did I just see? Paige with her high achieving family in January of *this year* right before she disappeared. That means, this month, if it's still January. Paige, an award-winning creative writer, whose parents are supposed to be recently deceased in a train derailment with a little sister who she is desperately worried about, a little sister in foster care with abusive foster parents. Paige's family in the photo seemed to consist of an older brother, not a little sister. But maybe she has one too, and Kimmy was just not shown.

The article said Paige got the award *right before she vanished*. So, even if there is a Kimmy, Paige's parents are there with her and very much alive. Which means their deaths were a lie, as is the need for foster care. So then, there *isn't* a lecherous foster father staring at Kimmy while she sleeps or a foster mother beating her. If there is a little sister, she's not in any danger. She's just a normal girl whose older sister is a liar.

Damn. The bitch played me, trying to earn my sympathy.

But why would Paige lie to me about it all? I don't get it. Why did she want me to feel sorry for her? She made up this bullshit sob story to win me over *before* I won my round. And *before* we knew of the Second Survivor Secret. It's like she somehow *knew*.

I freeze, chills shooting up my arms. *Is Paige part of The Game?*

"Hey, I'm not finding any more clues," Paige says in my ear.

“Nah, me neither,” I manage, barely able speak. “But let’s meet anyway now at the Dow Building. I’m close by.”

“Okay, but why? We still don’t have enough letters.”

“Just meet me.”

She asks again, but I ignore her and walk past several more sculptures on my way, trying not to stop and examine each masterpiece or admire the students working on them who seem to know what to do to defy laws of physics with snow and water and some rudimentary tools.

“Hey, what’s up?” Paige says, coming around a corner. “You okay?”

“I just saw something very interesting.”

“Oh, me too. There was this whole Little Mermaid sculpture under the sea with coral and lily pads and all kinds of fish, and then Ariel was on this rock with Prince Eric embracing her. It was beautiful! I hope that one wins. But man, how are they even going to choose? Each one is better than —"

“I’m not *talking* about sculptures,” I say through clenched teeth. “I saw a news article.”

“Yeah? You used technology?”

“By accident.”

“Well, what are they saying about us? I can only imagine.”

“Oh, just that *you* won some creative writing award with your very-much-alive family with an older brother instead of a little sister *right before we were taken*.”

Paige gasps. “What? Why would they say that? They’re full of shit. It’s not true!”

“Paige, there was a picture of you! On MetaApplesoft! With a brother, not a sister, and *alive parents*, holding a goddamn trophy with *this month’s date on it*!”

I’m dying to see her expression as she covers her goggles with her hands and her shoulders bob.

“Oh, working on your crying? Your technique is way off. You’re taking too long. Throw in some sniffles.”

She exhales. "I can explain," she whispers.

I cross my arms. "So, it was all bullshit. Your whole story. How? Why? Are you part of Azure Dragon, Inc.? *DO YOU WORK FOR THEM?*"

"No! No way! I'm not part of this!"

I sit on a wall, staring at a scene of Mario Brothers as students in rainbow clothes add ice bricks to a section of a castle turret. Princess Peach of the Mushroom Kingdom hangs out a window waving to Mario and Luigi who are jumping over turtles to save her.

"You've got to believe me! Mallory! I'm not part of Vermilion!"

I shake my head, blowing through my lips. "I thought we were friends. How could you —"

Paige scoffs. "Friends? Really? *Friends*?! You think I want to be your *friend*?" She snorts with indignation. "Boy, you are even stupider than I realized, thinking Ollie is into you too. You're so full of yourself. I don't care to be your *friend. I'm trying to save my own freaking life*!"

Her words slap me across the face, and I burst into tears. "But why me? And how did you know?"

"Karyn-Bot whispered the Second Survivor Secret to me in the bathroom during Orientation. I knew the winner would be able to save someone. I don't think she told anyone else."

"Huh. Why would she do that?" Paige could be part of Azure Dragon, Inc., and this is another way to mindfuck me.

She shrugs. "I've been wondering myself, but you know very well I have NO chance of winning this thing. Maybe it was to give me an up so I could contend. I'm not sure."

"So, you lied to get my sympathy."

"I tried, but I don't have a penis."

I recoil like she slapped me again. "That's so not fair."

"Hey, I did what I had to do so you would pick me. You should feel complimented that I had confidence in you winning. Ollie's doing the same thing, you mark my words. He's not interested in you, only you helping him win."

“Oh, I should feel good because you chose me since Camila doesn’t like you and would pick Keondra or Ollie or even Jiro over you?”

“No. I didn’t know that then. You just seemed nice and might like me, and you’re fit, maybe enough to win. And then when I saw Ollie space out and Sammi died, I knew I made the right decision to align myself with you.”

My mind flashes to her asthma inhaler with another girl’s name. “Your asthma story was bullshit too, wasn’t it?”

She clears her throat. “I happened to have my friend’s inhaler in my pocket. She’d asked me to hold it for her and I forgot all about it until I discovered it in my hoodie that first day on the bus. It came in handy.”

I sigh. “I just can’t believe this. You truly are a fabulous creative writer, and actress. If I didn’t hate you so much, I’d ask you for tips.”

Paige exhales. “Wow. Thanks.”

“Find the coin without me.” I stalk off as Paige calls behind me that she’s sorry, but she did what she had to do.

Seething, I summon Ollie with a Walkie-Bot.

He answers right away. “Hey you. What’s up?”

Just as I’m about to tell him what happened, I turn the corner around large shrubs and smack right into some people.

I slip on the ice and go down, grabbing onto one of them and dragging them down too.

“Hey!”

“Oh, God, sorry!” I say. “I need to look more where I’m going.” I scramble to my feet and offer a girl about my age a hand, helping her up. Just then, I realize I’m staring right into the face of my sister Davina.

My heart practically bursts out of my chest as I notice she’s with that guy Snake with the huge snake tattoo wrapped all around his head and face, the one who mugged our parents on Valentine’s Day. *What the hell?*

“Oh my God, Mallory! Is that you?” Davina squints at me.

Even though I’m wearing my goggles and mask, she can tell!

I desperately want to hug her, to tell her everything, to beg her to save me. But I know they're watching me through my Mirror Egg. They'll know. And then, I'll be subject to the Punishment Wheel for revealing my identity and trying to seek help. Brutally aware of what these maniacs who have us are capable of, sure they'll torture Davina in some insidious way, I turn and run as she calls after me.

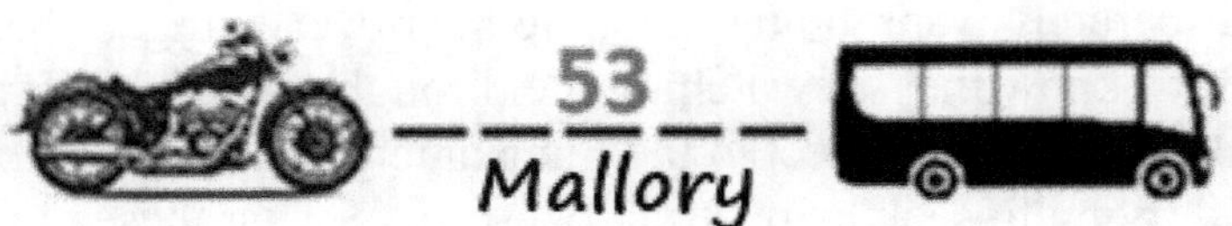


Davina and Snake give chase, but they are no match for me who by now is so used to escaping people, and I eventually lose them when I duck into a huge crowd of rainbow-clad students gathered around some broomball rink yelling at the players thrashing around inside.

I go to the west region of campus, and through Walkie-Bots, I find Ollie at the Administration Building poking around in the bushes. "Hey."

"Hi," Ollie says. "It's locked, so it must be the weekend. I figured there might be at least some clues outside."

I nod and tell him I found one in a row of hedges. While I help him search, I explain what happened with Paige.

"Wow, you serious? Her story was all bullshit? Even her asthma?"

"Yeah. I'm in shock. I mean, we went to bat for her, stole a freaking kid's inhaler for her, and it was just to gain my sympathy. She targeted me from day one. Isn't that so creepy?"

"Why would she hear the Second Survivor Secret before the rest of us?"

I shrug. "Maybe because she was weak. Perhaps to see what she'd do. I have no clue. Or, she's part of Vermilion, works for whoever has us. I think she's a plant, here to fuck with us."

"Bitch, why you here?" Camila asks, coming up out of nowhere.

She punches her fist toward me, and I twist away before it lands. "Leave me alone, you psycho."

"We don't need your help with this coin. Go!" She lunges for me again.

Ollie blocks her. "Hey, we need her help. We only have a few letters and there are a million places to look."

Camila crosses her arms. "Fine. But stay the hell away from me."

“Fine. You too, or next time, I bite.” I chomp at her, my teeth clicking loud, and she backs away.

Mark-Bot tells us we only have thirty-seven minutes remaining in the round, and we scatter, knowing we must find the White Tiger coin, but also the Vermilion Bird.

After we gather more clues, we have:

U ___ ___ O ___ B ___ ___ K ___ ___ O ___ E ___ E ___ L ___ N ___

“Man, I don’t know. This one’s hard,” Ollie says.

“No, it’s not,” Camila says in our ears. “Because I’m standing right in front of the Memorial Union and Bookstore.”

I investigate the puzzle behind my eyelids. “Shit, it fits. I think it says ‘UNION BOOKSTORE’, but what’s that last word?”

“It could be PEELING,” Ollie suggests.

“That makes no sense,” Camila says. “UNION BOOKSTORE PEELING.”

I stare up at the red brick building with the cylindrical, two-story entrance as Ollie and Camila join me. “It wouldn’t be peeling since it’s made of brick. But maybe inside it is.”

“It’s not PEELING,” Ollie laughs. “It’s CEILING.”

“Hey, that’s not funny at all,” Camila says. “The coin’s in the freaking ceiling?” Her desperate voice sounds like she might wig out any second.

I feel like I might too. Mark-Bot reminds us that we have thirty minutes now. We rush inside with no plan in mind, quickly finding the bookstore.

“Is there a ladder anywhere?” Camila asks.

“Good idea,” I say, hating to compliment her. I scan the student lounge areas, but I don’t see any.

“We could use a chair,” Ollie suggests, grabbing one nearby. He stands on it, reaching upward.

“You’re not tall enough,” I observe.

“But you and I are,” Camila says, and she grabs Ollie’s hand, pulling him through the doors into the bookstore.

I follow them inside to find Camila already jumping up on Ollie’s hands. He props her up so that her feet are even with his shoulders, and she pushes at a ceiling panel. The good news is that the ceiling is the drop-panel kind where there are removable rectangles on a metal grid. The bad news is that there are about a million to check.

“Um, excuse me, but what are you doing?” A chubby man in a sweater, shirt, and tie with a shiny gold badge that says “Raymond, Assistant Manager” on his pocket approaches with an alarmed expression on his face.

“Oh, hey. We’re with Campus Operations,” Ollie says. “Damn electrician left his wedding ring here last week when he was working on some wiring in the ceiling, if you can believe it, and he forgot exactly where.”

“Um, what? Who now?”

Ollie shrugs. “I don’t know his name, just that I was sent here with my coworkers to find his ring. Guy’s off on assignment today but needs it bad.”

Ollie lifts Camila up again to check another panel as Raymond frowns at us.

“This is highly unusual,” he says. He presses his Hollaphone. “Now, who did you say sent you?”

I climb up Ollie as the assistant manager keeps questioning us and we ignore him.

“Uh, guys, I’m sorry, but I can’t have you doing this right now. There are students around and —"

Just then, Camila lifts a ceiling panel and screams. A huge rat pops out and runs down her body, then Ollie’s, scurrying away on the floor behind a huge bookcase as I jump into Raymond’s arms.

“Oh, God. I thought they exterminated,” Raymond says as I let him go and move away. “Well, anyway, I can’t have you doing that right now. Can you come back after we close?”

"No," Ollie says as he lifts me to check another panel. "The man's wife is real upset. It's their anniversary, and she thinks he lost the ring and is lying. He wants to surprise her with it tonight."

"Oh, well, that's very nice, but..."

We go round and round with Raymond for a while, but he finally puts his foot down. "No, I'm sorry. I'm going to have to call Public Safety if you don't leave."

Suddenly, Ollie lowers a surprised Camila and practically drops her, throwing her into me who catches her and sets her on her feet. "Excuse me, Raymond, is it? Can I have a word?"

Ollie leads the assistant manager away with his arm around him. I haven't a clue what he could be saying, but he seems to have the man's attention.

After several seconds, Ollie separates, clapping Raymond on the shoulder. Then, he spanks the assistant manager on the butt. "I'll see *you* later."

Ollie walks toward us, motioning for me to climb up onto him again., as the assistant manager retreats into the back room and lets us continue.

"What the hell?" Camila demands. "What did you say?"

"Oh, I just made a fair trade with him."

"Trade?"

"I told him if he looked the other way right now, I'd take him for drinks after his shift. We're meeting at the Downtowner Lounge at six."

I laugh, and even Camila chuckles a bit.

"How did you know?" I ask, incredulous that Ollie's so buff and fit that he can even attract someone through his rainbow outfit.

"Good gaydar, I guess," Ollie says. He crouches down, and I run into his hands again.

We rush all over, and students stop to stare at us. Just as Mark-Bot reminds us we have eighteen minutes left, Camila finds the coin in a ceiling panel all the way at the end, near the bookstacks.

We hurry out of Memorial Union, summoning Keondra and Paige through our Ear-Bots to check in with them. They both confirm they got the other two coins, so now it's time for the Vermilion Bird. Rushing to the south region, I pray that we'll have enough time to get the clues and find it. I certainly don't want to be the randomly eliminated player when I'm so close to winning this thing.

We communicate through Ear-Bots and divide up the southern region, everyone looking everywhere they can. I gain many enemies as I pry open people's bags, whip off a few hats to check inside them, and kick over a snowman some kids just built, sure there's a clue in there (there wasn't). I even climb onto an ice sculpture or two and topple them, earning many choice words and even a few people chasing me throwing things.

We check in with fourteen minutes remaining to see we have the following letters:

___ R ___ O ___ B ___ L L ___ A ___ L

"What the hell is it?" Camila cries.

No one knows, and so we continue scrambling, me earning more enemies. Any manners or politeness I've ever learned are out the window as my life is potentially nearing its end.

I find an "L" in some ice fisherman's tacklebox, the vermilion tag sticking out from a package of bait hooks, and then Paige reports she found a "B" in a food truck's napkin dispenser. We look at the puzzle board now and see we have:

B R ___ O ___ B ___ L L ___ A L L

"I think I got it!" Keondra says. "Is it, BROOMBALL MALL?"

"Maybe," Paige says. "So, there's a broomball pit at the mall? How far is the mall?"

"No," Ollie says. "The mall is not in the south region. I think it's not 'mall' but 'ball.'"

"Ball? BROOMBALL BALL? What the hell does that mean?" I wonder.

"I think the coin is in the ball of a broomball game somehow," Camila says. "A broomball pit in the south region. How many are there even?"

"The map shows several," Keondra says, her eyes clamped shut. She divvies them up, and we each disperse to the one we're assigned.

I approach mine and see several students gathered around the perimeter, yelling as others inside chase a red ball with their brooms.

I hop in as Mark-Bot tells us we only have eleven minutes left, right in time for someone to hit the ball to the other side of the rink. I try to chase it, but I feel like I'm in a cartoon; my feet moving yet I don't go anywhere.

I latch onto a girl in a blue coat with a black and gold MTU cap on, and I try to use her to propel myself forward.

"Hey!" she yells as she loses her balance and lands hard on her side.

I do the same with a large guy in a black and red checked flannel, then a girl in a purple coat, a guy in a wool peacoat, and another guy in a puffy green vest, and as I grab each person, I get closer to the ball — until someone hits it to the opposite side of the rink.

Sighing, I turn to find a bunch of people I'd grabbed onto, some of whom I made fall, glaring at me. They look ready to attack, their brooms raised, and teeth bared.

I try to run in a different direction, but I fall to my knees, cracking one hard enough to bring tears to my eyes.

I feel a broom come down on my head, then another, and another, as those I'd grabbed onto pay me back with a good whack.

I curl into the fetal position on the ice and shield my face with my arms as they continue pummeling me, but then I see a person run by. I grab his leg, and he pulls me with him. Adrenaline helps me practically climb up the guy as the red ball rolls by, and I dive after it.

Someone swats it away.

I stumble after it, using people left and right to help me keep my balance, and as I glance back, I see the entire rink of broomball players is chasing me instead of the ball.

"Get her out of here!" someone shouts, and before I can look to see who, I feel myself being lifted — and thrown over the side of the rink into the snow.

"And stay out!" someone calls.

I exhale, trying to steady my ragged breathing, when Mark-Bot tells us that we only have seven minutes left.

I shoot to my feet, stars still swirling before my eyes, and peer over the side of the rink. The red ball is nearby, not close enough to reach but on my side. I run on the outside of the rink after it, following its motion as people swat it around, waiting for it to come toward me.

When it does, I dive over the side and cover it with my body before anyone can hit it again.

"Hey! What are you doing? What's she doing? That's not allowed!" someone complains.

I grab the ball and shove it into my shirt, then hoist myself back over the wall as people call after me all sorts of names, telling me that's not how broomball is played.

I couldn't care less. I flee the rink before anyone can catch me.

I duck into a bush and shake the ball. I can hear something inside. "Guys, I think I got the coin," I report, searching around for something sharp enough to cut the ball open.

None of the branches will work; they're too flimsy. I scurry out of there, going the opposite way of the broomball court, and I see a few students on a frozen pond making wide figure eights around one another.

I put the ball in the back of my pants, safely tucked into my underwear, and dive toward the skaters, bowling two over.

"Hey! What the —"

"Give me your skate!" I yell at a startled girl.

"What? No!"

I dive at her foot anyway, yanking. It's tied too tight. As she claws at me and her guy friend tries to shove me away, I attempt to undo her laces.

"What the hell's your problem? Get your own skates!" she says, kicking toward me.

I pull off my gloves, realizing they're too thick to grasp her laces. When she kicks again, she connects with my arm, her blade slicing me.

I scream, but then as I hear the time ticking down in my ears, I realize it'll be better to use the blade while the skate's on her foot. I reach around and pull the ball out of my pants, then continue fighting with her. As her foot comes toward me again, I block with the ball, hoping she'll slice it open.

I get cuts all over my hands as I continue with two and then eventually three, trying to go after their skates as we flail around on the frozen pond. The ball gets sliced, but not enough to break open.

"What's your issue, weird girl?" one of the boys demands.

Eyeing the ball, I see there's enough of a slice that perhaps I can pry the rest open. I push away from them and off the frozen pond onto the snow, then get to my feet, dusting myself off. "No issue. All good. Thanks for your help."

I run away as they call me awful names like the pissed off broom ballers. Diving into a bush, I hunt for a strong stick. Just as I find one and get it into a hole made by the blade, a hand grasps my shoulder.

"Miss, you'll have to come with us," someone says.

I look up to see two guys in Public Safety uniforms. Oh no. Not again. They hoist me to my feet, each taking one of my arms.

The ball drops to the snow with the stick in it, and I still don't know if it contains the coin.

I thrash as Mark-Bot tells everyone I'm detained and only have fifteen seconds to escape before being eliminated from The Game. They're too strong, and I cannot get away.

Mark-Bot counts down my time in my ear just like he did when the cop on Mackinac Island tried to cuff me to his HoverSeg. Knowing I have mere seconds left to live, I bend toward a hand holding my arm, twisting my head as far as it will go, and bite down hard through my mask on the fleshy part near the man's thumb.

He screams and releases as I'd hoped, and I kick the other in the shin and rush away, searching in the snow for my red ball. I find it under a tall pine tree and hide behind it, then poke the stick further inside, splitting it apart as much as I can — only to find a rock in there. No Vermilion Bird coin.

"Miss, you're under arrest," the campus police say, finding me behind the tree and rushing at me with cuffs.

I throw the ball as hard as I can and hit one square in the nose. He keels over groaning as his partner lunges for me.

My instincts bend my knee, and he lands right on it. "Oh!" he cries, holding his groin and falling over into the snow.

I race away, wondering if I even have time to find another broomball pit. I stop to search the map behind my eyelids when I hear Keondra report that she found the coin.

I open my eyes to find the campus cop with the bloody nose coming after me.

This time, I stick my arm out, fist clenched, and the man runs into it, connecting again with what is surely now a broken nose.

"Sorry," I say as I run off, feeling badly for what I did as the two campus cops just doing their jobs writhe in the snow behind me. Little do either know that getting their asses kicked just saved my life — at least for now.

We race to the map's center and get our coins together. They glow red hot and elongate to form the firescope, hopefully for the last time.

Sucking in my breath, I know that it's now or never. Soon — within the hour — someone *could* win Vermilion. Camila, Keondra, or me. Who will claim victory? I'm dying to see, but hopefully not literally.

The finish line is at a place called Bridgeview Park, which from the map is right near the Houghton-Hancock Bridge. I can also see that the distance is two miles, which is twice as far as normal.

I get the scope first and race down the street with everyone on my heels, bracing for a glitch or someone to strike me. I know better than to climb something high like Jiro did before Keondra killed him. I've also learned not to run near traffic.

It's hard to stay away from busy streets as the map shows College Avenue is the most direct path to the park and it's through the downtown area. With everyone after me, it's difficult to study the map in my eyelids and plan an alternative route anyway.

I pass a row of shops, and in the mirrored windows, I see Camila, Keondra, and Ollie right on my tail. I pump my arms now, going faster than I could ever imagine. Someone in my periphery goes down, and I glance to find Keondra sprawled on her stomach. Camila and Ollie jump over her, still on my heels.

A group of older ladies exit a restaurant, suddenly in my path.

"Excuse me!" I call, but they don't hear. I try to dart around them, but one moves right in my way, and I knock into her. She stumbles into her friend, and they both slip on the ice and fall.

My first instinct is to help them, and as I turn to do so, Camila swoops in and steals the firescope from me.

I fight the urge to chase her, instead trying to help one of the women up, but as she grasps for me, and I try to hold her, my arms won't work, and she falls back down again. I try again with the same result. Shit. Damn Spaghetti Arms glitch.

I've wasted too much time, and after assessing both ladies are startled but seem alright, I run away calling I'm sorry and then chase after Camila, knowing I can't grab the scope from her even if I can catch her since my arms aren't working.

I pass Ollie sitting in the snow rubbing his head. I don't know if it's his TBI again or if he has a glitch. I consider helping him, but when I see Camila dart across the street toward the water, I know it's more important I follow her and try to win this thing already — because she's seconds away from doing so herself.

I jump between two cars, making the rear one slam on its brakes and honk at me, and I see Keondra, who somehow caught up and passed me, and they're playing tug of war with the firescope.

I run full speed, hoping to surprise them and grab it, feeling my arms working again, but I trip, and my momentum pushes us all down the hill. We slide on the ice into the frigid waters of Portage Lake.

Camila surfaces and screams, "Mallory, you bitch!"

I'm too freezing to respond, but my adrenaline kicks in. I grasp for the scope, which floats nearby on a thin layer of ice.

Someone tugs my hair and yanks me back.

Keondra swims toward it, but then Camila grabs it from her and with her other hand, she dunks her friend under the water.

I paddle toward her and try to get it, but she punches me in the nose and lunges for the dock.

I catch Camila, and we struggle. She tries to push me under like Keondra. I claw at her arm as it tries to tread water while holding the firescope.

"Ow!" she says, her fingers releasing, and I snatch it before it sinks.

"Mallory, give it to me!" Ollie yells, suddenly there and reaching from the edge.

I blink at him as Camila comes at me again. I slap her away.

Ollie wriggles his fingers toward me. "Trust me, Mallory! I'll save the scope for you so you can win! I promise. Give it to me!"

Treading water, I have about a millisecond to think about it before Keondra and Camila charge toward me. Either he's going to screw me over to win and take us to a tiebreaker, or he'll save it for me like he said.

I thrust the firescope at him just as Keondra and Camila dunk me under. And then it occurs to me that Ollie could also save the firescope for someone else. Maybe he's in cahoots with Camila, or Keondra, or even Paige, although that wouldn't help either of them.

I thrash under the water, fighting my way to the surface. Pushing Keondra and Camila away from me, I see Ollie on the deck. He takes off with the firescope, racing to claim his first victory.

Paige said to mark her words, and she was right. Asshole Red Car Guy totally played me.

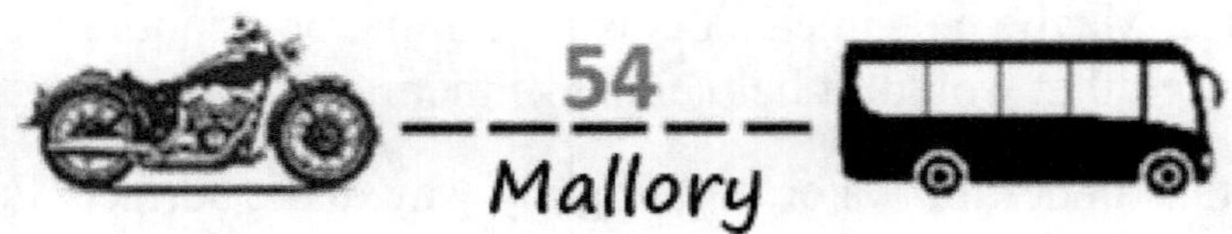


"What the fuck?" Camila shouts. She's sputtering, her teeth chattering, staring after Ollie in the distance. "He got the scope, you stupid idiot. You gave it to him!" She splashes water at me. "Now, he's gonna win, and we go into overtime. Can't believe this shit."

I blink, incredulous that I trusted Ollie and he fucked me over, when a muscular arm thrusts between us. It has a tattoo of the five Olympic rings on the wrist. "Mallory! Take my hand! Let me help you!"

I grab it, and Ollie pulls me out of the water and into his arms. He kisses me quickly as I shiver like I might freeze to death. He pushes me away from the water and points down the street toward the bridge. "Go! Win! I told you I got you. Now go beat Vermilion!"

I glance behind me, and Camila and Keondra are trying to climb back onto the dock. "Where's the firescope?"

"There." He points. "In that snow pile near that tree. I buried it so I could come back for you without anyone getting it. Now go!"

I run where he says, get the scope from the snow pile, and race toward the finish line down the street, eyeing the awesome Houghton-Hancock Bridge in the distance, the one my mother showed me long ago on her Hollaphone.

Soon, I see some benches in a circle and then four columns. Between the middle two, there's an arch over them that says "Bridgeview Park." Under it, a girl wearing rusty orange bell-bottoms, a long patchwork poncho, and white-blonde curly pigtails waves, a huge smile on her fake freckled face. I race toward her and put the firescope in her hand like it's the easiest thing in the world.

She grins in her adorable Sandy O'Grady way, the mask on her so realistic, I can't believe it. "Congratulationssss," she says, her last "s" lisped, before turning and walking away.

"Who are you?" I shout after her with tears streaming down my face as the realization of what just happened settles over me. Then, I remember the bus driver from the Tech Tour bus had the very same lisp. The bus driver was Sandy O'Grady — or someone pretending to be.

She doesn't turn, and I consider following her to see where she goes, but Ollie comes up behind me as Mark-Bot declares me the winner of Vermilion. Ollie spins me around, kissing me and telling me he knew I could do it.

"I couldn't have done it without you," I say, and I hug him back, seeing over his shoulder Paige in the distance scowling at us. Ollie saved me, doing what he said, not lying to me and using me like Paige did. And because of him, I won. *I FREAKING WON VERMILION!!!*

A massive weight falls upon me as I remember I'll now have to decide who lives and who dies. An impossible decision. As Keondra and Camila and Paige approach, Mark-Bot asks who I will pick as the second survivor. I think about each person and who deserves to live the most. At Mark-Bot's insistence, I give him my answer.

Seconds later, everyone else clutches their chests and falls to the ground as I cry out and sink to my knees. I clamp my eyes closed, not wanting to face my decision, but the Eye-Bots show me behind my lids anyway.

All but me and the person I've chosen to live disintegrate into nothing right there in the snow at Bridgeview Park. As I gawk at what just happened, that three out of four of my bus mates who were just standing there no longer exist, some man and his Rottweiler come up. The man sits on a bench and stares at his Hollaphone while his dog pisses right onto Camila's sparse remains. I collapse in a puddle of tears that feel like they'll never end, despising the decision I was forced to make. Simultaneously, I've become a winner, a savior, and a killer.

# 55

## Mallory

As Mark-Bot tells us to go back to Home Base where we'll be given all our possessions and the antidote to disintegrate our Rover-Bots before we're released, I pull out a slip of paper from my fanny pack where I put Paige's foster family's address. She'd given it to me at the Rock & Roll Hall of Fame, asking me to save Kimmy if I won.

I stare at some address in Warren, Michigan, remembering Kimmy, who I'd been so worried about, doesn't even exist. Or if she does, she's not in any danger. Paige lied to me about everything, although admittedly, she played the game well. But she used me and got me to care for her, which I do even if she was a stone-cold liar, and that's why I couldn't pick her no matter how good her reasons. Since she's now dead, I no longer think she was part of The Game. That tears me up even worse than Krystall and Sammi.

Without meaning to, I've literally become a serial killer.

Ollie hugs me to him as we walk in silence, both of us sniffling behind our masks, me reliving all three of their deaths, plus Jiro's, Sammi's, and Troy's. My mind whirs through the details as my stomach turns inside out.

"That was truly terrible," he says. "I didn't expect it so soon like that, and to think, it could've been me just as easily." He snaps his fingers.

"It was the worst thing I could ever imagine," I agree. I'll never be able to erase from my mind how Paige, Keondra, and Camila screamed as I told Mark-Bot to save Ollie, those words serving as their death sentence. And I thought of Paige's family, her brother and professor parents instead of who she said, and then Keondra's mother the Red Wings superfan, and of course Paulo, Camila's brother who she raised. I wonder how they'll ever be the same. Because their loved ones are now specks of dust in the wind. "I don't think I can stand what happened." Tears scald my eyes. "What I did. It's because of me that they're gone."

"Yeah. What you did." Ollie stops and turns, taking me into his arms. "Because of you, my six brothers and sisters will now have a real chance. You saved us all, and I'd like to be able to tell you how thankful I am forever, until I can't talk anymore. How does that sound?"

I gaze up at him and he removes his goggles so that I can see his beckoning sea blue eyes. "Like a dream," I say, and I pull off my mask while he lowers his, then kiss him like I've never kissed anyone before, right there in front of Home Base as it idles at the curb. He presses me up against it, lifting me so I'm his height and hugging me to his huge chest, whispering that he's so happy to be with me.

"Ahem, Mallory," Karyn-Bot says in my ear. "That's not very lady-like behavior."

"Fuck you, Karyn-Bot," I say, kissing a laughing Ollie again.

The doors to Home Base open, and we rush inside. I find my original clothes on my bed in a bag, the ones I wore that first day on the Michigan Tech bus tour. I dump the bag out while Ollie does the same with his, searching through everything for our Hollaphones, but more importantly, for the green amulets with silver spiderwebs containing the antidote we've worked so hard to get. I'm so anxious to get those damn Rover-Bots out of me finally.

I find my phone, but not the necklace. Instead, I see a piece of paper with my name scrawled on it.

I unfold it to discover a receipt for an Etsy purchase:

**Item:** Green glass amulet with silver spiderweb harness

**SKU#:** 10594287

**Cost:** $39.95 + $6.99 standard shipping = $46.94

**Customer:** Ionia Lemon

**Location:** Fort Lauderdale, FL

**Purchase Date:** 12/23/2029

"What the hell? Did you find yours?" I peer over at Ollie, and he turns to me with a similar receipt in his hands.

Shaking his head, he shows me his. “No. Looks like I gotta’ go to Buffalo to find some dude named Trent Diablo. He’s got my antidote.”

# PART 15

## DAVINA, SNAKE, AND THE O'GRADY KIDS

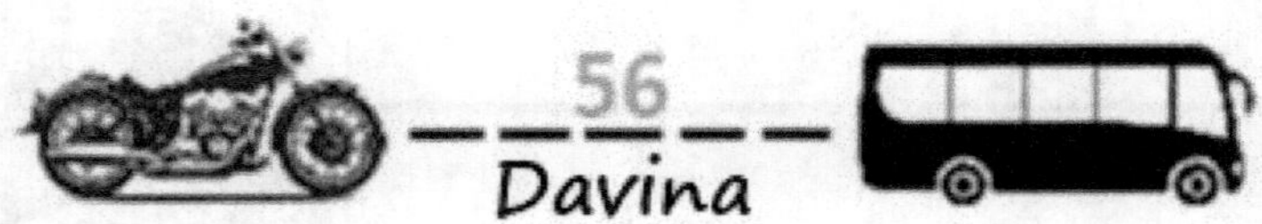

# 56

## Davina

**Saturday, February 2, 2030**

As Mallory runs away, slip-sliding through intersecting lines the sun painted onto the snow through the icy trees, I try to chase after her, but Snake pulls me back.

I fight him, but he's stronger and holds me to him.

"Stop! Let me go! We need to get her!" Tears fill my eyes and I'm unable to see him nor my kidnapped sister who just ran away from me.

"She ain't comin' to us! We can't save her!"

I pound my fists into his chest as he tries to embrace me. "You're wrong. We can! Don't lose faith now!"

"No, listen!" Snake grabs my wrists, stopping me from bolting. "We can't save her. Like you said, she's full of them bots. She won't come to us cause they got her all scared. We need to find that antidote and get it to her."

"Antidote? What antidote?"

"Rocco told Dad 'bout it. That's what they's all playin' for. Some antidote in a necklace to kill all them bots."

"Are you serious? And you're just sharing this now?"

"Sorry. Thought I told ya'. We gotta' get to them people running this thing and make them give it to us. We know where they's at, right?"

I nod. They're all at the fancy Airbnb condo on the water that they brought Rocco and I to before I ducked out claiming another bout of food poisoning. It's where all the VIPs and people running things are, as far as I know. They came to meet us and all the other criminals, six people dressed as The O'Grady Kids in creepy, realistic masks. I'm not sure why they're dressed like that. Super weird, especially since it's my parents' favorite show.

"But how do we know who has the antidote? How're we going to force them to hand it over? They probably have weapons and tons of security to help them, and we don't even have a gun."

Snake bites his lip. "You be right about that." We walk along College Avenue, watching students frantically tend to their ice sculptures while others sled, a few skiers glide by, and a lone figure snowboards down a huge snow mound piled up to a building's roof.

"I don't think we can force them the way we imagine," I say, defeated.

"I hate sayin' it, but I think you're right. Don't mean we can't still stop 'em though."

"Stop them? From running The Game? From possibly killing my sister and the others? I don't see how. Not without the antidote."

Snake stops and looks at me with a grave expression on his face. "Think we gonna' hafta' pull another Winston Churchill."

I groan. "What do you mean?"

"Sacrifice a few of 'em to save more of 'em."

"Who? What?"

I feel slow, mentally, and physically, as Snake hurries forward, leaving me behind. "I got me a plan. Come on."

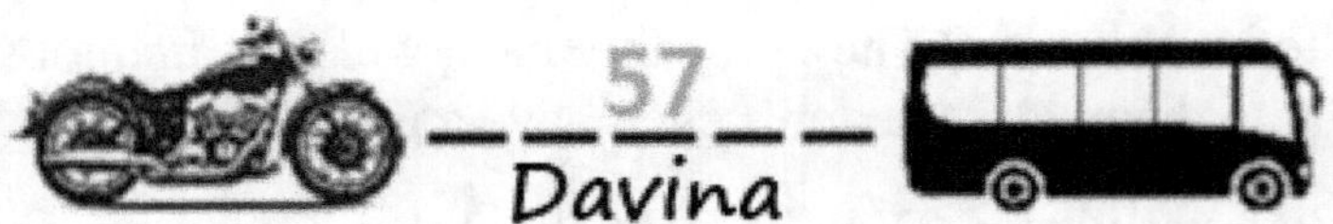


We stop on the way to a hardware store downtown, and there, Snake buys a bunch of rope. We visit a drugstore, and he purchases a package of giftwrap tissue paper. He grabs a lighter at the register.

"What's this all for?" I ask a silent Snake. "Jonah, what are we doing?"

He waits until we're outside alone to answer. "You ain't gonna' like it, but it's all I can figure."

"What?"

"We gotta' kill 'em."

I stop walking. "You serious?"

"As a heart attack. It's the only solution that makes sense. They ain't givin' up that antidote. And without it, they be doin' whatever to your sister and anybody else unless we stop 'em, like forever. Otherwise, what'll they do next? Sounds like them bots be pretty advanced. Them people runnin' this thing, whoever they are, they's gonna' be able to control anyone easily. That means they could take over the whole damn world pretty quickly."

I shiver, knowing he's right. "But what if there are people in their company who aren't at the Airbnb condo?"

Snake shrugs. "We gotta' take that chance, 'less you gotta' better idea."

I think about it as we walk back to the condo, but I can't come up with anything else. "I don't want to kill anyone," I whisper as we see the Airbnb in the distance.

"Hell no, me neither, but they started this shit. And we can't finish it any other way, except get guns somehow and try to force them to give us the amulet. And I ain't sure how we'd score a gun. I ain't know anyone here. We got no Rebel Demons chapters 'round these parts."

"Can we steal one? Is there a gun shop we could break into?"

Snake shakes his head. "They'd have too much security. And how many guns would we even need? I ain't in no mood for no gun fight. Are you?"

I frown.

"And even if we do get they's antidote, they still be knowing how to control them nanerbots. Just think all the terrible things they still can do, to your sister and anyone they want. It's the only way, far as I can see."

I nod with a sigh, hating that he's right. "So, what's with all this rope?"

Jonah doesn't answer. He's texting on his Hollaphone.

"Who's that?"

"Rocco. Just told him to get the hell out of there, and leave a door open for us. I know he's mad as shit at us right now, but I ain't doin' nothing 'till he's out."

"And then what?"

We approach the condo, and Snake ducks down, motioning for me to follow him. He runs around the side, and we find a pair of glass doors. Snake takes some rope out of one of the bags, then produces a pocketknife from his coat. He cuts the length off and ties the rope around both door handles, making several knots. "Locked doors, leaked gas, and a match should do it."

I'm incredulous, unable to accept what we're doing even though I know we must.

We peer in, and we see some people through a window sitting around a large screen. The fake O'Grady Kids chat with others while watching. Marci is next to Robbie staring into a Hollaphone together, and then Sandy and Craig and Janice are on a sofa munching on snacks. Skeeter is in the corner mixing a drink at a small bar while chatting up some pretty girl. "What the hell? Those masks are so realistic. Those can't be the real people. The actors are much older now."

"They be really good," Snake says. "I ain't never seen ones like that."

"I know. What do The O'Grady Kids have to do with anything?"

Snake shrugs. "No clue."

I think of my parents obsession with that show and wonder if that has anything to do with Vermilion, if the two are somehow connected. Putting it out of my mind for now, I gulp and then muster all the courage I have. "So, we doing this? Are you ready?"

Snake claps his hands together, sucking in a huge breath. "Ready to blow up The O'Grady Kids? Hell yeah. Never liked that show."

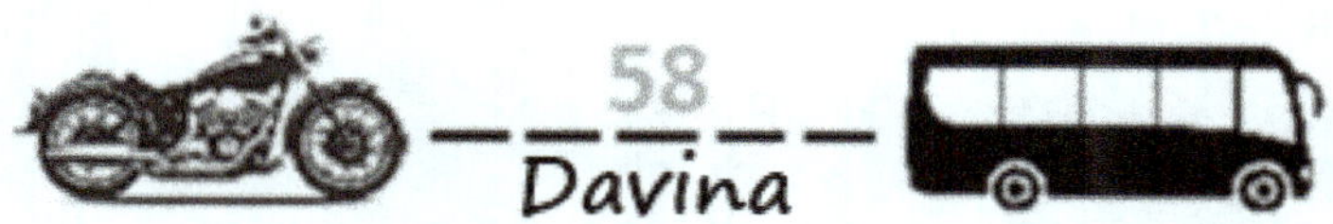


I wish I could leave this whole mass murder we have planned in Snake's lap, but that's not fair to him. Even if he thinks he needs to repay our family, to which I disagree, Mallory is *my* sister, *my* responsibility. I'm the one who was supposed to be on the fake Tech Tour anyway, so there's that, but it's not the only thing.

Snake and I enter the condo through the door Rocco left open and sneak into a utility room on the lower level. Snake fiddles with the furnace, turning some knobs. I smell gas instantly and wonder how long it'll take for everyone upstairs to notice.

"Wait here," Snake says, and he creeps toward the stairway.

"Where are you going?"

"Kitchen. Saw a huge gas stove in there when we peeked in. I'm gonna' go turn it on too."

I rush after him. "No. Let me. No one knows you're here. I'm supposed to be. People saw me."

"Too risky," he says, but I shoot forward in front of him and open the basement door.

Snake squeezes my shoulder. "Fine, but hurry."

I do, and thankfully, no one is in the kitchen when I get there. I switch all the knobs on the stove to high. As I turn to flee, someone taps my shoulder.

I whip around to find Janice O'Grady staring at me through her mask, which up close you can tell is not real skin but pretty darn similar. "Thought you were sick. Just what do you think you're doing?" She wriggles her fake Janice nose.

"I was going to make some popcorn," I say, turning and pulling open a cabinet. I find it full of pots and pans.

"We have popcorn out there. Didn't you notice? There's some at like every table."

I shake my head. "No. My bad."

"Aren't you supposed to be ill? Why would you be —"

"It always settles my stomach."

Janice beckons me toward the other room. "Well, come on back. They already crowned a winner, but there's more to see."

The voice is not familiar. Janice O'Grady slings an arm around me, attempting to lead me back into that huge room with the others, telling me I don't want to miss anything.

I pull away and she turns, her brow creasing. "It kind of smells like gas," she says, her faux nose wrinkling. "Do you smell that?"

I answer by grabbing a pan and whacking her in the fake face until she stumbles backward. Thinking of what she and her siblings put my sister and the others through, I charge at her, jumping on her and wrestling her to the ground. I clamp my hand over her mouth before she can scream for help.

She wriggles around, kicking and flailing, but I pin her down, using every limb, and I finally grab the frypan that fell and smack her in the head again and again until she stops and begins whimpering.

It's too loud, so I hit her again until she's silent. I fear I may have killed her and reach for her throat to feel for a pulse, but then I remember I'm there to kill them all and rush outside to a pacing Snake.

His eyes question, and I mouth "tell you later." We rush around the perimeter, tying the remaining doors shut.

When we're done, we go out to the street, hiding behind a large bush.

"Where's Rocco?" I ask.

"He texted that he left."

"I'm surprised he's so compliant, being as how he hates us. You were right all along too. He didn't give a shit about my sister being a contestant. Telling him wouldn't have worked." I turn to Snake, taking his hand. “I’m sorry how it all went down though. I don’t want our blackmailing him to come between you two. He’s your only family now.”

Snake kisses me. “This is more important, and he’ll come ‘round in time. And if not, hey, at least your sister’s gonna’ be alive.”

“Thank you.” I swallow, overcome with all sorts of conflicting emotions. “You’re a really good person, you know that? Even if you’re about to commit mass murder.”

Snake bears his fangs. “Back a’cha.” He rubs his hands together. “Okay, let’s do this shit.” He reaches into his pocket and produces a lighter, then pulls endless pink tissue paper out of his pocket like a circus clown.

“What’s that?”

“Watch.” He unfolds the paper and twists until he has one long piece. He glances at his Hollaphone. “It’s time. Gas been on long enough. The house should be full up by now.”

I shrug. “I guess.” I swallow, realizing this may be the last moment before I’m officially not a killer, and my nails practically impale my palms.

“Wait right here.” Snake runs up to the front door and slides his long, twisted strand of paper into the mail slot so the end sticks out. He lights it, then turns and races toward me.

Behind him, I see some of the O’Grady Kids and VIP’s at the windows, tugging at the locked doors, trying to get out. They must smell the gas.

Just as Snake is about to reach me, someone comes out of nowhere and tackles him to the snow. As I scream, the Airbnb with the VIPs and fake O’Grady’s explodes, shooting a fireball way up high into the grayish afternoon sky.

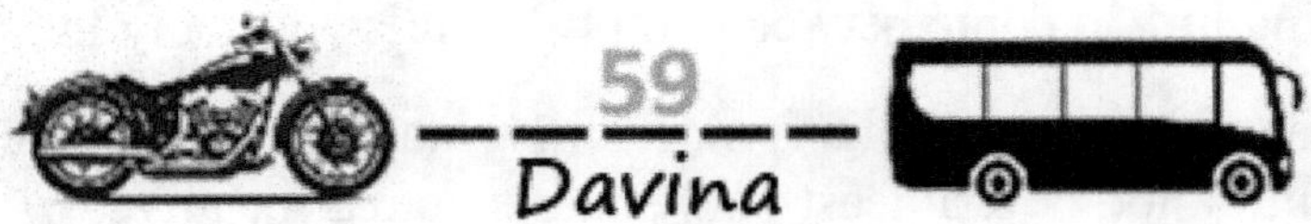

# 59

## Davina

Without thinking, I rush over and tackle whoever jumped Snake, and I get a fist full of white-blond hair.

Snake's attacker twists around. He has circular glasses and a pudgy freckled face, resembling a kid from the neck up, but a grown guy otherwise, a very muscular one. At first, I think it's Miles, the brother of Paige Tellison, because of the light hair, but when I look closely, I can tell the person's wearing a good mask.

He shoves me back and then continues with Snake, flipping him over and pounding on him.

I attack the guy again, but he's very strong, pushing me off easily while he wails on Jonah, who can't do much since his arms are pinned.

I stumble back, catching onto some shrubbery, then find a huge stick on the ground. I whack it against the guy's head, and he falls over enough for Snake to get out from under him. Snake whips around and forces the guy into a chokehold.

The guy, much stronger than Snake, pushes him into the bushes and comes at me.

As I struggle against him, I notice a tattoo of the five Olympic rings on his wrist.

"You killed my entire family," he snarls. "There will be consequences, just wait and see." He strikes me, and I feel myself falling back before the lights go out.

# PART 16

## SOMEBODY FINDS JACK

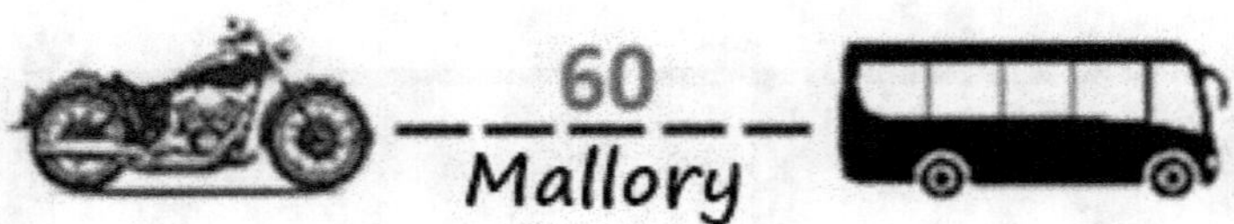


**Saturday, February 2, 2030**

The night I beat Vermilion is surprisingly upsetting. While Ollie leaves me in the motel room to go buy food and a change of clothes, I call my parents, desperate to talk to them. I get their voicemails and leave a message on both letting them know I'm okay and to please call me back, that I have my Hollaphone now and will explain everything.

I get Davina's voicemail too, and I tell her since maybe she knows why I'm here that I won The Game. How does she even know I'm in Houghton? I hang up, floored that none of my family is answering their phones after all I've been through. I've only been dying to talk to them all this time, which my phone calendar says has been over three weeks.

Next, I listen to my voicemails, and my supposed boyfriend Blake did not call once to see if I was okay. Everyone else I know left worried messages but him. He's probably too busy with that other girl. A pang travels through me, and I sigh, trying to accept it. Well, good riddance. I have Ollie now. Worked out for the best.

I reach some friends, like Santos and Liza and the other Majik 8 Balz, who are so glad to hear from me and that I'm okay, but no one knows where my parents or sister are. I call my grandparents in St. Paul, wondering if I should tell them I saw them during The Game, but I get their voicemails too.

I'm even more shocked as I lie in Ollie's comforting arms all night that none of my family has called me back. I'd think they'd be desperate to talk to me. Ollie says he doesn't even want to phone his siblings yet until he gets his antidote and makes sure he is okay. He doesn't want to get their hopes up until he verifies all is cool, but I'm aching to hear my mother's voice, to make sure my father is alright, and especially to apologize to Davina about being such an insensitive bitch our whole lives.

I watch Ollie snoring softly next to me so peaceful and beautiful, but I'm a wreck, worrying about my family and wondering why none of them has contacted me.

All night, I switch between dozing, crying over those we lost — especially Paige — and puzzling over my family's lack of response.

An hour after the sun rises and pokes through the curtains, Ollie finally opens his eyes. A slow, sexy grin spreads across his face, and he reaches to kiss me. "Good morning, beautiful. Thank you for saving my life."

"Hey, you made it possible," I tell him. "And you saved mine too, more than once." I think of the polar bear who almost ate me, and when Ollie made me go almost topless in front of the world on live TV at the Red Wings game, and I shake my head, incredulous that I'm here in this bed with him, alive and almost out of danger.

I hug him, wanting to feel his body against mine, but he pops up from the bed before I can, clapping his hands together. "Let's do this! Let's get to the airport now, get our antidotes, and then I say we meet up at the Grand Hotel in two days, same time."

I giggle. "Room 310?"

He laughs. "Where else? I'd love to try lying *on top* of the bed with you this time instead of underneath it."

I crack up, thinking of the lovers Charles and Myra, who we got to know *way* better than we ever wanted to. "Yeah, me too."

Ollie pulls me in for a hug, whispering in my ear, "I think that's when I really fell for you."

"Yeah?"

He smiles. "You were so brave, and calm, and beautiful, dying with laughter right when we were minutes from dying. Oh, and that was after doing your unbelievable head spin in the snow. That was incredible. Yeah, I think it was then, for sure. I wanted so badly for it to be *us* in that bed, not them."

I put my cheek on his chest, so glad I chose him to live, even though I feel awful about Paige, and even Camila and Keondra. "Well, now you'll get your chance." I slide my arms around him and grab his rock-hard butt Myra-style, squeezing with both hands. I was never so sure with Blake if I wanted to sleep with him, hesitant even though he was so sweet for a while, but I have no doubts with Ollie. "I want you to be my first."

"Yeah?" Ollie pulls back and looks into my eyes. "You serious?"

"Oh yeah. I cannot wait to be with you, for real."

"Oh God, me neither. I know I should probably wait until then to say this, but well, Mallory, I love you."

I exhale, tears stinging my eyes. "I love you too, Ollie." And as I say it, I realize that this horrible game Vermilion brought me love of all things with a guy who may just be the best thing to ever happen to me. Just like Dad's horrible sledding accident that permanently messed up his leg and hip brought him Mom. All because my parents forced me to go on the Michigan Tech Tour against my will. I guess I need to thank them now — if they'd ever answer their damn phones. Dad said if I went on the Tech Tour, I'd be pleasantly surprised. I had no idea just how much.

Ollie and I grab an Uber to the airport. I buy our plane tickets on the way with my Hollaphone, paying for the cab and last night's motel too, with Ollie promising to reimburse me when he gets the money he stole from the Darby's. We enter the United terminal, and after we go through security, we must separate to different gates.

Ollie grabs me for another hug, talking in my ear. "Let's not speak until then. We'll get our antidotes, meet at the Grand Hotel, and call our families together. And then, we'll really celebrate." He nuzzles my neck until my knees practically give out. "How does that sound?"

I kiss him in response, and then we part ways. As I walk toward Gate G, I turn back just as Ollie disappears around the corner. Checking the time on my Hollaphone, I start counting the minutes until I can see him again.

When I step off the plane in Fort Lauderdale around one in the afternoon ready to find this Ionia Lemon who has my antidote, I notice I have a new voicemail message. Excited to hear from my parents or sister, I check the details, but I don't recognize the number. I click to listen, wondering if it's any news about my family.

"Hi, Mallory, this is Snake Riley. I'm the guy who you think attacked your parents. I didn't. It's a long story, but Davina and I worked stuff out. She got your message but wanted me to call you. She's kinda' out of it. She's got herself a concussion. We at the UP Health System on Campus Drive in Hancock, across the water from Michigan Tech. We hope you're okay. Real glad you won that game. Davina will call ya' just as soon as she gets up. You can call me at (248) 555-1242 or just come here if you can. Thanks."

Stunned, I sit down, trying to process everything. Snake Riley, the guy who attacked our parents, was with my sister when I saw her. I totally forgot. That doesn't make sense that she'd be with *him* of all people. She's always hated him, ever since she saved him from that dog attack in fourth grade, and he never thanked her. I call Snake's number, and someone answers on the first ring. "This is Jonah."

"Hi. It's Mallory. Why are you with my sister?" Scary images surface, and I worry he kidnapped her or something.

"She'll tell ya' everything when she wakes up. She's with me but sleepin'." A text comes through, and I open it to find an image of Davina in a hospital bed with her eyes closed. Snake's head is next to hers, the colorful snake tattoo with its tongue forking into his pierced eyebrow prominent, his fang-like teeth showing as he smiles. Much of his face is covered by bruises in various shades of purple. "Just took it. I got a little roughed up, as you can see."

I pinch and expand, looking for restraints like maybe he tied Davina up, but I don't see any. "Okay. Is she alright?"

"Yeah. She hit her head and got herself a concussion. They doin' some tests to make sure it ain't worse. She been too dizzy to walk. They knocked her out for her MRI cause she was too scared, so I'm gonna' have her call ya' the minute she wakes. You still in Houghton? We saw you in that Vermilion game, you know."

I tell him I couldn't talk to them and why, and Snake says he understands. "Figured it was some threat. So, where you at so I can tell her?"

"I'm in Fort Lauderdale to get the antidote, and then I'll be there right away." We chat a little longer, him telling me about my mom and dad and why they're not answering their Hollaphones. Snake promises Davina will call me the second she opens her eyes, and we hang up.

I walk a bit, trying to process the news about my parents, wondering why we're all being punished. I say a silent prayer for their welfare, just in case someone up there cares.

Afterward, I dial Ollie, his number now in my phone since we traded before we left. Even though we agreed not to talk until we meet at the Grand Hotel, our romantic reunion will have to move to Michigan Tech. God, I can't seem to get away from that place.

Putting my Hollaphone to my ear, excited to hear his voice, I hear: "Do, do, do! The number you have dialed is no longer in service. Please check the number and try again."

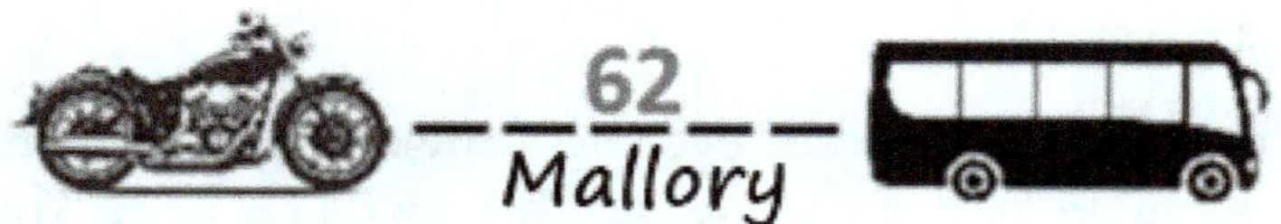

# 62 Mallory

I burst out of the Fort Lauderdale International Airport terminal desperate for fresh air as my head swirls about me. It is sunny and sweltering. Squinting, I rip off my fleece pullover, hot and flustered. I dial Ollie's number again, which he had typed into my phone himself, but the number is not working. Maybe he entered it wrong, or perhaps something happened to his Hollaphone account.

Or he faked his number because he doesn't want anything to do with me anymore. Paige's ominous warning about Ollie using me to survive The Game ring in my ears. She said to mark her words. *Was she right all along?*

But no. Ollie saved me. He pulled *me* out of the water and helped me to win. He could have just as easily claimed the round for himself since all of us except Paige were in the water or he could have given the scope to Paige or rescued Camila or even Keondra. But he chose *me*. He told *me* he loved me, not them. Maybe his phone is broken or something. I don't know right now.

But first things first. I need the antidote. Sitting on a bench, I try to regulate my breathing while looking up Ionia Lemon from Fort Lauderdale on my Hollaphone. The only one I can find happens to be the conductor of the Sunrise Symphony Orchestra. I check again and again, but the only thing I find when I search that name in all South Florida is articles and links to the same woman. Squinting at her picture, I see she's an older lady with short blonde spiky hair poking out of dark roots and lavender-tinted glasses with lime frames. I try to imagine if she'd be a person who would buy a heart-shaped amulet with a spiderweb from Etsy.

It's hard to say, but I see that she's performing tomorrow at an awards luncheon for the Ladies Auxiliary Club of Sunrise, and I decide I'll have to get the amulet then unless I can somehow find her home address and finagle it from her sooner.

After a fruitless hour of searching online for her whereabouts over a vegan muffin and coffee in an airport café, I conclude tomorrow's daytime symphony concert will be where I'll have to corner her and somehow get the antidote.

For the rest of the day and evening, I wander Hollywood Beach's Broadwalk, trying to reach Ollie, unsure what's with his unworking number, and wishing my parents and sister were well enough to talk to. After I spend more of my dwindling savings to rent another motel room, I close my eyes, trying to plot out what I'll do tomorrow to get the antidote from this Ionia Lemon person. I pray this will be my last night with the Rover-Bots inside of me and start to dream of a life with Ollie free of them, where we can be together and happy without anyone forcing us to play some deadly game.

# 63
## Mallory

When I arrive at the Ladies Auxiliary Club's banquet hall the next day, the orchestra is warming up. They're in a large room seated in four rows facing the audience who will be sitting at several round tables with floral centerpieces. Above the orchestra, a screen announces the awards ceremony and the special symphony performance, led by conductor Ionia Lemon. Several different people, mostly women, wander through the three sets of double doors with drinks and hors d'oeuvres, finding seats at the tables.

On the way to today's affair, I'd splurged with even more of my savings and bought a skirt, blouse, nice tights, and decent shoes, knowing I couldn't just show up in the wrinkled jeans and sweater I was wearing. I try to blend in, sitting at one of the round tables in the middle with a pleasant smile.

"Hi there," some of the ladies say.

I smile. "Hello."

The one closest to me asks if I'm new to their Auxiliary. "Haven't seen a pretty face like yours here before."

"Oh, no. I'm uh, well, I'm the kid of that guy there." I point toward the musicians. "Yeah, um, I just came to hear my father. It's his first time playing his clarinet since he got out of the hospital, so it's a big day for him."

"Oh, now isn't that sweet?" One of the ladies puts her hand on my arm. "What was wrong with him?"

Ugh, why did I tell such an elaborate lie? "Oh, he hurt his hand. He, uh, he slammed it in a car door. Couldn't play his clarinet until he had surgery. He's so thrilled to be back."

Now, I just picked the clarinet at random, the first instrument which came to mind, but as we look at the symphony again, we see that all the clarinet players are women.

The ladies turn back to me with confused expressions. “Well, now which one is he?”

My cheeks burn. “Oh, I guess they’re having him play flute instead.” I point to some guy in the front row. “Yeah, there, second chair from the aisle. The balding guy. He must be really disappointed with all he’s been through.”

“That’s your father?” They look at each other with confused expressions and then back at me.

I nod, but then a blonde woman’s eyes crinkle as she studies me. “But that’s my father.”

I shrug. “Oh, well, oops. Guess cat’s out of the bag.”

Her mouth drops open as I slip away, me the unintentional homewrecker. I approach a table closer to the stage when some loud voice comes over a loudspeaker. “And now, the moment you’ve all been waiting for. Introducing the Sunrise Symphony Orchestra, led by the internationally acclaimed Ionia Lemon!” The lights dim as a woman walks out wearing a tuxedo with long tails, a skinny white stick in her hand. We’re a bit far away, but I see something there under her bowtie. Is that a heart necklace, a stain, or something else?

She turns her back on us and the music begins. I won’t be able to tell from here, so I abandon my seat, ducking down and finding one closer on the side near the musicians. I move to another table, then another, and another, but I can’t get a good view.

“Is something wrong?” A man leans over toward me, chewing on a dinner roll. “I noticed you’re moving around a lot.”

“Hard of hearing.”

He nods. The symphony suddenly crescendos louder than I can stand, and I clamp my hands over my ears as the guy shoots me a quizzical look.

Ionia the Conductor is very lively, her arms raising up, her body moving all over with the music, but the woman never turns toward me once. I must get in front of her somehow. I sneak away and move toward the side of the room. Creeping along in the shadows, I try to see Ionia’s front better, but I’m still too far.

I come closer, and a man playing a trombone notices me, his eyes wide. I slide next to him in his chair, scooching him over. He stops playing. "What the —?"

"Shh…" I say with a finger over my lips, squinting and leaning forward. I think the conductor does have the necklace, or *something* is dangling below her bowtie, but I can't tell if it's green or heart-shaped from my angle.

"What do you think you're —"

I push past the trombone player, sliding further into the second row, tripping over people's feet and music stands as I try to get a better look.

I stumble forward and fall all over a bassoonist who pushes me off with anger twisting her face. "I beg your pardon."

The music dwindles to nothing as Ionia Lemon and everyone else glare at me.

"You there!" Ionia points her conductor baton at me. "Who are you? Why are you interrupting our performance?"

Well, the jig is up. I worked my ass off to win Vermilion for this moment. Nothing worse can happen to me now, and once I get the antidote, even if I get arrested, at least they won't eliminate and disintegrate me.

I break between two flutists in front of me and lunge for Ionia's necklace. I rip it from the stunned woman and twist open the little top. Tipping my head back, I drink what's inside.

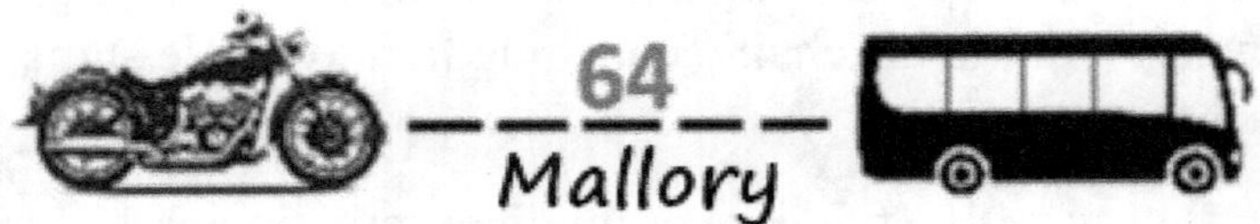


It takes me a second to realize it's not liquid; I just drank something ashy. "What the fuck? Where's the stuff that was in here?" I wipe my tongue and lips with my sleeve.

Ionia Lemon, the refined composer, bursts into tears. "Why on God's green Earth would you drink my beloved Jack's ashes? What is *WRONG* with you?"

"*Jack*? Who's Jack?"

"My dog! Why would you do that?" She wipes her eyes. "Someone, call security!"

I grab her by her bowtie and shove the amulet toward her. "Where's the liquid that came in here?"

Ionia flinches and pushes against me. "I don't know! I spilled it out when I got it. I bought it to hold my dog's ashes."

"Are you freaking serious? YOU SPILLED IT OUT? *It's all GONE?"*

An invisible shoe kicks me in the gut as I realize I risked my life all this time, and the others died, so I could win to get the antidote, *the antidote which doesn't even exist anymore?!?!*

I shake my head, so floored I should be carpet, and suddenly it's the funniest thing I've ever heard.

Keeling over, I laugh so hard, I pee in my pants in the otherwise silent hall. When I can stop enough to straighten up, urine trickling down my tights and forming a puddle beneath me, I see through my tears the audience's shocked expressions and a few men in dark uniforms approaching, ready to pounce.

With all my Vermilion experience, it doesn't take much to outrun a few pudgy security guards without guns. I sprint outside into the sunshine and find a place of safety down the street behind a large bush. When I catch my breath, I dial Ollie again, my hands jittery, hoping that somehow his phone will work now. I get the same message saying his number isn't in service.

Breaking down, I hold my head in my hands while I sit there in the grass, bawling. What the hell am I going to do now? I'm still full of nanobots, there's no freaking antidote or any way to get some, so I'm still at someone's mercy. But whose?

We never found out who did this to us, who made us play The Game. Whoever it was got away. Oh, and everyone including Ollie is out of sorts or missing except my sister. She's in the hospital with her mortal enemy Snake Riley, who insists Davina forgave him and sent me a selfie with her unconscious body.

After some more freaking out, I debate whether I should go see Davina who is perhaps being held captive by Snake or go see Ollie to find out if he got his antidote and why his phone doesn't work. I finally decide to go to Ollie on Mackinac Island since he's on the way to Davina in Houghton, because we're supposed to meet tomorrow morning. I grab an Uber back to my motel to collect my things and then catch another to the airport.

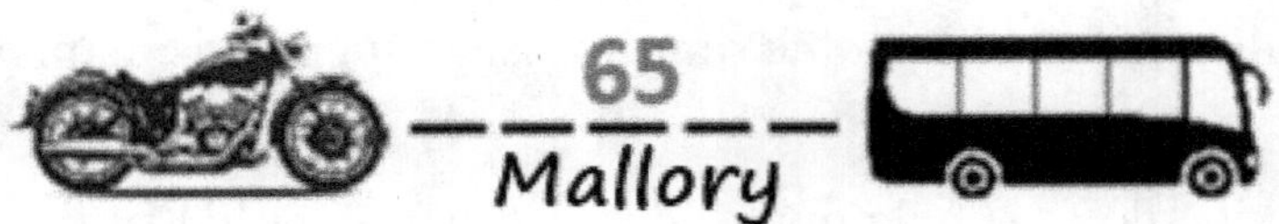


I spend a day and a half waiting for Ollie at the Grand Hotel while my sister is lying in a hospital somewhere. I finally reach her after lunch the first day, and we talk for a long time. Davina tells me they found some bleeding in her brain, so she must stay a day or two more while they observe her, but they say she should be okay.

She fills me in on my parents and Snake, or Jonah, assuring me he doesn't have her held captive and he's a great guy. She tells me about his letter to her and our parents, explaining how he gave up everything — even his relationship with his brother Rocco — to make it up to our family, helping to save me. She describes blowing up The O'Grady Kids and all the VIPs, hoping they got everyone responsible for The Game, although there was the mysterious person who attacked them right after, so she's not sure. That's why Jonah's face is all beat up. I'm glad she's not being held captive by Snake and that he helped her so much. He sounds like a good guy, and I'm quite surprised.

I tell her a bit about what me and the others went through, but I don't get into Ollie or Paige or anyone. It's too raw right now.

"Also, I owe you a huge apology." I bite my lip, trying to figure out the best way to say what I need to tell her.

"What? No, you don't."

"I do. I've been insensitive to you a lot, and I recognize that now. I wasn't the best in The Game, and I realized how I usually —" I stop, unsure how to proceed.

"Kick my ass at everything?" Davina asks.

"Yeah, that."

"Hey, you are who you are," she says. "I realized that, and for once, I was glad for it. Snake helped me to understand that there will always be people better than me and worse than me, but I'm my own special person, and it does no good to always be comparing myself to others."

"I know, but you're not the only one who does. Mom and Dad need to tone it down too."

"Yeah, and Bubbe," Davina tells me, revealing how our grandmother keeps mistaking her for me and telling me how much better I am than her.

We talk about it some more, and I vow when this is all over to have a chat with them.

"No need," Davina says. "I know my worth now. Their actions and opinions don't have to define me. And I owe you an apology too."

"What? No, you don't. You saved my ass or tried to. You somehow found me when no one else could."

"Yeah, well, Jonah was mostly responsible. But I'm sorry it was you on that tour and not me. I should have spoken up to Mom and Dad about it, but I let them force you instead. I was just so hurt."

"I get it, and I'm not mad. I was, but I dropped all that. Not worth holding onto."

She thanks me, then tells me she's dizzy and tired. We say goodbye for now.

I sit in all different spots in the hotel lobby and out front as I wait for Ollie, moving around so no one will question who I am and why I'm there. Much to my dismay, after spending the night outside on a bench keeping a watchful eye, Ollie never shows.

What could possibly have happened to him? He was supposed to find Trent Diablo in Buffalo for his antidote and then meet me. Did Trent do something to him? Perhaps he's in charge of all this, the ultimate Game Master. Diablo *is* Spanish for devil, after all.

I Gaggle a Trent Diablo in Buffalo, and I find three. Staring at their pictures, I wonder which of them would be most likely to buy a heart-shaped amulet necklace. They could have purchased them for anyone, a wife, girlfriend, daughter, niece, or even themselves. Part of me wants to go to Buffalo now, blow more of my savings and fly out there to track down these three Trent Diablo's, but I need to see Davina more and make sure she's okay, followed by my father and mother. I called the hospital to check on them, and Mom was in therapy, so I left a message, and Dad is still unconscious on a ventilator in the ICU.

I fly from Mackinac Island to Houghton, and as we land, I'm incredulous I'm arriving again in the city I was trying *not* to go to in the first place. I grab a Lyft from there to Hancock across that huge lift bridge near the park where I won Vermilion and everyone except me and Ollie died. As soon as I get dropped off at the hospital, I dash inside.

I find Davina on the second floor, with Snake Riley sitting next to her bed holding her hand, his eye black and jaw all bruised. I've never been happier to see anyone in my life. I rush to Davina, hugging her and bawling.

She cries too.

Even though we talked about a lot yesterday, I need to apologize to her face. "I'm sorry I haven't realized how tough it must be to always be compared with me, to feel like we're in competition."

She puts up her hand. "It's not your fault you are who you are. I'm proud of you and all you can do."

I hug her. "I feel the same way about you. You have all your strengths and talents too. It doesn't matter if others also do, there will always be people better and worse than you, and me too." I think of how tough of opponents Sammi and Ollie were, Camila and Keondra too, and know I won't always be the best, especially when I get to Broadway. "You should be proud of yourself for who you are. I know I certainly am. And I'm so thankful to you both." I smile over at Snake, who reveals interesting fangs.

Davina beams at me, then faints against her pillow.

I look at Snake in alarm. "Is she okay?"

Davina pops up. "Sorry. Just in shock. First compliment from you and all."

I bop her head and hug her, so glad to be with her again, sure it would never happen. I think of Ollie and Paige and the others, who I'm torn up about and miss, but there's nothing like family. "I love you, Davina. I'm so glad you're my sister." I give her a huge hug and kiss.

## PART 17

### DAVINA RECEIVES A VISITOR

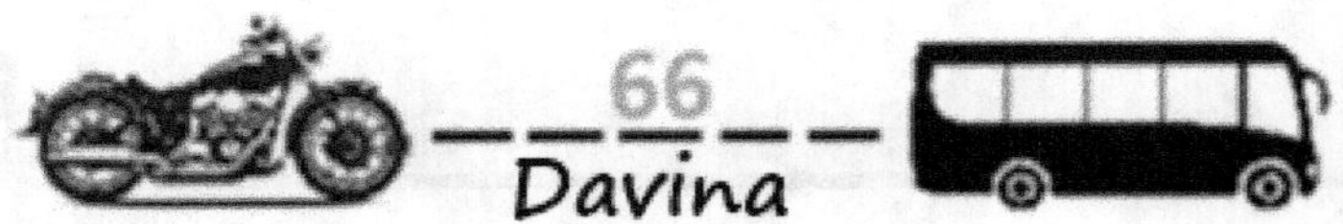


**Sunday, January 26, 2030**

Even though I'm still dizzy as hell and worried about my swollen brain, I'm thrilled to be with Mallory and Jonah. Although we still don't know how my parents will be, at least we're together.

Mallory and I agree we won't be taking any more buses if we can help it.

Jonah is sound asleep in his chair even though it's barely dark yet. He looks so adorable, like the little boy I remember from the first grade, I wish I could hug him, but he's too far. Mallory is between us, so I hug her instead.

She strokes my hair, telling me about Ollie, this great guy she met and fell in love with during The Game, and how she doesn't know what happened to him after she chose him to live instead of Paige, her other good friend out of the group. "She really wasn't my friend I discovered at the end, but I still care about her." Mallory wipes her eyes. "I just don't get it. Ollie told me he loved me and then fell off the face of the earth. Paige said he was using me, and I think she was right." My sister buries her face in her hands. "Either that, or maybe he was killed by Trent Diablo. Who knows?"

"I'm sorry," I say. "That must feel terrible."

She waves her hand. "Tell me more. Make me feel better. Describe again how you blew up those asshole O'Grady Kids. Who the hell were they? That's what I want to know. Who did this to us?"

"I don't know. I'm not sure we ever will unless the police identify them through dental records. And there were a lot of VIPs too, so it'll be hard to know who was who, unless those crazy realistic masks don't burn for some reason."

"Well, tell me again how they all went kablooey, how they burned. It does my heart good."

I go through it again, up until that weird-looking albino guy attacked us right when we blew up The O'Grady Kids.

"Who was he?"

I shake my head. "I don't know. After he said that we killed his whole family, he knocked me out, and then Snake told me later that he tried to strangle the guy, but the much bigger and stronger attacker got the upper hand and knocked him out. When Snake awoke, the guy was gone."

"So, he was a Game Master too then? One got away?"

I nod. "Yep, I think so. He had straight, white-blond hair. Must've been a wig. Round glasses. Realistic mask with freckles all over. Looked like that other O'Grady kid, the annoying little cousin they brought in for the last season. Remember him?"

"I do. He was annoying. What was his name? They said putting him on made the show get cancelled."

"I don't know." I grab my Hollaphone and Gaggle it. "It says here his name was Cousin Tolliver."

Mallory exhales, slumping in her chair. "I can't believe this. *Tolliver*? Really?"

"What?"

Mallory's stares down at the bedding as tears stream down her cheeks. "Oh my God."

"What?"

"His siblings. Their names. Duh. It was there the whole time. I just didn't put it together." Mallory smacks her head, sucking in air between her teeth.

I shake my dizzy head at her, which makes it worse. "What about them? You lost me."

"His siblings were Meg, Weaver, Dobby, Darcy, Candace, and Mandy. And he's Ollie."

"Oh shit. The O'Grady Kids are Craig, Skeeter, Robbie, Marci, Janice, and Sandy. And the seventh O'Grady kid, Cousin Tolliver. And he's Olliver."

“Ollie must have come there when he was getting us food and clothes and stuff,” Mallory whispers, putting her head in her hands. “He’s the one who attacked you and put you here.” My She grits her teeth, her hands balling into fists. “He almost killed you, and he did kill all of them. All my bus mates.You should have seen their last terrified looks before they fell and disintegrated. Hard to forget something like that.” She shudders and then puts her hands over her face. I let her have a moment while she cries. She looks up with red eyes.

“What? I don’t get it. Are you sure? Just because it’s a similar name doesn’t mean anything.”

“Do you remember anything else about him?”

I think back, and then the five rings of the Olympics come to mind. I saw them right before I passed out. I tell Mallory.

She glances at a sleeping Jonah near her and grabs a pillow nearby, holds it to her face and screams.

“What?”

She finally takes it away. “That was Ollie’s tattoo. He used to be a gymnast.” Her fingers bend into air quotes. “‘Cousin Tolliver’ was him for sure. Ollie’s the one who put you here!”

“Oh shit. I’m so sorry. So, he was *in* the game but also one of the Game Masters? How? Why?”

Mallory punches the pillow now, her face skewed by rage. “I don’t know, but he’s the one who could have killed you, and who subjected me and the others to all that torture. He killed them all! Troy and Darla, Sammi, Jiro, Camila and Keondra. Krystall Nykkolls. And Paige. *He’s* part of The Game, not her! Or maybe they were in cahoots. Maybe she’s the eighth O’Grady! Hell, maybe she’s not even dead or none of them are and that was a visual hallucination! What if it was all bullshit and everyone’s alive? Maybe it was all a prank on me for some reason and no one really died.” Mallory closes her eyes, a tear escaping down her cheek.

“I don’t know,” I tell her, squeezing her arm. “But I do know that Paige is not an O’Grady Kid at least because I met her family. Her parents are architecture professors and work at Lawrence Tech with Mom and Dad.”

“Excuse me.” Mallory bolts out the door. I get up to try to follow her, but the room spins, and I fall onto Snake in his chair.

He awakens with a start. “What? What happened?”

I send Jonah after Mallory as I settle back into bed, hoping she’ll be okay and wishing everything around me would stop moving so fast.

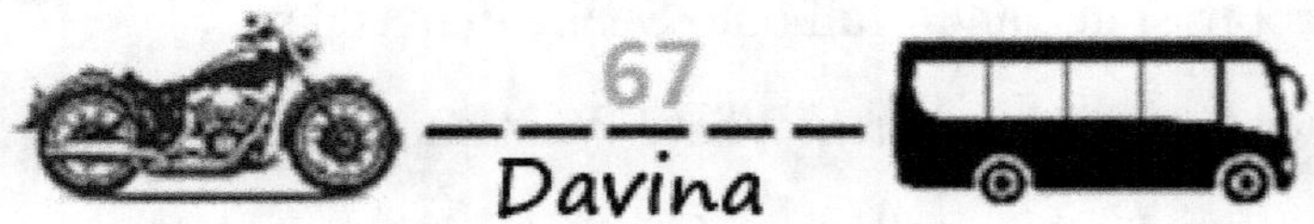

# 67
## Davina

A while later, as I'm wondering if Snake found Mallory and if she's okay now that she discovered this Ollie that she fell for is part of Vermilion, a nurse comes in pushing a cart with a computer on it. His face and head are covered in a mask and cap, but his eyes seem friendly behind their square frames.

"Hello. I'm your evening nurse, Shane. We just had shift change." He grabs a clipboard at the foot of my bed and flips through it. "How're you feeling tonight, Ms. Rosenbaum?"

"Okay. Just very dizzy. I tried to get up and – "

"Oh, you shouldn't do that. You have an order from the doctor to stay in your bed. Didn't they tell you?" He pulls up the sides and locks them into place. "Just call us if you need to use the restroom, okay? We'll help you there safely."

I nod and start to explain about my sister and how I tried to go after her, but he takes a huge syringe with a long needle off his cart and depresses the plunger, expelling a spittle of fluid, which shuts me up as he comes at me.

I shrink away. "What the – "

He sticks the needle into the I.V. port in my arm. I exhale a sigh of relief. Snake said they put the I.V. in my arm while I was unconscious when he brought me into the ER, which is a good thing since I hate needles so much. "I thought you were going to stick me with that."

"Oh no. That would hurt too much." His eyes smile. He points to the I.V. port. "We try to stick only once, if we can help it."

I start to ask him what's in the syringe, what do they suddenly think I need since they haven't given me anything since I awoke two days ago, but the words won't come out.

I try to calm down and speak again, but my mouth won't move.

"It's a weird feeling, isn't it?" The nurse's grinning eyes turn dark.

"What?" I try to say, but I can't. What the fuck?

"You're feeling the succinylcholine chloride I just injected," Shane the nurse says. "It's a common paralytic used in tracheal intubations in addition to general anesthesia given during surgery."

As he says this, I notice his wrist bears the five Olympic rings, and my heart explodes out of the gate. It's Ollie! I try to flee, but I can't even move to blink. "Help!" I scream, but no sound comes out of me.

As I stare at my nurse, really Ollie and not Shane, he tells me that he needs to explain. "Please tell Mallory when you can. I really can't see her again. It's just too hard. So, pass it on, k?"

I pray she comes back soon and catches him, preferably with Snake.

"My brothers and sisters and I invented the game Vermilion, you see, to do good eventually. I know it doesn't seem like it, but my family and I have done something great. Revolutionary. We improved the current nanobot technology by leaps and bounds, but obviously, these good things can be used in bad ways."

Ollie shuts the door to the room and lowers the shades. "My siblings, who are older even though I told Mallory they were younger, none of us are very educated. My older sister Meg did some classes at Oakland Community College, and Dobby and Candace went to Michigan State a few semesters, but we got too obsessed with what we were able to learn and do on our own. See, we were rich growing up, then poor and forced to watch rich people while cleaning up after them. I was too young to know, but my siblings weren't. This thing they started, this Azure Dragon Inc., was for us to get rich again, to use AI in a way no one had ever seen, bringing in lots of money. But now, it's become so much more. It's how we can do good for society, to change the world for the better."

"Better?" I try to ask, but my face is stone.

"After all the years we spent developing our Invader Patch and Rover-Bots," Ollie continues, "giving up friends and fun and everything else to work around the clock, my siblings and I shopped our Invader Patch around to reputable biotech companies, but no one wanted it."

Ollie strokes my forehead while I scream in silence.

“No one legitimate, that is. They didn’t take us seriously because we were a bunch of kids with no real education telling them we developed this super advanced patch. They didn’t even give us a chance to show what it could do.” He clucks his tongue. “So rude.”

“So, one day, Weaver, the smartest of all of us, says, why don’t we get criminals to invest? Show them what our Rover-Bots are capable of with a fun interactive game, where we get hostages and shoot them up with nanobots and let our potential investors try before they buy.”

He waves a hand. “Meg had once gone on a bus tour to Michigan Tech, and she suggested that’s how we get our hostages, by creating a fake tour. Everyone thought it was a great idea, because it would be easy to do, but also because most on the bus tour would likely be relatively young and smart enough to want to go to Michigan Tech, so we’d have good test subjects. We could study them at the same time to collect data on various things. And well, you pretty much know how it worked. Mallory will fill you in on the specifics.”

Ollie squeezes my dead hand that I’m trying like hell to move so I can strangle him. “We had to find a way to get the criminals to invest, so we made The Game so we could eventually accomplish our good goals. Weaver said criminals will throw a lot of money at stuff they think will make them more, and he was right. We did net quite a bit, enough to now do some of what we planned, but we still need more, which is why we’ve been developing Vermilion 1.2 with our improved Invader Patch. There are other VIPs to be had, and many other things we will make the bots do.” His eyes get even darker. “Or at least, I will, since the rest of them are gone and all.”

This guy thinks he’s all noble and stuff. I can’t believe it. I try to relax my frantic heartbeat before my chest explodes, praying Mallory and Snake arrive soon.

“The whole O’Grady Kids thing, I’m sure you’re wondering, and Mallory will ask, so let me explain. Our mother, who was a maid when her husband died suddenly and left her with nothing except seven kids, killed herself trying to support us working for her best friend, a wealthy socialite. I didn’t know Mom well because I was only five when she died, but from what my siblings tell me, she was obsessed with that O’Grady Kids show. She named all us kids after The O’Grady’s, even me, her youngest, who she named Olliver after Cousin Tolliver, the seventh kid they brought in for the last season. Mom even legally changed our last name to maid Allysin's last name, Melson, after our father screwed us."

"Meg and the others said the only time my mother was ever happy after my father died was when she was watching that show and eating her Luckster Gems, which she won a lifetime supply of long ago and was often all we had in the house to eat. That show was always on growing up, even after she was gone, and I feel like those kids were my siblings too, we know them so well."

"So, we had to of course incorporate The O'Grady Kids in The Game, and it was perfect since we planned on six rounds and needed to disguise our Game Masters to collect the firescopes. And then when the Rebel Demons brought us that Krystall chick they captured because she tried to rip them off with some drug deal or whatever, we made her into Luckster for an extra fun challenge for the contestants. Janice was the one who came up with the whole 'leprechaun chasing rainbows' thing and thought to dress everyone that way. She was always the most creative, even though everyone always paid more attention to Marci because she was prettier."

"My dad was really into astronomy when he wasn't being a lawyer or secretly gambling his fortune away, and he taught my siblings all about the Four Auspicious Beasts of the Chinese Constellation, with the Azure Dragon in the East, the Black Tortoise in the North, and the others. Since there were directions involved with their names, we thought it was perfect for the coins in The Game."

I can't believe how he's talking as if this is all reasonable, everything they did to my sister and the others. From what Mallory told me, it was awful to watch people she knew suddenly die and then disintegrate before her very eyes. Plus, all the stress and worry. I can't even imagine, although I sure had my own share of stress because of this guy too, and so did all the other families. And soon, they'll be going through more hell since no one except Mallory and Ollie survived.

"Now, I know you're thinking me and my siblings were awful because we did all this. And it was bad, I know. I was there. But it was the only way to get the money we needed to do good, and to make sure that the nanobots of the future are not hackable so that no one can ever do this to anyone again and can only reap their benefits. Don't you see? We had to do it like this. It was the only way."

I get it, but I don't. And I don't approve. Although in some ways the game Vermilion was a genius idea to accomplish their ultimately good goal, it hurt a lot of people. Like Churchill's bombing of Coventry, Ollie and his siblings used their little game Vermilion to sacrifice a few for the good of the many. I used that same justification for using Rocco's bisexuality against him, and killing Ollie's family, but those were for good. I guess in a way, I can see Ollie's viewpoint and understand a little of why he thought his use of The Game was for good, but I still hate him and his family for all they did.

"We sent Mallory and me to Ionia Lemon and Trent Diablo, who were two random customers who ordered the amulets with the supposed antidote, but they didn't really have it, you see. I mean, I still want control of Mallory. Even though she won, she wouldn't have if it weren't for me. And as a dancer with a high level of physical fitness and tremendous intellect, she's a great test subject for our Vermilion 1.2, which will be coming very soon."

Ollie turns around and takes something else off the tray, then comes toward me with another syringe with a long needle. "I have your sister right where I want her. I was in the game to test out the bots and the contestant experience, but also to manipulate things from within to study social interactions and other factors. My siblings made me since I'm the right age. I didn't mean to fall in love with your sister. She was a huge distraction I didn't expect."

He rubs an alcohol swab on my I.V. port. "I'm not worried though. I'm developing a way for AI to target emotions in the brain, and soon, I'll be able to delete all the feelings I have for her. It'll be part of our new Emo-Bot. So, I got Mallory," he says, and then injects my I.V. with the syringe. "And now, my dearest Davina, I got you too."

The liquid empties from the vial into the little plastic thingy in my arm. "Yep, millions of itty bitty nanobots are filling your insides as we speak." He shrugs. "You kinda' killed my whole family." He takes out the syringe and walks over to a sharps bin, putting it in. "What's fair is fair."

I hear some voices, and Ollie's head whips around.

Mallory and Snake are chatting as they walk into the room.

"I'll be in touch," Ollie says. He straightens his mask and walks right past Mallory out the door. She doesn't even notice him, still talking to Jonah.

And I can't move to say boo.

"I told them my father was a clarinet player, but when we looked, they were all women!"

Jonah laughs. "So, what did you do?"

Mallory frowns at me. "Davina?"

I try to blink, but I can't even do that.

"You don't look right." Mallory turns to Jonah. "Does she look right?"

He bends over and peers at me. "No. Her eyes ain't moving. Something's wrong. Call that nurse back."

"Okay," Mallory says, and she runs out the door after him.

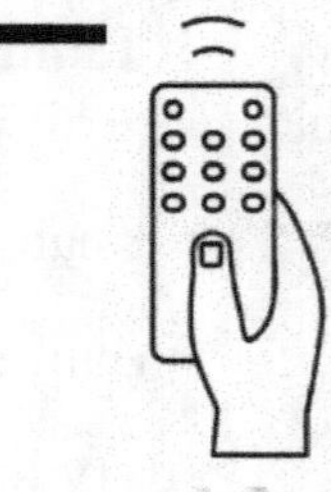

# PART 18

## A VOW IS MADE

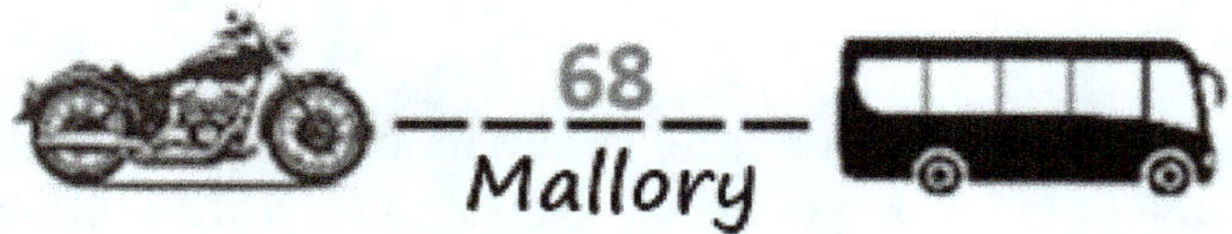


**Thursday, February 14, 2030**

I never found whichever nurse was there. I didn't even pay attention to who it was and just got anyone. After they put Davina through every test under the sun and couldn't figure out what was wrong, thinking her sudden paralysis was a complication from her concussion, they started talking brain surgery. Thank God she eventually snapped out of it and told me and Jonah and the doctor what happened. The police put out an APB on Ollie Melson, if that's even his real name. Much to my surprise and dismay, he was the ultimate villain in The Game.

I had to sit down after hearing all Ollie said, how he wants to control me as a test subject and invent a way to forget his feelings for me, and my eyes haven't been dry since. So, he did love me, but it doesn't matter. I'm not sure if it's worse if he did or didn't.

Davina said she thought it all had to do with our parents, or even my rivalry with The Purrrlz Gurrrlz. I told her between tears that I was convinced too, that it all seemed too coincidental, but it was all really inconsequential. I was never a target, and my parents didn't have to do with anything. Ollie and his siblings would have done what they did whether I was there or not.

The doctors eventually released Davina after they determined her brain was fine. We flew home and discovered that my dad is awake now and out of quarantine. They're keeping him for observation and more tests for his lingering issues with breathing. Davina and I visited him and told him a bit about what happened, but not everything yet. It's too overwhelming. Then we left to see Mom.

When she noticed me, she lit up and ran to hug me, holding me, crying, and apologizing forever until I had to pry her off me. She told me I can be a dancer or a clown or a street cleaner or a stripper, she doesn't care, so long as I'm alive and happy, and she apologized for trying to force me. “I’ll be there at opening night of your first Broadway show with bells on!”

Davina and I explained a little to her about everything that had happened to each of us, trying to answer her questions without overdoing it and getting her too emotional.

Sadly, we discovered Zayde is still in a coma, so he’s oblivious to anything that went on. He’s still a big stressful question mark, but Dad says we’ll hire a nurse to help, no matter what it costs, even if he must take a second job. Me and Davina said we’ll pitch in and work to contribute if needed, and he says we’ll see.

A week later, exactly a year since Snake “mugged” our parents on Valentine’s Day, he shows up at our front door with his arms full of flowers.

I peek outside as he steps through the threshold, yearning to be able to just go to the mall or to a hip-hop practice, something beside this house. For now, though, the police and my parents want me staying inside, my return from The Game still unknown except to my few friends I spoke with who are sworn to secrecy. The police and the lawyers and PR people are trying to figure out the best way to present what happened to the public and the families of my murdered bus mates. They don’t want me to become a target of scorn or retaliation, people upset that I’m the only survivor.

Davina rushes to help Snake and gives him a kiss. “Thought I was coming to see you later. Why are you out in the open? Aren’t you supposed to be in hiding?”

He presents me with beautiful white daisies, my favorite, then hands Davina a bouquet of lavender tulips, her favorite, without answering. He’s left with a huge bunch of wildflowers, which he sets on the table. “Please give these to your mom when you see her. You can tell her they’s from me, or not.” He looks at his shoes. “Happy Valentine’s, ladies. Thought I’d get’cha somethin’ better than last year.” He looks to my sister. “And don’cha worry. We can plant them in the yard so we don’t poison your kitties.”

“They’re beautiful,” I tell him, hugging him and kissing him on the cheek, and then Davina kisses him for real. I turn away, blushing. I can’t help but feel a little envious and think about Ollie, but I also feel happy for my sister that she seems to have met a great guy. I can’t get over that it’s the one my family has hated since he attacked our parents, but it is, and he's shockingly awesome for my sister. I've never seen her so happy.

And Snake has the cutest snake ever. Lola loves to Slither Smile for me. I'm thinking of incorporating her into a Majik 8 Balz routine and dedicating it to Camila and Keondra, maybe inviting the rest of The Purrrlz Gurrrlz to be in it or join our group, although we couldn't be the Majik 8 Balz anymore because we'd be too big. Santos would love Lola for our next competition. I think we'll dance to Paula Abdul's "Cold Hearted" and maybe sample some of Heart's "Barracuda" and Nicki Minaj's "Anaconda."

"So, are you going to keep me guessing about why you're risking your life to give us flowers?" Davina asks. "What if the Eastside Boyz see you? Where's your cowboy disguise?"

Snake grins ear to ear. "Don't need it no more."

"What?" Davina asks. "Why not?"

Lola bobs on Snake's shoulder, Slither Smiling, in on some secret. "Last night, Rocco bought out the contract the Eastside Boyz had on me. Said he'd give them the 50% that Hawk always wanted instead of the 40/60 split like before if they'd leave me alone and reunite with the Rebel Demons, stopping their stupid civil war. Hatchet, now their President, says Hawk was an asshole, Shailene a bitch, and he agreed. Hatchet will run the east."

"Why would Rocco do that? Isn't he so mad at us?"

Jonah nods. "He is, I'm sure, but I ain't gonna' care. I had to do another bad to do good. Told him I'd tell everyone 'bout him and Cody if he didn't get that contract off me and let me out, and then I promised I'd never, ever use it against him again."

"Out? Out of what?" Davina asks.

"The Rebel Demons." Jonah exposes his fangs. "I'm officially out, no hard feelings, no retaliation. Rocco said I can even go to Blades Cave and Rebel Demon events, but I can't go to no meetings or hear club business, which is fine with me. And I must get my Rebel Demons tatt blacked out, which will suck, but at least I ain't get the huge one on my back yet, so —"

Davina hugs him, kissing his cheek. “This is such great news! I can’t believe it!”

“I got me even better news. Rocco said he’d let me finish high school and pay for me to go to college and vet school. And he said this ain’t because he’s afraid of being outed, but because he knows I take great care of Lola and can help a lot of them other animals too.”

“Huh,” Davina says. “He turned out to be a decent guy after all, even with what we did.”

Snake shrugs. “Yeah. I’ll always be feelin’ bad, but there wasn’t no other way. I told Rocco and Cody that they better tell Corrinne, or I will. I feel bad as shit, but she’s gotta’ know.”

“All your future patients will thank you,” Davina says. “I feel bad for Corrinne too, but she’ll land on her feet. Hope she finds some great guy who deserves her and won’t cheat.”

“Me too,” Snake agrees. “And as for my future as a vet, I can’t freaking wait.” He takes Lola’s head in his hand and kisses it. “And this one here will be my assistant. Isn’t that right, widdle widdle Lola Girl?” She Slither Smiles, bopping around as he scratches her belly.

Davina tells Snake she’s thrilled for him and offers to be his permanent math tutor. “I won’t even charge you if you continue building Lola’s Waterfall. I’ll even help steal boulders.” He laughs and they start making out, not caring that I’m right there. Lola wraps herself around them like she’s tying them together.

Davina reaches over and embraces me who’s trying not to see, and Snake and Lola wrap around both of us. I smile despite everything because Lola suddenly discovers she loves burrowing in my hair, which tickles.

When Snake lets us go, Davina picks up the wildflowers Snake brought for Mom. “I think you should bring them to her yourself.” She hands them back to him. “I gave Mom your letters, and my Dad read them too, and they want to meet you and thank you for all you did. They totally understand what happened and say they completely forgive you.”

“You serious?” Snake asks.

Davina nods, and then he hugs and kisses her again. "That's the best news ever." He glances at me. "Well, except of course that we got Mallory."

"Mark-Bot, signing on," I hear in my ear.

Davina's eyes widen as she hears Mark-Bot's voice for the first time. Jonah is the only one of the three of us who are not shot up with nanobots, so he's not privy to it.

I told Davina to expect that Ollie would be making contact soon, but after a week of silence, I think she doubted me. Until now.

"Mallory? Davina? Are you there?" Ollie asks in Mark-Bot's voice.

We don't say anything, but Davina's eyes are wide. She presses her ear and frowns.

Suddenly, my heart is a racehorse, trotting faster and faster until I feel like it's going to take off without me.

"Do you feel that?" Mark-Bot asks.

"What's going on?" Davina gasps, clutching her chest while Snake tries to prevent her from falling.

"Ollie, stop!" I scream. The exploding pain behind my ribs suddenly goes away. Davina cries and grasps for Snake.

"I don't like being ignored," Mark-Bot says.

"What do you want from us, you psycho fuck?" Davina demands. Suddenly, she drops to the ground, gurgling as she writhes around.

"Ollie, please! Leave her alone!" I bend down, trying to hold her still.

A few seconds later, Davina stops and looks up, bawling now. "What's happening?"

"Ollie is messing with us from the inside," I tell her. "Ollie, please, let us go! We won't tell anyone. Just give us the antidote."

"Uhhhh, nope," Ollie as Mark-Bot says. "Me and my sisters and brothers have voted and — oh, wait. No, what? Oh, they're all dead? Because they were killed by your sister and that guy with the snake on his head? Oh, right. Nope. Sorry. Jury's back. Can't let you girls go. Oh, also, there is no antidote. There never was. I'm sure I can invent one though, but it's not high on my priority list. I'm working on Vermilion 1.2. There's lots to do. So, anywho, that's my plane. I'm off for a little vacay and then it's back to work. I'll be in touch with details about the next game. I'm really working on more mind control stuff for it. It'll blow your minds, maybe literally!"

Mark-Bot laughs as I wonder which airport Ollie's flying from.

"Should be soon, so get ready," Ollie warns. A laugh track plays along with some campy interlude music while the fake audience whistles and claps. "Mark-Bot, signing off."

"Goodbye, and good luck, Vermilion Contestants!" Karyn-Bot says. Since Ollie's whole family is gone, I wonder if the voice is Ear-Bot generated, or if he's already replaced me with some other girl the way Blake did.

The O'Grady Kids theme song starts: "Here's a fun tale of a super cool gal who was raising up three kiddos of her own…"

I close my eyes and look behind my eyelids to see all the O'Grady's faces in a grid on the screen – Mark, Karyn, Craig, Skeeter, Robbie, Marci, Janice, and Sandy — but instead of Allysyn's face in the middle like usual, Cousin Tolliver appears, and evil laughter drowns out the song. It fades and then the words appear: "Vermilion 1.2, coming soon!" The letters drip like red blood off the screen, and the image fades to black.

Davina exhales, running her fingers over her arms like I did the first time I realized I was full of bots. "I can't believe this."

"What happened?" Snake asks, his Lola brow scrunched.

I explain it all to Snake and Davina, that Ollie has us both now because he wants to use us as his nanoslaves for his invention, or the next game, or whatever, and he's super pissed because Davina and Snake killed his family. "I'm worried he'll get you too, Jonah. He knows you helped blow up his siblings. We must get him and force him to make an antidote this time."

"He won't," Davina says. "I don't know how we could make him. And there's no one to hold over him if he's telling the truth and we really killed his whole family. We have no leverage."

"But he's shot up with the bots too," I say. "He was able to hear us all on our Walkie-Bots. He spoke Japanese to Jiro with Talkie-Bots. They're in him. That wasn't fake. Maybe we can use them to —"

"What if that's all he's shot up with?" Davina asks. "Maybe he doesn't have the bad ones you told me about, like the Med-Bots and Soldier-Bots and stuff?"

I bite my lip. "I don't know."

"I agree with Davina," Snake says. "He'll just fuck with us and find a way to escape. He's too smart to have those bad bots in him and make himself vulnerable. No, I'm afraid we gotta' save people from his mad games. He's too smart for the world's own good, no matter if his intentions be noble and shit. No, only way to get rid of the problem is to well…" He looks at us and winces. "Get rid of the problem. Once and for all."

I gulp, knowing what he says is true. "He claims he wanted to help people, ultimately."

Davina and Snake raise eyebrows at me. "You believe that?"

I shrug. "I don't know. Part of me does."

"Even so, it ain't an excuse what he did. What he's capable of," Snake says. "His siblings are all dead, but he knows where all the code is for they's Invader Patch and how it all works. He can train others. Maybe there be cousins. God knows what's gonna go down in Vermilion 1.2. Mind control now? Ollie's gotta' be stopped, or it could be the end of like freaking humanity."

"Totally," Davina agrees. "Believe me, I'm not looking forward to killing anyone else, but he's too dangerous. No way can we let him live. Only *one* in Vermilion may live, remember? Is it him, or is it you?"

I nod begrudgingly, knowing they're right, and I must choose myself — and potentially the rest of the world — over him. I think of Paige, Sammi, Jiro, Camila, Keondra, Darla, and Troy, then Krystall Nykkolls, the surprise captee, who Rocco finally admitted the Rebel Demons did capture and donate to the Vermilion people to spice up their game. Ollie killed them all, even the ones he got to know, and I can't believe that he can be that cold.

As I squeeze Davina's hand, I try to ignore the aching in my heart for the guy who played me like a fiddle and screwed me like a lightbulb. I'm glad at least I didn't let him screw me for real. If we'd reunited, he would have had the chance.

I look over at Snake, the bad boy who turned out to be good, and then think of Ollie, the good boy who turned out to be bad, and I smirk at the irony. Ollie truly is Asshole Red Car Guy; I should have trusted my instincts. Remembering all the things he put us through, I vow to find and destroy him as my sister and her boyfriend intend to do. I know we must, or he'll take over the world very soon with his Vermilion 1.2. The problem is that I still love him, and that really, really sucks.

Stay tuned for Two in Vermilion May Die, coming soon!

Dear Reader,

If you enjoyed this story, kindly spread the word on Goodreads, Amazon, social media, and other sites to let others know! Thanks ver-milion!!!

Also, please sign up for my Reader's List on my website at https://authorjenniferjaxxonlouis.com for fun contests, a monthly newsletter, and exciting giveaways! Looking forward to seeing you in my inbox!

~ Jennifer

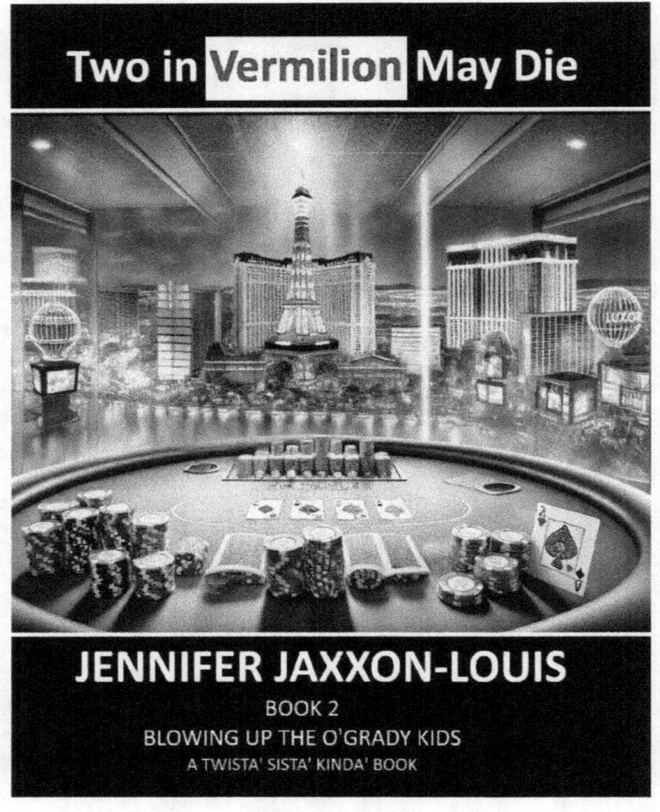


(Temporary Cover)

Mallory and Davina are back with new ally Snake hoping to kill those responsible for the Vermilion game before they take over the world. But since the Rosenbaum twins are full of nanobots which are even better than before, they have no choice but to play a whole new game.

Teaming up with members of Mallory's Majik 8 Balz and the Purrrlz Gurrrlz, Mallory, Davina, Snake, and a few surprise guests race around Las Vegas playing a deadly version of Texas Hold'em. In between impossible challenges, they race to find and destroy the new O'Grady Kids Game Masters before the unthinkable happens and everything they've ever known implodes.

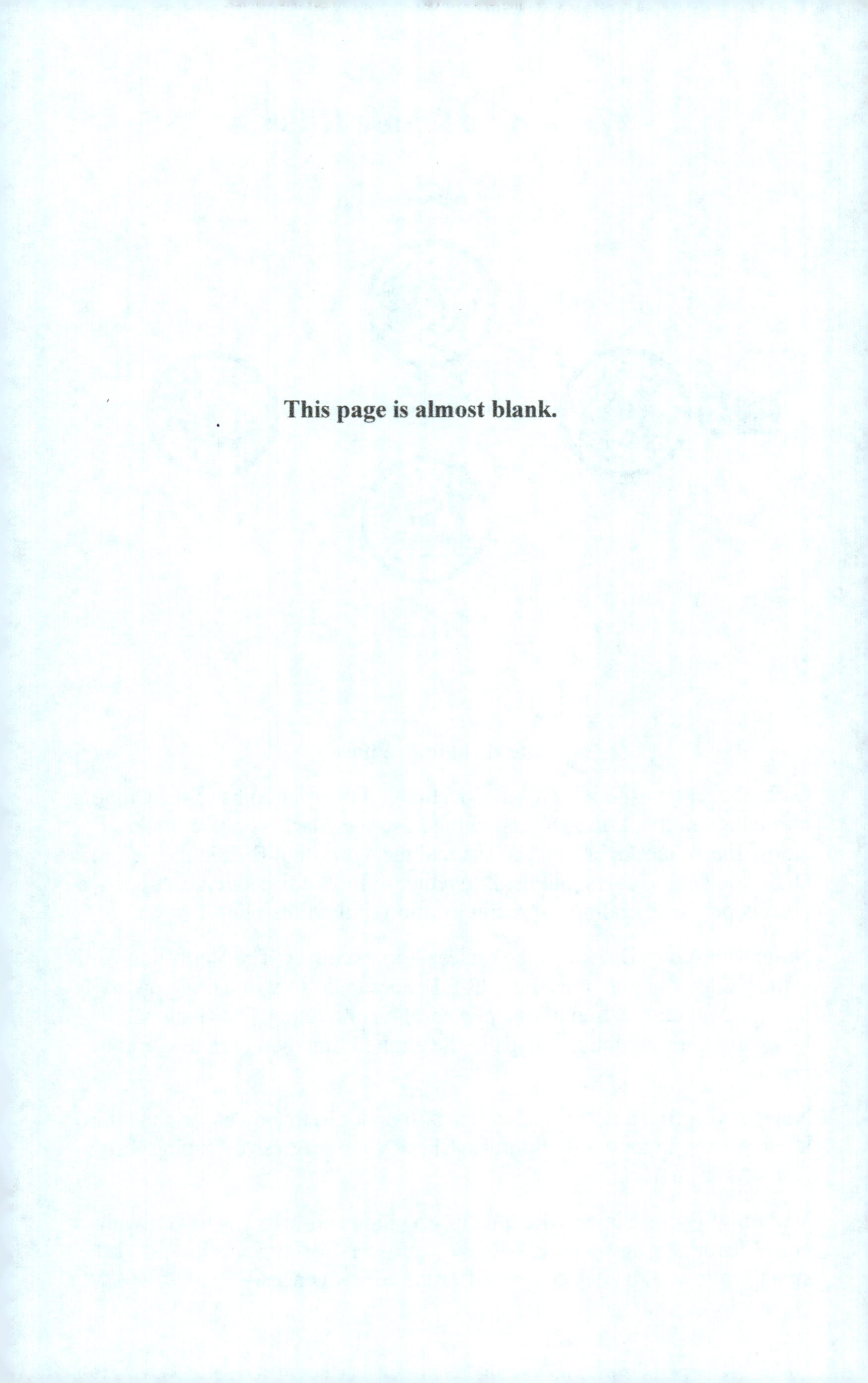
This page is almost blank.

# Vermilion Game Rules

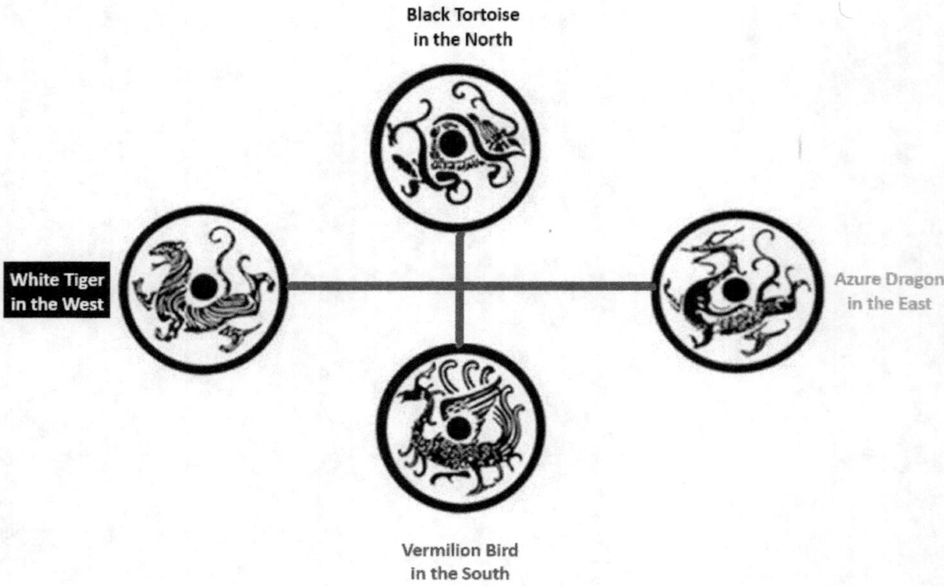


### The Hangman Phase

Gather letter clues to identify the locations of the four coins of the Chinese constellation: the Azure Dragon in the East, the Black Tortoise in the North, the White Tiger in the West, and the Vermilion Bird in the South. Once you get the coins, put them together to form a fire kaleidoscope — a "firescope" — revealing the secret location of the finish line.

**Note:** The Azure Dragon is the easiest coin to collect. The Vermilion Bird is the hardest, so you must get it last. Failure to do so will cause you to face random elimination of one player. Not completing The Hangman Phase and forming the firescope in the allotted time will earn the same result.

**Note:** If you find a letter clue with a 3/10 under it, that means it's the third letter in a ten-letter word or phrase. Check your progress by asking Karyn-Bot to "see puzzle."

**Warning:** Game Masters are *always* watching and listening to you with your Mirror Egg and your Ear-Bots (see Rover-Bot Types below), so be sure to follow all game rules or suffer the consequences.

## The Vermilion Hour

If you pass The Hangman Phase, you and your opponents must walk backward from the firescope until a proper circumference is achieved. When Karyn-Bot announces The Vermilion Hour has begun, whoever gets the firescope to the Game Master at the secret finish line within the sixty-minute time limit has won the round.

**Warning:** Watch out for your enemies! They want to win as much as you and it is *not* against Game Rules to rob, injure, or kill your opponents.

**Note:** Any injuries sustained in a round will be erased during Nap Time. The Soldier-Bots will carry appropriate drugs from the Med-Bots and repair any broken bones or torn ligaments. If you die, however, there is no Rover-Bot who can remedy that, and you are officially eliminated from The Game.

**Note:** If no one hands the firescope to the Game Master within the hour, one random player will be eliminated after Karyn-Bot spins the Player Wheel.

## Who Wins Vermilion?

The player who wins the most rounds will survive — if they make it until the end. They will receive the antidote to destroy their Rover-Bots in a beautiful green amulet — theirs to keep! — and set free. The losers will receive lethal doses of potassium chloride from the Soldier-Bots, and then hydrofluoric acid will disintegrate them into specks of dust.

## Vermilion Game Warnings

1) You may <u>not</u> use any technology or communication device, attempt to seek help, or tell anyone you're participating in this game. Always wear your provided disguises and do not reveal your identity to anyone. Violation of this warning will result in a family member being subject to the Punishment Wheel while every contestant must watch. Ask Karyn-Bot for details.

2) If you're arrested or detained, you will have fifteen seconds to escape, or you'll be eliminated from The Game.

3) If you attempt to flee, automatic elimination is a certainty.

### Rover-Bot Types

**Eye-Bots:** They allow the Game Masters to see what you see and show images behind your eyelids. They can display things that aren't there and alter your vision for better or worse.

**Ear-Bots:** They enable Game Masters to hear what you hear and can play different sounds at various volumes.

**Walkie-Bots:** These special Ear-Bots connect to other game players so you can hear one another, providing an internal messaging system. You can summon anyone by saying, "Walkie-Bot, call Skeeter," or whatever their name is.

**Soldier-Bots:** The Soldier-Bots destroy and repair bones, ligaments, and tendons. They collect various bodily substances like urine, bile, mucus, and saliva for the Med-Bots to synthesize into any quantity of any other substance and then distribute it to targeted locations.

**Med-Bots:** They collect fluids from the Soldier-Bots and change them into poisons, medicines, hormones, and the all-important dust cloud of the highly reflective aluminum or "lightning sheeting" that makes the Mirror Egg work. They pass newly transformed substances to the Soldier-Bots to deliver.

**Skin-Bots:** They form your Mirror Egg by shooting microscopic lasers out of your skin's pores of all different lengths to form an ellipsoid surround. They also emit a fine dust of highly reflective aluminum. The millions of reflected images catch on the laser web, and then the Eye-Bots peer out your pores to assemble them like a huge jigsaw puzzle and read the continuous feed.

**Mirror Egg:** Since the Vermilion challenges occur in public at very crowded places, the Mirror Egg allows the Game Masters to watch you while you roam free by accessing the continuous feed provided by the Eye-Bots.

**Mark-Bot:** This Game Announcer provides maps, gives warnings, and does countdowns. He's sometimes cranky and likes to lecture. He and Karyn-Bot sometimes bicker, and he always signs off with corny interlude music. It's his thing.

**Karyn-Bot:** This other Game Announcer provides helpful tips, good news, and instructions on completing tasks. She argues with Mark-Bot at times, but it's because she cares about everyone's welfare. She also often signs off with campy transition music, claiming Mark-Bot stole her exit strategy, but sometimes, she's a pathological liar. It's her one little flaw.

## Vermilion Glitches

VIPs can bend things to their favor in The Game by applying various glitches to any player they wish. You can suffer up to two glitches per round, each lasting a minute and spaced at least sixty seconds apart.

**Spaghetti Arms** ($13,000): You won't be able to pick up or hold anything.

**Hobbling** ($14,000): You won't be able to walk or run, only crawl.

**Tactile Hallucinations** ($12,000): You'll feel that you have roaches or spiders or other bugs or vermin all over you.

**Auditory Hallucinations** ($14,000): You'll hear loud polka music, an Italian opera sung in a high falsetto, a blasting foghorn, or another pervasive auditory disturbance.

**Visual Hallucinations** ($16,000): You'll see things that aren't there.

**Blindness** ($20,000): You won't be able to see anything.

**Deafness** ($14,000): You won't be able to hear anything.

**Muteness** ($11,000 + $13,000): You won't be able to talk, and your hands won't help you communicate. A Spaghetti Arms add-on is required for this glitch.